Thera

Zeruya Shalev

THERA

TRANSLATED BY

H. Sacks &
Mitch Greenberg

The Toby Press

Thera

First English Language Edition 2010

The Toby Press LLC
POB 8531, New Milford, CT 06776-8531, USA
& POB 2455, London W1A 5WY, England
www.tobypress.com

Originally published in Hebrew as *Tera*
Published by arrangement with The Institute for the Translation of Hebrew Literature

ISBN 978 159 264 266 3, *hardcover*

A CIP catalogue record for this title is available from the British Library

Printed and bound in the United States

Chapter one

I'm dead, he shouts, his voice ringing, his lean body convulsing before me, I'm totally dead, dead forever. His mouth is open, exposing rickety baby teeth that hang by a thread. I'm a dream, he sings, and you're always dreaming, in the end you'll see that you don't even have a child. For a moment he falls silent, examining my face with his swimming eyes, his glee magnified by my panic, his new malice, born this morning, six years after him, draped over him like the capes he once wore.

A ring of limp stuffed animals surrounds him, their fur lackluster, their eyes brimming with eternal expectation, and he prances between them, light as a bubble, a cut-out paper heart with his name printed in block letters bounces on his chest, so the new teacher will know, so she won't get confused, so the children will know, so the walls around them will know, the still-bare walls that in a few days' time will be covered with drawings of animals and plants, heroic tales and legends, smeared in colors of blood, earth and soot, like the caves of prehistoric man before the invention of the written word.

I look at him and purse my lips, they taste of dry rubber, charred at the edges, the house reeks of it, as though a tire were smoldering in the corner, licking us with its foul flames. The bookshelves catch my eye, only yesterday they were crammed from end to end, but now they're punctuated with voids that glare at me like the vacant eye sockets of a skeleton, how little we leave behind us, a trace of bone-white dust is all that remains of the books that watched us in silence year after year.

He thinks he has lost my attention forever and he teeters in front of me, testing his strength again, amplifying his message, you're dead, he trumpets, really dead, dead forever, you're only dreaming that you're alive, this house isn't for real, this chair isn't for real, I'm not for real, it's just a dream, soon you'll see that it's just a dream.

His small, perpetually dirty hands with their closely-clipped nails fumble with the space around him, seeking their way to me, here he is, kneeling on the carpet at my feet, apparently defeated, the crown of his head craning toward my lap, but then he straightens up, grabs one of the stuffed animals and hurls it at me. I catch the soft yellow teddy bear, bring it to my heart, and rock it in my arms, hoping to arouse his jealousy, to retrieve, even in this manner, the soothing powers of his innocence.

Give him to me, he's mine, Daddy got him for me in Scotlag, he says, but I hide the bear behind my back, Scotland, I say, my voice creaking as if it hasn't been used for years, say Scotland. He draws closer to me, seeking to receive the shadow of an outdated embrace, and at once I spread my arms to envelop him, but he leaps toward me and snatches the captive bear with a shrill, triumphant bleat, I fooled you, he gloats, a cunning gleam in his eye, and he's already off dancing around the coffee table, holding the teddy bear aloft like a torah scroll, Scotlag Bear, he sings, you're only mine in a dream.

Surprised, I examine him as if for the first time, his vivid, vehement existence more baffling this morning than usual, he's a real boy, it seems, not a figment of the imagination, not a character torn from a yellowing children's book, not a complex toy. A child who was born, I stress, as if his birth were different from that of other mortals, from the children he will soon meet in a classroom with bare walls, a child who pierced the skin of reality with clenched fists, and I sift through the six years of the intimate knowledge I've amassed, setting the swirling, precious details aside to focus on the most marginal ones, which will, as in a complex criminal investigation, inevitably crack the case: he refuses to have his hair cut and his curls fall over his face at night, filling his mouth with hair; he likes to eat while walking, waving his arms, toying with his food like an animal with its prey; he furrows his forehead as darkness approaches, grows stooped with worry about the encroaching night and all its dangers, and wakes each morning triumphant, as if his victory were final and absolute. He loves his stuffed animals, dresses them in his old baby clothes, separates them into family units and assigns each its own increasingly complex history.

He flips through our photo albums, looking only for himself. A picture in which he does not appear brings tears to his eyes, events in which he did not participate stoke his anger, everything that happened before he was born outrages him, all the cakes I baked that he never got to taste, all the snow days that he never got to enjoy, all the trips taken before his arrival in the world, especially if an airplane was involved. Where was I then, he asks, in your tummy? As if his presence within me might enable him to share in the pleasure, and I am forced to admit, that no, you were not in my tummy yet, and he wallows in his gloom; so where was I, he demands, defeated by the possibility of his non-being, and I rush to appease him, you were in my heart, from the day I was born you were in my heart.

He is a strict, zealous historian of his own short life, sanctifying his memories, endowing every event in which he took part with great significance, poring over the details. What time was I born? Who saw me first? Here I am, he melts, when his little face appears for the first time in the album, who took that picture of me? Who bought me that hat? And at the same time he is ashamed of his cross-examinations – I remember everything, I'm just asking, he announces, I remember what happened before I was born too, because inside your heart there was a little window, and I looked out of it and saw everything, *everything,* he emphasizes, almost threatening, as if, from his hiding place, he noted all the inappropriate behavior too.

He sleeps in a room with three night lights guarding his windowsill and a bed full of stuffed animals. He wakes up with a grunt, his look, like theirs, smooth, clear, and full of anticipation. He watches over his possessions – old pacifiers, baby clothes, knitted booties – refusing to part with them, as if the course of his life is reversible and he might need them again soon. He detests change, clings to old habits, every one-time event becomes a binding ritual, a chance visit to an amusement park, a memory game before bed, everything we did once must be done again and again until the end of time, he hates being watched while he's playing; he hates the sunlight in his eyes; tries to shoo it away like a fly; he doesn't know how to swim; he doesn't know how to tie his shoelaces; he's scared of riding a bicycle; his parents separated yesterday.

Come here, Gili, I say, my head spinning from his perpetual circling, but he is already far from me, his attention turned toward the door, where keys jingle; Mommy, a robber, he whispers, taking a quick inventory of the stuffed animals scattered over the carpet, which to take with him, which to leave, and I get up and go to the door, looking for the key, but to my surprise it's thrust open, creaking. Daddy, I thought you were a robber, Gili rejoices, his fear giving way to a jubilant feeling of achievement and relief, as if he alone had bested a boatload of pirates, and I am quick to spoil the fun, saying, in a stern voice, Amnon, how did you get in? We agreed that you would leave your key here.

What do you mean, he says, feigning innocence, an explanation perched on his tongue, I left you a spare key, just in case, but I made a copy for myself, and immediately he bends his full frame down to the child, eyeing me from behind Gili's thin neck; what was your plan, that I wouldn't have a key to my son's house? What if I'm walking down the street at night and I hear him crying, I won't go to him? What if I see smoke billowing out the window, I won't go in and put out the fire? And Gili throws all his support behind him, of course, Mommy, otherwise all my stuffed animals will get burned, do you want Scotlag Bear to get burned?

We'll talk about it later, I sigh, you'd better get going, he's late for school, but Amnon rises heavily, looking at me with a deprived expression; just a second, what's the matter with you, you've already had your coffee, right? I haven't, and he goes to the kettle, fills it to the brim with water, as if there were dozens of guests sitting and waiting in our living room. Don't ask, he grumbles, I didn't sleep a wink, the fridge in that place sounds like a bulldozer, and I look at him, surprised, unable to read the tone of his voice. Has he forgotten that I'm responsible for his misery? Yet he innocently confides in me, as though our sentence has been decreed from above.

So sleep here tonight, Daddy, like always, our fridge doesn't make any noise at all, Gili says, stationing himself proudly in front of the fridge, like a smooth-talking salesman, opening the doors wide, until its frosty breath fills the kitchen. Our fridge is quiet, Daddy, he puts his little ear to it, it won't wake you, and neither will I, he declares in a hesitant voice, I won't wake you up any more if you get back together. I go to the kettle, pour out almost all the water, Gili, we've been through this, we've talked about it many times, our separation has nothing to do with you, nothing to do with your waking up at night, parents separate because of their own problems, not because of their children; on the contrary, they will always love their children more than anything in the world. How convenient it is to hide behind that word – parents – that grown-up, authoritative word, not Mommy and Daddy, not Daddy and I, not we, the two of us, Amnon and Ella.

The kettle steam billows into my face, and I bustle through the coffee preparation, careful to play the role of hostess, flooding the cup with cold milk, drink fast, I mutter, he has to get there on time, he doesn't know any of the kids in his class, how will he fit in if you keep coming late, and Amnon smirks, I don't think that by eight thirty they'll have forged unbreakable bonds already. He always makes light of others' difficulties while magnifying his own. How will I teach today, he sighs, I didn't sleep a wink, and I ignore him, fixing my eyes on the pale brown liquid, too pale for his taste, only when it has been drained will he get out of here, take his complaints, as he took his books yesterday, and be gone.

Gili, it's time to go, I announce, but he is no longer parading around, where is he, I go to his room, his feet are sticking out of the closet, old costume parts are strewn around the floor, look at me, he cries, I'm a magician. He pops out of the closet with a tall black hat on his head, a blue wand in his hand, and a starry cloak over his shoulders, this past year's costume, and I recall how I rummaged through the costume stalls with Talia, pushing and shoving through dozens of women and children in the pre-Purim madness, and only there did I dare tell her, purposely there, where it was impossible to hear, I whispered the stark words in her ear, and Talia covered her mouth with her hand and screamed, you're crazy, Ella, don't even think about it, do you want to ruin your kid's life?

I'm the Great Magician, he announces again, the hat covering his forehead, hiding his chestnut curls, making his face look older, like a rabbi in a grave black hat he stands before us, a midget rabbi waiting to marry us, to re-consecrate our union with his wand, and Amnon glares at him, is that how you're going to school? What's the matter with you, it's not Purim today, take that off right now. I don't care, this is what I want to wear, he shoots back, the glistening potion of grief already pooling in the corners of his eyes, where it always lurks, waiting for the right moment, and I say, who cares, let him go like that, what's the worst that can happen? But before my eyes I see him coaxing the classroom door open, the children looking at him in surprise, the ridicule spreading across their faces, look at him, a magician on a regular school day, bashful and wispy, a magician who can't cast a single spell.

But when they leave me, Gili enthroned on his father's shoulders, they are transformed into a single two-headed creature, vanishing as one into the stairwell, the lower one baldheaded, the upper one in a hat, an endangered species. I listen tensely to the echo of their footsteps, to the shrill, birdlike warble of his voice, and it seems to me that a burglar has indeed been in the house, quick and covetous, looting everything I have amassed, all the age-old family treasures, leaving me empty drawers, gaping shelves, childish pajamas hidden between rumpled sheets in the double bed, where the scent of his night fears has been trapped. Again I remember the moment when we became three, when we brought baby Gili to this house in a borrowed wicker cradle, his thighs bare because Amnon brought two tiny cotton shirts instead of a shirt and pants, and the intense desire, unlike anything I had ever known, to lie in bed with the two of them, to cover the new born family with a thin sheet, me on one side, him on the other, and the baby in the middle, separating us, while we stroked his miraculous skin, the soft autumn sun creeping in between the covers, licking the tips of our toes with its transparent fire.

Only it wasn't like that, we never had time for that, and now we are no longer three, will never be three, and suddenly it seems that the new rift turns us into four, two separate couples, me and my Gili, Amnon and his Gili. He will be completely different with me and with him, two couples growing further and further apart as the child grows older. Half of him is no longer mine, and I imagine him cut in two, which part will you choose, Mommy, the top or the bottom, the right or the left, because I won't be whole anymore, even if I look whole, half of me will live only in your imagination.

He'll be scarred for life, Talia said, her coal-black eyes widening in rebuke, her arms full of costumes, queen of the night or a lovely bride for the little one, she wonders, Robin Hood or Tigger for the big one; you're hurting Gili and yourself, it will be much harder for you without Amnon, how can you leave a husband for nothing, with no other prospects? How can you break up a family for nothing? But it's not for nothing, Talia, I protested, you know it's not for nothing.

You have no idea what you're talking about, she insisted, the plastic-wrapped costumes sliding out of her arms, and I watched transfixed to see which of them would fall, if the bride falls, my marriage is over, if the queen of the night falls, my divorce is off, but Talia clasped both of them to her chest, you don't leave a husband for vague romantic notions, she pronounced, and the swarm of women pouncing on the costumes looked at us curiously, ready to voice an opinion, to contribute their two cents to the course of my life, and I dragged her away from the stalls, stop shouting, calm down, it's not like I'm leaving you.

It isn't about romantic notions, I said on the way home, it's something completely different, more basic, it's about oxygen, I have no oxygen, all I want is to be without him, without arguments, without fights, without accusations, not to insult or be insulted, not to disappoint or be disappointed, I'm tired of this constant friction, like sandpaper rubbing against itself, why do I need that, tell me, why do I need him?

You haven't convinced me, she said, biting her nails like a teenage girl, if you didn't have a child, I'd say, go ahead, you're not risking much, but now, with Gili barely six years old, to leave Amnon because he gets on your nerves?

He doesn't get on my nerves, I corrected her, he suffocates me, he harasses me, he wears me down, at one point I used to admire him so much, and now every word that comes out of his mouth seems irrelevant to me, it isn't just that I no longer love him, I no longer respect him. I'm sick of his demands, of his complaints; he's unhappy with himself and he takes it out on me, and ever since Gili, it's gotten worse. I have neither the strength nor the interest to take care of both of them, and if I have to choose, I much prefer Gili; at any rate, I've been raising him practically alone, it took me years to understand that Amnon isn't going to change, that our life isn't going to change, I don't want this life anymore, it's my right.

You're talking about rights and I'm talking about obligations, she said quickly when I stopped next to her house, I was brought up to regard family as sacred, maybe I'm narrow minded, but I still believe that; I'm worried you'll only see the error of your ways when it's too late. You're about to ruin a family, Ella, and you still don't have a clue as to why, you don't have a clue about the stakes, about how much you're losing and how little you're gaining, and I said, that's enough, Talia, calm down, I'm not getting a divorce tomorrow, I'm just toying with the idea, you're the first person I've told, and she gathered up the costumes with a sigh, the miniature wedding dress needling me with its sheer whiteness; I'll be happy to be the last, she said, you'll get over it, you'll see, it's a kind of virus that attacks us once in a while, when it seems like if we get rid of our husbands all our problems will disappear, but forget about it, Ella, it's an illusion.

Where's that wind coming from, I wonder, gathering up the trail of stuffed animals he left behind him in the living room, a soft path of golden footprints, throwing them onto his bed where it seems there is hardly room for another creature, certainly not a whole, real, flesh-and-blood child, and again the chill wind sends a shiver down my spine, a surprising autumn wind, early this year, where has it come from, the windows are shut and I closed the door after they left, but now it's wide open again, and he enters, light footed and silent despite his size, quieting the jangle of the keys, locking the door behind him. Amnon. For a moment I am alarmed to see him without Gili perched on his shoulders, like a tree without its birds, what's going on? Where's Gili?

He's at school, where else could he be? he answers with a sour smile, leaning against the door, his eyes wandering over my face, leaving an unpleasant tingle in their wake, but I'm here, I brought you coffee, he holds out a cardboard tray with two lidded cups.

That's exactly what I wanted to ask you, I say dryly, what are you doing here? And he, as usual, launches into an attack, I don't understand you, Ella, you told me to come here, don't you remember, half an hour's gone by and you already forgot? And I deny it immediately, what are you talking about, I have to go, I never told you to come here, you're delusional, and it seems to me that the cups of coffee are trembling with insult when he says, you said we'll talk later, don't you remember? You asked me to come and talk to you.

Amnon, come on, I meant in general, that we should talk sometime, it wasn't anything definite, I have to be somewhere soon, I don't have time to talk now. I take the tray from him and put it down on the kitchen table, a menacing murmur accompanies my steps, this is how I'll take the marriage contract from your hands, I'll walk, head bowed, into the vast hall, escorted by hostile glares, long white beards matted on black robes, divorced, divorced, they'll cry, no longer consecrated, and you'll stand there, effortlessly linking arms with my enemies, and below us, on the main street, the cars will growl, mounting each other like animals in heat.

When is your meeting, he asks, glancing at the clock we received as a wedding present, treading gingerly toward me, just as he'd treaded around the shards of pottery on the dusty gray archaeological dig where I first saw him. Our movements have to be as careful as a doctor's, he would remind us repeatedly, because the past, strewn here before us, is just as helpless as a sick body, and I would gaze at him admiringly from the depths of the excavation pit like an animal from its hole, praying that he would notice my existence.

In an hour, I say, frowning at the tired blue eyes twinkling at me, why do you ask? And he whispers, so we have enough time. His lips twitch in a nervous spasm, the buttons of his gray shirt open almost of their own accord, exposing a heavy flushed chest, and I back away from him until I bump into the kitchen table, squashing the still warm coffee cups and flooding the table with a frothy aromatic liquid, no, we won't sit facing each other sipping at our leisure, curling our fingers around the lukewarm cardboard, complaining about the unseasonable autumn, we won't linger over the events of the night, reconstructing a moment of intimacy as if recalling a miracle we managed to perform yet again, we won't indulgently moan about our son's broken sleep, how many times he woke up and who he woke, we won't relish something he said this morning, some dream he recounted in all its details, we won't look at each other with a sigh of resignation before we begin our day, a discontented sigh, but also a complacent one, a sigh that says, here we are, in spite of everything, Amnon and Ella, and we'll be here tomorrow too, and the next day, and next autumn.

Don't worry about it, he says, I'll clean up later, as if this was still his house, his rights and obligations intact, and I feel the warm seat of my pants, the spilled coffee spreading over my thighs with a tingling sensation, but the anger is spreading through my body even faster, why did you bring that coffee here, why did you come at all, look what you've done, I fume, averting my eyes from his big, clumsy figure, his unnecessary and disruptive presence. Now I'll have to shower again, get dressed again. If Talia were here maybe she'd finally understand how oppressive his presence can be, how easily you can be robbed of your freedom, even when it entails nothing more than changing your pants.

I have to change, I snap, turning my stained backside to him, heading for the bedroom with a display of annoyance, but he follows me down the hall like the scent of the coffee, stopping in front of the closet, his breath drawing close, let me help you, he says, going down on his knees and tugging on my pants, his shaved head pressing against my thigh, his tongue stretching out to lick the drops of coffee, his breath steamy on my skin, and I try to free myself from his grip, leave me alone, Amnon, what do you think you're doing? And he whispers, I'm cleaning you, you wanted to be clean, didn't you? And I scold him, enough, stop it, you're making it hard for both of us, leave me alone, it's over between us, it's completely dead, dead forever.

His bald head is between my thighs, as if it has just this moment been pushed out, maybe for you it's dead but for me it's alive, his voice creeping up my body, sticky and hostile as a poisonous caterpillar, why do your wishes count more than mine, who do you think you are? And I say, I thought we were done talking, I thought you understood that you can't force yourself on me; and he snaps, shut up, I don't ask you before doing something just like you didn't ask me, what you did to me was a lot worse than changing a pair of pants, I have to change my whole life because of you.

Leave me alone, Amnon, I try to push his head away, my hands slipping off his bald head as if it were wrapped in nylon, let me get dressed, I'm in a hurry. My hands stretch toward the closet, fishing out a pair of slacks, but my legs are caught between his arms, pressed to his shoulders, to his thick neck and the elongated turtle head at the top of it, a giant sea turtle has me trapped and I beat the armored shell of his back, trying to escape, enough, Amnon, enough, I don't want you, don't you get it, I do not want you anymore. I see his empty shelves next to mine, the closet seems to have lost its balance, slanting lopsidedly, like weighted scales.

But you're my wife, we're married, he murmurs in astonished innocence, suddenly loosening his grip, and I attempt to leapfrog clumsily over his back, spreading my legs and sliding over his head as if he were a vaulting horse in a gym. To my surprise he doesn't react, remains on his knees, head bowed, as if kneeling in supplication before some imaginary being, begging for mercy, continents of bitter sweat spread across his gray shirt, plastering it to his body, and I am mesmerized by their sudden, shameful advance, I'm not the one who will wash your shirt, not the one who will hang it in the sun to dry, not the one who will put it away in the closet, this closet will not be its home, and as I disentangle myself from the fate of the shirt, I am filled with a bubbling joy, as if it alone had been keeping me from happiness all these years.

Amnon, listen to me, I cast my words toward his damp back, you can't force me to stay with you, I don't want to live like this anymore, I tried to talk to you so many times and you barely listened, but now, all of a sudden, you remember, when it's too late. When he doesn't answer I take my leave of his back, step over the coffee tracks to Gili's room, sit down exhausted on his bed, dozens of dry beady eyes peering at me, inspecting me with inquisitive, disapproving looks as if I am the odd one out here, with my smooth, furless skin and my moist eyes, and without much thought, instead of hurrying to the bathroom and locking the door, I begin to arrange them like he does, in families, lion, lioness and little lion cub, tiger, tigress and little tiger cub, cheek to cheek, fur to fur. Disturbed, I notice the absence of his favorite teddy bear, it must have disappeared in the upheaval of the covers, and I shake out the blanket, move the pillow, peek under the bed. What are you looking for, he asks, his smooth bare chest rising and falling heavily, the shirt crumpled in his hand like a rag; this was how I first saw him, ten years ago, half naked, squinting at the royal compound as it was gradually unearthed, only then his chest had been covered with dust so thick and dark that I didn't notice it was bare.

Scotlag Bear, I reply, and he says, he's in my car, I'm taking him to my place so Gili will have something to play with there, and I sit up straight, but Gili can't sleep without him, why should you have him, you can't separate families like that. Well, well, well, he says with a sneer, you think breaking up a family of teddy bears is wrong, but breaking up a family of human beings is okay? Maybe you're confused, maybe it's the other way around? Maybe you've got a toy heart, like them, come on, he draws closer to me, his lips open, his eyes hooded, his hands stretched out in front of him like a blind man's, pulling my shirt collar apart, let's see once and for all what you've got there, a toy heart, a malfunctioning toy heart? And I am thrown back underneath him onto the crowded bed, where there isn't even room for a small boy, his hands gripping my chest as if to tear it from its place, his voice hoarse, I'll fix you, you'll see, I'll fix your screwed-up heart, I'll give you a new heart, you'll love me, you'll love me like you once did.

When I was a child I had no husband. I slept alone in a narrow, single bed and I woke alone. The sky changed in front of me, dousing the fire of sunrise in the sheets with its blue radiance, and when I went to school I had no husband, and when I came back from school I had no husband, and when I did my homework on a dark Formica desk I had no husband, and when I lay in my bed next to the window and looked at the moon I had no husband, the sky reached for me with black hairy arms, like a giant prehistoric creature, a Cyclops, with one eye slowly opening and closing, and like the priests of On who stood barefoot on the cliff waiting for the rising sun, I would pray for its second eye to open, knowing that only then would sleep descend upon me like manna from heaven, and then, too, I had no husband.

Bitter male sweat seeps into my hair, crudely spreading his scent, his shoulder collapses onto my arm with a sigh, his hands struggle with my smarting breast, let me, he groans, let me fix your heart, the dark curtain stains the sunlight an unseasonable gray, and I stare at the wall, sad, autumnal brown eyes looking out at me from the framed picture of Gili on his last birthday, watching us, and it seems that this is not the picture taken a few weeks ago but a picture from the future, a picture of the boy he will grow up to be, bitter and remote, and long threads stretch painfully from my eyes to his, threads that have been torn from my body, and I close my eyes, Amnon's rough hands are on my face, kneading my cheeks, patting my neck, pinching my belly, searching under my skin for the decision forced on him a few months before, the decision he still can't grasp, the decision to leave him, and he tries to pull it from my body like a thorn, and I no longer try to break free because my body is crushed beneath his weight like a loaf of bread on the bottom of the basket, and it is not the weight of his body alone but the weight of our life together, day after day, year after year, from the time I first saw him on the Tel Jezreel excavation site up until this morning in Jerusalem, the weight of the love and the fights, the enmity and the compassion, the attraction and the revulsion, the weight of our son who was born, and the weight of our children who will not be.

His shoulders are slippery and damp, his breath blazing, his face the dark purple of an eggplant, the same troubling color as Gili's at the moment of his birth, and I'm lying on my back in the agony of reverse labor, with a powerful, overgrown bald baby trying to invade my body, an unwanted baby imposing his presence on me, is there a word, a look or a movement, that will get him off me, that will remove this coarse clumsy body from this child's bed full of stuffed animals? It seems that the word has not yet been invented, and perhaps it's for the best, because the memory of this morning will sustain me during my new life, safeguarding me from regret, from longing, because it isn't as a stranger that I regard him now, the expression on his face changing like the sky, it isn't the shock of strangeness but the shock of familiarity, for this morning is no different in its essence from the other mornings of our life, for even though he's never before forced himself on me, it's clear to me that already last autumn I could have found myself lying underneath him, immobile, reverently recalling those days of old when I had no husband.

The lioness's eyes hold me as I clamp my lips together, I won't even give him my voice, and it's like sharp stones are stabbing my back the way they did on our first nights, on the dig, by day burrowing beneath the earth and at night beneath the skin, his pale eyes shining above me, anointing me with all the light they soaked up during the long, hot day, the smell of ancient dust rising from him, and the hands that scrupulously sorted the pottery shards wandered my body, trying to decipher its inscriptions, letter by letter, and I'd think of the Sidonian queen who was there before me, as if there were scarcely a generation separating us, how she looked out the window, her eyes painted and her hair combed, watching the enemy approach, how her eunuchs betrayed her and let her fall, how her blood spattered on the palace wall. Their calamity was our good fortune, he had said, this settlement was destroyed shortly after it was built, and it never recovered, its short life lends it enormous importance, and I had taken his hand, during the long day we were strangers, and during the short night we were the heirs of kings stepping among the ruins of their palace, reconstructing the monarchy's golden age, and when the digging season was over, I didn't think I would see him again, I thought he would steal out of my life the same way he had entered it, with the glory of the enigmatic past trailing behind him, but a moment before I boarded the minibus he pointed at me and said, with the gravity of a general selecting his soldiers, you're coming with me.

It seems that the ancient image swaying before me sways before his eyes too, but it fills him with rage, who do you think you are, where do you get the gall to leave me, without me you were nothing, a miserable volunteer on a dig, I handed you a career and this is how you thank me, let me be clear here, it's over, finished, just as I built you up I'll tear you down, and then like a final, crushing curse he sways above me, spewing his protean-white liquid onto the slope of my belly, and immediately buries his face in the fur of the lioness lying by my side, as if felled by a blow to the head, panting and whimpering, without a moment's respite. Ella, I'm sorry, I don't know what came over me, I've been wracked by grief, let's try again, I know it isn't all smooth sailing with me, but I love you, don't think it's so easy to find love, there isn't much love out there and there's love in our home, don't belittle it, Ella, answer me, he fondles my face, his fingers on my lips, trying to pry the right words from them, don't cry, he begs, I'm sorry I jumped you like that, it won't happen again, just give me another chance, Gili's so little, do you want to ruin his life already? I'm silent, the memories of the old days cave in on me, suffocating me in a landslide, covering me with mounds of earth, priceless earth that holds, frozen inside of it, the raw, idle data that has been waiting thousands of years for interpretation.

Through barely open eyes I look at his flickering features, his beauty and his ugliness jostling for superiority, the change in him is immense, Gili's narrow bed presses us to each other and I silently intone, I solemnly swear, oh, I solemnly swear, you will never come near me again, and with surprising ease I liberate myself from the bed, shoving his body off me. It's soft and airy, as if he has turned himself into a spongy stuffed animal. His head is still buried in the lioness's neck, his back heaves above the furry animals now saturated in his smell, which will accompany Gili as he sleeps at night and during his day-time games; what do you want from me, he moans, I'm not so bad, so I can be moody, what's so terrible about that, what's going on with you, I don't understand what's going on with you? And I say, get up, I don't want a thing from you anymore, and I have no interest in explaining to you what's going on with me for the thousandth time, do you even understand what you've just done? If there was any chance of us getting together again you've destroyed it, you only have yourself to blame. With practiced composure I watch him rise, wrapping his creased shirt around his chest, sullenly pulling his jeans up his thighs, his face heavy, his jaw thrust forward in shame, and it seems that dressing beside him is the woman who once lived here, vulnerable, bitter, disappointed, and the very possibility of withdrawing from her has a heady, supernatural redolence.

I'm sorry for what I did, he says, his voice flaring up, but what you did was much worse, you have no idea how sorry you'll be, you're playing with fire, Ella, you're feeling reckless and you're playing with fire, but you'll regret it. Spare me your threats, I hiss, just leave the key here, and he takes the key out of his pocket, waves it in front of me like a juicy bone in front of a dog, this is what you want? This is all you want from me? Then know this, you're not going to get it, this apartment is mine too, if you don't want to see me here, then get out, and he goes straight to the door, yanks it open and locks it behind him with three sharp turns of the key, as though he were leaving an empty house.

Chapter two

You're late again, he declares, his face smooth and bright as a Pharonic bronze statue, his eyes flashing silvery warning signals, and I mumble, sorry, I had a really important meeting at work, relying as always on the pretext of professional obligations, the only thing he's ever respected. At the entrance to his room he stands, making authoritative gestures with his hand like a policeman directing traffic, and I follow him into the brightly lit room where books line the walls, towering all the way up to the vaulted ceiling. They too, seem to be watching me from above, provoking me in their absolute immunity, as they alone are shielded from his barbs; after all, he always preferred them to us. He sits down at his spacious desk, facing the computer and the glass bowl, which, as always, cradles a peeled, sliced apple. He runs his fingers through his untarnished white hair, crossing one solid thigh over the other as I look out the window towards a tall, slender palm tree that basks in the mounting heat of the sun, nodding its lion's mane at me in understanding.

This is how I sat before him in my youth, chastised in advance. Ella, there are a few things I have to say to you, he announces officially, always to say, never to talk or listen. He would summon me to his room, which in those days seemed as suffocating and hopeless as an interrogation cell, and I would steal a quick glance at my mother, what have I done this time? What does he want? And she would don a sympathetic face, I have no idea, but the door would shut before her eyes, and only I would hear the rattle of his warden's keys, and then he would deliver his speech in a stern voice, slow and emphatic, as if a large audience was listening, he is under the impression that I am not interested in my studies, he is not satisfied with my grades, he is not pleased with the clothes I wear, with the company I keep, with the books I read. He understands from my mother – this is how he puts it, like a secret understanding, as if there's no talking between them but a mute secret language of signs and expressions – that I already have a boyfriend, and he wants to warn me not to go too far, not to do anything that I will regret.

I understand from your mother that you and Amnon are thinking of separating, he thunders, scolding, as if it's not just me sitting here in front of him, his only daughter, but a large audience of women, a revolutionary mass movement that must be silenced by any means. Is it final? he inquires, as if he expects that the very posing of the question in so penetrating a way will lead to an immediate denial, and he will be able to put a swift end to the meeting and return to his affairs. I admit it, feebly, immediately adding a reservation, that's what it looks like, we're going to try and live apart for a few months, and he clears his throat, am I permitted to ask why or is it too private? The word private is enough to make him jiggle his bare foot nervously, and I say, we're simply not right for each other, we aren't happy together, we've decided there's no point in going on like this, the false first person plural smoothing things over, as if Amnon himself is right here beside me, backing me up. We no longer see eye to eye, I say, trying as always in his company to elevate my language, so that he won't say, I see that your vocabulary is deteriorating, what have you been reading lately? And then I fall silent, not willing to contribute more than three stilted sentences to the conversation, since it isn't a conversation at all, we've never had one of those, and I stare at the pendulum of his leg, swaying sturdy and slender as the palm tree, coming closer to me, in a moment it will hit my knee, as if by mistake, in a sharp, well-aimed kick, impairing my mobility, spoiling my plans.

You know that I have never interfered in your private affairs, he says, chilly and authoritative, but this time I see it as my duty to clarify the situation, since it concerns not only you and Amnon, two adults who can allow themselves to err, but a small child, who will have to pay the price of the error, one who has no means of paying it, Ella, his purse is empty. He falls silent and inspects the effect of his words, the effect of the opening blow, prepared well in advance, like his lectures, as if he expects me to whip out a notebook and pen and take down his bits of wisdom like a diligent student, word for word. It concerns a small child, who will have to pay the price of the error, one with no means of paying it, his purse is empty, empty.

And so he will be put in debt, he says, resuming his lecture, his voice accustomed to big halls, beating reluctantly against the confinement of the walls, owing a debt that cannot be paid, and soon the creditors will arrive, I am speaking of the creditors of the soul, Ella, who are even more dangerous than the underworld, and they will take the little he possesses, the little soundness of mind he possesses, do you understand what I'm saying?

You're exaggerating, Daddy, I protest weakly, times have changed, today people don't make such a fuss over divorce, I know lots of children of divorced parents and nothing happened to them, they have a father and a mother and they learn to cope with life. The most important thing for a child is for his parents to be happy, I say, it's better to be happy apart than miserable together, but he waves his hand in disgust, as if I am speaking utter nonsense. These are the frivolities of the new age, he announces, people today are as thoughtless as animals, slaves to their passions, there is nothing as dangerous as passion, as I explained to you when you were a girl. Just as a car needs brakes, so too does a human being; just as a car crashes without brakes, so too will a human, and I tell you, he points his finger at me threateningly, that I know your son, he isn't like other children, he is a weak, sensitive child, and if you don't apply the brakes now, I'm warning you that it will end in catastrophe.

Catastrophe? I mutter, what are you talking about, what kind of catastrophe? He'll have a hard time for a while and then he'll get over it, like everyone else, children survive worse things than divorce, but he raises his voice again, his lips turning blue as if his blood has frozen in his veins, a catastrophe! Pay attention, Ella, your catastrophe is certain, and your happiness is doubtful, completely doubtful, what guarantee do you have that you'll be happy without Amnon? I do not recall your being so happy before you met him. Listen to me, I'm only asking one thing of you, to think things over and reconsider. Amnon was here this morning, after he left you, he reveals, contentedly shaming me, like a cunning interrogator who took the time to cross check witnesses' statements. I understood from him that it was you who initiated the separation, that it all depends on you, and only on you, so I have a proposal for you, a simple, effective solution, to which Amnon already agreed this morning. You must make a pact, in the deep sense of the word, promise each other that you will never separate, because you brought a child into this world, giving birth to a child is the greatest commitment there is, and from the moment you have a child in common, you have to stay together. You'll see that after you make this pact everything will become simpler, you'll overcome your difficulties easily because you'll know that you have no alternative, you won't believe what relief you'll feel once you've completely removed any possibility of another life and other partners. I'm offering you the option of complete happiness, Ella, this is the change you're looking for, difficulties await you everywhere, living alone is difficult, establishing a new family is difficult, I'm making things easier for you by helping you to renounce dangerous options, wherever you go you will have to overcome difficulties and cope with problems, so why not make an effort for the sake of the family you already have, for the man you chose to father your child.

Enough, Daddy, you don't understand, I say, shaking my head and covering my ears with my hands like when I was a child, helpless in the face of his bullying lectures, his immovable confidence. I can't stay with Amnon, it's over between us, what pact are you talking about? We're separating, not getting married, but he silences me immediately with a patronizing wave of his hand, his leaden eyes cold and impermeable. Listen to me, Ella, I know you better than you think, every few years you have an attack of self-destructiveness, up to now it was your own affair, I didn't interfere, but now it's Gili's affair. I see myself in this matter as representing Gili's interests, and I tell you that the child will not withstand your separation, and if you compel me to put it plainly – the child will not be able to cope with the situation, he won't survive, he'll be annihilated.

Annihilated?! I whisper, what are you talking about? Can you hear yourself? And at last he places his bare foot on the floor, on the black and white chess-board tiles. You force me to speak plainly: we're talking about a matter of life and death here, you want to look for happiness – he spits the word out as if it were an obscenity, a bitter almond – the only happiness lies in commitment to the family you created, and don't fool yourself by thinking I am indifferent to your feelings, if you had a violent husband, God forbid, I would of course advise you to leave him, and I would help you, but I know Amnon, and I can imagine the kind of difficulties involved. It's self-indulgence, he thunders, the insufferable self-indulgence of your generation, and it will exact a terrible price from you. Do you understand what I'm trying to tell you, or do I have to make myself even clearer?

It's late, I have to pick Gili up from kindergarten, I say, as if it's only the lack of time that's standing between us, preventing us from continuing our pleasant conversation, and when I stand up my legs tremble, and it seems to me that the walls are slanting, the bookshelves bending over me, seizing hold of me with their scholarly, venomous grasp. I will be buried among his books today, under the thick stone walls, and then who will pick up Gili. It seems that this daily task has suddenly become of the utmost urgency, to get there in time to pick up Gili, before disaster strikes, and I advance toward the door of his room like my life depends on it, and he hurries after me, unrelenting, just promise me to consider it seriously, as befits a matter of life and death, he shouts. If he had a more invasive method of forcing his words into my ears he would employ it, he wouldn't hesitate for a second. I quickly open the door to the hall and encounter the gray head of my mother, stooped and intent, eavesdropping, what did he want, what did he want from you? she asks in a whisper, offering me her fearful, insubstantial sympathy on a crumbling tray, and I can't stay another minute in this place; we'll talk later, Mom, I have to run and get Gili from kindergarten.

Kindergarten? He's in the first grade! she cries in alarm as if she has caught me in the midst of a terrible mistake that casts a gloomy and suspect light on my motherhood, why did she say kindergarten, I hear her saying in astonishment to my father, a moment before he returns to his spacious desk, and it seems that all the questions and wishes, the perplexities and difficulties, have been narrowed down to one, completely marginal, complaint: why kindergarten, he's already in first grade?

Defeated, I descend the steps of their house, like a prisoner who escapes too late, his ability to enjoy freedom gone. The blazing banister burns my fingers but I don't let go, step after step, till on the last one I collapse, hugging my knees to my chest, dread swelling inside me, squeezing and crushing internal organs, the presence of the catastrophe as concrete as if it had already taken place, sealed the moment his blue lips said, your catastrophe is certain, your happiness doubtful. I lay my forehead on my trembling knees, the daylight seems to be fading before my eyes, drowned out by a mourners' tent, the dark pain of everlasting orphanhood.

A noisy taxi swerves to the edge of the curb, its honking mingling with the wail of a distant siren, and I rise heavily to my feet. You free? I ask the driver, and he says, someone called, was it you? And I say, no, but do me a favor, take me to the center of town, it's right here, and he says, hang on a minute, I'll just see if it's on my way, and striding rapidly toward us comes a stout man in a dark suit, his thick hair neatly combed. How quickly he changed out of his shorts and put on his reserved expression, how deftly he succeeded in concluding our nightmarish talk just in time, giving me the impression that I was the one who ended it. He slides rapidly into the air-conditioned taxi, waving at me with captivating courtesy, as if I were one of his students whose name he had forgotten, or which he had never known, and I stand at the edge of the street. With a perfect stranger I would have gotten into the taxi, but not with you, Daddy, the simple word as forlorn as the barking of a dog after the crack of an explosion, Daddy, Daddy, bark the dogs in the lull between the roar of the explosion and the nearing wails of the ambulances, Daddy, Daddy, what did you say to me?

He won't survive, he'll be annihilated, you said, as if summing up the fate of the great powers of the ancient world, the Hittites, the Babylonians, the Sumerians, the Akkadians, entire empires vanished from the world, but we're talking about a little child, barely six years old, a child who hasn't learned to ride a bicycle yet, who has difficulty tying his shoelaces, a child who's afraid of the dark, and it seems to me that I can hear his night voice, the voice that rises from his bad dreams, shrill and terrified, Mommy, come, come quickly, and I obey, my feet slapping the hot asphalt. I need to see him right now, to save him from the catastrophe decreed here, at the top of this cloud-covered mountain of steps, as if it were the smoldering Mount Sinai where the sight of the glory of the Lord was like devouring fire, fierce and certain and almost justified, yes, how terrible, almost justified.

I run through the streets like a woman whose house is on fire, spraying disquiet around me, sowing seeds of panic in the hearts of the passersby. Perhaps some secret knowledge has reached me and is the cause of my haste, knowledge of an impending terrorist attack, an earthquake, a trail of anxious stares follows me, growing longer all the time. For some reason running seems slower than walking, the gray streets ensnare me like meddlesome old men, an occasional windowbox of flowers in full bloom tries to soften the hard hewn stones, but it seems that the flowers, too, are turning gray, ossified.

A short-haired cyclist strains as she rides uphill, her shirt as damp as Amnon's this morning, how carefully he must have buttoned it, smoothed its creases when he stood outside the house I am fleeing from now, betraying me to the authorities with a pious face. I widen my stride, looking fearfully behind me, for it seems that I am not running alone through the streets, that the curse set out alongside me at precisely the same time, that very curse that leapt from my father's throat, and I am neck and neck with it, must overtake it, on black wings it glides by my side, and even if my ribs hurt, and my breath burns, and my knees give way, I have to reach the finish line before it does because a little child is waiting for me, barely six years old, a child who refuses to cut his hair, who hates the sunlight in his eyes, whose parents separated yesterday.

Through the open windows of the classrooms the roar of the school rushes like the waters of the sea, suppressed and angry, gathering a savage strength, hundreds of children sitting on little chairs, holding pencils and crayons in their hands, and one of them is mine, and I have to see him at once. I push the gate, try to open it, but to my surprise it's closed, a heavy lock holding the gates together, and topped with an awkwardly written note, *the guard makes his rounds, please wait passiontly.* The misspelling makes it seem like one of these ancient inscriptions with an unexpected meaning, and maybe a few hundred years down the road researchers will wrinkle their brows, offer an array of explanations, until another such sign will be found, shedding light on the conundrum, please wait passiontly, sounds like a worthwhile endeavor, but not for me, not now. I gauge the bright green gate, cheerful and challenging, as if it was built to separate me from my son and not to protect him. I size it up like an adversary, I have no choice but to overcome it, no intention of waiting for the guard to complete his lazy rounds, I look around me, making sure that nobody is watching, I place my foot on the handle, and take hold of the closely set bars.

The climb is easier than I expected, a strong hand seems to have grabbed me by the crown of my head, to be pulling me upwards, and in an instant I have reached the top of the iron gate, at the foot of which, to my annoyance, stands a girl with fair, curly hair, looking up at me in surprise and following my progress with an amused expression, and I ignore her and carefully swing my leg onto the other side, but on Gili's side there is no purchase at all, the surface smooth and flat. I'm at my wit's end, an additional, unanticipated obstacle has arisen between us, my child, and were there not an audience I may have tried to go back, but this girl, rooted to the spot below me, waits patiently, just as the sign says, and I decide to stay where I am for the time being, as if I had only scaled the gate for my own amusement, in order to get a better view of the deserted yard, and indeed, from my new vantage point, I am able to take in the entire school; I can even see the elderly guard proceeding slowly and deliberately along the fence, full of a sense of purpose, for the safety of hundreds of children has been entrusted to his hands, and I give him a friendly wave, so that he won't mistakenly draw his weapon.

The sight of the figure perched on the gate immediately interrupts his leisurely patrol, and he approaches me at a rapid pace, his paunch wobbling before him, making gestures of disapproval with his hand, what, you are crazy, he yells, you not have patience? It says on sign to wait patiently. I hang on to the top of the gate, I'm really sorry, it's just that I'm in a terrible hurry, I left a baby alone at home and I have to get his big brother, but the desperate excuse only seems to increase his rage; who leaves baby alone at home, he grumbles, everybody's crazy here, he says, judging parents in general for my crime, and it seems that he is about to punish me for my appalling negligence by leaving me suspended between heaven and earth, hanging on top of the gate in eternal disgrace, to be made an example of for all other parents. Shaking his head in disgust he opens the lock and lets the girl through, and she steps into the schoolyard with calm pride, as living proof that patience pays. I try to climb down the same way I climbed up, but my leg, groping blindly for the handle, misses the mark and I drop onto the hot asphalt pavement, just barely missing a baby carriage, almost crushing it beneath me.

Even if I'm hurt I won't let him see, it takes an effort to stand but I do and I straighten my clothes, smiling pleasantly, as if my leap had been planned, the very reason that I climbed the gate in the first place. I try to proceed with affected dignity, telling myself that if I deny the pain, it will disappear; the main thing is that I'm inside and in a moment I'll rescue him. I hurry to the basement classroom, where I am greeted by the pale mango curls I saw from the great heights of the gate, that girl again, I say indignantly to myself, what's she doing here, I hoped never to see her again. From close up she's not so young, it turns out, and not as short as she looked from above either, and not a girl at all but a mother, which means that I'll have to see her every day, and she examines me with amused curiosity, indicates the closed classroom and says, they haven't finished up yet.

But it seems I have already proven today that neither locked gates nor closed doors will stand in my way and I give the door a forceful push. Dozens of pairs of eyes turn to me and I recognize his autumnal ones immediately, under the wizard's hat. He jumps up and runs across the classroom, and only when he is gathered in my arms do I breathe a sigh of relief, he's all right, nothing has happened to him, I sniff him like a cat, a smell of steamy childish sweat and chocolate spread, glue and sand, pleasure and longing rises up from him; the smell of my love.

Excuse me, Gilad's Mother, we haven't finished yet, the teacher interrupts our joy, and I am obliged to apologize, trying to come up with a new excuse for my haste; it's just that we're in a big hurry today, we have a family affair; but she insists, you'll have to wait another thirty minutes, we're in the middle of an activity; go back to your seat immediately, Gilad, but he clings to me, whimpering into my neck, I want to go home, I don't want to go back to my seat, and I try to coax him, its all right, Gilili, I'll wait for you here outside the door, we'll go home soon, suddenly conscious of the magnitude of my mistake, why did I have to put him to the test in front of the other children, to wake the sleeping tiger of his tears, and I stare shamefaced at the teacher as she advances on us, stern and decisive, and snatches him from my arms, the wizard hat slipping from his head as he slinks back to his seat, embarrassed by his tears, exposed to the ridicule of his peers.

Like him I, too, retreat, rushing out of the classroom, almost falling into the arms of the curly-headed woman, who looks at me open-mouthed as if I were a circus animal performing astonishing tricks, the amazement on her face is about to morph into words, and I have no choice but to preempt her, to correct the impression by firmly demonstrating my awareness of the situation, and I smile at her; believe me, I don't always behave like this, I say, today is an unusual day, and she smirks, you don't need to apologize, when you leave a baby alone at home you can't afford to dawdle, her voice is low, hoarse from cigarettes, and I stammer, look, that's not exactly the case, but her smirk has already turned into cackling laughter, don't worry, it's obvious you don't have a baby at home, and I join in her laughter, and then ask, why is it so obvious? And she scans my lean body, lingering on my small breasts, you really don't look like a woman who's just given birth.

I've never left a baby alone at home, I promise her, I just had to invent something on the spur of the moment so the guard wouldn't get mad, and she looks at me pityingly, I don't think it helped, on the contrary, but I pounce on her sympathy, as if she, a total stranger, can grant me clemency. We have another half hour, why don't we go out to the lawn, I propose, and she nods, climbing the stairs next to me with rapid steps, swinging her arms as though she's rowing a boat downriver, resplendent in her fruit-scented curls, and I try to keep up with her because she, remote and absent-minded, seems to represent a sane, logical world from which I have been momentarily torn and to which, with her help, I shall return.

The guard watches dubiously as I walk past him, limping slightly, ignoring his presence, silently wishing him a new job so that I won't have to encounter his reproachful stare every day, but she greets him warmly, covering for me with her politeness, and we've arrived at the sparse park adjacent to the school's gate, spotted with patches of white rock and surrounded by olive trees with twisted limbs, gnarled as old rheumatic men. We used to come here with Gili when it got oppressively hot, he liked dunking his bare feet in the water canals, sailing his floaty toys, but now the canals are dry, last year's arid winter demands water conservation, and litter is sprinkled among the patches of yellowing grass, and the park, speaking through the coarse cawing of the nesting ravens, seems to be warning us off as if from a plague. Nevertheless, we make our way through it, searching for a clean, shady spot, and there we stretch out. The pain in my leg is piercing, but I ignore it, sprawl out beside her and ask, so whose mother are you? Immediately I admit that, regretfully, I don't know any of the children in the class yet, nor does my son.

Yotam's all set this year, she says, he arrived with a group of friends from kindergarten, and, by the way, my name is Michal, she adds, taking a pack of cigarettes out of her bag. Her lips, painted a pale orange, encircle the cigarette, and then stretch in laughter, it was great seeing you stuck on the gate like that, like a treed cat, and when she laughs she claps her hands enthusiastically, her eyes fixed on mine until I join in her laughter, mildly resentful, was it really so amusing, was this truly the most entertaining thing she'd come across recently, so much so that she has to bask in my humiliation. I apologize again, as if it were the gate of her house I had climbed, its lock I had tried to break. I had to see my son right away, I know it sounds strange, but I didn't have a choice, I say, and she gives me a sidelong glance from a pale, slightly faded eye, the color of the thirsty lawn, her lips still clinging to the leftover smile, and I fall silent, waiting for the question that will inevitably be asked, trying to think of how to respond, how much detail to go into. I feel an urge to tell her everything – about this morning, about my father's curse, even to ask her opinion on divorce, whether it's really a malignant disease that kills children. But to my surprise she doesn't ask anything, just stretches out on her back, her blue linen blouse spread out like a mirror against the cobalt of the sky, her hair fanned out around her head. It looks as if she is about to take a little nap after the enjoyable drama she witnessed earlier, a drama that provided relief from boredom, but whose meaning she has no intention of going into. I observe her movements with sudden hostility, she shows no sign of having heard my words, is it excessive politeness or lack of interest that makes her close her eyes, lying flat on the spiky yellow grass, where ants toil away, advancing toward us in a rear column, marching greedily toward her hair, as if there are breadcrumbs hidden inside it. I don't warn her. There are ants in your underwear again, my mother would cry angrily, fishing my panties out of the laundry basket, waving the blackened cloth in front of my face, the ants swarming to and fro, covering its length and breadth, it's only your panties they come to, she would cry, as if it were my fault.

With her eyes closed I can inspect her thoroughly, her black wrap-around skirt exposes pale feminine thighs, her slightly receding chin is turned to the sun, the gold watch, a bracelet, hangs around her limp wrist, covering her forehead, the broad wedding ring firm on her finger, and I glance at my own hand, a pale band of skin has replaced the ring that was slipped on nearly ten years ago and removed yesterday. A metallic black raven hops toward us on strong legs, as if coveting her jewels, glittering in the sun, and I watch it, its audacity, in a moment it will tear the gold ring from her finger with its curved beak, fly over the park with a hoarse caw of triumph; look, she sits up and points, apparently noticing the raven, but then says, at your foot, if you can call it that, and indeed it looks more like a swollen lump of colored dough forgotten in the sun, bursting out of my sandal straps, and only now do I acknowledge the pain that comes as a kind of astonishing, liberating relief, external confirmation of a growing sense of suffocation.

You took a serious fall, she says, the smile finally leaving her lips, you'll have to get that X-rayed, her hands gently feeling my ankle, testing the movement of the toes; I don't think the bone is broken, she pronounces, it looks like a sprain, when you get home put some ice on it, and admiringly I ask if she's a doctor, and she says, no, not really, her lips drooping as she glances at her watch and jumps quickly to her feet, look at that, we came so early that we're late, you wait here, don't get up, she instructs as I try to get to my feet, I'll bring your son to you.

But he doesn't know you, I protest, he won't just come with you, and she says, trust me, and only when she walks away do I remember that I haven't told her who my son is, maybe she'll bring another child here, and maybe I won't even notice the mistake, and maybe I'll even love him like I love Gili, because the greatest love on earth isn't personal, it doesn't depend on the object of the love but is a reflection of the needs of the lover, and Gili, too, will be picked up by another mother who won't notice the mistake, and perhaps this way he will be saved, for she'll be a mother who doesn't leave her husband, a mother who doesn't tear her family apart.

It seems that I have been left alone in the huge park, alone with the ravens and the piles of fermenting garbage swaying like humps on the back of a giant camel, sending sour smells of rot in my direction. The only others in the park are a distant pack of soldiers next to the main road, their uniforms melting into the grass, lying motionless in the shade of the olive trees, the ravens hopping between them, perching on shelves of rock, cawing ceaselessly, menacingly, telling each other bad news, like the raven who told Adam about the murder of his son Abel. I have landed on Planet Raven where their strict rules apply. Ravens are the most faithful of birds, they stay with the same mate their entire lives, which is why the ancient Egyptians chose them as the sign for marriage in their hieroglyphic script, and now I have broken their laws, and they are gathering around me as if I were a corpse; soon dozens of ravens will grab my clothes in their beaks and carry me away, gliding over my house, which I will soon have to leave, over my father's and mother's house, which I will never see again, and over the scarred squares of the impoverished city that has set itself above richer and more beautiful cities, the haughty, arrogant city that is nourished by the glorious past it invented for itself, which succeeded in convincing the whole world of its importance, and failed to foresee that its importance would become its curse. I will look down on its antiquities, which are more familiar to me than its new neighborhoods, until they drop me on the cusp of the desert, where the city abruptly ends.

Shrill, clear voices approach at a run, on little sandaled feet, scuffed by the summer, they cavort like a pair of clowns, holding half-melted ices in their hands, the gaudy watermelon coloring trickling down their fingers. For a moment I can hardly tell them apart. I had expected to see a little boy with a mop of wheaten curls at her side, but to my surprise his hair is black and straight, like a glossy forest mushroom, his eyes are dark, serious, and he is a little shorter and leaner than my Gili, and still strangely like him. Gili skips by his side, slender legged as a grasshopper, his tears gone. Proudly he shows me his splendid popsicle, as if by the sweat of his brow he had attained it, and mostly he is proud of the new friend who has suddenly come his way. Out of the dozens of strange children whose names float through the air like hats that have not yet landed on the right heads, one distinct child has materialized, and he examines him with satisfaction and vague apprehension, lest he vanish as unexpectedly as he appeared, casting him back into the desolation of his loneliness.

She drops her load next to me – two schoolbags, one wizard's hat, wand and cloak, two water bottles – and flops down again, in exactly the same position as before. I sit up and thank her. You don't look much alike, I say, and she looks her son up and down; no, she says, he looks like his father, and I stretch the little boy's limbs in my mind's eye, setting by her side, with some disappointment, a lean, very upright, serious man. They asked me to tell you that there's a get-together with the parents to welcome the Sabbath tomorrow afternoon, she remembers. Tomorrow? I ask dejectedly. Why, what's the point? And she looks at me in surprise, you know how it is, the beginning of the year, they want the families to get to know each other, it's not so terrible, but I grumble, it's very inconvenient for me at the moment, I won't be able to make it.

Because of your foot? she asks, and I say, no, it's not because of my foot, and again I wait for her to question me, and again she says nothing, her teeth clenching the filter of another cigarette. Maybe it isn't terrible for you, I think sullenly, you'll take your husband and your son and afterwards you'll go home together for dinner, but I – the thought of socializing with all those functioning families when I'm busy dismantling mine brings bile to my tongue – I have no desire to sit next to Amnon and pretend to be a normal family, to sing Sabbath songs with a crowd of smug, self-satisfied strangers. Only a little while ago it would have been natural, simple as breathing. Is this but the beginning of the transformation, I wonder. Is every day in the lives of the divorced strewn with obstacles, must every little event be fumbled over? Amnon will take him without me, I decide, after all, I can hardly walk, and I lie down on the grass again, at her side, silently watching our children jump like puppies over the empty canals. A pleasant breeze brings Gili's laughter to me, deep and mirthful, it weaves between the squawking black ravens and instills a deep serenity in the chambers of my heart, why were you in such a panic, no catastrophe is going to happen, everybody is in the process of getting divorced, is already divorced, or going to get divorced in the future, maybe this woman lying next to me is planning her new life at this very moment, don't let anyone scare you, he'll be fine, he has a mother, he has a father, he has a friend, he has a popsicle in his hand, what else does a boy need.

I have to get going, she says, jumping up again, and it seems the more time passes, the older she gets, right before my eyes, in the space of a single hour, she has changed from a girl to a woman, and while before I was surprised that she already had a child, now, with the sun hitting her straight in the face, her skin sags, and I am surprised that her child is so young. Yotam, we have to pick Maya up from her class, she shouts, her voice harsh, as though she had been calling him repeatedly, and Yotam drags his feet in our direction, complaining, but Mommy it's fun here, and she says, we'll come back another time, let's go, Maya's waiting for us.

We're going too, I say quickly, and she turns to me, can you walk? She holds out a white hand, blue veins running along it like winding riverbeds, and I rise heavily to my feet, walking has suddenly become a complicated project, demanding care and deliberation. She appraises me, I'll give you a lift, she offers, where do you live? Not far from here, I say, leaning on her arm and limping to her car, a sudden burden on the tranquil life of a family of strangers.

Mommy, is Daddy home already? I hear Gili ask from the back seat, and as I attempt to formulate an appropriate response, she replies. Turns out it was her son asking, even their voices are alike, not yet, he'll come home in the evening, and to my horror I hear Gili whisper, Yotam, does your father sleep with you at your house? And Yotam says, yeah, it's his house, except when he's in reserves or out of the country, and Gili carries on in a clandestine, conspiratorial voice, my father sleeps at night in a fridge, but the fridge makes noise and he can't fall asleep. Don't be silly, Gili, I say with a forced laugh, you're confused, you didn't understand what Daddy said, but he ignores me and adds, you're lucky that your parents aren't splitting up, and Yotam says, sometimes they split up and sometimes they don't, everybody's parents split up sometimes, and Gili says, but my parents are spitting up forever.

That's it, this is us, I announce, even though it's only the beginning of the street and we're too many strides from my door, come on, Gili, they're in a hurry, thanks a million, Michal, you saved my life, and she casts a pale green look in my direction, her face lit with surprise and curiosity again, as if I'm back up on the gate. Do you want me to help you get home? she asks, and I say, no need, it's pretty close, I can manage, but her eyes follow me as I hobble, and they're full of wonder and concern and even sorrow, as if a long, sad letter addressed to me has reached her by mistake.

Mommy's limping, Mommy's limping, he skips around me, flapping his arms like a bat in his black cape, and I plead with him, give me your hand, Gili, I can barely walk, but he's not eager to take on the role of savior, and even when he agrees, at last, to give me his sticky hand, it seems that all his weight is tugging me toward the leaf strewn sidewalk. The pain peals through me like the clear, heavy ringing of a church bell, and I listen to it in fear and astonishment, almost in awe, so sharply does it focus my attention, marking a clear division, growing greater every minute, between what was up to now and what will be from now on, between who I apparently was until a few hours ago – a married woman with a family and an apartment, all of whose possessions were tangible but limited – and what I will shortly become, a divorcee with a child, without a mate, without an apartment, who, for the time being, has almost nothing, but may soon have it all, and that uncertainty intensifies, present in my life after a long absence, and it possesses the power to alleviate pain, to put a fresh sheen on reality, and when I lie on the sofa with my foot raised on the tower of cushions Gili playfully arranged for me, it seems to me that these are the labor pangs of my new existence, that from the blocked womb of my former, fossilized self, a new life is emerging, born in a joy-tinged torment, a life as yet unfamiliar, but nonetheless beckoning, with a newborn's initial sob, to grab hold of it with both my hands, to clasp it to my breast.

Mommy, kick, come on, you said you'd kick it to me, he demands, crouched in front of imaginary goalposts between the two walls, waiting for the ball, and I sigh, maybe tomorrow, Gili, I can barely stand up, how can I play like this; but he insists, not tomorrow, today, I'm bored at home, his face grows redder, in a minute it will be contorted in weeping, and the tears will fall onto his shirt, clear and as full of importance as the season's first drops of rain, and I try placating him, let's play something else, Dominoes or Monopoly, but why should he give in when his purpose is so obvious, to force a blind person to compete against him in marksmanship, and while I go on listing possible games like a waitress offering items on the menu, he allows a cunning smile to appear between his tears as he announces, I already called Daddy to come and play soccer with me because you can't, he'll be here soon.

The sudden, sharp contradiction between his wishes and mine hits me like a blow to the chest. My little cub, flesh of my flesh, my soul, my only child, almost unbearably loved, for years his wish was my wish, his joy my joy, his sorrow my sorrow, and now this sudden conflict has sprouted between us, like a skyscraper erected overnight. His wish is no longer my command, and it seems that this tear, like the gash in a mourner's garment, is the true chasm in my life. It's not the growing estrangement from Amnon, but the estrangement from Gili's wants and desires that place me in the opposing camp, and it seems that the rare, precious harmony that existed between us for six whole years is wilting in the corner of the room next to the unwanted toys, to be replaced by a growing web of tension, overlapping and opposing needs, alien and extraneous considerations. I regard him resentfully as he clutches the ball in his hand, looking expectantly at the window, his milky face set in an expression of pride and apprehension, like a hungry child who has just succeeded in obtaining a hot meal, but cannot help but worry about where the next one will come from.

When Amnon arrives I pretend to be sleeping, and perhaps I really am sleeping because their voices are distant and muffled, as in a dream, the pain in my ankle separates me from them, exempts me from any obligation, limits my ability to move, but frees my spirit. Their conversation bounces around the room, soft and malleable as the Nerf ball rolling between them. Cheers and cries of victory trail behind the ball and, wrapped in the twilight of the pain, their identity blurs until it seems to me that they are my father and mother tiptoeing around me in the living room of our house as I lie ill, free to bask in fantasies of love. Like a cat with her litter I would lie and lick my fantasies, fawn over them, paint my adult life in flaming colors, with my parents a couple of exhausted sailors rowing the unsteady lifeboat of my childhood, trying with the last of their strength to lift me onto the ship of my adult life, and the minute I climb onto the deck I wave goodbye until they disappear into the blue horizon. Stretched out on the sofa, covered with a thin blanket, it seems to me that I am indeed waving lazily to this pair as they recede into the distance, giving way to other figures, still blurred, completely mute, only the murmur of their conversation still echoing in my ears, and perhaps only now I realize that the warm, natural hum that has accompanied me for the past six years will no longer be heard here, the ambient sounds of a father and his son, a son and his father, and though they will still murmur to each other, I will not hear them, and the purr of our conversations will also be left without a listener, drifting from the open windows into the street, swallowed up among the other voices, among the sounds of families preparing for the night.

Tonight I've been granted a final opportunity to share their lives without me, to be a spectator, to see how they will play in the afternoons on his days of the week. Mondays and Thursdays? Sundays and Wednesdays? We haven't decided yet. This is how they will eat their awkward dinners, facing each other across the kitchen table in another apartment, and he won't bother to peel his cucumber for him, like I do, and he won't cut the crust off his bread in brown rings, and he'll give him a soup spoon instead of a teaspoon, and they'll agree to go without bathing, like now, and without brushing his teeth. They'll put his dirty clothes next to his bed for him to wear again the next day, but the bedtime story will be long and generous, as will their conversations, and when I'm not there, as if I've left for another archeological conference, I need not fear that he will lose his temper, or hurt the child with his jagged tone of voice, because when I'm not around he always makes an effort, and Gili himself tries so hard to flatter him, to fully ingratiate himself with his sole guardian. From my place on the couch in the dark living room I hear them putting the toy animals to sleep by family, lion and lioness and little lion cub, tiger and tigress and little tiger cub. Does Gili detect the bitter smell that clings to their fur? I hear Amnon announce, and here's Scotland Bear too, a hasty family reunion on the narrow bed where I lay this morning parting from his body for all eternity, but this body, which now revolts me, is so loved by Gili. At this very moment he nestles up to it, grunting happily in its arms, and I lie rigid, afraid of moving my foot, trying to get used to the complexity that will become part of my life, to be able to contain both my revulsion and Gili's love for the source of my revulsion, to accept Amnon as the beloved father of my child and at the same time to keep him away from me. It seems that in order to do so I will have to duplicate myself, or sever myself, and the weight of this new task tosses me back into a scared, moonstruck sleep because it's all up to me and yet nothing can be changed, because this family murmur, with all its pleasantness, grows ever faint, drowned out by the trumpet call of my new life, the loud notes blaring as from a ballroom in the bowels of a ship.

When I wake up, shivering with cold in the middle of the night, a gray but still radiant river flows before my eyes. I will never cease to be astonished by the sight of a river, the sight of moving living water, as in the European port city to which I traveled for the last conference I attended, carrying with me the echoes of a fight, of sentences hurled too many times, dulled by overuse: don't threaten me, you're only threatening yourself, who do you think you are, I'm sick and tired of your complaining, I'm sick and tired of you, there's no way I'll go on like this, I'll leave you, this time I'm serious. The elegant hotel room window looked out on the river and the vast iron bridge above it, and the smaller model next to it, like a distorted mirror, and on both bridges a constant flow of traffic, rushing trains, red and toy-like, and light rails holding one arm aloft, tearing the spider web of the high-tension wires, and beyond the river, the facades of brightly colored buildings, narrow and fragile, and ships sailing, seemingly hovering over the water. Was it there that the decision was made, sudden but predictable, facing the river that bore the weight of the ships with surprising ease. The sounds of the last fight swirled around me, hoarse, bitter, as if we were there together, violating the silence of the room with our voluble hostility, he stood in front of me, aggressive, accusatory, ugly with rage. This is not the man I wanted, this is not the life I sought, and even I am profoundly different from the woman I thought I'd be, something has gone irrevocably wrong between us, must I really reconcile myself to all this, will I never live differently, too soon it becomes too late.

Silently his shadow glides from room to room and switches off the lights, the house rendered dark and still, a passerby in the street might imagine a family slipping into the night's sleep, pulling the autumn blanket around its body. The bedroom door closes behind him like the most natural thing in the world and I am on the sofa far from them both, as if I were still in the hotel room overlooking the radiant gray river, a continent away; is this what my life will look like, I asked then, is this how my youthful dreams will die, giving up the ghost with a soundless sigh. Gili will grow up, gracefully evading the role I intended for him, filling a void whose depths I never even imagined, and then what, a new child? A new dig? A new trip? A new love that will blossom in secret like a primrose in a bed of shale – fragile, seasonal, short lived? No, I promise the ships gliding along the river, it's not too late, I can still hope for more, and I fling the windows wide and announce, as if trying to persuade a large audience watching me from across the river: it is over, ladies and gentlemen, it is stone dead, dead forever.

Chapter three

The sound of hesitant singing, like a prayer with no hope of being answered, one that knocks limply on the gates of heaven, greets us as we enter the yard, late, taking up a spot behind the other families, all seated in a vibrantly colored circle, crowding onto blankets and straw mats like miniature versions of Noah's Ark, raising their voices in faltering song. We don't have so much as a blanket, and Gili clutches my fingers, Mommy we have to have a blanket, he mutters, everybody brought a blanket. Nobody told me, I say self righteously, casting a reproachful look at Amnon, as if he is responsible for the omission, while he pushes forward, impatient as ever, signaling us to follow him with a ludicrous gesture, like a general gloriously conquering a piece of land for an army that's already disintegrated.

Shabbat Shalom to the Miller family, the teacher chimes in her candy-coated voice, come over here, sit down and we'll continue, she says, pointing firmly to a vacant spot right next to her, and I drag a reluctant Gili behind me, hopping painfully between elbows and knees, stepping on the corner of a desirable blanket, a leaky bottle of water, a gaping bag of diapers, and we sit down next to Amnon and the teacher, our separateness obvious to everyone in the absence of a blanket of our own, that shabby, homely blanket that creates a common ground for each family, something only we lack, not belonging to them or to each other, planted on the bare pavement of the yard, the miserable Gili between us, looking around with surrendering eyes.

Hey, we're the shortest family, he whispers, and the force of habit compels me to stand up for our honor, why short? Daddy's very tall, and so are you, but he immediately explains, because we're only three, and indeed when I let my eyes wander over the scores of strange faces, I find big sisters and little brothers, babies and adolescents, grandmothers and grandfathers resplendent in white shirts, even several well-groomed dogs, and the anomaly spreads across my forehead like a scarlet letter, this is how we will remain, for, like someone cut down in the bloom of youth, we will never grow again.

Harden not your heart, as in the provocation, as in the temptation in the wilderness, they sing haltingly from the photocopied pages of the prayer book. The teacher hands me a stack of pages and I look at them, trying to lend my voice to the group effort, but the words crack in my throat, *They are a stray-hearted people, and they have not known my ways: As I swore in my wrath that they should not enter into my rest.* Under the cover of the singing a continuous conversation is being conducted, free words infiltrate the verses, and it is to them I listen: so, how have you been doing, why don't you come over tomorrow, how about going to the beach, where did you spend the summer, what an awful location for a school, right in the middle of town, try not to think about it, everything's equally dangerous these days, it's all fate. It seems that most of the people know each other, and have accumulated common memories, attended school functions together, an aromatic warmth rises from the blankets as if a secret stew is simmering on a hidden stove, each family bringing with it the smell of its home, its breath, its cooking, its laundry powder and its shampoo, the smell of negotiations and compromises, intimacy and habit, ancient power struggles and friendships forged almost absent-mindedly, and I look at them, leaning on each other, forming complex geometric shapes, soon they will no longer be foreign to me, perhaps I will even know what their various poses hide, but in the meantime only one smile is cast in my direction, and it comes in the dreamy form of sealed lips and narrow, pale green eyes. She is sitting cross legged, her arm around her son's shoulder, an older girl in a red velvet dress is splayed across her lap and behind the fan of her radiant curls looms the forehead of a pale man with graying hair and dark, deep-set eyes, shaded by thick eyebrows, his hands massaging her neck and her shoulders as they sway to the singing.

Your God will rejoice in you as a groom rejoices in his bride, the voices of the adults try to accompany the teacher's voice like a slow convoy, obedient but listless, while the children giggle, beginning to lose patience, *Come in peace, crown of her husband, both in happiness and in jubilation, amidst the faithful of the treasured nation, come o bride, come o bride,* and for a moment it seems that now, of all times, we have wound up at a wedding, and on the Sabbath of our separation, we are obliged to sing emotional marriage songs, and, indeed, the teacher confirms my suspicions, asking in her commanding voice, kids, if the Sabbath is the bride, then who do you think is the groom? She poses her riddle to the baffled children. I know, I know, God, declares a little girl with wild-red hair, and the teacher says, no, not God, listen, she tells them, after the world was created, Sabbath complained to God that she was the only day without a mate, and God soothed her and promised her that the people of Israel would be her mate, her groom.

How's that possible, Gili says, squinting at me, so many grooms for one bride? But the teacher is not interested in petty details, she has apparently told this story dozens of times and she continues rapidly, you know, kids, hundreds of years ago the rabbis would put on white clothes and go out into the fields in order to receive the Sabbath, she says, heaving herself up, beads of sweat glittering on her upper lip, why don't we go out, too, and see who discovers the Sabbath first. Most of the children rise to the challenge immediately, abandoning their family blankets and clustering around their teacher, and I try to push the hesitant Gili, who clings to me and buries his head in my lap, go ahead, I say, go with all the other kids.

Like a pack of gangly colts they gallop past, in a minute they'll trample him, but one of them pulls up in front of him, his narrow grown-up face set on frail shoulders, come on, Gili, come with me, it'll be fun, and in a flash the timidity is gone, even the absence of the blanket is no longer important to him, and it's as if another child has jumped into his skin and he pops to his feet, forgets our doleful presence, and sets out with his new friend Yotam to meet the Sabbath queen, the beautiful bride who marries her husband every week anew. When I look for Michal I see that she's already staring in my direction, she must have sent her son our way, and I shape my lips in a thank you. To my disappointment, she doesn't react, staring ahead with a glazed look in her eyes, her mouth slightly open, unaware of the words mouthed in her direction, but above the golden crown of hair her husband sends me a questioning, almost indignant look, as if I'm disturbing them with my muddled messages, and I sweep my eyes away, careful not to send an additional glance in their direction.

Throughout, he is behind me, uncharacteristically silent, and I am careful not to relax and lean back against his knees, like most of the women around me, but to sit up straight and rigid as if there is no one there. The whisper of his breath on my neck, the cool air that has churned around in his lungs and emerged thick and hot, incites such revulsion that it feels as if my skin is sprouting tiny thorns of resistance. Even with my back turned I can sense his eyes panning his surroundings in supercilious disdain, on the way back he will condemn the ritual as primitive, the ridiculous songs, and what the hell is that supposed to mean, going to look for the Sabbath, what a load of crap, I told you not to register him for that school. But I won't have to listen to that anymore, I won't have to see the happy memories wiped off Gili's face, and I won't have to try to persuade him that perhaps we should start welcoming the Sabbath at home too, nor hear his contemptuous snort, come on, Ella, I'm surprised at you, what do we have to do with this idol worship, this Jewish haggling?

How sweet it will be to go home without him, to talk to Gili without him interrupting us, urgently reporting every scrap of a thought that occurs to him, to look at the newspaper without him saying, leave that garbage alone, to speak on the phone without him cutting me off for God knows what, and all this, of course, isn't the essence, but the essence grows increasingly blurred and it's taken the shape of an eternally locked gate, that's how I'll see him, through a closed gate. I glance around me, there is a look of aggressive pride on the faces of the women, most of them no longer captivating, peasant women with beefy thighs running the farmyards of their lives, and still they are proud to display their achievements, written in blurred writing on the domestic blanket with its accumulated stains of wine and coffee, urine and vomit, tar and milk, and behind every stain lies a happy memory of adversity and triumph: you remember, when the kids were little, how we took a trip to the Golan, and the baby almost drowned, you remember how we once got lost in an Arab village, how scary that was. I look at them with a defiant expression, you won't believe, ladies, what I'm going to do, I'm going to begin again, a completely new life, to be a girl again, to be filled with fresh feelings again, to abort before my hair goes gray and my back is loaded with a sack full of rotting resentment, of resignation that ferments like garbage in the sun. Wait and see, I turn to my unaware audience, as if a marvel is being revealed for my eyes alone, an astonishing, chance discovery like turning sand into glass, reversing the irreversible, I will beat time, I will break the laws of nature, while, on the other hand, my silent audience remains in an inferior stage before the advent of fire; look, the dull matter is becoming pure and transparent, and you don't see it, and in this manner I veer between arrogance and dejection; you, what do you have to look forward to, a promotion at work, an annual vacation, a new apartment; for me the future is an open horizon, and an impatient joy surges inside me, I can't wait for this future, all I need now is to shed the cranky nuisance whose breath stings the back of my neck. We haven't exchanged a word all day, from my place on the couch I followed his movements with hostility, the pain in my ankle forcing me to endure his presence, but now that the pain has somewhat subsided, my resolution returns in full force. No, I will not retreat, in spite of all the warnings and threats of the past few days, even if his hand rests on my back, even if his voice calls to me with surprising softness, saying, Ella, what's wrong, what is this madness, don't you care about Gili, don't you care about us? At any moment, it seems, he is going to call on the bored parents to judge between us, and I whisper, stop it, Amnon, that's enough, you woke up too late.

Behind my back his voice hardens, without turning my face I know that his broad jaw is drooping sullenly, his eyes are narrowing, what's going on with you, tell me, what's the meaning of this wanton behavior, you think you're sixteen years old and you feel like rebelling against your father because you didn't dare do it at the right age? I'm sorry, honey, it's too late, twenty years too late, what right do you have to ruin all our lives? His voice rises and the last words are not for my ears alone, the adjacent families on their blankets look at us uneasily, wondering at the jarring notes we are sounding in the middle of the family get-together, what right do you have to ruin all our lives, and I get up quickly and remove myself from the circle, but to my chagrin my aching ankle prevents me from moving with the imperial disdain I strive for, and I am forced to clumsily hop my way to the gate, like a stunned bird that has narrowly escaped a predatory cat.

How different this place looks in the evening, as if it has woken from a nightmare, in the wild tangle of the ravens' park human bushes are growing, illicit couples embracing passionately between the branches, whispering like hot coals, harboring a secret that pours a welcome and sad heaviness into their blood. In the fading light it is hard to distinguish between trees and people, people and rocks, it seems that the same yearning has taken hold of the inanimate objects and of me, but his words pursue me, and behind them his clumsy body, too, in the faded striped shirt and the short pants whose deep pockets always hold a few grains of leftover sand; look around you, Ella, he says, his hand reaching for my shoulder, the difference in height between us lending him a paternal air, look at all these women, they seem satisfied, no? What do you think, that they're all married to angels? You'd be surprised, but they make the best of what they've got and try to keep their families together, only you insist on thinking that you've been deprived, that you deserve more, only you don't appreciate what you have, every woman here would be happy to live with a husband like me, and I shrink back, the fence pressing into my back; you see, that's exactly your problem, you're so pleased with yourself that you'll never bother to change, you don't even try to understand why I don't want you anymore, you never ask in order to hear an answer, but to prove me wrong, I'm sick of your contempt, I'm sick of you, I'm not going to bury myself with you in the middle of my life, is that clear?

You're a monster, he says quietly, in astonishment, as if to himself, you're not human, and I whisper, great, so be happy that you're getting rid of me, why should you live with a monster, and he says, believe me, it's not myself I'm worried about, I'll get along just fine without you, it's only Gili I'm worried about. Suddenly you're worried about him? I interrupt, for six years you've neglected him and now you remember to worry about him? And he bares his big teeth at me, I can see the fine cracks running down them. I neglected him? I'm the best father there is, just because I don't prance around him all day like you, that means I'm not a good father? Look how attached he is to me, no less than he is to you. Of course, I say, you're the only father he has; he doesn't know any different.

So that's what you're looking for, he says through clenched teeth, a new father for my son? You're out of your mind, I'll take him away from you, I'll go to the rabbinical court and get them to give me custody, and I chuckle, you really scare me, an egomaniac like you to bring up a child on your own? And what about your lectures and your articles and your sleep and your basketball and your buddies? Up to now you haven't been willing to give up a thing, if you'd only given up something we wouldn't be splitting up at all, I shoot the poisoned arrows feverishly, one after the other, his heart seems outlined in crude red brush strokes on the material of his shirt and I aim and shoot, mildly doubtful of their validity, but unable to stop; is there any point in listing the disappointments that piled up one on top of the other, each slightly varied, like clay bricks made by hand and dried in the sun, shaped like so many loaves of bread.

The sinking sun paints the ravens' park in soft crimson shades, the lawns pink as the blanket of a much-awaited baby girl, the feathers of the circling ravens a fiery black. His face comes closer to mine, flushed and exposed, as if flayed, I don't intend to beg anymore, he says, trying a new tack, just allow me to remind you that you can only excavate a dig once, and if you don't exhaust its possibilities there's no way of going back again. Great time for an introductory lecture, I say, yawning, what's that got to do with anything, and he opens his eyes round and red as cherries, I'm simply warning you that I'm not as erratic as you are, when I move on, it's over; I know you, you'll regret this and you'll want to come back and I'll already be somewhere else, so take it into account, when I go, I'm gone, and, this time it is he who turns his back and walks away, while I try to shoot one last arrow, don't threaten me, the days when your threats upset me are over, but this time the arrow seems to have missed his broad, rapidly receding back, and it crosses the sky with a whistling sound, yes, the days are past when every argument drilled a hole inside me, when I would be beside myself with sorrow, when I couldn't bear the resentment and the hostility, when I had to appease you even if my anger had far from cooled, I will never miss those days, I'd rather live alone than like that, vulnerable whenever I faced you, always facing you, never beside you.

Is that the way you all live as well, I ask of the transient encampment, wandering in agitated impatience like the children of Israel before the giving of the Torah, from strife to insult and from insult to strife, from suffocation to hostility and from hostility to suffocation, waiting for a lull that will awaken in you distant memories of love, trying with gritted teeth to keep the family intact, weary and disappointed, and nevertheless clinging to one another as in a deep sleep, or is there perhaps something you know that I don't. Perhaps your mothers spoke a secret in your ears, a magic spell passed on from generation to generation, for some reason withheld from me, tell me what it is that makes your breath mingle, what makes the cells of your bodies produce the mists of tenderness, yes, that is what we so sorely lack, tenderness.

In the distance I make out a woman removing a shawl, draping it around her husband's shoulders, a simple gesture that squeezes a sigh from my throat, and I lean against the fence, contemplating the oval structure created by their seated bodies, protecting the little ones gathered in their midst, like the remains of an ancient settlement discovered on a mountain, a row of rooms joined together in an encircling belt to protect the flock at night. I survey them stubbornly, searching for a hold in the strange faces, as if standing in front of ancient ruins; what can I learn about the reality of this transient life, for these are not structures that can be measured by the Egyptian cubit or the Greek foot, defined as a temple or a house, identified by the telltale vessels of clay or stone. The few clues are on the surface and they are itinerant, when they go they will leave nothing behind them, perhaps the pit of a peach that has just been eaten, a coin from a pocket, a pacifier whose absence will cause an upheaval. Is it really easier to decipher the fossilized results of human activity than these vital, animated artifacts, when our purpose, after all, is not to find the remains but to explain their significance, to reconstruct the reality of a life that has passed from the world? Well, yes, the findings are on the surface, changing from moment to moment, for example Michal's blanket is suddenly emptying, she is alone now lying on her back, while her husband paces somberly to and fro, holding their little girl's hand, and I watch him absent-mindedly as he paces, the profile facing me is hard but at the same time fragile, why has he abandoned the family blanket? Not far from there stands Amnon, tall and slightly stooped, a woman in a long dress engages him in conversation while I scan the lawns, trying to locate the children.

Does no one sense their absence, even their voices are no longer heard; perhaps the Sabbath queen has abducted them to another country, pure as the driven snow, where they move about clad in white robes like angels, holding long candles in their hands, the wax dripping onto their fingers, onto their bitten nails, sliding down their arms, their slightly protruding stomachs, collecting in the round pools of their navels and sliding down their slender thighs and along their calves. Look, our children are covered in wax from head to toe, our children have turned into candles, into wax statues, and we will all be left here until daybreak, orphaned of our children, a vulgar, motley crew, in our grief we will come together, and in an instant the curse comes back to me, swaying from side to side like the pendulum of my father's foot, commandeering a megaphone until it seems to me that everyone can hear its call, he won't survive, he'll be annihilated, more certain even than the jubilation of the children coming back to us, skipping on their thin legs, like white ravens before they were painted black as punishment for not returning to Noah's Ark. Mommy, the Sabbath is as beautiful as a bride, Gili shouts, running excitedly toward me, his cheeks flushed, his hands full of candies, she has yellow hair and a bride's veil, and her face is pink, and we saw her in the sky, she threw candies from the sky, and I clasp him to my heart, stroke his sweat-dampened hair; dear child, in your small body I built myself a home, the only home in which I am safe, free, loved, for this is the face of love and these are its features, love has autumn-leaf eyes, and teeth hanging by a thread, its nose is thin and delicate and its cheeks are smeared with chocolate.

He leaves a sticky jellybean in my hand and runs to his father. I hobble after him to the teeming camp and as we reassemble we are obliged to return to our places and to introduce ourselves, as per the direction of the teacher, each family saying their names and, to my horror, their hobbies. It's our turn, and Gili pipes in his high voice, my father's name is Amnon and my mother's name is Ella, and I'm Gilad but I'm called Gili, and when the teacher asks, and what do you like to do together, he hesitates a moment and then mumbles in a whispery voice, divorce.

Speak up, Gilad, the teacher says, we can't hear you, and he mutters, we like divorces, and the teacher strains to hear his words, horses? how nice, she says, you like horses, and she breezes along, to the families that like having picnics, traveling, swimming, diving, seeing movies together, and I look shamefaced at the women as they follow their children's words with tense smiles. Perhaps Amnon is right, they, too, must have problems, fights, frustrations, and still they seem content, as if they have come to a unanimous decision. Perhaps all of them have really made a pact like the one my father recommended for achieving perfect happiness, a pact that limits expectations and deadens hopes, but in return bestows great peace of mind; is that how I, too, should have behaved, and again I feel the kick of rebellion, no, their way is not my way, their life is not my life, and it's as if I am declaring a secret competition, beginning this evening, between me and them, between my way and theirs. The year has just begun, we'll all meet here again at Hanukkah and Passover, Purim and Shavuot, then we'll see where I am and where you are, and in the meantime I realize that the tedious ceremony is over, and refreshments are being served, the children are circulating among us like little waiters, offering slices of late-summer watermelon, sweet challah bread with raisins, and one of the women stands up, towering slim and supple in tight jeans and a white tank top, her hair long and straight, a beautiful toddler in her arms, and she says, embarrassed and enthusiastic, hey, we're having a party tonight, anyone who wants to come is invited.

What's the occasion? someone asks, and she looks at her husband and giggles, as if sharing a secret with him, a faint blush on her cheeks, nothing special, we just feel like celebrating, she says and gives their address, there'll be lots of wine, good music, should be fun, and her husband, youthful and handsome, stands up next to her and, with his hand on her shoulder, he explains to everyone how to get there, and soon enough a jolly throng forms around their happiness, sure we'll come, why not, as long as we can find a babysitter, should we bring something, I've got a delicious cake, where did you say to turn, the first one after the traffic circle, left or right, and I avert my eyes from them, staring at the thin flames of the Sabbath candles trembling in the evening breeze, like a pair of eyes, yellow with age and illness, malicious, conspiring.

Bless me in peace, ye angels of peace, ye messengers of the Most High, they sing with their mouths full of the sweet bread, *may your departure be in peace, ye angels of peace, messengers of the Most High,* and already they are shaking their blankets and folding them up, some neatly and some in untidy bundles, collecting their knapsacks, their children, their dogs, their baby carriages, and scattering like clouds dispersed by the wind, getting into their cars or walking light-footed to their homes, to their Sabbath dinners, to their parties, to their routines. Some will eat at their grandparents' house, some at their friends' house, some will invite friends over to their house and their children, Gili's future friends, will enthusiastically set the table, enjoying the bustle, while we proceed slowly in the fading light to our first weekend apart, to our new, severed lives, and I know that soon this ritual will be the norm and that our former lives will fade into incomprehensibility and Gili will hardly remember what it was like, when we were a real family. It will take another ten years for our lives apart to catch up with our lives together, but well before that our common past will morph into legend, once upon a time we had one house, many years ago, and one fridge, and one dining table, and we would come home to our house as if it were the most natural thing in the world, without coordinating, without discussing where he would sleep or who he would spend the day with. As we approach the house, a new and unfamiliar tension rises from my ankle to my forehead, as though an operation was scheduled for early the next morning and, despite the fact that the preparations have been completed, the warnings given, the chances of recuperation clarified, a small unknown factor claims the mind, wakens doubt, perhaps it would be better not to operate, perhaps the disease will pass of its own accord, perhaps the hardships of the cure outweigh the hardships of the disease.

Leaning on a stick I found along the way, I trod, as I will in my old age, without any future ahead of me, and with only one asset in my possession, the one I so sorely lack now, knowledge, and from the top of the hill I'll peer down at days long gone and I will know whether all this was obligatory or gratuitous, for the best or for the worst. Gili and Amnon walk on ahead and I look at them, as though I just happened to be behind a tall father carrying his son on his shoulders, and there is no mother by their side, the mother is waiting for them at home, busy making supper, and soon she will greet them with a kiss, or perhaps she was taken from them cruelly, snatched away in a fatal accident, a malignant disease, or perhaps she left of her own free will, to find herself a new life, to break the laws of nature, to go back to being a girl.

When I was a girl I had no child. Without him I would fall into the darkness, swim every night in churning waters, river stones across my back, and wake up bruised in the morning to a smoky fiery sky; without him I would escape to the orange groves, leaving behind me my father's face, blue with rage, his tirades sawing through the body of my youth, and I would find a dry branch there and dig in the ground, perhaps if I dug deep enough I would discover a home, and it would be my home and there I would find the bones of a girl, and she would be my sister.

Daddy, let's wait for Mommy, I hear Gili whine, and I see Amnon stop reluctantly, fix his eyes on the pavement, bend down and unload the child from his shoulders. When I reach them Gili holds out his hand to me and his other hand to Amnon, and he says, you're the best parents in the world, better than all the other parents, and I hunch my shoulders uncomfortably at this groundless praise, trying to gage the extent of the anger behind it. Yes, he repeats to our somber faces, really, I know that sometimes I make you mad, but remember that I love you best in the world, and you do so much for me, and I stop him with suppressed impatience, I can't bear to hear one more word, it would be better for him to curse us out, lash out at us with his fists, and in that way do we proceed in silence, his narrow body unwillingly transmitting currents of hostility between us. Families glide past, returning from synagogue, the perfumes of the women mingling with the voices of the children, in the middle of the street they walk, begrudgingly giving way to the few cars because even on the main road the traffic is dwindling, the city falling silent at last, like a baby calmed from his crying, and only his shortness of breath, his sudden damp sobs, bear witness to the grief that has passed.

The child's narrow hips shiver in the evening breeze and I press him to me. Lights flicker one after another on the exposed mountain ridge to the east, bright as fruit drops, lemon and orange, grape and raspberry, a thick light lies on the walls, seemingly emerging from the depths of the earth, sharpening the crosses at the top of the church spires, like those menacing wooden crosses the Romans planted on the hills around the besieged city to scare the rebels, to demonstrate what would happen to them if they refused to surrender, *O sanctuary of the King, o royal city, arise and depart from the turmoil, too long you have dwelt in the vale of tears, and He will take pity upon you.*

And already the door to the stairwell opens before us and Gili drags the two of us after him like a stubborn little wagon pulling the horses behind it, but I make haste to say in a firm voice, the voice of the new teacher, Daddy isn't coming up with us, Gili, he's going now, tomorrow he'll come and take you for a few hours, and to my surprise Amnon doesn't argue. His face frozen, he bends over him, kisses him on the top of his head and leaves almost at a run, without saying a word, without hearing Gili burst into tears as he climbs the stairs, the embarrassment of the door opening onto the empty apartment, the groan of the heavy evening hours, the bitter, adult weeping, soured and despairing, like that of an old man lamenting the failures of his life.

How did this heavy, impermeable stone heart take root within me this evening, how in the face of his grief do I steel myself, repulse his tears, belittle his pain, despite the feeble emissaries of mercy pleading on his behalf. Among the families I gave in to weakness for a moment, under the mantle of the Sabbath, but here, at home, I recover my strength, and I embrace my resolution and press it to my heart, my new baby, my unadulterated hope, because it is not for Amnon that I long when Gili corrals his tears and falls asleep at last, not he I wish for by my side, with his feverish verbosity and his endless grievances, covering for his neediness. Like a young girl left alone at home, I celebrate my sudden freedom, nobody speaks to me, nobody needs me, nobody watches what I do, my presence does not wreak havoc in anybody's heart, and I warn myself, don't be tempted to believe in the lie of families, or those artificial pacts, don't be alarmed by prophecies of wrath, just think how simple and pleasant this domestic freedom is, and it seems to me that the apartment is a warm, perfumed orange grove, dotted with modest wildflowers, and this time I won't return, I won't even hear my parents searching for me, begging, this time I won't return.

Stretched out on the sofa, exhausted but content, as if I have come back from a backbreaking military maneuver with a promotion, I listen to the silence waft down the street, practically hearing the leaves disconnecting from their branches and drifting down until they drop to the pavement, I listen to Gili muttering in his sleep, to the fragments of liturgical songs flickering in my memory, bless me in peace, angels of peace; from time to time I hear the phone ring, the sound of the recorded messages piling up like the cushions piled under my foot, messages in tense voices charting Amnon's unhinged, erratic course. I listen unwillingly, no, no, I'm not here, I'm not available, you won't be able to do as you wish with me tonight because tonight is not like all other nights.

Ella, answer me, I know you're there. Amnon was just here and he's in a terrible state. You have to get in touch with him, I'm afraid of what he might do to himself. Believe me, I wouldn't say so without reason. I've known him since he was six years old and I've never seen him in such a state. Think about what you're doing, he's the father of your child after all. Do you want your son to be left without a father? I think you have to give him another chance, otherwise you might regret it.

Ella, this is Gabi again, I wish you'd answer. I promise you that he'll make an effort. I know it's not easy for you with him but he really loves you. Maybe you should try marriage counseling, what have you got to lose? You have to know, for Gili's sake, that you did all you could, otherwise it will haunt you for the rest of your life.

Ella, it's Talia, Amnon's just left, he asked me to talk to you, I'm really worried about him, even though I'm on your side. He's completely broken, you have to hold off on the separation, call me as soon as you get this message, kisses.

And when I don't reply their voices remain in the air, pecking at my peace of mind, flying between the walls, stubborn and somber, robbing me of the solitude I sought. Reluctantly, I host Gabi, and Talia, listening to their arguments and not answering them, afraid of the moment when they will invade me, when their voices will turn into mine, and it seems that I have only one answer for them, but precisely these words cannot be said: When I was a child I had no husband, I breathed alone, dived alone into the smoky caves of books, alone and barefoot on the blazing dirt road, alone on the wet fence in the cloudy night, surrounded by yellow jasmine flowers that had no scent.

Hi, Ella, this is Michal, Yotam's mother, he wants to know if Gili can come and play with him tomorrow morning, if it's still hard for you to walk, we can come by and pick him up.

Ella, I have to talk to you right away, I'll try to drop in later, after your father goes to bed. I have something important to say to you.

But when I was a child I had no husband, how could you forget, Mother, you had a husband and I didn't, and that was almost the only difference between us because you wanted to be a child too, bowed beneath the weight of his personality you would escape with me to the orange grove, join in my lonely game of hide-and-seek because I could still sometimes hide from him and you couldn't, and there you would lay out your case before me, turning me into a judge in the tribunals we held behind his back, your suffering howling like a jackal between the trees: what could I offer you, instant sympathy, inconsequential and lacking in authority, just as you offered me, always in stealth and always at a heavy price.

And she arrives, bursting in without knocking, as if my home is hers, my life her life, wrapped in a coat although winter is still far away, smelling strongly of spicy roast chicken, facing each other they sat and chewed slowly, he talking and she listening, filling his plate and nodding, and under the coat she is wearing wool slacks, tight on her heavy thighs, and a thick tasteless sweater she knitted for me many years ago. You see, she boasts, I never throw anything away, you remember how I knitted this sweater for you? It took me months, and I look at the crude combination of colors, olive green next to red and cut with a yellow stripe; that's how you sent me to class parties, and I believed you that it was the most beautiful sweater in the world, that I was the prettiest girl in the class, and it was only to your arms that I could return, burying my face in the ridiculous, wide sleeves. I was the only girl nobody asked to dance, I was the only one nobody talked to, and you would console me and predict, wait and see, one day men will fall madly in love with you.

Look how well it's kept, she boasts, perhaps you'd like it back? It always lit up your face, and I say, God forbid, not letting the wide sleeves come anywhere near me, sitting opposite her on the sofa, sadly examining her pathetic figure, an overweight woman in old clothes unbefitting the season, unbefitting her age. So what did you want to tell me?

Daddy told me about your conversation, she sighs, and I interrupt her, conversation? Since when do you call that a conversation? It was a warning, or more precisely an obituary, and she says, all right, Ella, you know your father, he is always sure he's right and you won't change that, especially since he usually is right, but I can't listen calmly any more to the familiar phrases, enough with this cult of personality already, I upbraid her, do you have any idea what you're talking about, do you have any idea what he said to me yesterday? And she sighs, well, you know what he's like, he's a little extreme, he takes everything to heart, but it's out of concern, he's concerned about you and the child.

I don't buy those slogans, he's only concerned about himself, I say, I don't plan on talking to him again about that or anything else, I'm not sixteen anymore, he can't tell me what to do, I'll bring Gili to you as usual, but I'm not talking to him, and she lowers her eyes, her fingers pleating the shabby wool, listen, Ella, that's what I came to tell you, it's not so simple, you won't be able to bring Gili to us for the time being, he doesn't want to see him.

What does that mean, he doesn't want to see him? I say, he's his grandson, he needs him now more than ever, he needs your support, and she squirms, it's not that he doesn't want to, he says that he can't, he won't be able to bear the child's sorrow, he's afraid of causing him harm, precisely because he's so concerned about him. Don't judge him, Ella, it isn't fair, and I breathe into her face, don't judge him? Once upon a time you weren't so eager to defend him, once you liked hearing from me how wrong he was when he hurt you, and now that he's hurting me I have to accept it, and you still take his side?

I'm not completely on his side, she mumbles, he made me promise that I wouldn't see you either, but don't worry, I'll come to you when he's abroad, lucky he goes so often, or when he's sleeping. But when he's sleeping Gili's already asleep too, I protest, what kind of madness is this, are you trying to tell me that you actually promised him you would not come see me? And she says, I had no choice, you know what he's like when he wants something, it's impossible to resist him, but I'll come to you without him knowing, I'll say I'm going shopping, and I'll come here to see Gili, lucky we live nearby, she says cheerfully. Swirling with rage I stand in front of her, I don't need your clandestine visits, what am I to you, a lover you can only see when your husband isn't there? Do you even comprehend what you're saying to me? I can't wrap my head around it, if he's really concerned about the child why can't he help him, Gili is so attached to him, he should be a source of stability now for Gili when his home is breaking up, so what if it's hard for him, let him overcome it, and she says, apparently he identifies with him too much, at the moment he can't help him, but don't get so upset, in a few weeks he'll calm down and everything will be all right.

In a few weeks' time I won't even know who you are, I yell, and Gili will forget you too, you know what it's like with children, they have short memories, and now get out, I won't see you under these conditions, the only way you're coming here is if you come in the open, and she stands up in alarm, wraps herself in her superfluous coat, you're taking this too far, Ella, I didn't think you would react like this, you exaggerate just like he does, that's why it was so hard for you two to get along, she groans, because you're so alike, and I shriek, alike? Oh my God no, how can you say that I'm like him? Can't you see that he's heartless, that he's inhuman?

He's your father, she says, as if this is my fault and my responsibility, as if I, not she, had chosen him. I hope you change your mind, Ella, you don't have to punish me because of him, and I say, but what he's doing is much worse, he's punishing my child because of me, and you accept it, why don't you stand up to him for once in your life, what did you get from submitting to him all your life? Nothing but more and more compromises on your part. Let's see you stand up to him and say, this is my house too, and Gili is invited to come here whenever he likes, and if you don't like it, you can get out, let's see you say that.

I stand up to him in my own way, she says in a wavering voice, and I snort, your way? Coming here behind his back? That's not called standing up for yourself; you let him trample you, how come you don't see it? I'm going to divorce Amnon for far less, for fear of becoming like you I'm divorcing him, and she contorts her full, doughy face and holds her stomach as if it hurts, her braid thin as a rat's tail encircling her head in her stubbornly old-fashioned style, I hope you have a better reason for your divorce than that, Ella, just remember that two people can't live together without giving something up.

Really? I say, what did he give up exactly? He's never given up anything in his life, and she says, he gave up marrying a woman as brilliant as he is, he preferred a wife who would take care of him over a wife who would be his equal, don't think I'm not aware of it, and sometimes I even feel sorry for him because of what he gave up, and you know what, in my eyes that's love. She squares her shoulders defiantly, in your generation love has become something that's weighed on a scale, a currency, he's inconsiderate so I'll stop loving him and love somebody else, someone more considerate, for my generation it's different, for us love is fate, something you can't argue with, and I look at her and shake my head, horrified to discover once again how proud she is of this pathetic achievement, the privilege of serving the professor, feeding him and keeping his clothes clean, a pride that only seems to grow greater with the passing of the years.

When she comes up to me and tries to kiss me on the cheek I evade her with practiced agility, and she sighs, then I'll say goodnight, I hope you'll change your mind, and I say, when he changes his, I'll change mine, not a minute before, and I quickly lock the door behind her, staring through the spy hole into the darkness of the stairwell, hearing her fumble for the light switch before giving up and descending the stairs in the dark, and when she's gone something remains on the armchair, a hairy creature of repulsive colors. Did she leave it there deliberately or was it a mistake? I hug the sweater, it smells of murky frying oil and of old age mixed with the scents of my youth, and I take a pair of scissors out of the drawer and slowly cut it up, slashing it into strips of colored wool that fall to the floor like tresses of hair pulled from their roots.

Chapter four

The veil of his raw grief is shed with the coveted invitation, dropped straight onto his bed like a present from the tooth fairy. Yotam wants you to come play with him, I announce as soon as he opens his eyes, and immediately his face breaks into an amazed smile. Really? Today? He stands up in bed and hugs me, his bare feet on the lioness' neck, his slender body pressed against mine, his warm head on my shoulder, his hair brushing my cheek, and the two bodies clutching each other seem to be wrapped in a soft cocoon. Is there a more perfect, absolute intimacy than this morning embrace, when he rises to me from his sleep, swaying in my arms as if climbing a narrow rope ladder, warm and yielding as a baby, his lashes encrusted with a yolky film, his face calm, without a trace of last night's heavy weeping, its swelling complaints. We get dressed quickly because Yotam's waiting, he called before, twice, when you were sleeping. I brandish his name like an entrance ticket to the new class, to the friendship of his peers, a guarantee of the beginning of a blessed routine. He'll be busy with his buddies, won't notice his father's absence, the disappearance of his grandparents. His determined gaiety encourages me as we emerge into the radiant autumn morning, pale clouds crossing the sky like feathery sail boats. We too seem like a resolute little boat, a two-person craft, when we were three we rocked, capsized, and now without him everything is light and easy, mother and child, child and mother, what could be simpler.

You're hardly limping any more, he says admiringly, circling me like a butterfly, it's because I kissed it all better, I bet I'll have fun with Yotam, he persuades himself easily, the most fun in the world, but you'll stay there with me until I get used to it, right? And I say, I don't think so, I hardly know his parents, but he refuses to allow the doubtful note to bother him, skipping from building to building, maybe this is the house we're looking for, maybe it's this one, his eyes wandering over the plain, heavy façade of the stone buildings, some flaunting their red-tiled roofs and the others, the drab majority, flat and gray. The long summer has brutalized the municipality's meager flora, wiped the color from the street like a faded painting, stripped the playground equipment of its vibrancy, a slide and two swings, a strip of mangy lawn, right opposite the park, she said, and indeed overlooking it is an imposing apartment building that seems to have been recently renovated, for it looks both antique and new at once, its bricks shine in the sun, long, narrow balconies jut into the street, and high up on the topmost balcony stands a small friendly figure waving his hand and shouting, Gili, I'm over here.

Why don't you go up by yourself, I say, overcome by uneasiness at the sight of the grand building, the street given over to the Sabbath, people milling around, dressed in their finest and holding prayer books in their hands, on their way back from the synagogue service. They seem to be the exact same figures as I saw yesterday on our way home, apparently there is no need to search for the Sabbath, for the Sabbath is pursuing us, clinging and tiresome, like a guest overstaying her welcome. I don't feel comfortable disturbing them now, I say, remembering the reserved look on the face of the man who sat behind her on the blanket, massaging her neck, they invited you, not me, I hardly know them, but Gili insists and I climb the stairs behind him, just a few minutes, I warn him, as his back disappears behind a bend in the staircase. I think I hear Yotam skipping down to meet him, huffing and puffing, when a large object plunges past me and splatters onto the marble floor below. What was that, I demand, but their laughter rings out, telling the tale, we're throwing water bombs, they say, as Gili joins the exploit, but I am still shaken by the sight of the pale object, big as a baby, rushing past me to its doom, and I scold them, don't lean over the banisters or you'll fall down too, go back inside, that's a really dangerous game, and I follow them through the wide-open door without ringing the bell, as if it's my house and these are my two children, my beautiful empty house. Despite the polite cough I produce to announce my presence, none of the doors open and the door to Yotam's room actually slams shut, only to open again immediately so that Gili can remind me, Mommy, don't go yet, wait until I feel okay, and I hurry along the trail of his voice, Yotam, where are your parents? They're still asleep, he says, and I stand there at a loss on the edge of the living room, surveying the handsome apartment resentfully. A brown leather sofa sits comfortably on the wooden floor, a large Persian carpet spread at its feet, topped with an antique looking rocking chair, dark modern photographs adorn the walls, separated by a big mirror in a wood carved frame, which reflects my anxious, unmade face, my disheveled hair, an uninvited guest.

A black-patterned Armenian bowl stands on the dining room table, full of cracked crimson pears that look as if they're made of clay, and I reach out to touch one of them, to see if it's real, it feels hard and cool, and I look around to make sure nobody's watching and then try to bite into it, preparing my teeth for the harsh encounter with baked clay, but to my surprise it's soft and juicy, an unexpected burst of sweetness fills my mouth, and I bite into it again, roaming around the room. So, this is how they live, these are the traces they will leave behind them, these are the artifacts that will be found trapped in the ruins of the house if it should suddenly collapse. Once again I force the inanimate findings to speak, reconstructing the character and class of the inhabitants through them, as if I am standing before a home dug out of the ground, trying to ascertain if the scene before me reflects a peaceful routine or an upheaval.

A door opens with a creak and I prepare a friendly smile for Michal, quickly swallowing my half-chewed plunder, but to my embarrassment it is a lean, sleepy man who approaches me, straight hair rumpled and clad in a black t-shirt and a pair of polka-dot boxers, red as the pears and far too big for him, like a boy trying on his father's shorts, and he strides toward me with a measured, mechanical stride, erect and tense, lost in thought, dazed, his eyes almost closed. Still not noticing me, he goes into the bathroom facing the living room and urinates with complete concentration, in a faltering stream, and with the door wide open, I can't take my eyes off him, digging my teeth into the pear so as not to burst out laughing, I watch as he bends his knees and crouches over the toilet bowl like a cat about to drink the water, his head lingering over it, moving from side to side as if puzzled by the findings, and then, straightening up, he walks out without flushing and proceeds to the kitchen, where he flips the switch on the kettle and looks around him intently as if to make sure that nothing is missing, and only then does he notice me.

If I hadn't suddenly burst into wild, embarrassed laughter he might not have noticed me, but I can't control myself, leaning against the wall and giving vent to the pent-up laugher until it hurts, pouring out of my throat like food chewed but not yet swallowed, and he confronts me, his face hard as if carved from wood and his skin rough, his hand absent-mindedly stroking his taut chest, and I hold the red pear up in front of him as if it's a glass of wine and I am drinking to his health. What wonderful pears, I say, I was sure they weren't real. He examines me suspiciously, do we know each other? he asks in a cold voice, clarifying that he does not share my amusement, and I say, not really, I'm Gili's mother, Michal invited Gili to play with Yotam, apparently we came a little early, I'm sorry I embarrassed you, I add, the wave of laugher rising again, and this time I submit to it, in the mirror opposite me I see my mouth agape, deep and red and dotted with teeth. But he maintains his resistance, refusing to join in my laughter, tossing his head back in an equine gesture. You could have said something, good morning for instance, he says sulkily, to let me know that I wasn't alone, I had no idea I was being watched. He hurries to the toilet and quickly flushes, and it, too, seems to be laughing at him, gurgling at the top of its voice, and I say, I wasn't watching you, I was simply here, I'm sorry, let's forget it, just tell me what you were looking for in the bathroom, and he says, traces of blood, and I repeat in surprise, traces of blood? And he says, it's just a habit, some people have troublesome genes.

Did you find any? I ask, suddenly anxious, and he says, no, thankfully, I did not, but tomorrow morning I intend to check again, you're welcome to come and watch, and only then does he finally consent to produce a slow, cautious smile, dawning first in his eyes, which soften slightly. Do you want coffee? he asks, you're already here, you might as well have something to drink, and I quickly refuse, no thank you, I have to go, Gili doesn't seem to need me any longer, but he insists, becoming friendlier from moment to moment, wait, the coffee's ready, and he pours the boiling black liquid quickly into two ceramic mugs, a strong coffee aroma filling the air between us. I give in to temptation, sit down at the modern kitchen bar, well designed, re-examine the pictures on the wall, this time with permission, the notes on the fridge, all in order to avoid looking at him, as he seems to be beginning to enjoy the striptease act imposed on him this morning, standing tall in his underpants, pouring coffee, setting out coffee and milk in matching Armenian ware and a plate of star-shaped chocolate cookies, and I send a nervous, sidelong look to the hall, in a second she'll come out and see me sitting opposite her husband in his underpants, what will she make of that?

Perhaps you should put something on, I suggest to the man whose name I don't know, what will Michal think, and he grins, exposing fine square teeth, you had no problem embarrassing me, now it's your turn to be embarrassed, and I rise to the challenge, actually what do I care, it's his problem, not mine, and nevertheless I wish her a long, sound sleep. I try listening to the sounds of the house and for a moment I think I can hear a faint sobbing from one of the rooms, bubbling beneath the noise of the children, and I look questioningly at my host, but he ignores my glance, concentrating on the cookies as he dunks them one after the other in his coffee and rushes them toward his mouth before they fall into the cup, but in spite of his efforts they slip through his fingers and sink into the boiling coffee, leaving him broken bits of stars. He doesn't try to make conversation and neither do I, focusing on his game with the cookies.

Have a cookie, he urges me, and I say, I'm not hungry, and he asks, would you like something else, do you want another pear? I shake my head, the half-eaten pear I took without permission is still hidden in my hand, warm and sticky inside my fist, and I look for an opportunity to get rid of it without finding one, and I can't find anything to talk about either, and neither can he, perhaps he is deliberately avoiding any attempt at conversation, contenting himself with the most basic gestures, as if pleasantries are already behind us, as if we're a married couple waking in comfortable silence from our sleep. From time to time a thin, uncontrollable trickle of laugher still sprays from my mouth, and then he puts down his cookie and looks at me with a faint smile, which completely alters the expression on his face, and we seem to have become partners in a highly entertaining prank, just like Yotam and Gili throwing a bag of water into the stairwell. I cooperate with surprising ease, not bothering him with polite questions even though I would be happy to obtain a little information, examining his lean body, trying to content myself with what I can see, his tense shoulders, his bare boyish thighs, his long face, hard as if carved in wood, the two lines cutting into his cheeks, his sunken eyes widely set under their heavy brows, his full, dark lips, and if he kissed me now I would be swallowed up in a sweet euphoric void, and I would forget the mountain of worries weighing me down for just a moment, the volcano threatening me and my son. His lips would cover mine like a blanket in winter, soothing and satisfying, and I stare at them as they busy themselves with the cookies, I have never seen such vital, expressive lips, I have never known this wish, to be suddenly kissed, a totally random kiss not meant for me, like merging into the wrong lane and driving on nevertheless. Suddenly he stops chewing and looks at me, licking his brown fingertips, his eyes framed by crescents dark as rain clouds, his gaze deep and thorough, he searches my face as though hunting for traces of blood, and asks, is everything okay? I try to smile, why do you ask? And he says, because you look worried, and instead of answering I take a paper napkin in my free hand and wipe my eyes where the tears are already welling, everything's fine, I try to say, the old laughter and the new tears mingling in my mouth in an impossible concoction of syrup and brine, and I tighten my lips to stop the sigh stretching in my throat, but it doesn't emerge from there, instead the same faint, stifled sound wanders through the rooms of the house.

Do you hear anything? Is one of the kids crying? I ask carefully, and he says, no, I don't hear anything, but his voice has lost its calm, the words rolling from his mouth, deliberately bland, words intended to blur the clarion sound, were you at the *Kabbalat Shabbat* yesterday, I don't remember seeing you. Oh, wait, you arrived late, what a contrived celebration, it's always the same, can't they think up something new for a change, I've been through enough ceremonies like that with my older daughter. Is Gili your first child? he asks, and I say, yes, the first and last. It's that bad? he smiles, and I say, no, it's that good, and he says, I don't understand, when a door creaks open and we both stare at the entrance to the hall, he has a suspicious expression on his face, as if another strange woman is about to appear there, but our children burst out of the room in a torrent, and again I marvel at the resemblance between them, does he see it too, an undefined general resemblance, not found in the details. Daddy, can we have chocolate milk, Yotam pipes, can we have cookies? And his father pulls him toward him and hugs him, can I have a kiss first? I haven't had a kiss yet this morning.

Like an agile little monkey his son climbs onto his lap and kisses his neck where the skin sags slightly, and at the same time the beautiful full lips tasting of coffee and cookies press the child's forehead with a loud, ostentatious kiss, but the eyes are looking at me, and I pass my tongue over my lips, an agreeable flutter unfurls inside me like a tender memory, a forgotten one, of an old love, not as it was but as it might have been. Daddy, your kisses are too wet, Yotam says, squirming away, extricating himself from the embrace, and grabbing the plate of cookies for Gili, here, take one, me and my mom made them together, but Gili doesn't put out his hand, only now I notice that his eyes are examining me with a hurt, adult look, like Amnon's look in recent weeks, and he says, I'm not hungry, even though he has never refused a cookie before, and Yotam takes hold of his arm, come on, let's go back to my room, but Gili suddenly clings to me, lays his head on my lap and mumbles, I want to go home.

Home? repeats Yotam in surprise, but you just got here, he protests, we haven't had time for anything yet, let's go and play with the computer, let's go and stick cards in the album, anything I have doubles of I'll give you, but Gili refuses, his merriment has deserted him all of a sudden like the soul leaving the shell of a body and he is rendered limp and spiritless. My dad's coming over in a little while, he claims, I want to wait for him at home, and Yotam says, so what, you'll see your dad later, and Gili explains sadly, but my dad doesn't live with us anymore, later he won't be there because my mom won't let him stay, and all their eyes are on me, including the dark ones with the black rings around them, and Yotam looks at me, shrinking as though he faced a monster. Why won't you let him stay? he asks, and I try to smile, it's not that I won't let him, we have a kind of arrangement, but it really isn't a problem, Gili, I promise you that you'll see your father today, I'll call him right now and tell him to come later, but it seems that Gili is already trapped in his foul mood, even Yotam's threat falls on deaf ears, if you go now I won't invite you to come and play with me ever again, we won't be friends anymore.

Hey, what kind of behavior is that? his father says, can't you see that he's having a hard time, is that the way you help a friend? Yotam begins to cry, hurt by the scolding that's hurled at him before the kisses on his brow have dried, and Gili, too, bursts into tears, disappointed in himself, fearing the consequences of his rash decision, his standing with his desirable new friend. I inhale heavily at the sight of the two drooping heads, whimpering like a couple of puppies, it seems that my way has suddenly been blocked, not by a barrier with blinking lights, but by a small child, three feet tall and weighing about fifty-five pounds, who's prostrated himself on the road to stop my advance, and a strong tide of resentment runs through me, you won't force me to stay with your father, you won't force me to give up everything for your sake, to go back to the life that now sickens me, but the resentment immediately turns to pity, how yearningly he looks at his friend as he's gathered back into his father's arms, how enviously, as if he never had a father.

Like a water bomb bursting to the seams we tumble down the stairs, crash onto the floor. The puddle we walk through can't climb up the stairs again and crawl back into the tap, and neither can we pass through that door again, an unusually tall steel door, as if the inhabitants are giants, and as we slump along the sidewalk another bag of water comes crashing down and explodes at our feet like a furious farewell. It seems to me that I can hear a taunting voice, but I don't raise my face, concentrating on the unruly head of my son, who sniffs accusingly, hurting the hand that holds his so that I won't forget for a minute the misery from which he succeeded in momentarily escaping.

From the windows come sounds of forks clattering on plates, snatches of conversation, children's laughter, a late breakfast moving from window to window, its smells mingling, the smell of the omelet and the salad and the toast and the coffee, and I think of the almost full cup of coffee I left behind me and again I am engulfed by rage; how could you behave like that, Gili? In the end you won't have any friends, Yotam was looking forward to playing with you so much, he wanted to be your friend and you let him down, it's not like you to behave like that, and it seems he was only waiting for the rebuke in order to respond with a heart-breaking wail, disturbing the peace of the street. I want Daddy, you promised yesterday that Daddy would come this morning, I don't care about Yotam, I don't care about you, I only want Daddy. I clench my fingers into a fist of rage, and realize for the first time that the remains of the red pear are still hidden in my hand, and instead of throwing it into the nearby trash can, I cram it into my mouth and chew it fervently. The taste of my laughter, and the coffee I didn't have time to drink, and the question I didn't answer properly, and the cookies I didn't taste, and the kiss that didn't materialize fill my mouth instead of reassuring words to soothe my weeping son, and I turn the skeleton of the disintegrating pear over in my mouth, refusing to part from it even when we enter the apartment, which echoes to the sound of a familiar male voice. Daddy! Gili shouts, and runs to the kitchen opening the fridge, as if his father will pop out of it, but the voice is not Amnon's voice, it's Gabi's, coming over the answering machine, going on and on as usual, recording his detailed message, the end clarifying the beginning.

In any case, Ella, if you hear from him tell him that I'm really worried, he said he was going out for a walk, but he stayed out all night and he doesn't answer his cellphone, and yesterday he was really down in the dumps, I told you, he said he didn't have anything to live for and all kinds of things along the same line that I've never heard him say before, and I pick up the phone reluctantly, hi, Gabi, I just got in, what's going on?

What's going on is exactly what I was afraid of, he says glumly, the guy has completely fallen apart, you know him, he's used to things falling into his lap, no woman has ever left him before, he's never failed at anything in his life, so now he's broken, he doesn't have the means to cope.

He was fine, I got the impression he was pulling himself together, I say, refusing to join in the wake that Gabi, despite his genuine concern, is obviously enjoying, but he is quick to dismiss my words; what are you talking about, pulling himself together, he was trying to put on an act for Gili's sake, but over here he sat around like a zombie, he wouldn't eat, he wouldn't talk, he just cried like a baby, believe me I've got good reason to worry, I've known him since he was six years old, I know him far better than you do. I try not to be dragged into the ongoing competition between us, have you tried Uri and Tami? I ask, or maybe Michael? And he says, of course I have, I've tried everyone.

So where can he be, the alarm is already beginning to creep into my voice, much to Gabi's delight. At last you understand that this is serious, he exults, what did you think would happen? That he would say goodbye like a good boy and go on his way and keep on being a wonderful father to Gili? You haven't got a clue, he's not as tough as he seems, inside he's like paper, tears in a second, I've known that for years, and that's why I cut him some slack, which is exactly what you should have done, I tried to tell you, but you wouldn't listen.

You're blowing this out of proportion, Gabi, I try to lend my voice a note of assertiveness, are you saying that I should stay with him for the rest of my life out of pity, out of fear for his well being? Do you think that he could live with that?

Yes, he answers confidently, he could have lived quite well with that, and believe me, so could you, it's better than anything waiting for you outside, are you suddenly in a hurry to join the singles market? You have no idea what goes on there, the kind of psychos you're liable to meet, compared to them, Amnon will look like the bargain of a lifetime. Why don't you spare yourself all that trouble, let him come home, end of story, and let's just pray that it's not too late, that he hasn't done himself any harm.

You don't get it, for some reason I insist on explaining, I'm not in the least interested in meeting anybody else, I'm not looking for a new husband, I want to be by myself. He snorts rudely, don't kid yourself, there isn't a woman in the world who doesn't want to live with someone in the end, a woman of your age who doesn't want to have another child before it's too late, I don't buy it, but it doesn't make any difference anyway. At the moment you can't leave him, you married him of your own free will, nobody forced you, on the contrary, if anyone pushed it was you, he says, landing a jab, and marriage is no joke, and a child is definitely no joke.

What century do you live in, I protest, people split up, we're not Catholics, you got divorced yourself, why is it okay for you and not for me, because you're a man and I'm a woman? And he answers immediately, no, because I knew that the results of my divorce would be tolerable, and yours won't be; I know that Amnon won't survive it and you'll be responsible for that, above all toward your son. I breathe heavily, Gabi, that's enough, don't threaten me, let me try to find out where he is and I'll get back to you right away, but instead of getting on the phone I stumble to my bed, dizzy, and only when I stretch out on top of the rumpled sheets I abandoned not long ago do I remember Gili, for a moment I forgot all about him, as if I had left him happy and laughing at his friend's house. I heave myself up and see him bending over the answering machine, apparently he succeeded in pressing the button and playing the recorded message, which was not intended for his ears, and now it's too late to stop the exchange being conducted all over again, this time in a hushed tone, and I hear Gabi's voice again, and my voice, Amnon won't survive it and you'll be responsible for that, above all toward your son. Gabi, that's enough, don't threaten me, let me try to find out where he is and I'll get back to you right away, a conversation that only took place a minute ago, and already it sounds like a historic legal document, incriminating evidence in a celestial court, and then he straightens up and comes toward me, his stride rickety, Mommy, I'm tired, he whimpers, can I come to bed with you? And I say, of course you can, darling, stretching the arm of the blanket out to enfold him, let's rest a while and calm down, and he lies down next to me in his sandals, in his clothes, turns his back to me and to my surprise falls right asleep.

I will never tire of gazing at these features, this small assertive creature, a cub with clipped nails, as if he has just been born I examine the topography of his body, the failure of the temporary bond between us etched on his face, will his eyes, which resemble mine, forever quarrel with his lips, which resemble Amnon's? The child's very features have been marked by divorce. He looks just like me, Amnon would insist at every opportunity, he doesn't look like you at all, you're just the surrogate womb, honestly, just look at him, he would say, eyeing him with satisfaction, as if he were his representative on earth, but he had trouble coping with Gili's emerging personality, so clearly different from his own. He's such a crybaby, he'd say, I was never a crybaby, he gets that from you, at his age I was already reading and writing, I don't understand why he can't grasp it, he would announce, oscillating between absolute pride and absolute disapproval, while Gili clung to me apprehensively, knowing how fleeting fame can be.

Amnon, he isn't you, for better and for worse, make your peace with that already, I would say, trying to persuade him not to hurl the child from one extreme to the other, accept him as he is, and he would immediately attack, look who's talking, you, incapable of accepting me as I am, should not preach to me. It's not the same thing, I would say, with children it's completely different. You're not helping him by protecting him all the time, that's for sure, you give in to him too much, he would say, bringing him up as if he's some kind of prince, that's not the way to prepare a child for life, and I would say, but that's exactly how you were brought up, maybe you're simply jealous that another little prince has been born here, and he would snort contemptuously, spare me your theories, and turn the back of his shaven neck to me. Perhaps we should bring him up separately, he would propose arrogantly, all this friction isn't healthy for him, and I would say, no problem, let's separate, but the words would dissipate without the force of intention behind them, it was as if they hadn't been said, until the intention ripened almost imperceptibly, joined the words and made them as clear and penetrating as the barrels of a gun aimed at him, yes, let's, and he ran for his life, hiding from them.

Listen to this, Gabi, I'm not going to play along with his game, that's exactly what he wants, for my anxiety to welcome him back, like an adolescent boy trying to bend his parents' will. What will he come back to, endless arguments, spite, friction? Sometimes when a great love fades it is replaced by friendship that can be even rarer and more precious than the love itself, but in our case it was antagonism that grew on the ruins, bitter, petty, rancorous antagonism, like a couple of siblings that never stop bickering. Is it really Gabi I am talking to now, it's not his face I see before me but the face of a tall, handsome boy, his hazel eyes like autumn leaves, his lips sensitive, a beauty spot on his milky cheek, it is to an older Gili that I am talking now, to the youth who will sit facing me in the not-too-distant future, his parents' only son, a youth whose life was cloven when he was six years old, who is trying to make sense of the chronicles of his family's brief history, only to him I am talking, for only before him will I stand in judgment.

On my marriage bed I move from side to side, careful not to wake the child, the dark linen curtain flaps in the afternoon breeze, hiding and revealing the light, and it seems that a capricious finger is holding the heavenly light switch, turning it on and off alternately, until my eyes hurt. Carrot-beaked blackbirds assemble shrilly on the branches of the graying cypress tree out the window, the green of its foliage diminishing with each passing month, the worms eating into its branches, drilling tiny holes. It will have to be cut down before winter because this time it seems it will not withstand the force of the winds. Last winter it was covered so thickly with snow, swaying stiff and surprised out the window, that it seemed that at any moment it would collapse right onto our bed, whipping us with its frozen branches, angry and jealous, how is it that you're still alive when I am already dead.

I turn onto my stomach to escape the anger of the tree, a deep hunger rumbles inside me, in a moment it will reach out of my throat with a greedy hand, and I remember the star-shaped cookies chewed so greedily before my eyes, if only those cookies were next to me now, and with them the lips that never let them go, smacking and licking, and my lips reach for them now, stretching and pouting, growing thicker all the time, my whole face has turned into hungry lips. How provocatively he kissed his son on the forehead, measuring me with his eyes, and I giggle softly under the blanket like a young girl keeping a passionate secret that will never be realized, nor does it have any need to be realized, for it's a patient secret that needs no partners, and I lean over the sleeping Gili and kiss him on the forehead, a long, wet, tender kiss.

Right over my head, like a bubble of memory rising from consciousness, hangs a picture in a frame. I peek at it and pull it from the wall, the wobbly nail it had rested on falls onto Gili's cheek, powdering his face with whitewash. I blow it away, examining the picture resentfully, while it points at me with three smiling faces like three accusing fingers, disturbing proof that we might still have had moments of happiness, and that they are not so far away. We're crowded under a black umbrella spotted with snowflakes, Amnon strenuously stooping, holding the umbrella as if sheltering us, the furry black hat on his head like a mop of hair emphasizing the lightness of his eyes, Gili sitting on his lap, his cheeks glowing, his mouth full of snow, and I, I have to admit, it is indeed me, smile contentedly between my two men, my hand in a red glove on Amnon's arm, sunglasses over my eyes. No, no one would have guessed, there is nothing in the picture that could have borne witness to the approaching end of this threesome, how we went down to the yard on that surprising white morning, infected by Gili's delight, asked a neighbor to take a snapshot of us, took the trouble to frame the picture and hang it on the wall, mistakenly thinking that it was the snow we had to immortalize, while we, in fact, were the fleeting phenomenon.

Yes, there was a time, not so long ago, when all I wished was to be three, three in the house, three in the car, three in the airplane, how protected I felt between my two loves, like a little girl between her mother and father, stay with us, don't go, I would plead, and Amnon would evade me, don't nag, I have work to do, or an urgent phone call, or a meeting, first let's be two, he would grumble, you've already forgotten what it means to be a couple. And yet how natural, self-evident, was that threesome planted in the snow, sitting in the moving car, around the dinner table, whereas from this day forward every meeting of the three of us will be as poignant as a memorial service, and even when the years pass and the pain dulls, a perfectly ordinary word, a routine glance, will be enough to remind us that today it's a hundred days, two hundred days, five hundred days since the burial.

In one fell swoop nothing remains innocent, neither the sleep of a child nor the look of a strange man sympathizing mutely with a grief not his, neither cookies melting in coffee nor a phone that doesn't answer, everything has become terrifying or unbearably attractive, and one minute the new life dazzles before my eyes with an intolerable glare and then the next minute it is as dark and frightening as an impenetrable forest. We step between the trees, long and slender as spears, searching for a grave in which to bury our love before evening falls, so as not to delay the dead. With our bare fingers we dig in the loose soil, where will it find a place, who will know its measurements, was it massive in size, as I believed in the beginning, too big for the entire forest to contain, or tiny and shrunken as it seemed in the end, a wizened love, a sick love, its body like the body of a man who in his prime was tall and strong and when he is borne on the stretcher to his grave he is as tiny as a bird and everyone who knew him is amazed, is it really him? how he shriveled during the moons of his sickness. Soon the earth will swallow him, but we are sentenced to build the home of our new lives right on top of the fresh grave, like the inhabitants of a city destroyed in an earthquake or a war, returning to build a new settlement on the ruins of the old one, and so on and so forth until, through the years, a steep mound of archeological remains will mark the spot. Unthinkingly we will tread on it with our feet, in the summer we will tread on it with sandals and in the winter with boots, we will spread new carpets over it, and set furniture upon it, and only occasionally will we remember the corpse under the foundations of our home.

The cold shivers of an autumn evening wake me from my sleep, the bleak sleep of someone who has heard bad news, the blanket is wrapped tightly around Gili, and I am shivering in my clothes, but my limbs are still asleep, how will I get up and take a blanket from the closet, and again I look at the dead tree, gray as smoke, perhaps it will be so kind as to collapse on top of me and cover me with its branches in a final symbiotic favor before the heavy, burdensome winter. Again I fall asleep, embracing the tree's dry branches, and out of the dusk of this strange, deformed day, a day whose smile froze prematurely, Gabi's voice emerges again from the answering machine, my old rival, who for years has been inciting Amnon against me, trying to excite him with stories of a carefree bachelor existence. Ella, he's disappeared, he isn't anywhere that I can think of, nobody's heard from him, and his cell phone isn't on, you have to help me think of where he could have gone, or else I'm calling the police, and only then do I get out of bed, the languid sleepiness is dispelled in an instant and in its place I am overtaken by a feverish alertness, my heart kicks in my chest like the knees of a muscular fetus, and I prowl around the house as if seeking a sign, go through the names in the address book, dial the numbers hastily, without thinking, embarrassing myself with pointless conversations, only in order to cross name after name off the list, and remain without so much as a clue.

Where have you gone. I will not call you dear because the heart that you were dear to is closed to you now, nor will I call you the love of my youth because I had other loves before you, nor will I call you my husband because I'm sick of the word, nor father of my child because you never wished for the title, and all the other words of endearment and possession lie before us like the useless toys of a child who has outgrown them, we have no words left and no tender feelings, only faded, stained memories of love, like the tablecloth after a festive meal.

For ten years we were together, and it seems that with each passing year the words grew fewer, like a troubled child who instead of acquiring words loses them to the terrible anxiety of his parents, and the syllables he still uttered in his first year were wiped out by his third, and it seems as if when the baby was born he sucked in all the good words, all the words of affection and admiration collected in his little bed and our bed emptied out, and legions of bitter words armed with weapons rushed in to fill the void, like armies of imps going to war. What were we fighting for. It seems that the words were fighting for us, while we went about the increasingly onerous tasks of daily life. Like wars between nations fighting for freedom and independence, for territory and equality, for domination and recognition, while around us various interested parties, and one anxious child, negotiated.

Where are you, Amnon, only your name remains, without the additions of affection and title, the name I always loved, which I did not give you and therefore cannot take from you with the disappearance of my love, the name of a lustful and volatile son of a king, and I almost said then, when you introduced yourself to me, my name is Tamar, I so wanted to be a king's daughter too, a half-sister, to connect you to me by an ancient story, which ended badly, but I only saw its attractive beginning then in my imagination, *And it came to pass after this that Absalom the son of David had a fair sister, whose name was Tamar, and Amnon the son of David loved her.* You took off your sunglasses in my honor and your blue eyes sparkled from amidst the tan, you bent down to give me a huge, bony hand and asked, are you here with the class? And I realized that you thought I was still a high-school student, and I corrected you with relish, what class? I'm at the end of my BA already, and only then I noticed that the gray shirt clinging to your skin was nothing but dust, and when you went on looking at me, I ignored you, tapping the layers of dirt with the pick in my hand, as if knocking at a door, one meter below the surface of the earth, thousands of years below our present time, I'll find a little house there and it will be my home, I'll find the bones of a young girl there and she will be my sister.

Sitting safely in the excavation square, whose sides were packed with sandbags like a trench in wartime, I went on brushing the dirt with ostentatious diligence, watching you walk thoughtfully among the squares, your great height making the whole site feel secure, your jeans cut carelessly on your calves, frayed threads dangling from them like ritual fringes, and then you returned to me with rapid strides, pointed at me with satisfaction, as if solving a riddle; now I know where I've seen you before, you've been painted on the wall in Thera, in the Minoan site, they call you the Parisian, and I asked, where? And you said, in Thera, that's the ancient name of Santorini, the island that exploded, haven't you been there? Exquisite frescos have been preserved there, and to my surprise you pulled a slide out of your pocket and I examined it in the sunlight, seeing my expression, set haughtily, on a pale, elegant face; it's incredible, you muttered, bending down to me again and looking into my face, you've existed for four thousand years.

Perhaps that's where he's gone, back to the ruined, devastated Tel Jezreel, to the royal compound surrounded by a deep fosse overlooking the rich valleys of the north, whose cities went up in flames one after the other, Beit She'an, Ta'anakh, Megiddo, leaving us a layer of devastation that links them to one another. Perhaps he's gone back there, to the site that was destroyed only a few years after it was built, which never regained its bygone importance, to the excavation squares covered in dirt, how quiet it is there at night, quiet and dangerous. I cling to the wall, seeing before my eyes his body covered with a suit of dust from top to toe, lying cold and still at the bottom of the trench as if in an ancient burial cave, how little we leave behind us, and the terrible vision shakes me violently until it feels as if my hips are breaking, and I try again and again to dial his number, leaving him tender messages, call as soon as you hear this, I'm worried about you, I never thought you would take it so hard, I thought it was the right step for both of us, you threatened to leave me so many times, I didn't mean to hurt you, and from minute to minute it becomes clear to me that perhaps it isn't a trick, that perhaps this is only the beginning of the disaster my father predicted, and from minute to minute I realize that only one thing is required of me, and it is the hardest, but also the easiest, and it is the most noble, but also the basest, the most logical, and also the most absurd, I am required to relent because it's a question of life and death, because the disaster is certain and happiness is not, to give in as the mothers who sat on the blankets and sang *bless me with peace ye messengers of peace* gave in or would give in, to give in like our mothers gave in, to give in unquestioningly because this is the verdict of the supreme judge, *harden not your heart, as in the provocation, as in the temptation in the wilderness,* and then I stand up straight, stiff and serious as if standing to attention on the stage at a memorial service. All eyes are upon me, and in the background the heartbreaking sound of the sirens is heard, drawing the agony out in an endless thread, and I recite the vow out loud to the dead tree gray as smoke, to the sleeping child with the saliva dribbling from his mouth: I, Ella Miller, daughter of David and Sara Goshen, swear before God and man, trees and stones, that if Amnon returns safe and sound, I'll let him come home, and I'll accept him fully and live with him as his wife as long as he wants me to; I swear to put my intention to divorce him behind me and never to bring it up again, neither in my thoughts nor on my lips.

Chapter five

Is it really him I am sitting next to now, here in the cramped one-room apartment he lived in then, reading the ongoing excavation report about the potshards discovered in Tel Jezreel that are identical to those found in the City of Palaces in Megiddo, potshards of incalculable importance, which prove that the glorious Kingdoms of David and Solomon were nothing but a tiny tribal kingdom, that it was not Solomon who built these cities but the kings of the House of Omri, and he smiles his open-mouthed smile at me, perhaps I'll write about how I discovered you there, he says, my most important find, a Minoan wall painting that came to life in the land of Israel, a four-thousand-year-old woman.

Don't answer, I whisper when the phone rings next to the bed, and he says, maybe you should answer, bringing the receiver to my ear, Amnon's not at home, I chirp to the despairing female voice on the other end of the line, I have no idea when he'll be back, but the phone keeps ringing well after the conversation is over, thrusting me into this morning's reality, Amnon's not at home, I have no idea when he'll be back. I leap out of bed and grab the phone, disappointed by the sound of Gabi's voice, mysterious and choked with pride, as if he has been awarded a medal of valor, for service beyond the call of duty, everything's okay, Ella, I got a sign of life from him.

Thank God, I sigh, where is he? And Gabi purrs condescendingly, celebrating his victory over me, it doesn't matter, he asked me to keep it between us, I just wanted to let you know that he's okay, and I taunt him, you see, you let your hysteria get the better of you, and he says resentfully, when you love someone you worry about him, apparently you've forgotten this fact, and I say, and you've forgotten that Amnon's love is mostly for himself,and he's the last person who would ever do himself harm.

Stop it, Ella, he sighs, I don't want to argue with you first thing in the morning, and anyway, you'll be happy to know that our paths part here, his next wife will have to put up with me, not you. Feigning indifference, cloaking the lash of my curiosity, I say, what, he's already with someone? Gabi guffaws, I didn't say that, all I said was that when you part from him you're parting from me too, and neither of us will be too sorry about that. I try to soften my tone, in spite of my strong desire to end the conversation, so similar to our previous conversations and at the same time so alarmingly different, listen, Gabi, I have to know where he is, at least the telephone number, his cell phone is switched off, and Gili wants to talk to him, and he resumes his patronizing tone, taking obvious pleasure in every word, my dear Ella, I would be happy to give it to you, but Amnon explicitly asked me not to, he doesn't want to talk to you, what can I do, there's a limit to the sway I have over him.

You're taking this too far, Gabi, I snap, he has a child here, Gili misses him, he's been trying to get in touch with him all morning, and Gabi, sighing piously, says, what can I tell you, Ella, you should have thought of that before, you can't kick the father the hell out of the house and still expect him to be like clockwork with the child, you probably won't be able to count on Amnon for the time being, but in any case you always said you were bringing Gili up alone, so what's the big difference, you're already used to it, and I exhale long and hard into the receiver, you meddling creep, you did all you could to come between us, and before I have to hear him lap it all up, I put the phone down, grinding the receiver into its cradle in order to obliterate all traces of the conversation, but it goes on between my ears, scattering a heavy handful of tacks and pins inside my head. He doesn't want you to know where he is, he doesn't want to talk to you or to Gili either, it's been said, it's happened and there's no way back. This is parting, this is its language and these are its sounds, this is parting, planned but unexpected, a body that has ceased to struggle and emits only a thin silence, systems that have collapsed, a string that has snapped, a field that has been set on fire, it's happened and there's no way back, there is no need for my belated pledge of allegiance, there is no need for my vows, they are null and void, retracted and revoked.

Where is the relief, from whence will it come. Like a glass broken as soon as the package is opened, the promised relief has collapsed, its shards scattered all around, sharp and stabbing, glittering spitefully. I tiptoe around them, picking up the teddy bears lying on the carpet like I do every morning, throwing them onto the bed where Gili tossed and turned last night. From moment to moment my movements become disconnected from my body, my arms float in the air, holding the stuffed animals, while I myself lean against the wall, my breath blazing, it seems that a lighted match has been thrown inside my body and the flames are raging in my stomach as if it contains a hidden oil well, here you are, whisper the flames, you got what you wanted, you're free, he's safe and sound and he won't bother you anymore, the gate is open, the barrier has been lowered, why don't you pass through it.

I stir a bubbling stew of contradictory feelings with my bare fingers, without so much as a glove to protect my skin, with bare hands over the steaming cauldron, a fairytale witch concocting a poisonous brew, and this brew is meant for you, for you and your little son. Am I doomed to stand red-faced over the cauldron, waiting for a resolution? Soon the seething porridge will boil over and spread through the house, fossilizing its contents, trapping this moment in time, this, of all moments, when I was ensnared by contradictory feelings and crossed the border unthinkingly, to be swiftly ensnared, this moment, which has redefined the difficulty, the insulting, incomprehensible difficulty of identifying my true feelings. When my eyes, melting in the heat, scan the familiar living room of our house, the gray sofa that looked used on the day we bought it, the two light-canvas armchairs looking at it wearily, as if they are engaged in an exchange of tedious banalities, and again at the empty spaces in the bookshelves, like the hollow eyes of a skeleton; it seems to me that, above all, I long not for Amnon himself and the broken sequence of our lives, but for the simple feelings that accompanied us, a hunger that could be satisfied, a thirst that could be quenched, a weariness that could be allayed, a love that could be realized, and like a little girl whose lies have been believed, I walk angrily about the room, flinging myself onto the sofa and kicking the cushions, which respond with clouds of provocative dust.

He's just punishing you, I try to console myself, anger and insult are behind his absence, he's trying to use that absence to magnify his presence, but it's obvious that if you want him, he'll come back, it's still up to you. But the charged tone of Gabi's voice claws at me, the glimmer of the presence of another woman. How, in the course of one weekend, another woman has begun to emerge from the woodwork, warning bells swing between my temples, it's happened, I've lost control over his life, the rules of the game have changed. It's happened, for better or worse, it's real, it's beyond a heart-to-heart with a girlfriend, beyond the familiar argument, beyond the seductive fantasies, the bliss of blowing off steam, for opposite the mount of blessings looms the mount of curses, so close, so hard to discern between the two.

Even the cold water is steamed by my skin in the shower. My hands burn, my tongue blazes in my mouth like a torch and I drink the scattered water, fatigued from its journey. The telephone comes to life with a persistent ring, accompanied by knocking at the door, the inner turmoil dons outer apparel, somewhat more promising, and I leap out of the shower, my hair dripping onto a now-clinging dress. I ignore the telephone and run to the door, drops of water evaporating on my skin, which is alive with the agitated anticipation of seeing him standing in the doorway.

What are we going to do with you, Ella, when will you learn to answer the phone, he says, the cell phone still at his ear, its buzzing underscoring my refusal to reply, I tried to let you know I was on my way, but as usual you didn't answer, maybe it's better this way, otherwise you wouldn't have let me in, he smirks, stepping inside, his short, thick body encased as always in a dark lawyer's suit, his sparse hair combed back and stiffened with gel, his cheeks giving off the stinging smell of cologne, his protruding teeth sticking out of the grimace of his smile. He surveys the living room with a prying, mocking look, as if everything that has transpired here since our conversation is laid bare before his eyes. His gaze lingers on my bare thighs, not bad, he remarks, if you like petite, maybe you'll manage to find someone after all, and I make an effort to cool my voice, what are you doing here, Gabi, I don't remember inviting you, and he waves the familiar key, glittering like a stolen jewel between his fingers, it's okay, darling, you don't have to entertain me, Amnon gave me the key, and I try to snatch it back, give me the key, I say, it's mine, and he says, calm down, I'm here on Amnon's behalf, this apartment belongs to him too, I drew up the contract when you bought it, remember?

It belongs to him too, but not to you, I snap, what do you want here? Relishing every word, he says, Amnon asked me to bring him a few things, are you going to help me look for them, or should I find them myself, and I say, get out, Gabi, if he wants to get something let him come over, and he chuckles, what's wrong, darling, you pining for him already, so soon?

Not at all, I say, I'd just rather see him than you, and he ignores me and proceeds grandly to the bedroom, flinging open the closet doors. He needs a few sweaters and long pants, it's getting cold in the evenings already, he states, where do you keep the winter clothes, here? His freckled hands, pale office hands, rummage in my underwear drawer, you need a new wardrobe, Ellinka, he announces with affected sorrow, it's not nice to say so, but in the flesh market you have to invest, no one will come near you with something like this, he waves a pair of frayed, pale green panties in front of me, and I feel myself flushing as if I have been slapped; get out of here, you pervert, get your hands out of my closet, but he goes on rooting; I asked you to help me, he says innocently, pulling out a bra that's gone gray with washing, dangling it in front of me like a fishing rod, you leave me no choice but to find things by myself.

Get out, I say, get out of my room, I'll bring them to you, and he says, fine, I'll wait in the living room, and he hands me a crumpled yellow note, the kind I used to sometimes find in Amnon's pockets, in his sloppy, downward sloping handwriting, like a list before going out on a dig, two sweaters, a pair of jeans, corduroys, a jacket, a blanket. I throw everything onto the sofa, where he sits, amused and pleased with himself; take it and get out, and if you ever come here again I'll change the lock.

Believe me it's no pleasure for me, he says, I have greater pleasures than seeing you, but you know that for me friendship is above all else, it's only now that Amnon is beginning to appreciate that, he boasts, give me a bag or I'll look for one myself, and I take a plastic bag out of the drawer and hand it to him, so where is he, here in town? I pry with affected indifference, and to my surprise I even get an answer, yes, he isn't far from here, should I give him a message?

Tell him that he has a child, I say, Gili needs him, he should see him soon, and he says, don't worry, I'll take care of it, his voice surprisingly gentle, but when I trap his gaze, I see that his eyes are moving over my body, his smile is broadening, covering his freckled face, his expression is very familiar to me but not the movement that accompanies it, for with one hand he pushes me against the wall and with his finger he pulls down the strap of my dress, which yields to him with annoying ease, exposing my breast, shrinking in embarrassment. Not bad, he remarks again, you have the breasts of a girl, and I try to push him away, astounded by his audacity; what do you think you're doing? Get your hands off me, and he lets go of my shoulder, relax, I'm not doing anything, I'm just looking. With narrowed eyes, like an assessor evaluating property, he examines me, and I quickly return the treacherous strap to its place, get out, how dare you! His lechery doesn't surprise me, only now for the first time it's directed at me, as if he was never my husband's close friend, as if I was never his friend's wife, and he breathes stifling manufactured air in my face, who do you think you are? he says, you'll beg me to touch you, your life has changed, darling, you don't get that.

I'd rather be a nun than come anywhere near you, I hiss, and he lets go of me and picks up the plastic bag; listen to what I'm saying to you, you'll still beg me to touch you, and he hurries to the door with his dandified walk, and I call after him, wait till I tell Amnon what just happened. What makes you think it will interest Amnon? he asks without turning his head, disappearing down the stairs, leaving me shrinking in disgust, holding my stomach as if I've eaten spoiled food. I watch from behind the curtain to make sure that he's really leaving, and I see him get into his luxury car, where someone waits for him in the front seat, probably another one of the interns that he's always trying to seduce, and I squint and see that, no, it's a man this time, tall and stooped in the front seat, Amnon, welcoming him with a raw smile, reaching for the plastic bag I took out of the drawer and setting it on his knees.

A dazzling silver light covers my eyes as I grope for the telephone, I have to stop them before they get away, as if they were a couple of burglars taking a prized belonging. I mean to ask for Amnon, but when Gabi answers in his nasal voice I hear myself say, you forgot something here, Gabi, and he says in surprise, what did I forget, and I say, there's another bag. Really, he wonders, puts his hand over the phone for a minute and then says, okay I'll be right there, and I see the car come into view, reversing carefully back into the street, parking with two wheels on the pavement opposite the house, under the poplar trees, and he emerges with great self importance, while Amnon, hugging the plastic bag, follows him with his eyes. Why don't you look up at the house that was once your house, at the big window that you loved, at the ivy climbing up the walls, only two weeks ago you pruned its stubborn branches and the window grew bigger and bigger until you could see the whole street from it, narrow and serpentine as a parched river bed.

Where is it? he asks, beads of sweat wobbling on his upper lip, and I feign innocence, what? I don't have the strength to play games with you, Ella, he says, where's the bag? I smile at him, slipping the narrow strap off my shoulder with an imperceptible movement, a movement that is not mine, there is no other bag, Gabi, and only then does an expression of proud comprehension dawn on his face, but his eyes are skeptical, his lips twitch, and I challenge him, what happened, you scared? Of you? he whispers, not in the slightest. With a quick grab, as if afraid he might regret it, he presses me to him, takes hold of my wet hair and pushes a fleshy tongue into my dry mouth and I sit on the windowsill, casting a sideways look at the car and the person sitting in it, who seems to be glancing uneasily at his watch, scanning the building, perhaps he will decide to come upstairs, walk through the open door into his house while his friend licks my neck with a tongue as rough as a cat's, thrusting a hand between my legs. You want me, darling? I don't answer, my eyes are fixed on the stooping figure, my back arches, in a minute I'll fall out of the window like an incautious child left alone at home, crashing onto the blazing roof of the car, terrifying the person within it. I always knew you wanted me, he mumbles, and I nod weakly, enveloped in a frightening, seductive haze but still riveted to the car, the breath of its engine calms me a little, like Amnon's breath next to me at night, and I try to breathe in time to it, my foot dangling down the outside wall, if I had a sandal on I would let it drop, like the last sign of life thrown out of the car window by a kidnapped person, assisting the rescue party with their search.

He lets go of my bristle-scratched face, his hands fumble with his belt, his eyes look into mine, as if waiting for an emotional confession, an admission of surrender, and only then does he notice the direction of my gaze, what are you looking for down there, he whispers, gripping my chin firmly and turning my face to his, staring at his car as if surprised to see it there, red blotches spreading across his cheeks, are you playing games with me, is that what you're doing? Abruptly he withdraws his hands, breathing heavily, his eyes darting over my face, don't play with me, Ella, he says, nobody plays games with me, you'll pay for it dearly, and he stomps away, wiping the sweat off his face with his hands, and then, as if changing his mind, he comes back, pushes his hand between my legs again, marking territory, and whispers hoarsely, I'll be back, but when I choose, not you, when there's nobody waiting for me downstairs. Glaring at me he backs stiffly out the door, and I don't even take the trouble to answer him. Turning away from him with my eyes still fixed on the car, I watch him slip into the air-conditioned interior that's steeped in Amnon's breath, and, to my surprise, they linger there, seemingly engaged in some sort of debate that is accompanied by sharp, cutting gestures with their hands. I follow the developments intently, hoping to see Amnon's tall body extricating itself in disgust, but instead I see Gabi's arm reaching out to give the shoulder next to him an encouraging pat. Are they laughing? Their shoulders are shaking as the car slides slowly off the pavement and drives away, leaving me silent and exposed to the sharp rays of the sun.

We were an odd, almost embarrassing, couple. He, tall and stooping, rather ungainly, his movements jerky and uncoordinated, like the body of an adolescent who missed the right moment to stop growing, and I, who stopped too soon, as if some accident damaged the mechanism and prevented it from completing its mission, leaving me shorter than my mother, narrow hipped and flat-chested, only half a woman, tense as an impostor afraid of getting caught, and sometimes it seemed as if each of us was drawn to underscore the shortcomings of the other, to inflict ridicule. Next to him I looked twice as short, next to me he looked more overgrown, together we made each other uglier, forced each other to make an effort. I stretched my neck up to him, he was obliged to bend down to me. In the beginning the difference was actually thrilling, as if we had come from two completely different races, the representatives of two tribes that had united, but over the years it grew burdensome. He liked to tease me with stories about his previous girlfriend, who was almost as tall as him. I only saw her once, when we went to her wedding, and when I remember her now, and try to reconstruct her appearance, all that remains is a long blurry silhouette, and the startled expression of the eyes in the made-up bride's face when we went up to congratulate her after the ceremony, as if she couldn't believe that he was attending her wedding as a guest and not as the groom.

Not long ago Amnon told me that he had bumped into her in the street, poor Ofra. He always called her poor Ofra. Her husband had bolted, leaving her alone with two children, and now that I am poised on the windowsill, utterly drained, with my leg dangling down, I realize that this is the answer, the only answer to the question that flared up this morning, the smoke still filling the house. This is how he resigned himself to our separation in the space of a single weekend, how he suddenly gave me up, for it is quite clear that he has given me up. Gabi wouldn't so much as lay the tip of his finger on me if he hadn't known that I was back within bounds. Without a woman he would never have let me go so easily, and no new woman could have gotten her hands on him in one weekend, only poor Ofra, who took in the refugee, poor Amnon, and in the blink of an eye succeeded in reminding him of the strength of her love, her infinite faithfulness and devotion.

So the world has turned, Amnon with poor Ofra, and me with poor Gili, two hopeless couples splitting off from one hopeless couple, and who knows if I am capable of re-establishing the old order, and if I even want to. I stretch my bare foot out along the windowsill, at the end of which is a plastic window box we received for a wedding present, blooming with hardy geraniums, and I reach out my foot and kick it, jolting it again and again until it plunges heavy and stunned to the pavement below, vomiting its soil in the exact spot where the car was parked, where both of them burst out laughing, with their arms around each other's shoulders.

I spread myself out on the wide windowsill, like a duvet aired out before the onset of winter. It seems that the faintest wind will send me flying, but no gusts approach. Below me, the usual routine unfolds, in short flashes of other people's lives, which always seem simpler than they really are, the recurrent procession of a baby being pushed in a stroller, a couple sauntering past, a woman returning from a shopping spree, bags in her hands, a noisy group of high school students. A gray cat pads toward the overturned window box, sniffs its soil, and when it is found worthy, it digs a modest hole, arches its back and does its business, immediately covering the results. I turn my eyes to the living room, the light armchairs face the sofa, the toys are scattered over the orange cotton rug that we bought in Sinai and, on the opposing wall, the picture of the Parisian, her pale face and her red lips, her dark hair carefully styled, her gaze haughty and her chin determined, a remote, aristocratic woman, what do I have in common with her? For a moment it seems that if I lie where I am long enough, in the midst of a silent, private strike, everything will go back to the way it was, and at noon the door will open and Amnon will come in, hoist Gili from his shoulders as if taking off a backpack, and I will gather the chattering child into my arms, listen eagerly to his stories, and again I will be seized with the joyful desire to fulfill his every whim, to make all his wishes come true.

All afternoon long I'll play with him, I'll invent new things to entertain him, I'll feast on sweets with him, and Amnon will watch us lazily, critically, from the side, you're just a child yourself, he'll say, you haven't grown up yet, you should thank me for giving you a toy to play with. I'll shut him up at once, so that Gili's sensitive nostrils won't detect the jealousy in the air, and only when he leaves the house to go about his business will I breathe a sigh of relief, at last, the day can take its familiar path, which even now I am unable to idealize, for even if we succeeded in avoiding friction until nightfall, until Gili falls asleep at last after interminable monster-banishing rituals and magic spells, and I hurry to the bedroom to get some sleep, Amnon will protest, what's the matter with you, come and sit with me for a bit, and without waiting for an answer he will launch an attack, for Gili you have time, for your useless research you have endless reserves of energy, for the whole world you have energy, only when it comes to me are you always tired.

Apparently you tire me out more than anything else, I respond, what do you want from me, I ask, but he won't leave me alone, following me to the bedroom with his heavy strides, you've forgotten the meaning of intimacy, he informs me as I undress. Don't be surprised if I hunt around for what I can't get here, you've turned this house into a nursery school, we're a family, not a kindergarten, and a family is based on a couple, if you remember what a couple is, that is: a husband and wife who make love, who go away by themselves for a few days, who take an interest in each other, not only in the functional sense of who does what chore. When was the last time you showed a real interest in my life?

Don't preach to me, I silence him in a cold voice, don't expect me to spend my whole life listening to your lectures, like my mother with my father, this may come as a surprise to you, but I believe in mutuality, when you start taking an interest in me, I'll start taking an interest in you. I'm through with making an effort, I've been making an effort for years and it's got me nowhere. When he gets undressed next to me I stare at him in astonishment, how did his body lose the powerful attraction it once radiated, how did it turn into this bundle of complaints and demands oozing from every pore, and I get under the blanket and pull it up to my chin so he won't think of touching me. Beside me, between us, the question mark grows, thriving like a well-fed animal, is this what my life is going to look like, is this what I wanted, to have a love affair with a little child at the side of a bitter selfish man, to witness the gradual erosion of our happiness, crumbling from the force of his careless, almost absent-minded blows.

In the morning he sulks, his eyes greeting the new day with unmasked hostility. He turns the radio on and listens to the news at full volume, grim, frightening news, even though I repeatedly ask that he spare Gili the experience. It's not for children, I say, there's a reason he has nightmares. Sometimes he prods him roughly, come on, how long does it take you to get dressed, I'll leave without you, and sometimes he delays their departure with long telephone calls while Gili waits at the door, lips trembling because he's going to be late. Thus I chart an entire day of our previous lives, like the world orbiting around itself, beginning my revolution with doubt and ending it with profound reservations. I try to encourage myself, to reinforce the decision that can no longer be revoked, give it time, I coax myself, don't break so soon, you're entitled to expect more, you have the right to change your life, the gate is open, the barrier gone, why don't you go through.

Give it some time, I mutter in front of the flickering computer screen in the bedroom, re-reading the reports of an excavation I didn't take part in, the last reports written by the Greek archeologist before he died in one of the chambers he was excavating, there on Thera, on the broken island, unwittingly adding his tragedy to the Minoans', a faint but lethal echo of the earthquake that changed the face of the ancient world.

Give it time, I repeat on my way to the school, arriving out of breath, slightly late. Luckily the gate is open, the guard has apparently already left, a few children are still clucking in the yard like abandoned chicks, but Gili is not among them, and I go ask the teacher, where's my son? He's outside isn't he? she says, slicing sour green apples with a thin knife. I take a slice of apple and go out to the yard again, in the distance I see him sitting on a pile of stones in a corner of the yard, he has a long stick in his hand and he is raking the dry ground. I run to him, hi, sweetheart, I didn't know where you were, let's go home, but when he raises his head I see it is another child, with a narrow, grown-up face on a slender neck, his lips slightly chapped, and I ask him, Yotam, where's Gili? He answers sullenly, I don't know, I'm not friends with him anymore. The marks of Saturday's kisses still seem to be printed on his forehead, the starry kisses of his father, and I stand in the schoolyard and yell, Gili, where are you? But he doesn't answer, and again the instant darkness descends, Gili, where are you? Perhaps he went out into the street to wait for me and some pervert persuaded him to go with him, perhaps he got lost, disappearing in the chaos of the children being collected.

A few pairs of concerned motherly eyes watch me, trying to offer advice, and I recognize Michal among them but I don't stop, heart pounding, I return to the teacher, where's my son? At long last she lays the apples to rest and enters the yard with the knife still in her hand, Gilad, she calls, waving the knife in the air, the fear and guilt already evident in every gesture; maybe he's in the bathroom, she suggests, maybe he left with a friend, and I say accusingly, he doesn't have any friends here yet, as if this, too, is her fault, and he's not in the bathroom, I already looked.

Taking their time, the mothers depart from the schoolyard, holding their children tight as sacred amulets, and only Michal remains, hesitating at the door, Yotam by her side, exhibiting demonstrative indifference, indifferent to the fate of the child who disappointed him, and she says, don't worry, Ella, the school is fenced, and there's a guard, he couldn't have left without being seen, and then she apologizes, I have to go and collect Maya from her afternoon activity, I'll call you later. Only the teacher and I remain in the yard, without any child to take care of, to offer apples to, to wipe his nose, to watch that he doesn't fall off the swing, and I stand there, my mouth dry, my hands sweating, looking around for traces, listening to every little sound, and it seems that my father's voice is echoing in the deserted schoolyard, loud and threatening as the voice of God in the Garden of Eden, he won't survive, he'll be annihilated.

Where's the guard, she mutters, her plump, cushiony lips trembling in her face. We run to the unmanned gate, looking at the bushes of the raven park, dark even in the afternoon sunlight, and I know that her fantasies of horror are already rivaling mine. Yosef, come here quickly, she shouts, and I say, he's already left, there's no point calling him, we have to call the police, but here he is, coming our way, heavy and sweating. One of the children is missing, she wails as soon as he is within hearing distance. He looks at me doubtfully, your child? I nod, thin with long brown curls, he was wearing a red t-shirt with a number on the back. I know him, he says, left long time ago, with father.

With his father? I repeat, how do you know it was his father? And he says, I know everybody here, his father is tall man, taking him on shoulders, and I suppress a shout of joy, yes, that's Amnon, he always carries him on his shoulders, I say to the teacher, trying to make up for the commotion I have caused with excessive friendliness. Thank you, Yosef, thank you for paying attention, I shake the guard's hand gratefully, and he says, you go home to look after baby, waving an accusing finger at me, and I back away from him quickly, he's confusing me with somebody else, I try to explain to the teacher, who takes hold of my shoulder. I'm so sorry, she says, I must have been busy with something else and wasn't paying attention, they didn't tell me they were leaving. Tell your husband that he was out of line, she says, going from scolded to scolder with surprising dexterity, taking a child before school's out without alerting the teacher is wrong. I am ready to bear any reproach as long as Gili is safe and sound, and I promise her that it won't happen again, apologize hastily and leave, making my escape from the empty schoolyard, which still smells of the children, their sweat and their farts, their breath in laughter and in shouting, the smell of the candy ground between their teeth, the smell of ancient schemes and insults resurrected on a daily basis, and it seems that the insults from my own childhood lurk here too, and that Gili is cultivating his own on top of mine, like a blind man carrying a cripple on his back.

Still agitated, I drop onto the lawn in the raven park, the catastrophe that didn't happen looming ever larger, dominating my thoughts like a final warning, as if the good news only magnified the bad, making it more concrete, as though the fact that he was saved this time only lessens his chances of being saved next time. I stroke the sparse hair of the lawn, which reminds me of Amnon's hair before he started shaving it, when Gili was born, as if he wanted to compete with the perfect shape of his skull, and as I lie there surrounded by faded blades of grass, it seems to me that the familiar park has completely changed, as though an earthquake has morphed the mild slope into a steep hill and if I don't hold on tight to the short blades of grass, I will tumble down and roll all the way to the ancient pool at its eastern end, accompanied by the terrifying caws of the ravens. So this is what the new life I wished for so rashly looks like, a plateau narrow and taut as a rope, seething with sulfurous fumes that paint the scorched earth yellow, and beyond it the chasm. If only I could make the hooked beaks of the ravens speak, have you seen an overgrown creature with two heads, one on top of the other, a double-headed beast taking broad strides, can you tell me where it went. Why don't you fly in front of me, show me the way, and I will follow silently behind you, a shortened afternoon shadow, the humbled tail of the two-headed beast. When I slowly sit up I know that the ravens are no longer afraid of me, their mocking caws will accompany me as I walk. My mouth fills with greenish spittle and gobs of cool phlegm when I fail to find them, when

I cannot hear them, and I march down narrow alleys, peer into gardens, clucking my tongue next to garbage cans, as if I am searching for a lost cat, and it is in this way that I find myself in the hazy afternoon, with the heavy stone walls giving off deterring waves of heat, like dangerous radiation, in front of the gate to Dina's house.

Will I barge in on her again, break into the routine of her lonely, orderly life that knows neither great joy nor great sorrow, as if throwing a stone into still water, and I remember how she shined on the roof of the house next door, her copper hair incandescent, her lips smeared with dark brown lipstick ecstatically puffing smoke, while she moved her arms in mysterious exercises, as if soaping her body without touching it, and then she would put out her cigarette in a flowerpot and go into the room on the roof, a ramshackle, illegal structure, and immediately a figure would appear, knock urgently on the door and disappear inside, reappearing an hour later, when someone else would go in, most of them youngsters, not much older than the girl I myself was then, and I would watch the comings and goings, and most of all I would wait for her to come out and stretch her body in the sun. How many friends this woman has, I would marvel, so many visitors, one after the other, and once I even expressed my astonishment to my mother when we were hanging up the laundry on the roof, and she smiled and said, those aren't friends, they're clients, she's a psychologist, and the new information only inflamed my imagination. I would sniff the laundry and imagine that this was how they left her, arriving in stained clothes and leaving clean and fragrant. All this was happening so close to me, such tangled problems were being discussed there, just like the knot in my hair, swelling and rising from the top of my head like a tumor, and I imagined her sitting behind me with a fine-toothed comb in her hand and brushing my hair gently and patiently, day after day, until she undid the knot. Picturing myself bridging the gap between the two roofs with a spectacular leap, I, too, would knock on her door and say, when I was a child I had no father and no mother.

And in the end she was the one who addressed me. After trying to light a cigarette in the wind, the matches extinguished one after another until there were none left, I heard her ask me, while I leaned on the railing, watching with interest, do you have a light? I rushed into the house before she could find another solution to her problem and brought her a lighter, threw it to her as hard as I could, hitting her on the shoulder. She waved her thanks and lit her cigarette with ease, and in my eyes this was a sign that our meeting would be a success. How old are you? she asked and I answered sixteen, and to my delight she didn't say what everyone else did, I thought you were barely twelve, but asked instead, would you like to exercise with me? And so, with the cigarette in her mouth, her stiff copper hair barely moving, she faced me and started doing her exercises and I, between the lines of laundry, mimicked her movements, bending and stretching my body without touching it, and so I laid in wait for her short breaks, learned when her last client left, and one evening I gathered up the courage and bounded downstairs, racing down the dozens of steps in our house and up the dozens of steps in hers, a moment before she locked her door, switched off the faint light over the entrance, and went to her real house.

Has anything happened? she asked, and I peered over her shoulder at our roof, astonished at the reversal in my point of view, as if it was the other half of the globe. I saw my mother coming outside with the wet laundry, she was always careful to hang his up first, his socks, his underpants, his pajamas, his cotton shirts, stretching them firmly with her hands, and only then applying herself to ours, mixing up my socks with hers, returning unlikely pairs to my closet, and in my embarrassment I pointed to this sight, as if it contained my story, a heavy-bodied woman hanging up laundry on the roof of her house in the gathering darkness.

I had often visited her unannounced, but now I hesitate, we have drifted so far apart lately, was it Amnon's heavy presence that had pushed her out of my life, or Gili's light body? Maybe I was at fault for failing to connect her to my adult life, content with short visits, snatched phone calls, preferring to leave her there, next to my parents, hanging between the two roofs like clothes forgotten on the line after the inhabitants had departed. With a heavy heart I survey her little porch, crowded with flourishing plants, growing riotously, unrestrained, the floor tiles covered with the freshly fallen stars of white jasmine, giving off a painful smell, reminding me of the faithful old geranium I had thrown from the window sill, how will I explain its absence to Gili, is there any point in ringing the bell, there's no chance she'll be at home in the middle of the day, and even if she is, how can she help me now, how easy it was then to stand next to her on the roof, when life had just begun to bud.

Delicate fronds of honeysuckle hide the doorbell and I fumble for it, startled by the long, loud ring I've inadvertently produced. She can't be home, but her face unfolds for me, Ellinka, what a surprise, I'm glad to see you, is everything okay? Thick strands of gray streak the copper helmet, the gleam tarnished, the bare arms stretched out to me are fuller than they were, but the wise, kindly flame that greeted me on that long-ago night still flickers in her eyes, and I fall around her neck, moaning in her arms, pouring out a stream of wet words; I'm so confused, Dina, I don't know what's happening, I was sure I didn't want him any more, but now that it's real I'm afraid, all these months all I wanted was to get him out of the house, and now that he's cut himself off from me I'm in a panic, suddenly it feels as if he's left me and not the other way around, and I regret everything, like a spoiled child whose parents took her too seriously.

It's not at all like a spoiled child, Ellinka, she says, taking my arm and leading me gently to the sofa, what you describe is completely natural and expected, separation gives rise to primal fear, irrespective of whether it's justified or not, you have to calm down, fear is a bad counsel, try not to be afraid of your panic, understand that it's natural, and it says nothing about what was or what will be, it simply takes time, give it time, be patient, she says, speaking slowly and thoughtfully as if to demonstrate her meaning.

I'm not afraid of the panic, I try to correct her, I'm afraid of the possibility that I've made a mistake, everyone around me judges me all the time, strips me of my confidence, I try to remember why I wanted a separation so badly, and suddenly it seems feeble, not in the least convincing, exactly like everyone said, so what if he gets on your nerves a bit, for that you break up a family?

Look, she says, sitting comfortably opposite me, it's clear that something very powerful pushed you to take this step, so it can't be a mistake, it was your choice, even if you find it difficult to stand behind it, often the real reasons for parting only become clear with hindsight, when we can allow ourselves to know them, just like the real reasons for coming together.

But I can't live with these doubts, I say, and what if I discover with hindsight that I was wrong, what will I do then? Tell me what you think, you treat cases like this all the time, did you think that we weren't good for each other, that we should separate? The truth is that I felt you were trying to tell me something, and I didn't really want to hear it, I say, trying to put the words into her mouth, which suddenly looks naked without the bronze lipstick, pale as a hidden limb exposed to public view, and as if she has read my thoughts she gets up and hurries to the little mirror in the hall, smears on a thick layer of lipstick with the practiced movements I always tried to imitate in front of the mirror in our house, with my mother's eyes watching me in perpetual rebuke, one would think you didn't have a mother the way you hang around that woman.

That's not what I was trying to tell you in recent years, she says, I tried to talk to you about your devotion to the child and its implications, and you really didn't want to hear it. I think what happened to you is what happens to a lot of mothers, you immerse yourselves in a perfect union with your babies, and that absolute harmony overshadows the relationship with your husbands, to a large extent makes it superfluous, and the more superfluous he feels the more jealous and resentful he becomes. I try to work on this with my clients because we have a triple tragedy here, the tragedy of the husband who is cut down to size, of the child whose father distances himself from him, and above all the tragedy of the mothers, who choose to give their all precisely to the person who will definitely leave them in the end, to rely precisely on the one whose abandonment is certain.

I didn't push Amnon away from me or from Gili, you're absolutely wrong, I protest. Can she really be describing my life, I wanted so much for us to be a threesome, for us to do things together, I wanted him at our side all the time, he was the one who always wanted to get away, you have no idea how much it hurt me.

But what role did you give him in that threesome? she asks, if you examine yourself, you'll see that it was a secondary role, you wanted him in the background, as an addition to your main happiness, while he was the one who lost out, he was actually left on his own, but I'm not trying to defend him, only to confirm that I really did notice the difficulty you had in changing from a couple into a family, I certainly understand your hurt as well, I understand that you didn't feel loved because, with him, possessiveness overcame love. This is also typical of many men in these situations, possessive behavior that relegates you to the status of an object. Clearly you were both reflected very badly in the mirrors you held up to each other.

But you're saying I was right, aren't you? I press her, I had good reasons to leave him, it wasn't just a wild impulse, right? If only I could gain her approval I would be able to calm down, to get back onto the path I had spent long nights planning, of a free, relaxed life, without arguments, without hostile radiation, and she sighs, listen, even the wildest impulses have deep motives behind them, it's clear that you weren't happy with him over the past years, but it's also clear that you still have a lot of ups and downs ahead of you, separation is one of the worst traumas a person can suffer, and you have to be patient, you chose a profession that demands a lot of patience, right? Try not to get involved in his games, there's no point in dragging the power struggles of marriage into the separation, and I drink in her words as if I am one of the plants she waters, looking around at the little apartment I haven't visited for months, crammed with knick-knacks, spectacular and decadent collections of miniature figures, blooming flowerpots and embroidered cloths. Is this what awaits me, too, at the end of all these decisions, to grow old alone, with Gili's visits growing further apart and the china animals multiplying on the shelves? I have to get back to the clinic, she says, let's talk in the evening, in the meantime try to calm down, you'll only be able to see the whole picture when things have settled down, be patient, give it time, her words command my steps, like a rhythmic marching song, give it time.

Next to the door I stumble in the dark on a hard object and I wonder what it can be, I haven't ordered anything, and when I enter the house with a clumsy hop I switch on the light and see the window box, which has surprisingly survived the fall, and inside it the earth has been collected and the geraniums replanted, some of them drooping, their thin arms broken, and I drag it inside, as moved as if I have received a meaningful gift, one I did not even know I wanted. I try to decode the mysterious gesture, who is trying to send me a message, and what message is it, when our wants and desires blur we look for signs under every rock, and in a rapid response to my question I hear footsteps racing up the stairs, galloping like a colt, Gili's joyful steps, and behind him must be Amnon. It was him, his way of telling me not to throw away what could still be saved, and I will respond with a cautious gesture of my own and invite him to stay for supper, and I hug the child and raise my eyes to the empty air behind his shoulders.

Where's Daddy? I ask, and he answers without feeling, as if reciting something he had to learn for school, Daddy's gone, he waited downstairs till I went inside, he was in a rush, and I look at the bruised flowers, his avoidance of me less hurtful when accompanied by so symbolic a gesture, don't throw away the past, he was trying to tell me, it's the soil we're planted in, and from which we will grow, and I kiss the field of curls on the head pressed to my waist, Gilili, thank you for bringing back the window box, did you help Daddy plant the flowers? And he says in surprise, what flowers, we didn't plant any flowers, and I almost try to coax him, what do you mean, Gili, didn't you find the window box that fell downstairs? Didn't you bring it up from the pavement? And he says, no, I don't know what you're talking about, and my glaring disappointment deflates him immediately.

So who did it? I cross examine him, and he looks at the window box lying unnaturally on the living-room floor, I don't know, he grumbles, annoyed that my joy in him is not complete, I'm hungry, make me something to eat. What do you want? I sigh, and he asks, what is there? I want to eat a lot, and I know that he hungers to see me working for him, and for the first time I have no desire to take part in our ritual pretense, to gravely list all the possibilities, most of which are redundant, omelet or fried egg, toast or cheese, salad, cereal. You know as well as I do what there is, I say, just tell me what you want, and he sends me a damp, sly look, if you bother me I'll go and live with Daddy, in another week he'll have a new apartment and I'll have a room there, and I look at him in astonishment, wondering at the speed with which he has adopted the manipulative measures of the child of divorced parents, reality has whooshed past me, surging ahead like a racing car, whistling as it goes.

Gili, don't threaten me, I warn him in a weak voice, it isn't up to you to decide who you stay with, and he says again, Daddy told me that next week he'll have a nice house with a fridge that doesn't make a noise, and I'll have a huge room there with new toys, he says, stretching his arms out sideways to demonstrate the size of the room, and I stand before him helplessly, am I supposed to share in his joy at the wonderful news, to congratulate him on his new home; for years I believed that it was Amnon's presence that was oppressing us, and now it seems that precisely his separate existence is what stands between us, preventing us from going peacefully about the evening's business, supper and bath, story and goodnight, a final kiss, and it seems that precisely by his blatant absence he has magnified his existence, he is present in all the rooms at all times, his voice loud, his protestations sharp.

Give it time, give it time, I murmur, leaning on the window sill, looking at the cars driving by, they all seem black and gleaming like the one parked here this morning, and they all have Amnon and Gabi sitting in the front seat and laughing with their arms around each other; will I ever be able to stand next to this window without shuddering at what happened here this morning, the burning breath on my neck, the purring of the car, the silence of the person sitting in it; but deep within the recesses of that retiring memory, I feel the sharp blade of excitement, shining like the blade of the knife the teacher held in her hand.

Chapter six

But what is time? ghostly, formless matter that shrinks and swells, thickens and dissolves, hastens and dawdles. It may be cut into seconds and minutes, hours and days, but the whole is nothing like the sum of its parts. A will-o-the-wisp is time, a failed cure, a river of suppressed tears, a hail of rocks, a continuous stoning, a cunning crook, an impostor, a daring highway robber. What can I say about this time, which day by day has robbed me of my possessions, of the blessing of an unquestioned routine, of the simplicity of days repeated like a prayer, the joy of nights heavy as rich black earth, the mercy of banished doubts, and now it is even trying to seduce my only son, reaching for him with strong hands laden with shiny poisonous sweets, trying to take him from me.

Is this what my father meant, was it the disappearance of the former Gili that he lamented and warned me about, for now there is a new Gili among us, a Gili who is not in the least like the child I loved, and it seems that amidst the barrage of blows, this is the most painful. He was the fruit of love, and with the disappearance of the love the fruit withered, shed its fragrant velvety skin, and before my eyes another child emerged, a thorny, prickly, stiff-necked child of strife and contention, a small-fisted but determined boxer, sharp-eyed and swift-tongued.

Within the space of a few days, the questions, requests and pleas were silenced, and a bitter resignation, dry and matter-of-fact, which he accepted submissively, almost unfeelingly, seemed to descend on our house; Daddy doesn't live here any more, and I, who was so afraid of his begging and pleading, stood amazed at the speed of his adjustment. He didn't try to coax his father to come upstairs or me to come down, he made no attempt to appeal to us, or bring us together on groundless pretexts, sober and open-eyed he accepted his fate as if he had been preparing for it since the day he was born. Quiet and acquiescent he said goodbye to his father at the entrance to the building, meek and obedient he climbed the stairs in the evening with his bookbag on his shoulders, as if returning from a long day at school, in a steady voice he told his classmates, my father lives in a different house, my parents are separated, as if this is how things were from the beginning of time, as if we had never been a family.

A family, is that what we were, the further this word recedes from my life the more it troubles me, casting its predatory claws in my direction, intensely present in its absence. The six-letter word besieges my heart like poison ivy around the trunk of a tree, sticky and venomous, accompanied by a host of collaborators, for its progeny, too, have become inescapable. Words seem to be my most bitter foe, not the moments of loneliness, the doubts, the memories, but the most common of words: Mother. Father. Family. Home. Brothers and sisters. Holidays and trips. Bedtime stories have grown frightening. Mommy in the kitchen and Daddy in the living room; Mommy drinking coffee and Daddy reading the newspaper; sleeping together in their double bed, and in the background a brother or sister, a cat or a dog. They are never the focus of the story, but for me there is nothing more disturbing, and when I read him the most banal sentences my voice trembles, worried that the words will arouse him from the trance of his resignation, remind him of what he had, what he lost.

Even the innocent things he makes at school scare me. He comes home from school proudly holding a sign he drew for the bedroom door, MOMMY AND DADDY'S ROOM is written in wobbly print, the letters suspended in thin air, floating in the void, and I try to smile, what a nice sign, and he says, hang it up Mommy, why don't you hang it up, and I almost say, where, my little darling, where should I hang it, haven't you noticed that we don't have a room like that anymore? But I purse my lips and hang it on the door anyway, fraudulently, and every night when I go to bed I encounter the fraud, fight the impulse to tear it off the door, or at least to take crayons from his pencil box and correct the form, THIS WAS ONCE MOMMY AND DADDY'S ROOM. You should have made two separate signs, DADDY'S ROOM and MOMMY'S ROOM, I don't dare say to him, whereas he, himself, pays no attention to the deception, proud of his creation as if it is an abstract painting without any obligations to the truth, a bunch of letters, devoid of content, claiming his right to be like all other children.

What's going on, aren't there any other children of divorced parents in your class, I wonder, only to discover that as opposed to the statistics published from time to time in the newspapers, and contrary to the impression I have gained over the years, there isn't a single other child in the vicinity whose parents are separated. When I accompany him to the homes of his new friends, who have been multiplying with surprising ease, I try to clarify the family situation as soon as I step inside, chatting with the mother while trumpeting my praise of the interior design, which enables me to wander around the house, and as I do so, I look around, seeking signs of a man. Sometimes it comes in the form of a pair of sandals in a corner of the living room, a jacket on the rack in the hall, sometimes the smell of shaving lotion, or that mysterious vibe of security and protection, evident mainly in its absence. Sometimes they themselves announce, my husband is at work, my husband is abroad, my husband is on reserve duty, and sometimes the husband himself appears, to my discomfort, as we grope toward acquaintanceship, and I hurriedly beat a retreat, without a single ally among the mothers, inevitably eyeing the bright sign, MOMMY AND DADDY'S ROOM, but only in my house do the letters cringe at the lie. And so I trail behind my son from apartment to apartment, examining at close quarters the families I first saw at the Shabbat party, trying to assess these couples' chances of survival; get divorced already, I mutter to myself, what is the meaning of this clinging to one another, come on, let the divorces commence, what do you care, give Gili a friend in the same boat, so he won't be the odd man out, I can't stand the thought that all these children, the tall and short, the fair and dark, the quiet and noisy, the neglected and well cared for, have something that my child lacks, a family.

But what is a family? A lasting partnership based on trust or fear, on common traditions from the past, common needs in the present, hopes for the future, a unit sharing a single address, fridge, washing machine, bank account, vacation plan, rights and obligations, beliefs and opinions, and if this is really all it is, and if this is really all we had, why is it then that these details upset me so much, as if the heart's sole desire is at stake, the summit of earthly aspirations, and within the space of a few weeks I see how everything I was dissatisfied with, everything I despised, is being built up inside me brick by brick as a high and mighty goal, a kingly acropolis, built of marvelously hewn stones, with crowned ornamental pillars and carved ivory plates set into its walls.

The more resolutely Gili resigns himself to the separation, the more horrifying it becomes. I wake up at night, stunned, the bed, pillows, blankets and boxsprings echoing the protestations of my raging heart, arteries flailing like the limbs of an infant in a terrible burst of fury – I buried a family. All alone, all for myself, in my own honor, I buried a family. True, it was a family that produced more difficulties than children, more fights than nights of passion, more disappointments than joys, but are these qualms sufficient, are they enough, because the bedtime stories imperil me and not him, the sign on the door threatens me and not him, the empty shelves stare at me and not at him; he's okay, father, he's fine, he won't be annihilated, but what about me.

He does not rebel against the decree of separation, but every other imposition incites flagrant protest, delivered with an unfamiliar stubbornness, born this autumn, six years after him. He refuses to get up in the morning, refuses to bathe, refuses to go to bed, refuses to clean his room. With the new friends who frequently visit him he is cheerful, jubilant, but as soon as they leave he turns a sullen face to me, and I look at him hesitantly, afraid to trigger his wrath. Back in those days, the days of the family, I would have been eager for the parents to come and take their kid home so that we would have time to play and talk before bed. As soon as the door shut behind one of his playmates, who would usually be removed kicking and screaming in his mother's arms, my little boy would put his arms around my waist and in his happy chirp, the voice of a honeysucker, he would detail his exploits at comic length, pull me by my hand and lead me to the carpet to play with him, or to the sofa to sit on my lap, or to his schoolbag to show me a picture he had drawn, and I would be spellbound, enchanted by his charm, entranced by his clear prattle, by the endless welling of the spring within me that I had never known was there, not wishing for anything else, only more and more of this unsurpassable intimacy. Every word his lips would pronounce I loved beyond bearing, his deep laughter, his candy-pink tongue, the spittle in his mouth, the beauty spot on his cheek, and now when he turns a sullen face to me, I fill the bathtub in silence, wondering what will remain of the love story that I never imagined would have an end, that was supposed to continue one way or another all the days of my life.

In the morning he wakes up tired and irritable, rubbing the sticky film of sleep from his eyes, peeking out angrily as though seeking grounds for a fight. Get dressed Gilili, I say, laying his clothes on his bed, but he twists his face, says he wants to wear what he wore yesterday, and pulls the dirty clothes out of the laundry basket, refusing to brush his ever-more entangled curls, refusing to eat. What do you want on your sandwich? I ask, and he complains, I'm sick of your questions, that's the most annoying question in the world. What's so annoying about it, just say what you want, cheese, peanut butter, chocolate spread? And he yells, why are you arguing with me, all you want to do is argue with me. I'm not arguing, I say, I'm just asking you what you want on your sandwich, and he mutters, I don't care, whatever you want, but when we're already on our way out, he rummages through his schoolbag, pulls out the sandwich, and throws it on the floor, I don't want cheese, he whines, I want chocolate, and I quickly make him a new sandwich, knowing that it's fate will be similar, and in the end I decide to avoid the inevitable confrontation by making two sandwiches every morning, but a new squabble always follows on the heels of the last one, materializing for no apparent reason.

Anything can provoke a confrontation, it seems, and in those first weeks after the separation we argued more than we ever had before, as if he had decided to take his father's role upon himself, to preserve the tradition of antagonism that had taken root between these walls, and I had imagined tranquility. When we naviagated our way between

Amnon's morning admonishments, when we played on the carpet in the afternoons under his roaming stare, when the echoes of the arguments penetrated the steamy air of the bathroom, where Gili sat immersed in white foam among his toys; I in his absence, imagined a home replete with tranquility, but now he is gone and the arguments remain, reincarnated, living alongside the enduring tension, except it is even heavier now because it is only split two ways, vanquishing only our love.

Is it, indeed, love? Under the heavy unhewn stones of guilt and regret, bereavement and longing, insult and disappointment, it is hard to perceive love, even the seemingly simple, most natural love of all, the maternal kind. This hallowed asset of mine, which astounded me with its intensity, which enveloped me like a bulletproof vest for the past six years and separated me from the rest of the world, even between me and Amnon, is slipping through my fingers, because when we lick ice cream on the steps of the house, it is no longer as sweet as it used to be, and when we play together in the yard I am no longer as engrossed as I once was, I no longer gaze at him in admiration and astonishment, hanging on his every word. With bleak boredom I look at my watch, how much longer till I can put him to bed, how much longer till I can be alone with my sorrow beyond the reach of his scrutiny, and I almost conclude that the love that flourished between us is incapable of sustaining itself between two, it's contingent on a third party, and without Amnon, without his meaningful looks, it has been stripped of content, turned into the routine and obligatory feeling a mother keeps for her child, pleasant and delightful at times, troublesome and tiring at others. It appears that, of all things, Amnon's presence, it turns out, magnified my love for Gili, breathed life into it. Was it a provocation, similar to my need to see him from the window with his best friend by my side, did I want to prove to Amnon how much I was able to love, only not him, or was I trying to transmit to him via the child a warm, simple love, a love that was intended for him, but that I was unable to bestow directly.

Flabbergasted, I follow the upheavals, amazed at my inability to foresee the future, stunned at the rapid cracking along the foundations of my life, and I can no longer tell if it was Gili who changed first and me in his wake, or whether he recognized that I was lost to him and therefore shuns me, or maybe these are parallel and even predictable developments that only I failed to predict, while time, that dexterous conman, watched me and laughed; give it time, she said, but time is a false cure, a continuous stoning.

Stop punishing yourself, she says now, with all that guilt you're not giving yourself a chance to recover, I told you, a powerful force compelled you to take this step, don't be in such a hurry to deny it, let things settle, you'll find your stride again, I guarantee it. In anticipation of the separation you denied everything that was good between you, and now it's come back in spades, these reversals are to be expected, try not to succumb to them, be patient. I listen to her distractedly, dying to bring the conversation to an end, with her and with all the others who call and want to know how I'm doing, and it isn't even pride that prevents me from admitting how deep my depression is, how great my regret, but the pointlessness of every conversation taking place in the sealed void of my sorrow is almost like talking to myself, I can barely move my lips, I nod with my mouth closed, make excuses for brevity's sake, Gili's calling me, I mumble, even when he's not at home, I have to see how he's doing.

Sometimes it seems that there's only one thing I'm prepared to listen to: how bad it was with him, how incompatible we were, how depressed we looked at that party, how we argued at that picnic, when Gili begged us to stop and we didn't even hear him, how everyone sensed the tension between us, how everyone knew that it was only a matter of time, but even when the right words are said, I listen to them doubtfully, with growing resentment, what do you know about it, you don't have a clue about what it was really like between us, nobody from the outside can know who we were, because there's only one person I want to talk to about our family life, to go around one evening to his rented apartment whose address I don't even know, to see the big room full of shiny new toys, to press myself against his long, ungainly body and to say, forgive me, my love, for I was wrong.

I chart the course of the evening on the nights when I wake up with my heart pounding, and in the mornings when a dense, late-summer heat covers my eyes with sticky fingers as if to ask guess who, and in the long hours in front of the computer, when I try to finish my research on Thera, and in the afternoons in the playgrounds, making small talk with the other mothers and plotting, this evening I'll go to him, he won't be able to resist me, I'll promise him that I'll change, tell him it's only now that I've learned how attached I am to him and how much I love him, I'll promise him that everything will be different, that everything he lacked will be supplied in abundance, every evening I'll sit next to him on the sofa and read his articles, and every night I'll make love to him, accept him as he is and never fight with him again. You'll give me a family and I'll give you a wife, I say, formulating the terms of the deal in my head, which now seems perfect for all concerned, never has a better deal been offered, and for a moment I'm excited as though everything has already been settled, imagining his return home, of course I'll help him pack, return the few things he took, put his books back on the shelves, his clothes in the closet, and when Gili wakes up in the morning his father will already be at home, like before, and this month of separation will remain between us like a warning sign, like a pillar of cloud, until our towering happiness renders it unnecessary.

Dazed by the happiness awaiting me, I sniffle, shake off the glittering drops of the illusion like a dog emerging from water, resume treading along the constricted paths of reality, and because I want it so badly, because I cling to it so desperately, I fear putting myself to the test, waiting for the right opportunity, the right time, the right place, and it seems that I will wait forever because I haven't seen the real Amnon, with his awkward body and beaming wide smile, since that Friday we welcomed the Sabbath, when Gili pulled us after him like a stubborn little cart, and I said in a firm voice, like that of his new teacher, Daddy isn't coming up with us, Gili, he's going now, tomorrow he'll come and take you for a few hours. The words were spoken crudely, callously, meanly, and ever since then he has been avoiding me, picking Gili up at school, accompanying him only as far as the first step, transmitting clear messages through him as if he were a pigeon carrier: Daddy's taking me this week on Sunday not Monday, Wednesday not Thursday. And I wonder, how long can he go on evading me, till the next Sabbath party at the school, till the child's next birthday, or perhaps even longer, till his bar mitzvah, till his draft day, till his wedding day, and perhaps he'll go on avoiding me forever, and I'll go on hesitating forever, afraid of facing rejection, but one day Gili announces upon his return home, Daddy says that on Friday he'll pick me up from school and I'll sleep over at his house, the bed he bought me just came, and then I know that this is the right night, because with Gili sleeping in the next room, his mouth open, his drool on the new pillowcase, his sleep crying out for a stable family, he will simply not be able to refuse me.

Where exactly is Daddy's new apartment, I ask in a sweet, nonchalant voice, is it far from here? And Gili says, not very far and not very close, a short drive in the car, and I ask, what does the street look like? And he says, kind of regular, like here, with trees and houses, and I suggest, why don't you try to read the name of the street, tell me the letters, and he protests, but it's still hard for me to read, and I quickly invent a new game for him, a quiz with prizes, and we go out for long walks in the neighborhood, with him trying to decipher the names of the streets, and me explaining as best I can, training him in reading and finding his way around, and although he enjoys the game, he makes no effort to apply it on his next visit to his father, and I am already at my wit's end, for in order to elicit a change of heart in him, I have to stand before him, and that has taken on the proportions of the impossible. He has severed all ties to our common friends, his cell is never on, Gabi is out of the question, will I try to find out my husband's address from the school secretary, but even after issuing some feeble excuse and obtaining a list of his classmates, I find only one address there for Gili, and I am baffled by this strange obstacle in the path toward the realization of my meticulous plan, for I know exactly what I will say and what I will wear, I know every detail of the ceremony, except for the venue where it is to take place, and still, not willing to give up, I decide to take the exceptional and eyebrow-raising, and yet apparently unavoidable, step of following them on Friday afternoon, when Amnon takes his son to his new home, to their first Shabbat without me.

I sit in Dina's little car with my head bowed, wearing dark glasses and a straw hat, next to the school gate, where empty cars loiter, soon to be filled with the shouts and laughter of children, returning sweaty and excited to the bosoms of their families. One after another the parents arrive, most of them already known to me, I have even visited their homes and admired their interiors, only a few are still strangers. Here comes the pretty Keren who invited everybody to a party after the welcoming of the Sabbath in a short dress and tan legs, her husband hurrying behind her, placing his hand on her shoulder, sparking my envy, crackling twigs within me, and here's Michal, walking slowly, unenthusiastically, she looks worried of late, but we barely speak, since Yotam has apparently lost faith in his finicky new friend and Gili has easily made other friends, and I rest my forehead on the steering wheel as if overcome by fatigue, looking out of the corner of my eye at the commotion, familiar and new, of a Friday afternoon. One after another they emerge from the wide-open gate, a bright, churning stream of children and parents, schoolbags and small talk, and only Gili's father is absent, late again as usual, and maybe he forgot altogether, lucky I'm here, but how can I execute my plan without him. The cars are thinning out; if I'm left here alone, my cover will be blown, furtively I look around, come on, where are you, more and more worries float to the surface, what if he doesn't come alone, if poor Ofra is at his side, if I've waited too long, if he came early and they're already in the rented apartment, Gili jumping barefoot on his new bed, but here he is, the red car pulling in right behind me, almost scraping Dina's bumper, and he gets out heavily and stretches his limbs, glances at his watch, smoothes his hand in a familiar gesture over his head, where to my surprise pale bristles sprout, like the lawn in the raven park. For four weeks I haven't seen him and my heart goes out to him, how dear and familiar he is, charming in his ungainliness, his deep-pocketed pants hanging loosely on his body, he seems to have lost a little weight, looks as boyish as in the old days, and he passes me with his cautious stride as if picking his way between the excavation squares, his dimensions lending an air of safety to the wounded site, while I carefully brushed away the dirt, stealing hidden glances at him, praying that he would approach me again, remove his dark glasses in my honor, that he'd call me the Parisian.

Here he is hurrying back again, the boy on his shoulders, not wasting a minute on chitchat with parents or teachers. Watch out for the gate, I almost shout when Gili's head comes close to the iron bar, but he bends down just in time, trust me, he would say, why don't you trust me, and I peek at them from under the straw hat, these are my two men, this is my whole family, his big fingers holding the child's ankles, covering his calves, Gili's hands on his head, playing with the new lawn of hair. When he carries my child on his shoulders it's as though he's holding me too, for this is the child I dressed this morning, these are the clothes I washed for him, this is the schoolbag I bought for him, the laces I tied, this child is all mine and when he rides so naturally on your shoulders, I, too, am there, by his side, don't you feel my weight, because I am still yours, and you are mine, because this child is ours and we are his, and I nearly jump out and rush up to them, take my place next to him in the red car, but instead I freeze, no, not this way, I can't let impulse lead to despair, I have to wait for this evening, to act according to plan. I take a few deep breaths, readying myself for the mission, as they get into the car and fasten their seat belts, I have never done anything like this, have no idea how the mission will be accomplished. What will I do if other cars come between us and I lose them, or if they don't and he recognizes me, and I pull the straw hat down and start the engine, setting out right behind them, praying that it won't take long. The possibility that they will get away and leave me without a clue as to how to carry out my plan on this long void of a weekend frightens me so much that I leave almost no space between myself and the red backside, light after light, and when he signals I signal, when he turns I turn, for a moment a broad smile gleams at me in the mirror of his car and my heart stops, until I realize it's Gili he's smiling at, Gili, the tip of whose head isn't even visible over the back of the seat, until it seems as if the car is empty, and when he slows down, alongside on a busy street I, too, smile, how typical of him to retrace his steps, I should have known, this is the street he lived on ten years ago, in a cramped one room apartment, this is where he invited me to come and read the excavation report he was in the middle of writing about the pottery finds discovered in the destruction layer of Tel Jezreel. When he parks, I pass him and stop a little further on, watching them in the mirror as they get out of the car, and when they disappear into a small building I turn around and cruise past, repeating the number out loud, even though there's no chance of me forgetting it, not the number and not the well-tended stone building with the two surprisingly stout palm trees stationed at the entrance like a pair of armed sentinels.

The approaching family reunification lends our home a warm glow, and I put the groceries away in the kitchen, beer for him and red wine for me and mango juice for Gili, and a sweet challah loaf and cheeses and fruit, as if a party is being thrown here tonight, as if this is not my first weekend without them but the last weekend of the separation. A bright and cheerful tale is told by the fridge, the kitchen cabinets, the clean sheets I spread on the beds, yes, I, too, am having a party tonight, just like the beautiful Keren, except that it is not the parents of the whole class that I am inviting but only one father, who I have chosen anew. What's the party in honor of, someone asked, and she answered with a shy smile, a light blush flowering on her cheeks, nothing special, we just feel like celebrating, and I admit that the details of my party are not yet clear to me, not even where it will take place; will we wake Gili in the middle of the night and come home together, or will I sleep there with them and come home in the morning all together, will the party happen at his house, and if so should I take everything there with me; but I don't allow these trifles to bother me, I wander around the house, beside myself with excitement, my body, which felt as though it had been cloven in a terrible accident, is mending itself, and it seems to me that the very walls are sharing in my joy, making the pictures dance, and even the furniture seems eager to receive the banished husband soon to return victorious, the fragment of the family floating in space like a comet that had lost its way, threatening the future of the world, but tonight he will be returned to his orbit, to his armchair, to his desk, to his bed, to his home.

Chapter seven

Ella, don't do it, she blurts as I stand behind her stooped back, jingling her car keys as if they were bells producing a festive score. She bends over the luxuriant plants on her little porch, picking off dry leaves, and I say, since when did you become such a defeatist, Dina, it's not like you, and she straightens up and looks me in the eye with her precise stare, it's just seems wrong, to take him by surprise when he's made it clear that he doesn't want to see you, and I say, you and your old-fashioned games, you're not reading the situation right, don't forget I was the one who left him, he begged for us to stay together, so why shouldn't I admit that I made a mistake.

But you still don't know if you made a mistake, she says, taking the keys from me with earth-stained hands, you're rushing to get him back and you're completely ignoring everything that led to this separation; have you given any thought to what will happen a week or a month after he comes back? Nothing's really changed, Amnon hasn't become more considerate or easier to live with, nor have you changed, listen to me, Ella, you're still confused, it's totally natural, during times of crisis we're inundated with fleeting emotions, it takes a long time to identify a true feeling.

What I'm feeling doesn't ring true to you? I interrupt her, you're totally wrong, and she says, of course you feel a need for him, but the question is what lies hidden beneath that need, fear, guilt, insult, and whether you're really willing to accept Amnon as is, or whether it's another illusion, another truce in your power struggles. You have no idea how misleading emotions can be, our emotional constitution is like a costume ball, it's only from the distant perch of time that we can begin to understand who masqueraded as what.

You're not updated, Dina, I say, I'm not the least bit confused, I'm absolutely sure that I want him back, and she says, but a month ago you were absolutely sure that you didn't; what changed since then, is it the fact that, contrary to what you expected, he can manage without you? Say he'd kept on pleading with you to take him back, would you still want him?

Maybe it would have taken longer, I answer cautiously, maybe I needed to be apart from him in order to realize how important he is to me, and she says, and maybe you just want what you haven't got; it seems to me that you haven't found your equilibrium yet, you're hurt by his indifference, you're afraid of losing him, the most convenient thing for you now is to remake the previous situation, but without really confronting the way things were between you, give it a few more months before you start another revolution in the lives of three people, and I say, you're not realistic, Dina, that's your problem, in another few months I'll have lost him completely, he'll get used to living without me, maybe he'll even have someone else, as it is I'm worried I've waited too long, who knows, he may have already gone back to his ex-girlfriend.

It seems she has retreated to her boldly-colored kitchen, treading thoughtfully on the orange tiles that climb the walls like vines, eat something, you're skin and bones, she says, anxiously inspecting my body in its tight, wine-colored dress, and I put my hand to my throat, as if trying to shield it from the flat blade of a knife, I'm having a hard time swallowing lately, do you have a sucking candy or something?

No, but I do have a cake, she says, producing a round tin with a thickly-iced chocolate cake from the fridge, cutting me a generous slice. I make do with the icing, licking it off the top with a little teaspoon without touching the cake, ignoring the dissatisfaction spreading across her face. Who did you bake it for, yourself? I ask, uncomfortable with the thought that a woman would live alone with a cake, and she says, I have guests coming for lunch tomorrow, why don't you come too, and I say, thank you, tomorrow we'll probably be busy moving his things back home, I don't know if we'll have time, and she sighs, giving me a doubtful, sidelong glance, Ellinka, in case things don't work out the way you think, just know that you're invited for lunch. Thank you very much, I say, a little condescendingly, what would I do at the contrived, solace-free get-togethers she organizes for her non-familied girlfriends. There's no doubt whatsoever in my mind that it will work out, I boast, he loves me, he can't have stopped loving me in a single month, you talk as if he was the one who left me.

At some point it no longer matters who left whom, she remarks, but who adjusts more easily to the new situation, and I snort dismissively, eager to get the sticky conversation over with, Amnon, adjust? He's so conservative, even the apartment he rented is on the street where he once lived, he can't stand any type of innovation. The fact that he's denying me now doesn't mean that he doesn't want to come back, more likely it means the opposite, he's just hurt, afraid to say what he wants, but if it comes from me, he'll be overjoyed, you'll see. Again she sighs, hugging her ribs as if a cold wind has suddenly blown through her, good, I hope for your sake that you're right, the truth is that I don't know what to wish you, and I say, what's the problem, wish me success. She smiles faintly, but what you see as success isn't what I see as success, and I kiss her on her desiccated cheek, which rustles beneath my lips like a dry leaf, come on, Dina, don't be so petty, and she says, I wish you success, Ellinka, her slightly bloodshot brown eyes watching me in concern as I depart, like my mother's eyes when I left the house on Friday nights to go to the class parties from which I returned humiliated, straight to her consoling arms.

How exciting and strange it is, to be treading now in my own ten year-old footsteps, narrow, hurrying footsteps, doubting their good fortune, finding it hard to believe that he really wants me, the big, arrogant man who directed the excavations with a high hand, focused and impatient, and at the same time exuding sudden, soothing gusts of warmth, and of all people it was me he singled out, me he invited to come and read the ongoing report, to make my comments. I pause for a moment next to the building where he once lived in a cramped one-room apartment full of books, potshards, gloomy etchings of Jerusalem landscapes from previous centuries, the whole place suffused with his rough, blunt charm. He'd purr with laughter at my comments, you're not an archeologist at all, he'd grin, you're only interested in fairytales, what are you doing in our department, and at the time it sounded like the rarest of praise. I have to take you to Thera, he'd say, will you come with me? And I would nod delightedly, to the end of the world I'll come with you, into the bowels of the earth I'll follow you, I'd sit on his lap and look gratefully into his soaring eyes, stroke his hands, as if I'd really been buried under layers of earth for thousands of years, covered with volcanic stone, until those big hands came along and rescued me.

Few cars pass me in the increasingly cold and cloudy, thickening night, but one of them slows down and a hand seems to wave to me but I don't try to identify the waver, flashing a quick hello to whoever it may be, absorbed in the voices fluttering out through the open window like a flock of birds into the street, and I permit myself to add my voice to the grace after the meal although I have not shared in it, *A song of ascents, when the Lord turned again the captivity of Zion, we were like dreamers, then was our mouth filled with laughter and our tongue with singing,* I sing as I stroll, at long last the holidays that came down on me this year like a heavy burden are over, holidays without parents, without a family, at the bottom of the high buildings, in the common yards, a few Sukkoth huts are left, hastily built and not yet dismantled, their dew-damp blankets giving off a deep autumn smell, their palm fronds withered. I peek into one of the empty booths, the carefully cut and pasted paper chains rustling in the wind, some of the links in the chain fallen at my feet. When was it, last year or the year before, that Gili begged us to build a Sukkoth booth on our balcony and Amnon refused, but I persevered, climbing onto the balustrade, stretching my short body, trying to surround the balcony with sheets, while he lounged on the sofa and read, indifferent to my efforts. For the whole holiday we did not speak, seven days and seven nights, and even when we made up in the end, the reconciliation was as bitter as the quarrel itself. I never asked him why he had refused, why it was so hard for him to make the child happy, perhaps I will try to find out tonight, without complaints or accusations I will say to him, it's so fleeting the chance we have to make him happy, to build him a Sukkoth booth and witness his joy, the day will come when his happiness will be independent of us; was it me who stood between the two of you then, prickly as the date frond you refused to ceremoniously shake.

I steal between the two palm-tree sentinels, lest they stretch out a prickly arm and bar my way, examining the mail boxes in the stairwell, here's his name printed in square letters on white paper, framed in black like the announcements of recent deaths, and I'm relieved to see that no parasitic female name has latched itself to his, and nevertheless the firmness of the letters oppresses me, testifying as it does to the depth of his intention to settle down, to an existence that is not as tenuous or transitory as I had hoped. He will be there forever, like the dead in the land of the dead, and I linger in front of his name, scanning the letters, rehearsing the words I've prepared, even though I still believe I will have no need for them, for the moment he sees me, his face will brighten, and there will be no need for words between us.

I press my ear to the wooden door bearing his name on the second floor, the identical name appears on our door too, in looping letters next to mine, and it seems that a silent battle is raging between these two doors, to determine which of them Amnon Miller belongs to, a battle that will be decided tonight. Soft music filters out through a narrow crack of light between the door and the floor, and I recognize with relief the disc I bought him, syncopated guitar chords accompanying the fading classical music, is this not an invitation, a sign that he's expecting me, and I knock softly, so as not to wake Gili, it's already late, he must be sleeping, there is no sound or movement behind the door. Perhaps they have both fallen asleep, I can easily see them sprawled out side by side, Gili, as always, lying on his back, Amnon, as always, on his stomach, as if they were two sides of the same coin, despite the difference in their size, and I knock again, every possible scenario passing before my eyes. Perhaps they are both fast asleep and I won't be able to wake them, perhaps I'll wake them both and Gili's presence will spoil everything, perhaps he has guests, or worse than that, a female guest, even though Gili has never reported a female figure at his side. I take small nervous steps backwards and sideways, to relieve the tension, and I knock again, recognizing at last the dragging of sleepy feet, and he doesn't ask who's there, maybe he's expecting someone else, because when the door opens and the light falls on my face, he recoils and mumbles, Ella, what are you doing here? But there are no traces of wonder or astonishment in his voice, only a cold and matter-of-fact surprise, what are you doing in a house that is not yours and to which you have not been invited.

Amnon, I say, raising my face to his, his inordinate height surprising me, my neck craning toward him with a creak, in the uncomfortable position I've managed to forget, and I follow him into the apartment as he retreats from me, Amnon, we have to talk, and he clamps his lips until they almost disappear in the expanse of his big face, his front teeth crushing his lower lip, his eyes avoiding mine.

Talk? About what? he asks, as if we have never talked about anything, and the very possibility amazes him, and I say, about us, about out separation, about our son, and he sits down in silence at the round dining room table standing in a corner of the living room, motioning me to sit opposite him, where Gili apparently sat not long ago, for his plate is still lying in front of me, cold leftovers of pasta and vegetable salad scattered over it, a half-eaten corn cob, beneath which the worried face of Winnie the Pooh, wobbling under a big balloon, stares up at me. I take a quick look around, as I have grown accustomed to doing in the houses of Gili's friends, to gather as much data as I can, to come to as many conclusions as I can from the material culture revealed to me, only this time the research opportunity takes on supreme importance and urgency, and suspiciously, surprisingly, I examine the coziness of the little apartment overlooking the monastery, which shines in the night like a giant meteor that has just fallen to the ground. The new furniture he has purchased, a thick rope rug, a sand colored sofa and two wicker armchairs, the electrical appliances and the kitchenware, how has he managed to put together a real home for himself and Gili in just a few weeks, he, who never partook in the demands of domestic reality, who never concerned himself with questions of furniture and interior decoration, who never bought a glass or a plate, who always said we have enough, leaving me to make up my mind in the stores alone, and condemned me, upon return, for yet again wasting time and money.

It's so nice here, Amnon, I say, did you pick it all out? And he admits with a careful smile, almost apologetically, yes, it's not as complicated as I thought, I devoted a few days to it and arranged everything, it was important to me to make Gili feel at home, to be able to bring friends, to feel comfortable here, and then he gets up and goes to the open kitchen, pours me a glass of water in a tall blue glass, and I drink it thirstily, even the water here seems to have a different taste, clear and clean as spring water.

Show me Gili's room, I ask in a sour voice, finding it difficult to admire his achievements, and he leads me proudly down the passage, on the way we pass a small bedroom, a bead curtain swaying at the entrance instead of a door, rustling. I look sullenly at the new double bed, covered with an embroidered bedspread, and immediately find myself facing a huge beautiful room, even more beautiful than Gili described, a night lamp casting a soft glow on the walls painted the color of golden wheat, its floor covered with a fluffy carpet over which are scattered new families of stuffed animals that have appeared out of thin air, for none of ours are missing, and in the corner of a room a wooden bed covered with new sheets, and on it a child, his brown hair thick and glossy and his cheeks flushed and his delicate lips parted. He lies on his back, his hands raised above his head, covered with a thin blanket printed with thick clusters of stars, his face fresh and sweet and his breath calm, and I bend over and kiss him on the cheek, trying to breathe in the warm air blowing from his slightly chapped lips.

A solitary tear falls from my eye onto his milky cheek because this seductive picture of a beautiful perfect child sleeping serenely in a beautiful perfect room spooks me, awakening a strong suspicion that something is being covered up, and I crouch down again and sniff him, instead of the familiar smell of his body, the smell of warm vanilla ice cream melting in the sun, I smell freshly painted wood, as if his soul has been taken away and without it he has turned into a wooden doll carved by a master, an identical double, and I feel his face, it's as soft as usual, and nevertheless a profound unease seizes me, what is this room, what is this house, far better equipped than ours, my child does not belong here, to this furniture exhibition, he belongs to me, to the house where he was born and grew up, what is he trying to do, buy his heart with toys and furniture until he forgets his real home, his real mother. Now he's proudly showing me the new closet, full of the new clothes he bought him, folded neatly on top of each other as in a store. He's even bought him a coat, getting his child ready for winter, and I try to hide the glumness, you never went with me to buy him clothes when the seasons changed, you always had more important things to do, what do I know, you'd say, wriggling your way out of it, and now without me everything is suddenly possible, why couldn't you change when you were with me.

Cool air steals under my dress, stirring the weighty scent of a new season, awakening vague longings, the memory of a clean life at its inception, a life which had order; do you feel it and shiver too, your big body at my side, endlessly familiar and yet impermissible, like the body of a child that's matured overnight, whose mother, accustomed to fondling him, must keep her hands off, as though his limbs were aflame. Together we stand planted by his bedside, like worried parents at the side of a sick child, his mouth opens in a yawn or a dreamy smile, and I notice a little gap at the back of his mouth, under his lower lip. He's lost a tooth, I whisper, stunned at not having been part of the event, even the last thread of nerve tissue tying the tooth to the gum has betrayed me, and he says, oh, yeah, when we were eating supper we found it among the corn kernels, and hands me the matchbox lying at the foot of the bed, where the tiny tooth rests. Now that it has been detached from his mouth, it looks yellow and stained as if it had fallen from the empty gums of an old man and not the fresh mouth of a child.

His arms stretch and it looks as if he is holding them out to me for a drowsy hug, and I bend down, his eyelids quiver, his lashes flicker, don't wake up sweetheart, not now. Amnon's look motions me away, and I obediently return to my place at the round table, to the glass of water that's no longer waiting for me, to the green fly that's beating its wings against the confines of the watery trap, and once more, with mounting hostility, I examine the lavish living room, the assertiveness of the furniture, much like the firmly printed name on the mailbox, challenges me, we're here to stay, you're transient, we're permanent, I attempt to circumnavigate the obstacle, to suggest creative solutions, actually we could all move here, start our new lives here, the apartment's smaller than ours, but we'll manage, and already I imagine us feasting at the table set with the new dishes he bought, drinking the pristine water, sleeping soundly on his brand new bed, why not, tomorrow I'll bring my computer and a few pairs of clothes, and already I can hear Gili's enthusiastic voice showing off the marvels of our new home, but why does his voice break, I shake myself alert, shards of weeping are coming from the room at the end of the hall and I hurry there, but Amnon signals me to stay away, with a rude gesture, as if I were a stray dog.

It's all right, sweetie, I hear him whisper in a warm voice, I'm right here with you, and Gili whimpers, I want to be with you in the living room, I'm not used to sleeping here yet, and my heart goes out to him, I'm here with you too, honey, I want to add, but the path to him is barred, and Amnon comes up to me, it's not good for him to see you here, it will confuse him, he whispers, scanning the air for a solution, and I want to say, what difference does it make now, that's all already behind us, but for the time being I have to obey him, a man so apprehensive it's as though he's been asked to hide a Jewess from a bloodthirsty mob.

Go into the bathroom, he hisses, lock the door, he can't know you're here, it would be really confusing for him, and I obey, seething, taking a seat on the toilet lid, locked inside the narrow cubicle, and then promptly the light is snapped shut, final as a verdict, much like a movie theater, but here only the voices reach me, while the sights, the child standing in his short pajamas, skinny legs peeking out, wailing, grief dripping from his eyes, as though he shall never know salvation, are screened on the surface of my oscillating heart. I want to be in the living room, he pleads, I'll sleep in the living room on the sofa, please Daddy, I'm not used to my room yet, I want to be with you, and Amnon says, I'll sit next to you in your room, don't worry, I'll stay with you until you fall asleep. But I can't fall asleep in this bed, it's too hard, he sobs, and Amnon says, it's exactly the same as your bed at your mother's, it's just new, that's all, and Gili insists, I want my bed, when I sleep at your place bring me my bed from home, and Amnon explains patiently, but that's impossible, you'll get used to it, you'll see, tomorrow morning you'll feel better.

I want water, he demands, and then says, I'm still hungry, I want to eat, and then comes the wish that I, in my insanity, so wanted to hear, I want Mommy, and I squirm on the toilet seat, what could be simpler, my little love, Mommy's here, just a turn of the key in the lock and she'll arrive like the good fairy in the story books, here to fulfill your most urgent wish. His face will shine, his tears will dry up, his smile will fill the house, and I almost disobey the instructions of my host and emerge from my hiding place, but at the last moment I demur, for this isn't an ordinary night, it is a night in the service of a noble goal, and I can't afford a false step.

His bare feet come percussively down the hall, just a drink of water and back to bed, Amnon says, beginning to lose his patience, and Gili shrieks in response, I want Mommy, I want to call Mommy, and his father says dryly, so call, and I, in my solitary confinement, a dark narrow room, redolent of disinfectant, hear him dial our empty house, waiting for me to answer, Mommy, it's me, he tells the answering machine in his most grown-up voice, I want to tell you something, I can't fall asleep, maybe you can bring me my mattress, and I curl up on the toilet seat, my face crushed against my knees, go to sleep already, I mutter, and let me patch things up here, how much longer is this torture going to go on, but it turns out that the main event is still to come. Daddy, I need to go pee-pee, he says, and my heart fills with savage glee at Amnon's predicament; how did you not foresee that, what are you going to do now; but to my surprise he recovers quickly, the bathroom's occupied, he announces, you can pee in the flowerpot on the balcony. Gili approaches the door and tries to open it. I can hear his bewildered hand on the handle, moving it up and down, so why is it dark in there? he asks, and Amnon replies, because the light went out.

So who's in there? he asks, apprehension and perplexity plain in his voice. Somebody, a woman you don't know, she's leaving in a minute, and Gili whines, I want to see her, and then his father's patience snaps and he scolds him, stop nagging and go back to bed, and to my surprise the scolding works and quiet is restored, a charged, threatening silence bringing the dead words back to life, somebody, a woman you don't know, she's leaving in a minute, and they terrify me as if they're foretelling my future. That's what he's plotting. I heard the cruelty in his voice, the gloating, all these years he's been jealous of the bond between us and now he means to seduce him with presents and treats until he forgets me; how, in a few weeks' time, have I been reduced to this, turning from a devoted, admiring, beloved mother into somebody, a woman you don't know, look how the separation is turning our lives inside out, until the most ordinary, natural circumstances, the three of us together on Friday night, under one roof, turn into an intolerable sequence of jarring mishaps, and it seems that the mission I have undertaken is becoming more crucial with each passing minute, for it was I who ripped the tear and I who must mend it tonight.

A few minutes later a faint knock lands on the door, I open it cautiously, emerging in tatters from my prison, my hair and clothes saturated with the smell of disinfectants. He sends me a cautionary look, puts his finger to his lips, tells me not to make a sound, and I tiptoe back to my place at the table, staring with a heavy heart at Gili's plate, the half-eaten corn cob displaying dozens of little yellow kernels like the one hidden in the matchbox, like all the other teeth that will fall from his mouth without me. Of the persuasive speech I prepared, only cold, tasteless leftovers remain, but I have no choice but to resurrect them, to season them anew, or else this is the fate that awaits me, bringing my son up through the locked bathroom door, turning into someone, a woman he doesn't know, who's leaving in a minute.

Amnon, listen, I whisper, trying to nobly ignore everything that has happened here, you have no idea how sorry I am for what I did, it's clear to me now that it was a mistake, I want you to come home, for us to be a family again, you were right, I didn't know how to appreciate what I had, I didn't understand what I was doing, please forgive me, I'm sure you won't be sorry, we have so much to gain, look at the alternative, hiding from my own son, separated from him twice a week. But I remind myself to concentrate on the two of us and not on Gili, he wants to be part of a couple, not just a father, that's what he's been saying all these years. For a moment I fall silent and glance at his face, which is not turned to me but to the big window overlooking the yellow-lit monastery, his straight, well-shaped nose, his narrow lips, his spectacular blue eyes focused on the ancient building as if my voice is coming from there, and I lay my hand on his, Amnon, I miss you, I want to spend the rest of my life with you. My narrow, nail-bitten hand is too small to cover his thick fingers, the very same ones that astounded me with their grace when cradling a potshard. Sharply, he pulls his hand away as if my touch is unclean, and says, without looking at me, listen, Ella, luckily for you I'll be more gentle with you than you were with me when I tried to persuade you to reconsider, you pushed me out of your way as if I was a gnat, a public nuisance, well, I won't do that to you because you were my wife and you'll always be the mother of my son, so I'll ask you but one question: who do you think you are; what on earth are you thinking?

I don't understand the question, I reply, already knowing that the conversation isn't going in the direction I anticipated, but still hoping for the best, and he says, and I don't understand your visit, do you really think I'm some chocolate-coated pawn in your games? That you can pick me up and put me down whenever you feel like it? When you threw me out of your life, you didn't think of me, and now, when you're trying to get me back, you're not thinking of me either, only of yourself.

Amnon, please, I protest, nobody leaves someone for the other person's sake or comes back for someone else's sake, married life isn't about altruism, and he says, I'm not talking about altruism, but about decency, you expect the whole world to conduct itself according to your changing moods, if you're tired of me, you have to get rid of me, at once, if you miss me, you have to get me back, at once. You think you can conduct experiments with human beings, when will you grow up? And I sigh, bowing my chastised head, you're right, I'm really sorry, and he waves his arm, I don't need your apologies, they won't help me now, I'm already in a completely different place, but you can't even see that, and I hear my voice quiver, what do you mean, what place are you in?

I'm here, he gestures toward the sofa and the armchairs, as if he were a carpenter and this was his workshop. I like my peace and quiet here, what happened between us through the past few years frayed my nerves, you distanced yourself from me and I felt threatened, so I reacted aggressively. Our foundations felt like they were crumbling and your endless complaints seemed like a thin veil for your true desire, to be rid of me. I had no chance of satisfying you, I stopped interesting you as a man, you only wanted me as a father for your son, and that, too, only on your conditions. You may be capable of falling in love, but certainly not of loving, the moment you're disappointed, your love cools, your constant criticism emits an icy cold. You're exactly like your father, you suffered so much under him that now you're just like him, and it's true, I'm full of shortcomings, but I loved you, and much to my chagrin that wasn't mutual. Now that I've gotten over the shock, I feel that I'm healing, my relations with Gili have improved, I like being with him without you, I like being with myself without you, without feeling that everything I do is put to the test and entered into a black list of sins, I'm sorry, Ella, but it's the truth, I'm over it, over you.

But Amnon, I'm not proposing that you come back to things as they were, I say generously, bridling my urge to dismantle the false picture he has drawn, of course we'll have to fix a lot of things in our relationship, but there's still love in the home, you said so yourself, and one doesn't give up on love so easily, it's better to invest in the fixing than in the separating. Then I take back what I said, he sighs, it hasn't been love for a long time, but a bad habit, I don't believe in our relationship anymore, in your last analysis you were infuriating, but right, it's over between us, it was over years ago. His blue gaze flickers over my face for a moment, and immediately returns to the window, and I listen to him doubtfully, finding it difficult to believe in the finality of his words, he didn't want to get married either, I recall, or to have a baby, there's time, he said, what do we need that official stamp for, what do we need that burden for, let's enjoy each other first, but in the end you always gave in, with a forgiving, patronizing sigh, and I was drunk with my power over you, as if I'd succeeded in taming a huge animal, double my size, a real Minotaur, a bull with gold-tipped horns, and now you'll give in too, I just have to find the right combination of words, like the right combination for a safe full of rings and bracelets and necklaces, the jewels of Helen of Troy, waiting only for me.

I understand that you were hurt and I'm really sorry, I say in a soft voice, but don't let that hurt control you, I promise you I'll do everything to make this work, we can be as happy as we once were. But he smiles bitterly and shakes his head, stop it, Ella, don't make promises you can't keep, I know you, I've learned that whatever you say is only true for the moment you say it, I don't trust you any more, it's clear to me that it isn't me you want, but rather to fill up the empty space in your life, and I'm the most obvious candidate because I've already been there, but it's not personal. You want a family, security, you don't want me as a person, you disapprove of me, have you forgotten already that I'm crude, selfish, insensitive, domineering, coarse, jealous? Well I haven't forgotten, and

I have no need to go back to all that again, so, in all matters concerning the child I'll always be with you, but in everything else you no longer exist for me, and I breathe heavily, my chest paralyzed with dread, for the first time the possibility of an absolute refusal enters my head, and it gores me, and I get up and lurch toward him, try to sit on his bare knees, to embrace his neck, his familiar scent, of soap and dust.

My love, I whisper in his ear, you have no idea how wrong you are, I miss you, I don't want anyone else, I know that I neglected our relationship, I was too absorbed in Gili, it happens to a lot of women, it's easier to love a sweet child than a resentful man, but it was an illusion, my complete life is only with you, we're the basis of this family. He shakes his head violently as if he has just heard an intolerable rumor, and removes my hand from his shoulder; I see things differently now, Ella, I think our separation was inevitable, living together put both of us in a situation of constant frustration, we took it out on each other, and I don't believe that it can change in such a short time, I have no intention of going back to that, I feel good without you, as far as I'm concerned it's final. Get up now, he says, go home, I'm trying to rehabilitate myself and I'm asking you not to get in my way, and I get up from his hard knees and stumble to the sofa, fall onto it and start to cry, staining the pale upholstery with my tears, my teeth chattering and my body shivering. Sickness has descended on me, mortal sickness, and there's nobody to take care of me, only a little wooden doll in the shape of a six-year-old child, and Amnon approaches me warily, as if I am a suspicious object left in his house, his unbuttoned black shirt reveals his solid pink chest, and I hold out my arms to him, come and sit next to me, but he stands planted on his heavy legs, I want you to leave, he says quietly, you're making it difficult for me and for yourself, I'm sure you'll get over it, you're stronger than you think, I'm sure you'll have a new family if you want to, look ahead, you have no choice, that's what I'm doing. I sob, beat the sofa with my fists, no, I won't look forward, only backward, I don't want a new family, I only want our family, you and Gili, how can you be so crass, so inconsiderate to him.

You were inconsiderate to him last month, when I pleaded with you, he says dryly, and I mutter, so for that you're going to punish us all? And he says, I no longer see it as punishment, I believe it's the right step for us, both of us suffered in the relationship and it must have affected Gili too, now we all have an opportunity to recover, and even if no great happiness awaits us, at least we'll have some peace and quiet, that's all I need now, and he holds out his hand to me and I try to pull him down but he's stronger than I am and he pulls me to my feet against my will, go now, Ella, go home, we don't have a chance, it's dead between us, dead forever.

Is it because of Ofra? I dare to ask, a question that didn't figure in the noble speech I had prepared, and he dismisses it out of hand, don't be ridiculous, Ella, I'm not like you, I don't start hunting around for a replacement right away. What do you mean, I mutter, a foul scene forming before my eyes, the blazing sun on the window sill, Gabi's feral smell, his tongue rough as a cat's, if your friend told you anything it was all lies, I say quickly, he was always trying to pit us against each other, and he interrupts me, he's not my friend anymore, and I don't want to talk about it, I want you to go, now, before I say things I'll regret.

Just let me kiss Gili, I request, and he refuses, no, I don't want him to wake up and start causing trouble again, I'll bring him back tomorrow evening, you'll have to pull yourself together by then, he shouldn't see you like this, and next to the door I cling to him again, and this time he responds, wraps his arms around me, be strong, he says, his voice warm and encouraging, you panic easily but you recover fast, as if he's the brother I never had, a best friend, a merciful father, and I lean on the door frame, halfway out of the apartment I was prepared to forever call home. Maybe I can just sleep here tonight on the sofa, I'll leave early in the morning, I make one last attempt, it's hard for me to be alone now, and he sighs, absolutely not, Gili might wake up and see you, it will confuse him, go now, and with a determined movement he pushes me out, switches on the light in the stairwell and shuts the door on my new life. I stumble down the steps, my wooden legs, hardly able to bear the weight of the sorrow and disappointment, pause again in front of his mailbox, where an arrogant notice in a black frame taunts me, Amnon Miller, and I yank it off the mailbox, ripping the stiff paper to shreds, so that not a trace will remain.

How will my legs know how to walk, my knees to bend and straighten, my hand to grip the rail, how will my heart know how to contract and expand, how will my blood know how to flow like a river of stifled tears, how will my lungs know how to hold the black air waiting for me outside, and I teeter between the palm sentries standing like the two towers at the front of the Canaanite temple in Meggido, like a monument to the ruined temple that was never restored, while the city around it was destroyed and rebuilt, destroyed and rebuilt. One by one the shreds of paper fall from my hand as I walk, my former footsteps meeting my future ones, and it seems that another decade has passed, only an hour ago they bore a stamp of hope, but now that hope has been obliterated, what remains, empty steps, wholly insignificant. If only I had listened to my father on that morning, gone back to him and made an everlasting pact with him, we would be sitting comfortably in our house now with Gili sleeping in his room, on his single bed, and tomorrow we would drive into the hills for a picnic with Talia and her husband and go look for quills and crocuses for the kids, and Gili would skip over the rocks with Yoav, no different from the other children, no longer the odd man out. From one step to the next the mistake grows and swells, like a catastrophe whose dimensions become evident only with the passage of time. The delicacy with which he treated me tonight as opposed to the rudeness with which I treated him, the coziness of the apartment, the softness of the rug, the effort he made for Gili's sake, his surprising ability to change, all this only magnifies my mistake, whose consequences will reverberate for the rest of my life, like that volcanic eruption that echoed from the North Pole to China.

Should I go to them now, wake them up and shout in their ears, save me, Mommy and Daddy, look what I've done, like on my fifth birthday party, when they put out a big table in the yard, covered it with a white cloth, and loaded it with sweets. I was only allowed to eat sweets once a year, on my birthday, and I sat and waited on pins and needles for my friends to come, drawn to the table as if snared by a lasso, my baby heart beating in excitement, my eyes examining the tempting dishes, my hand reaching out and touching until the sugar sticks to my fingers, taking a cookie shaped like a flower with red jam in its heart and putting it to my lips, and then into my mouth, the forbidden sweetness stirring my blood, until all of a sudden I was overcome with greed, and I couldn't control myself, reaching here and there, as if I had suddenly sprouted dozens of pairs of hands, dozens of mouths, biting and chewing and swallowing and spitting, heavy brown cubes of chocolate and airy waffles and chewy toffees, liquorice sticks and marshmallows, until the dishes were nearly empty and the debris piled up alongside the table. With dirty fingers I reached for the splendid birthday cake, a chocolate layer cake covered with little white sweets, and I bit into it, ruined it, and when the children arrived they found me wallowing in my vomit under the table, my face covered in food dye and tears and dusted with confectioner's sugar, save me, Mommy and Daddy, look what I did, I ruined my birthday, I waited for it all year long and look what I did.

Only when a man and a woman saunter past, engrossed in animated conversation, do I realize how empty the street is. I stare at them, he is tall and slightly stooped, she is small and slender, together they push a twin stroller toward me, a boy of Gili's age trails behind them, look at us, Amnon, here we are, continuing to exist in a parallel universe, bringing more children to the world, and I shield my eyes, the sights conspire against me, every random scene unsheathes cat claws, all that has been obliterated from my life, like findings destroyed during an excavation, with only written or photographic documentation remaining, turns into a perilous sight, couples with arms linked, pregnant women, parents and their children, and I look toward the road, a luxury car cruises past, provoking a feeling of unease, and then disappears, like the light going off in the windows, the singing dying around the emptying tables, people taking leave of their hosts, another evening coming to a close. But for me this is not another evening, it is the evening my expectations were dashed, the ones I had been clinging to for the past weeks, the ones that had been walking behind me and pushing my unwilling back up the steep slope, keeping me slogging along on this journey, which, not yet half over, has already lost my interest.

Weak-kneed I climb the steps to my house, what is this house to me, I want to live there, in his beautiful apartment overlooking the monastery, I want to sleep there, on the bed covered with the embroidered bedspread, behind the bead curtain. In the morning, the beads will sparkle in the sunlight as Gili stands before them and opens them, as if he can't believe the sight that greets his eyes, the sight he will never see again, his mother and father in the same bed, lying side by side, their eyes closed, just as the sign he made proclaims, MOMMY AND DADDY'S ROOM. How used the apartment looks, stained, faded, a body robbed of its soul. It no longer looks like a home, but like an orphanage, a homeless shelter, and they, being destitute, would not be concerned with the appearance of the place since the situation is only temporary, even if they remain there for the rest of their lives. I shut the light, take off my dress and fall into bed, exhausted and wakeful, and, above all, hopeless, deprived of the hope usually taken for granted like the beating of a healthy heart, and now its absence has exploded in the prairies of my consciousness, sending shock waves throughout.

An infinite rage fills the bed, stretching from one end of the world to the other, as if a furious bull is roaring under the mattress, and soon he will rise up with the bed, the street and the city on his back and carry us all to perdition, but unlike the ancient inhabitants of Thera, I am not afraid, let him stand up, aroused and terrible, let him overturn the intolerable order of the world, how have we come to this, that I am alone here in the house on Friday night, as if I were a spinster, as if I had never had a family, and they huddle without me, a father and his only son. How reality has been perverted, changed its face, like an attractive woman who's suffered a paralytic stroke. How could I have believed with such naive enthusiasm all those light-hearted, half-heard stories of divorce, how did I fail to understand that I was about to trigger an explosion whose ashes would cover the sun for months on end.

And then I hear the familiar, reassuring sound of the key turning in the lock, the door opens slowly so as not to wake me. This is how he would come in at night, and I, who couldn't fall asleep without him, would hear the creaking door and fall into a slumber, and now, too, I am tempted to seize hold of the reassuring creak and sink into the sleep I so sorely need, but tremors of joy surge from the tips of my toes to the roots of my hair, he's come, he couldn't resist me, just tried to make things a little difficult for me so I wouldn't take him for granted, he upped and left his new apartment with its comfortable furniture and came back to his house, and I jump out of bed and hurry to the door, my hands stretched out in front of me, parting the dense darkness. Amnon, it's you, right? I ask, but he doesn't answer, standing bent over at the door, looking short and stout. Amnon, I say, I'm so glad you came, I promise you won't regret it, everything will be different between us, and then a voice rises from the silhouette pressed against the door, a cracked, nasal voice, low and nasty, it isn't Amnon, you idiot, you must be in a bad way if you can't tell the difference between us anymore, and I quickly switch on the light, only to see Gabi's coarse body in a dark crumpled suit, black stubble climbing like ants up his cheeks, his eyes red. I look at him, stunned and horrified by his presence, by his intrusion into my home, by who he is and who he isn't, my throat hoarse with a sharp, shameful rage.

How dare you, how dare you, I growl, and he looks at me with his bloody eyes, breathing heavily, his breath weighted with alcohol. I warned you I would return at my convenience to settle the score, he rasps, and I see you were expecting me, he says, his eyes running mockingly over my underwear, and I hiss, get out of here before I call the police, one phone call and your career is over, don't mess with me. Why do I know you won't do it, he smirks, and I say, because you're a conceited little prick, stick around and you'll find yourself without an office and without any of your little interns, get out and leave me the key, and he leans against the door, measuring me with his eyes, don't worry, Ellinka, I'll go, but not before I teach you a lesson you'll never forget.

Like a wooden doll with scattered limbs, I am sprawled on the floor, the screws that hold my body together have been removed, I need a child to come and tidy up his toys before he goes to bed; you wanted to sleep with Amnon tonight, eh, that's what you wanted, his sour laugher fills my mouth, so now you've got me, everything you wanted to do with him you'll do with me, and I try to scratch the back of his neck with my nibbled nails, push his face away, you wish you could take Amnon's spot, I say, all you are is his trash can, and he doesn't even need you for that anymore.

He doesn't need you either, otherwise you wouldn't be here now, he chuckles, I saw you coming out of his building after he threw you out, and a picture comes to mind, of the slowly cruising car, you followed me, you pervert, but my voice is buried in the depths of my throat, what difference does it make, he followed me, I followed Amnon, both of us are lost, lost as the two skeletons found above the aqueduct in Megiddo, and his short legs push between mine as I lie beneath him on the bare floor, its touch as cold and hard as the lid of the toilet seat in Amnon's apartment, it seems that the entire floor of the house is a thin toilet lid, in a minute it will crack under our weight and all the city's stench, past and future, will rise in my nostrils.

Say Amnon, he exhales in my ear, say Amnon, I want you, and I see the words like broken boats rocking on the river of dry tears pouring from my throat, Amnon, I want you, the words have been said, and from the moment they are said it makes no difference who said them, who they were addressed to, like lost souls they will wander from incarnation to incarnation, seeking their redemption. Say, Amnon, come back to me, I'll do anything as long as you come back to me, his hand gropes the flanks of my body and I rasp, Amnon come back to me, Amnon forgive me, I'll do anything as long as you forgive me, it seems that his fingers are already straying inside the stunned cavity of my abdomen, upsetting the order of the organs, only an operation will restore them. Look at me, he grunts, I want you to look at me, I want you to beg me to be with you, and I murmur, be with me, Amnon, for from his face for a moment the face of the past shines out at me, but all of a sudden he lets go of me and straightens up, that wasn't convincing, sweetie, he leers, standing over me, his mouth gaping, you know what, I don't want you, why should I have Amnon's leftovers, and I get off the floor, panting, in a full body whimper, my head spinning alarmingly and I lean against the wall, watching him zip up his pants with trembling fingers, I'll say this before I go, he says with an effort, his speech heavy, slurred, you destroyed the only relationship I ever had in my life, I have no wife, no children and no real friends, I've only had one friend since I was six years old and you set me up, made him cut me off, and I'll never forgive you for that. My only consolation is that you lost him for the exact same reason, but it's not enough, and he shoves his hand into his pocket and takes out the key, throws it on the floor between my feet, take it, Ella, I don't need it anymore.

Like one facing his punishment I stand before him, punishment that is sometimes the Angel of Death and sometimes the flaming sword and sometimes a bull with gold-tipped horns, punishment that always comes unbidden and whose appearance is always accompanied by an awful, nauseating relief, and so he, too, stands before me, his face distorted, both of us partners in crime, both of us survivors in spite of ourselves, both sentenced to the same fate, we are brothers tonight, banished from the city like refugees in the dead of night, like lepers, he deserves me and I him. On slack legs I go to the fridge, take out the bottle of wine I bought in honor of Amnon's homecoming, uncork it with surprising ease, and pour it into the two deep glasses standing ready on the table, perched on slender legs, like herons fallen into a heavy sleep a moment before the hunters arrive.

Chapter eight

Overnight, the magical kingdom in the heart of the Mediterranean Sea vanished, leaving behind it a mysterious legend, a palace dizzying in its splendor, with hundreds of rooms, stunning murals of octopuses, dolphins, winged cherubs and bull horns, frescoes accompanying the guests from room to room, bare-breasted goddesses and muscled gymnasts, and among them the Parisian, her hair draped with jewels, her gaze haughty.

Sunlight was channeled into the vast palace, the most sophisticated in the ancient world, lighting the red pillars of carved Lebanese cedar, the exquisite ivory and jeweled traceries, the towering jars of olives and wine taller than a man, and all this breathtaking magnificence was built precisely on the chink in the earth's armor, and all this magnificence vanished overnight, buried by dozens of feet of volcanic tuff because, in the middle of the second millennium BCE, the worst recorded natural disaster in human history took place, and in the middle of the Mediterranean Sea the island of Thera was torn to shreds by unprecedented force .

Unfathomable amounts of lava and ash leapt from the mountain that turned into a gaping maw, burying a wondrously developed ancient culture, leaving in its wake a crescent of smoking cliffs, a forlorn, craggy smile in the heart of the sea, and a desperate yearning for the sun, which would not show its face for many long years, leading to religious revolutions in civilizations as distant as Egypt, where Aton, god of the rising sun, was elevated to the status of sole deity as the clouds of volcanic ash covered the light of the sun year after year, for seven consecutive winters.

This would also be the end of the great powers of the late Bronze Age – Egypt and the Kingdom of the Hittites – and in their place small nations would spring up, Edom and Moav and Amon, Israel and Judah, which would be forced to cope with the disintegration of the frameworks, with the spreading violence, with the thousands of displaced people wandering over land and sea in search of a new home, with the cold clenched fist of the Iron Age.

For this is how things would be from now on: from time to time he would pass beneath the olive-colored door frame, stooped and disheveled, a child perched on his shoulders, glance without regret at the home he had left behind, at the remnants of his broken family, exchange a few polite words with me, arrange the schedule for the next few days, kiss Gili on his forehead, tousle his hair, and he would always arrive on time and would always keep his word, always spread his expansive smile around the house and always leave behind him a deep, angry bewilderment. How had a new Amnon suddenly come into being only a few streets from here, reserved and pleasant, cool and polite, considerate and responsible and reliable; how had he suddenly sprung, at a not-so young age, in the middle of his life, from the shell of the old Amnon, ranting, hot-tempered, volatile and impatient.

Is this really what things will be like, during these days that shorten toward an endless winter, like the one that came in the wake of that shudder in the earth, as I grow weaker, receding further from life. When I occasionally drop in at the offices of the Antiquities Authority to collect my mail, visit the library that smells vaguely of dust and honey, reluctantly encountering familiar faces, it seems that an unbridgeable gap is widening between me and life. What's the matter with you, you're so thin, we could exhibit you here in the museum with all the other skeletons, my colleagues say to me, and I smile with chattering teeth, yes, that must be the solution, to steadily consume my inner organs instead of eating, even sweets sicken me now, like after that birthday party, when I couldn't bear the sight of candy for a whole year, until my next birthday.

Yes, that must be the solution, to wither, to shrivel, to shrink, to constrict, to wane until I'm a baby again, babbling meaningless sounds, kicking with unblemished feet, and my father and mother will take me under their protection, take care of all my needs, as they managed to do only in my first years, and it seems that this is the wonder that overshadows even the previous one, how did the devoted, patient, perfect mother I once was turn into a miserable lonely child, tense and irritable and sick. A dire weakness separates me from life, black dizzy spells bar me from life, and it seems that the only bridge that still connects me with it, my child, is melting too, like wax wings in the sun, for there are days when I can't even get out of bed, and I ask Amnon in a shamed voice to take Gili for another day, and he agrees willingly, with a veiled cheer of triumph. Now the truth is coming out, his voice says, and it's heart warming indeed, now when the chips are down we see which of us is the better parent, for six years you flaunted your superiority over me, and now in the hour of difficulty you brought on yourself, you stop functioning, lose interest in the child, and I, who was supposedly the neglectful, selfish father, turn out to be the more stable of the two of us, the only one who can be counted on. I absorb his hidden accusations in silence, it's only a phase, I try to console myself, soon I'll pull myself together and things will go back to what they were before. As soon as this phase passes, I'll look at him admiringly again, listen eagerly to his stories, sit on the carpet and build elaborate castles. It won't last forever, and Gili barely seems to notice because the lonelier I get the more he surrounds himself with friends, almost every day a new little boy joins him, and I breathe a sigh of relief, the double commotion enabling me to isolate myself, to avoid facing him in the dark afternoon hours when the air is constricted and stiff with cold, and after the friend leaves, the bath is quickly filled, and already the bed is waiting to hold him till morning, after the bedtime story that's growing increasingly short like the daylight hours in this autumn season, and thus day after day I avoid him and the intimacy that once existed between us, the perfect, secure, satisfying love that overshadowed, in its radiance and tenderness, the tense and conflicted other loves I'd known.

After he falls asleep I quickly clear away the dishes, swallow the leftovers on his plate, the remains of the hardboiled egg, the pita bread, and, after a slight hesitation, from his friend's plate, too, because the fridge is almost empty, inhabited only by souring milk products and ancient vegetables covered with a sticky frost in the far reaches of the drawer. Every evening I decide that tomorrow I'll go to the store, fill the refrigerator like I once did, but in the end I manage to squeeze one more meal out of the few remaining items, and I look around in irritated surprise, at the wilting window box with its drooping flowers, at the rotting apples in the fruit bowl, at the leaky tap, even the cats that sometimes used to steal inside in search of leftover food have stopped coming, as if the house had been abandoned, because the separation from Amnon has unexpectedly and inexplicably terminated all forms of life in this house.

No, I never imagined that this is how things would be, from time to time I still see flashes of the life I imagined living, a life of calm and tranquility, in the mornings I would do my research, in the afternoon I would play with Gili, and at night I would be alone, and if I ever felt an interest in any man I would be able to pursue it with ease, free and not alone, free with a child, isn't that the most desirable family situation. But when I squirm in front of the computer in the mornings, trying to document the most terrible natural disaster of the ancient world, all the ancient frescoes, so miraculously preserved, merely bring to mind our own story, how he called me the Parisian, pulling the slide out of his pocket. Come and see, he said, you're from there, from Thera, from four thousand years ago, it's unbelievable, and I put the slide up to the light, seeing my gaze set haughtily on the pale, elegant face, my lips painted red, my hair laced with jewels.

She was apparently a priestess, he said, but those idiots called her the Parisian because of the hairdo and the make up, as if women didn't decorate themselves in the ancient world, and he put his hand under my chin and turned my face from side to side, looking at the slide and back at me, and I remember how he said to me that evening, when we strolled for the first time around the gaping site that gave off the heat of the day like a feverish body, you're just putting on an act, you're not an archeologist, all you care about are stories, and now as I try to dress the findings in a scientific suit, I realize how right he was, only stories, only our story, which began in Tel Jezreel and ended in the city of Jerusalem ten years later, in a three room apartment, in one of the old neighborhoods, and as I narrow down our site it seems to me that the final excavation square, whose findings I must document in photographs and drawings, measurements and graphs, is there in Gili's room, in his bed, where his limbs covered mine for the last time, and where I return in the mornings, shivering with cold, trying to bring his burning body back to me, for as time passes the recollection grows docile, until it seems that precisely there our love rose to the heights of refinement and singularity, precisely there our bodies were distilled by an incomparable force, the force of his insult and heartbreak, the force of my resistance and obstinacy and lust for revenge, and when I press myself against the dead furry animals, stare into the lioness's blank, dilated eyes, I know that these are my eyes, the ones that I fixed on him, on what was most dear to me, a glassy gaze, dry and empty, and I try to bring him back to the bed, to draft a different ending for that day, the last of the days of our family.

Under Gili's comforter, smelling faintly of urine, I respond to his body, trying to revive an ancient pleasure buried amidst my organs, all I have to do is locate it, the moment I lay my hand on it, it will answer me, the familiar body becomes a maze as vast as the labyrinth in King Minos' palace in Knossos, where the terrible Minotaur dwelt, half bull and half man, craving young sacrifices, boys and girls, and then I fall into a sleep of burnt sugar, waking in a panic, I have to pick Gili up, and I look at my watch and only ten minutes have gone by, such a short time in comparison to the interminable waking hours gaping at me with purple, viscid jaws, and in the visions that come, much as they do in the twilight of sickness, it seems to me that my loves are there, my family is there, in the room next door, right on the other side of the wall, I can hear their relaxed voices, as in days gone by, Daddy, I'm hungry, what should I get you, a pita with chocolate spread, how about something healthier, fruit or salad, no, I want pita with chocolate spread, Daddy, look what I drew, that's very nice sweetheart, Daddy, where's Mommy, she's sleeping, she doesn't feel well, when will she be better, soon, I'm sure she'll feel better tomorrow.

Where is that promised tomorrow, whose wings are beating above me, beyond my reach, one long day confronts me like a ladder reaching to the sky, one long day in which I have to take Gili to school and pick him up dozens of times, prepare dozens of suppers, fill dozens of baths, write dozens of pages, stop up the sorrow hour after hour with a hard plug in my throat so it won't spray out like a fizzy drink from a bottle, and wait for night, not to sleep but to stop pretending, yet when I go to bed early at night, a dumb, demanding creature lies down beside me, spraying hate mail on the walls of my heart. The thin thread of sleep snaps again and again, its ends refusing to join, and I lie awake, the bed a battlefield of memories, the good ones fighting the bad ones like two muscled gladiators, and I find myself rooting for the defeat of the good ones, cheering the bad ones even as they dissipate, until it seems to me that only peace and other blessings filled our days.

Ella, it won't get better by itself, you have to get help, Dina says, I know someone who'll write you a prescription and you'll be back to your old self in a month, just say the word and I'll make you an appointment, but I refuse immediately, what do I need medication for? I'm not sick, I'm just in shock over what I've done. You're not in shock, you're depressed, she says, and no wonder, separation is one of the most severe traumas there is, it has the power of bereavement but not the legitimacy, you have to start therapy or take medication, preferably both, at least for the next few months, and I protest, why medication, it won't change reality, it won't bring me back my family, if I was simply depressed for no reason, I would need therapy, but I have a good reason to be depressed, which proves that I'm completely normal. Find me a pill that will return things to the way they were, and I'll swallow a bottleful, I promise you, but since there's no way to correct the mistake I made, what good will it do me, and she sighs, you're so primitive, Ella, the medication won't change reality but it will help you cope with it, that's exactly what you need now, I've told you before, I'm not at all certain that you made a mistake, and deep in your heart you're not sure either.

I didn't make a mistake? How can you say such a thing, I say, outraged by her blasphemy, look what I had before and look what I have now, I had a family, I had a husband who loved me, my child had a proper home, look how I'm coming apart without that framework, I had no idea how vital it was for me. You're getting carried away again, she scolds, I know those myths people construct in times of crisis, the further you get from the event, the more enchanted it becomes, soon you'll be telling me that you were a king and queen and you lived in a palace. I cut her short, explain to me how I could have been so blind, how I failed to predict what would happen to me, it's one thing for a person not to know the people around her, but to be so ignorant of oneself? I can't understand it, I was certain that I was going to be happy without him, and enjoy every moment of my freedom, and look what happened.

I admit that I, too, am surprised by the strength of your reaction, she says carefully, sitting on the edge of my bed, but stop condemning yourself, these are things that are difficult to predict, who knows what nexus of ancient grief you happened on, you fell into a pit that was always there, even if you didn't know it existed, who knows what you're really grieving for now. I'm grieving for my family, I say, what's so strange about that, why look for remote reasons when there are reasons close at hand? And she says, the mind doesn't recognize far and near, you should examine what you're going through now from a broader perspective, that's what I would do with you if you were in therapy with me, and I ask, is this the first time you've come across a case of a woman who initiated a separation and afterwards collapsed like me?

Of course I've come across it, she says, more than once, but it's generally a temporary state, which doesn't reflect on the past or the future, it doesn't mean you'll be sorry for the rest of your life, or even that there's anything to be sorry for, only that you're confronting deep and ancient forces now, like a disease that was dormant for years and has suddenly broken out. You need help, you owe it to your child, I have no doubt that he's aware of more than you know. It seems to me that he hasn't even noticed the state I'm in, I say, you have no idea how hard I try, I put on an act for him all the time, and she chuckles, then maybe he's putting on an act too, do you really think he buys your forced smiles, that he can't see what you're going through, what your eyes are saying? Children understand everything, Ella, pull yourself together, you have to start taking care of yourself for the kid's sake.

The kid. At times I forget his name and in my heart I call him the kid, the dear, forgotten kid, the shadow of the marvelous child I once had, a monument to the union that once existed and is no more. Sometimes I imagine him beaming at me as he did in the days of his dewy babyhood, a soft mistiness rising from him as I cradled him in my lap, it seemed we were both swaddled in sweet cotton, each welded to the neediness of the other, brimming with emotion. What does the kid understand, he resigned himself to all the upheavals but one, and he rages against it, protests with all his might and obstinacy and grief, until it seems that all he once had and lost, all his longings and wishes, the remnants of his stable world, the scaffolding of his security, all are hitched to a single point, to the book-lined rooftop apartment, with its arched windows and high ceilings, overlooking tiled roofs the color of earth and wine.

Mommy, I want Grandma and Grandpa, he whines almost every night, like a prayer before sleeping, I haven't been there in so long, we didn't even go for the holidays, and I'm evasive, this week it's impossible, Grandpa's abroad, Grandma's sick, maybe next week, and he remembers the feeble excuses better than I do, is Grandpa back yet? he asks a few days later, is Grandma better now? And at first I don't understand, oh, yes, I remember, that is, no, he went on a trip again, she's sick again, in the winter old people get sick all the time. But last winter she wasn't sick, he protests with a suspicious look, she used to pick me up at kindergarten once a week and make me chicken soup, and Grandpa used to teach me chess, it was so much fun, once I even beat him, he says, basking in his brief history, I want her to come and get me from school tomorrow; and I say, tomorrow's impossible, maybe next week, silently cursing both of them, that pair of heartless old wooly mammoths, why didn't I tell him they were dead, extinct, like they expected him to be, then at least he wouldn't nag me and ask, are they alive again? Have they come out of their graves already? But it's clear to me that his innocent orphaned voice is my own voice, for not a day goes by that I don't think of them, planning how I'll go there one morning, open the door without ringing the bell, burst into his room, here I am, Daddy, I'm your good little girl again, I tried to go back to Amnon but he wouldn't have me, I wanted to make a pact with him, but he refused, let's see you summon him to a meeting now, scare him, too, with your prophesies of doom like you scared me until it seems that I'll never get over it, tell him how disaster is certain and how happiness is doubtful, tell him about the fate of his son, about the cruel creditors of the soul. A fragment of foolish hope plays around me like a stray sunbeam, he can fix everything, if he only wants to, if I can only convince him that my intentions are pure, but whenever I pass by their house I find myself fleeing for my life, as if high-powered rifles were aimed at me from the windows, about to open cold, concentrated fire.

Their house is halfway between our house and Gili's school, and when I bring him home in the afternoon I take care to choose a different route, so he won't look up and burden me with wishes I can't fulfill, marching him around corners, confusing him like a kidnapper, if I could blindfold him, I would, but one day when we emerge from the gate, his schoolbag on my shoulder, his hand in mine, slanting gray raindrops from a suddenly dark sky slap at our faces, and I hurry him along, taking the short route, and as we approach their street at a run I no longer care, hope even stirs, grows stronger like the rain, perhaps today it will happen, perhaps they will stand at the window and see us running past, perhaps Gili will recognize their house and beg me to go up and I will have no choice but to agree.

When we approach the building I push him in front of me like bait, slowing down, anticipating his pleas, but he is staring at the pavement, telling me how he argued with Yotam, he's such a pain, he complains, I'll never go to play at his house again, he's a tattletale and a crybaby, and I remember the stifled weeping that rose from one of the rooms, the radiance of the morning that suddenly darkened, and it seems that the sun hasn't shone since, but then he raises his eyes and I see his face awaken, his sallow cheeks glowing as he says, Mommy, that's Grandma and Grandpa's house, right? And I say yes, we always go past here, it's on our way home, and he pulls my arm, Mommy, we're going to see them, even if Grandma's sick, I don't care, and I give in with a factitious sigh, without him I would never dare to climb these stairs, holding him in front of me like a hostage in the stairwell, my ticket into my parents' home, but when I was a child I had no child, barren was I in their midst.

Grandma and Grandpa, it's me, he shouts excitedly, banging on the door with his little fists, hard and brown as nuts, opening it himself, cantering like a colt down the hall, and she comes out of the kitchen to meet him, Gili, what a surprise, she murmurs, her white hair disheveled, her face divided, her joy at seeing us stained by her fear of him, holed up in his study. I'm so glad you're better now, Grandma, Gili says, hugging her waist, and she wonders, better? I haven't been sick for a long time, and when he gives me a look of suspicious bewilderment, I don't even bother sending signals over his head, for this is the least of our problems at the moment. You look terrible, Ellinka, she says, embracing me hesitantly, you're skin and bones, and Gili is riveted by her every word, the mere fact of my being somebody's child always sparks amazement and wonder, an enjoyable and annoying sensation, and he announces, then make her something to eat, she's your daughter, and my mother says, yes, come to the kitchen, and in the meantime she whispers in my ear, I hope Daddy won't be angry, he said he couldn't bear to see the boy, and I hiss, don't you dare repeat those words, when will you understand that Gili is what's important here, not you, he's suffering from being cut off from you, you'll get over your difficulties, you're the adults here, and she starts again, you don't have to convince me, Ellinka, the problem is your father, and I say, let me handle that problem, I'll speak to him.

Again that weakness in the knees as I confront the intent back, wrapped in a gray sweater rough as concrete, planted motionless in front of the computer, his fingers gliding over the keyboard, presumably polishing the new lecture he will deliver at one of his many conferences, at his side a glass dish holding a peeled and sliced apple, every hour she peels him another one, even if he hasn't touched the previous one, and I slam the door shut behind me and only then does he turn around, his bronze face slowly coming to life, and he shifts his feet, which are clod in thick wool socks like the knitted booties of an infant not yet walking, and slides himself toward me in his chair. Ella, he says, pedantically stressing the proper, second syllable, removing his gold-rimmed reading glasses, fixing me with his chilly eyes, which have both the color and feel of tin. He's remote as a god who has ceased to take interest in the world he created after the first sign of disobedience, see my gauntness, Daddy, see my paleness, hear the cry of my bones beneath my skin, the howl of my organs as they are eaten away, a pack of rats has invaded my body and is gnawing at it from within, ants are digging tunnels sharp and narrow as needles. How is Gilad? he asks, averting his eyes as if he can't bear the sight of me, and I say, he misses you, it's hard for him to be cut off from you, and my father justifies himself in an infirm voice, it's hard for me too, you know, it's only because he is so dear to me that

I preferred not to see him, I trust that's clear to you? It is not, God forbid, due to indifference or cruelty, and I say nothing, withholding my approval, which has suddenly become dear to him.

I felt that I wouldn't be able to bear his sorrow, he squirms, and that the severity of my reaction would only worsen his situation, I was afraid of doing him harm, you see, but I can tell you precisely how long I haven't seen him for, sixty-six days, he says, highlighting his longing, as if it's him we're talking about, and this time I prefer to avoid the confrontation; that's not the issue at the moment, I say, that's not the important thing, right opposite me the palm tree writhes like an epileptic, its slender trunk convulsing, its locks wet and wild, how both of us have changed since that last conversation, which hangs between us, heavy and metallic.

You know that it was only out of concern for you and Gilad that I tried to warn you, he goes on, concentrating as usual on himself, on the purity of his arms, as if he were the tragic hero of this melancholy affair, and I nod impatiently, waiting for him to conclude his defensive address so that I can have my say at last. When I told you that I feared for the child's future it was but, of course, a warning, a worst case scenario, intended to make you think about what you were doing, not a precise prediction, even if my words may have been blunt, and I look at him, unable to breathe, seething, that's what's bothering you now, that your prediction wasn't sufficiently precise, and he carries on as if reading my mind, of course I'm very happy that he's coping, especially now that the decree has been sealed and nothing can be done.

Daddy, listen to me for a minute, I interrupt him, lest he go on forever, preaching and weaving, protesting and warning until the end of days, I need your help, only you can help me now, you were right, I wish I'd listened to you, this separation is a catastrophe for me, you have to help me get Amnon back, and he shakes his head. Me? he exclaims with hypocritical modesty, how can I help? His hand runs through his thick hair, and I say, you've always had sway over Amnon, you have to talk to him about what can happen to Gili, about the pact that we should make, everything you said to me then say to him now, all your prophesies of doom, all your dire predictions.

But if it had no effect on you, how will it have an effect on him, he wonders with mixed feelings, proud of his potential role but loathe to undertake the mission, and I say, it had a delayed effect, you have to try, and he sighs, his feet rubbing each other in their woolen socks, I fear there's no longer any point, Ella, you have to strike when the iron's hot, that's why I asked you to come and see me urgently then, at this stage I'm afraid it has already cooled down. How do you know, I say, and he responds, I met Amnon at the university a few days ago, he told me that the separation has done him a world of good and I admit that I got that impression myself, he seemed calmer, he told me that his relationship with Gili has improved, I don't think there's any point in talking to him now, it's too late, and I listen to his authorial decree with growing dread, this is the last wisp of my hope, and my infallible father, who has opposed me my entire life, could render us invincible, if only, for once, he would take my side.

You have to help me, I sob, falling onto the neatly made bed, even though there are two empty rooms in the house, they choose to sleep in his study, you have to help me, I did everything you said, I promised him that everything would be different, I begged him to come back to me and he refused, he's to blame, he's the one who destroyed the family, not only me, like you thought, and he looks at me with undisguised horror, such an outburst has never been heard in our house, such bare emotions have never walked these floors in such embarrassing nakedness. I don't think that this is the time to assign blame, he says, and I insist, yes, it is the time, you have to tell me that I'm no longer to blame, only then will I be able to pull myself together. He sighs, his feet moving the chair toward me slowly and hesitantly, you know that I am a man of science, he says, I cannot bandy unfounded words about, if there's any blame here, or it would be better to say responsibility, then it must be shared by both of you. But above all it's evident that none of this makes any difference now, Ella, it's a lost cause, over and done with. You have to understand that you can't go back. You have to start to think about the future, not the past, but I refuse to relent, just say that it's not because of me, say that it would have happened in any case, and he jiggles his foot, there's no point in all this talk, it won't help.

So what will help, I wail, and he says, what will help is for you to stop picking at this and to finish your research before you go back to the field, and, by the way, at my last conference I met some archeologist who told me that the correlation between Thera and the exodus from Egypt is currently considered to be wholly unscientific, no serious scholar today believes that the exodus took place at all, I would advise you to re-examine your conclusions, why must you always go against the flow, and I close my eyes and listen to his buoyed voice tell me at length about how this archeologist had been smitten by his lecture, and of course he was not alone, in fact he had been invited right then and there to three more conferences, and as he talks I feel myself entombed in a thick layer of frost, a biting cold needling my limbs despite the heating, and I know that even if I were to depart from this life right here on their bed, he wouldn't notice and he wouldn't stop talking, dazed, I hear his loud voice beating against the walls, Gili's happy murmurings as he eats in the kitchen and the roar of the wind passing from house to house like bad news.

Bring me a blanket, I whisper through chattering teeth, and at long last he stops talking, what's that, what did you say? A blanket, I whisper, I want a blanket, and he raises his voice and calls, Sara, bring Ella a blanket, and she appears immediately in the doorway like a diligent chambermaid, Gili's head peeping in behind her. Grandpa, I'm here! he announces his presence ceremoniously, and my father stretches out his arms to him, rising at last from his chair, you're so big, Gili, do you still remember how to play chess? Sure I remember, Gili bleats, let's play, I bet I'll beat you, he says, his heart brimming over with the joy, and my mother spreads a red checked blanket over me, her inflated concern more oppressive than reassuring. What's wrong? She starts to cross examine me, you look sick, when did you last see a doctor, how many times have I told you to have a full physical, when will you listen to me? And she puts her hand on my forehead and lets out a shriek as if she's been burned, Ellinka, you're burning up, David, come and see how hot she is, and I try to sit up but a wave of nausea rises within me, get me a basin, I whisper, but she doesn't make it in time because it seems that whatever I haven't eaten for the past sixty-six days is climbing rapidly up my throat and spewing a bitter jet onto their bed, and all the words I haven't spoken for thirty-six years have been melted down and turned into a sour, gummy mush of unsaid syllables.

Sara, she's vomiting, he shrieks, as if it were actually a pack of rats leaping out of my throat, and my mother grumbles, *nu*, what do you expect, she doesn't take care of herself, she's never taken care of herself, get out, both of you, she chases them to the living room, shoves a laundry basin into my hands, it's too late, Mother, can't you see it's too late, the damage is already done, your mattress will sour beneath your bodies for many months to come, your pillows will exude the smell of my insides into your sleep. You went out without a coat again and got soaking wet, she complains, smoothing my forehead with her oily hands, you were always the same, ready to suffer from the cold for beauty's sake, how many times have I reminded you to dress properly, she says, addressing, as usual, not me but the girl I once was, and I am riding the empty waves of nausea, giant and dry and transparent as glass, retching over the basin, there's a reason I left you the sweater I knitted, she continues, I'm sure you didn't wear it even once, it isn't stylish enough for you, all you care about is how you look, never mind your health, it would have been better for you if you'd been less beautiful and more careful, look at your friends who weren't as beautiful as you, they're happily married with three children, and you, what have you got, one child and no husband.

My head falls heavy and feeble into the basin, her mumblings buzzing around me like a cloud of gnats on a still, oppressively hot day, but she won't let my eyes close, you have to wash up, she says, and in the meantime I'll change the sheets, come to the bathroom, and she takes hold of my crackling waist and drags me after her, undresses me in the big, white-tiled bathroom, examining me with open curiosity, look at you, like a young girl, she points out resentfully, you haven't grown since you were twelve years old. Although age has shrunken her, she is still much taller than me, and I shiver under her gaze, trying to hide my nakedness, why are you so surprised, mother, we both know the truth, it's because of him that I didn't grow, have you forgotten how horrified he was at the first signs of puberty, have you forgotten what he did to my first bra, when I left it by mistake in the bathroom, how he ran through the house waving it in his hand and yelling, I forbid you to wear such lewd garments! And in the end he threw it out the window, my black lace bra, the one I was so proud of, and you waited for dark and then you slipped out to look for it among the trees, but it wasn't there anymore, some other girl was trying it on in front of the mirror, free of the guilt and shame, and the next day you bashfully brought me a new bra, plain, as if you too understood that there was nothing to be proud of here.

How horrified he was at the presence of a young woman in the house, how he detested the budding signs of womanhood, smashing and shattering them like the prophets of the Lord in the face of the graven images of Astarte, and I, paralyzed by dread, stopped growing, since age twelve I've not added an inch or a curve, an aging girl under the hot water, under the boxy soap she hands me, grainy brown laundry soap, smelling of kerosene, which seems to have endured since those days, and when I step out of the shower, wrapped in a towel, she hands me a vaguely remembered nightgown, a brightly striped nightgown that I wore as a girl. She throws nothing away, who she's keeping these melancholy mementos for I don't know, but over the nightgown, with a cry of triumph, she drapes a thick woolen sweater, olive green, red, and yellow, smelling strongly of roast chicken, and I stare at it, too exhausted for surprise, can it be that the pieces of that lacerated sweater knitted themselves together, like a torn-up letter stuck together in the sky and returned surprisingly to the sender.

Are you all right? Gili asks nonchalantly when I enter the living room in my strange outfit. My illness seems only to have increased his merriment because he has already understood and assessed the wealth of possibilities implied by the new situation, and he has no intention of relinquishing them easily. We're sleeping here tonight, he breathes in my ear, beside himself with excitement, Grandma says we're sleeping here if you don't get better, he notifies me sternly, you're not better are you? And I appraise my new-old prison, we'll see how I feel, but he insists, unable to bear the uncertainty, say we're sleeping here, what do you care, just for one night? And I stand my ground, I'm not sure yet, why do you have to know in advance? Because I want to, he's already starting to wail, and then she comes into the room and cuts the argument short decisively, of course you're staying here, if Amnon was at home it would be different, but now that you're alone, how can you take care of the child like this, and who will take care of you until you get better? Your generation, she complains, you think you can do everything, mothers think they can earn a living and raise a child and take care of themselves as well, and they forget about all the troubles that the world has to offer, what about illness, and God forbid accidents and all kinds of calamities, how a mother can cope with that kind of trouble without a husband at home God only knows, without a father for the children, and I try to shut her up by pursing my lips, by looking at Gili, who is listening to her with a worried expression, and she as usual fails to understand, are you going to vomit again? She propels her heavy body out of the room and returns immediately with the basin, which she places on my knees, and Gili, whose face has fallen, climbs onto my lap with a cheerless smile, proud of his new trick, and seats himself cross-legged in the laundry basin that waits a fresh torrent.

The bed of my youth creaks discordantly as it spreads its wings to shelter both of us, not too close so you won't get him sick, my mother says, and I collapse onto the arid white sheets, which have never known a flower, never shone with any merry stripes, and Gili happily squeezes himself into a pair of pajamas left here from when he was much younger, look how much I've grown, he sings, pointing proudly to his knees peeping out of the pajama pants that once came down to his ankles; my illness is turning into a long, happy celebration for him, and I look at him in amazement, how can he not notice the oppressive gloom of every movement in this house, how can he not see that he is in a prison, his jarring cheers and his ridiculous dances are like an outburst of wild joy in the middle of a wake, and they busy themselves with us, for months they shunned us and now our presence has taken over their home, upset its order.

Glumly I stare at the room of my youth that has been turned into an additional library, a storeroom for the less desirable books. How hard it was for me to get used to this room, long and narrow as a hallway, overlooking the main road, and within a few years I left it for the crowded student dorms, where the air was steeped in the smell of old kerosene stoves in winter and in hormonal heat in summer. How hard it was to part from my old childhood home, sunk in the earth like a ship in the middle of the sea, with all my strength I tried to resist the move to the city, but how much strength did I have, my father's career was always more important than the whims of an adolescent girl. You'll get used to it, they dismissed my protests, what's the problem, a girl of your age, in a month you'll have new friends, at your own level, not like these country bumpkins, and you'll go to a decent high school at last and study seriously, but I chafed at the sound of their words, it's not the children, but the trees, the mown lawns, the smells, the citrus blossoms, the honeysuckle festooning the windows with perfumed tendrils, the colors, the sunlit carpet of autumn leaves rustling under my feet, the trumpets of hibiscus baring their red lips, you've brought me to a place without any smells, I would complain, there's hardly any difference between the seasons, a place without colors, except for the shades of the impermeable stones, but my father had been offered a post at the university and the city welcomed him gladly, and my mother was giddy with all the shops and cafes, and I, who once went to school barefoot on golden paths, learned to measure the sheets of hard asphalt with my feet, to change buses on my way to the prestigious high school where there were many outstanding students, not like in my regional country school where everybody knew that I was the only one, and how hard it was to concentrate in class and get to know new friends when my head kept dropping onto my desk because in the new house in the old-new city I had forgotten how to sleep.

The grunting of the cars, the way they flexed their muscles on the hill beneath my window, the desperate wanderings of noisy groups of would-be revelers in search of entertainment, the wailing of the sirens, the snatches of hoarse conversations, jarring laughter, the city's desperate cries rising to heaven, growing louder as night sawed in my ears, all amplified my longings for the gentle country nights, where only confused birds occasionally pecked at the blanket of the darkness, where treetops rustled, whispering distant green rumors to each other, bowed beneath the mysterious burden of their foliage, where the sprinklers did their transparent dance, cooling the heavy moist air, where cats in heat would howl under my window, pursuing their fleeting, frustrating pleasure for hours on end, and all these sounds rocked the cradle of my peaceful sleep to and fro. In the evening hours I would cast anxious sidelong glances at the bed in my new room as at an instrument of torture, and in the nights I would wait tensely for the first signs of tiredness and then I would huddle fearfully between the sheets, and within a few minutes the fragile weariness would flee from the din of the night and my whole body would throb as if an energetic heart beat throughout, a heart in my wrist and a heart in my ankle and a heart between my temples, and the noise stormed the iron shutters, as if the city were a giant field being ploughed under cover of darkness, its insides overturned, all the buildings destroyed one after the other, only to be hastily and noisily rebuilt at dawn, and in the mornings, I would sit in the classroom weak and shaky, my eyes red and narrow with sleeplessness, my cheek resting on the desk as if it were the softest of pillows and nothing, not the commotion of the class nor the scolding of the teachers nor the ringing of the bells, could rouse me.

Tonight, too, I lie stiff and wakeful between the covers, as if hiding from assassins, Gili clinging to me despite my mother's warnings, occasionally jabbing me with a scruff knee, parting his lips in an unintelligible mutter, while I prick up my ears to interpret the voices of his world, which is increasingly closed to me. From the hall comes the sound of feet slowly dragging back and forth, how long it takes them to prepare for sleep, as if it's a ball they're arranging, how rife with suspense the atmosphere; did you change all the sheets? he asks, and she replies impatiently, in one of those passing fits of rebelliousness I remember so well, the hoarse rebellion of the utterly subjugated, I already told you I did, if you don't trust me then change it yourself, and he snaps, why can't you give me a straight answer without complaining, and she retorts, because I've already told you twice, and he says, it wasn't twice, you see that's it's impossible to rely on you, you always exaggerate. Did you change the sheet and the comforter? he asks, and she says, the sheet was clean, she vomited on the bedspread, the cover got dirty and the sheet didn't. It doesn't look clean to me, my father complains, you should change the sheet too, that's what I'm trying to tell you, and she says angrily, but it's completely clean, what do you want from me, and I hear the doors of the closet creaking open, I want you to change everything, he demands, I can't sleep on an unclean bed, and if I don't sleep I won't be able to write my lecture. Then change it yourself, she says sullenly as she furiously strips the mattress, in the end she always does what he tells her, and he grunts, anyone would think I asked you for God knows what, and I cover my ears with my hands, knowing that this is only the beginning, nothing has changed since then, the echoes of the argument coming closer like an approaching thunderstorm, bearing on its wings all the arguments that went before, which would charge my small body with terror, would this be the one that smashes our family, the one that split my life in half, would they get divorced now, tomorrow morning, and I remember how I would make Amnon swear, when we have children we'll never fight, let's get all our fighting over before we have children, but in the end we were the ones who separated and not them, did I save Gili from nights of terror when I severed our family with the stroke of an axe, or will he forever long for the angry voices, proving beyond a doubt that there are two people close to his room, under the same roof, his parents.

With the last of my strength I return home in the morning, my bones shivering under my skin, I'll never recuperate here, I decline her pressing invitations, how can I get better without sleeping, but she'll pick Gili up from school, and maybe he'll stay there for another night as well, until I recover, so they discussed my recovery as if it were only a matter of time, and so I try to tell myself in the coming days, lying weak and exhausted on my bed, but then I remember that it's also possible not to recover, such a possibility exists and there are some people who never recover, and they become disconnected from the functioning world that was once their own, and in the end they are taken away to special institutions, where their cry will be swallowed up between the walls, cut off and isolated, so that it won't disturb the ebb and flow of their former world, and it seems to me that I see my soul fluttering between the two domains, no longer belonging to the one and not yet yielding to the other, a cruel hybrid creature, a reckless Sphinx. If only I could get rid of it, suffocate it, if only I could live without a soul, after all a person can live without a leg or a womb or even a kidney, and this is now my big dream, to uproot the soul raging uncontrollably inside me, to tear the malignant thing out of my body, all these years it has been masquerading as healthy, and precisely now, when I need it, it's infected, and I toss and turn on my bed in the inanimate home, where the computer has been turned off for days, and the messages on the answering machine have piled up and been erased without being heard, racking my brains, who can I ask to pick Gili up from school this afternoon, as long as I don't have to go there myself, facing the mothers when I am no longer a mother, for the moment I stopped being Amnon's wife, I stopped being a mother, I turned into a shirking babysitter, irresponsible and reckless, so Amnon today and my mother tomorrow and after that Guy's mother, Itamar's mother, Ronen's mother, in the end he won't be able to recognize me, what did Amnon say to him that night when I was locked in the bathroom, some woman, a woman you don't know, who's leaving in a minute.

Again and again I slog through the emptying apartment, yesterday he took the last of his things, removed the ancient landscapes of Jerusalem from the walls, the evidence of our lives together disappearing, soon I will remain without proof, no one will believe that this was home to three people. There is so much empty space in the house, on the book shelves, in the closets, in the bathroom sink, even the stuffed animals are gradually moving to the big beautiful new room, soon Gili too will be gone, and no one will believe that there was once a child here, and then I will be left with only the little that is truly mine, whatever that may be. How illusory everything was, how transient and temporary, be careful, I want to say to the people walking past under my window, don't delude yourselves, you have nothing, you had nothing and you will have nothing, only a sick, kicking soul, soon you will discover that this is your only possession, and a useless one at that.

From time to time it seems to me that my strength is returning in a feeble trickle and I make up my mind to spend the afternoon hours with Gili, prepare myself for the task all morning as if for a test, plan where to take him and what to do with him and how to hide my condition from him, and I get dressed and make up my face, the dry smile of my bones creaks opposite me in the mirror, but he comes running to meet me at the gate, Mommy, can I go to Ronen? And I try to object, why don't we do something together today, go to a movie, or to the playground, and he makes a face as if I am proposing a punishment, ugh, Mommy, why do you always have to spoil everything, I already told Ronen I'm coming, and I watch him walk away, brisk and edgy, so different from the tender, dreamy child I used to have. And now Keren, Ronen's pretty mother, opens the door of the fancy jeep and they both jump in and wave politely, and with the last of my strength I walk slowly to the raven park and fall onto a wet rock, the dark clouds all around me hang low as bushes growing from the lawn, and I find myself a little stick and dig in the ground, which exudes a warm, furry smell like a wild animal, unearthing wet twigs, pebbles, bits of broken glass, and already a mound of moist earth is rising at my side, as if I were a mole, I will find a ruined house there and it will be my home, I will find the bones of a girl there and she will be my sister.

My cheek is pressed against the cold rock, in a moment my portrait will be imprinted on it, like that of the little African monkey found on the east coast of Thera, how astonished the researchers were to discover that it was not a portrait at all but the skeleton of the monkey itself, whose skull was broken in the earthquake, and covered with a thick volcanic layer, and I close my eyes and try to pull a blanket over my body, and I no longer care what it is made of, volcanic tuff lighter than water, the panting breath of dogs, the stars of urban skies sour as lemons, earth smelling of warm fur, and I don't even know how I find myself in front of Dina's house, knocking on her door, wet and shivering with cold.

Ella, at long last, she says, embracing me, you know how many messages I left on your phone? Do you listen to your messages at all? This week I rang your doorbell twice, why don't you open the door? And when she holds me at arm's length to look at me she lets out a shriek as if she's seen a ghost, Ellinka, look at you, God help us, and she hurries immediately to the telephone, I'm making an appointment for you right away with my psychiatrist friend, he'll give you a prescription, I'll drag you there by force if I have to, and I hear her talking behind the closed door, apparently trying to convince him of the urgency of the meeting, and when she comes out of the room she waves her car keys at me, puts on her coat, and says, we're going there now, he agreed to see you right away, you're not getting out of this.

What difference does it make, Dina, where we go. Once I went there and tomorrow I'll go there, I saw this doctor and that doctor, I took this pill and that pill, I traveled to lands far and near, I met people like this and like that, I wore pant suits and evening gowns, I took part in excavations and wrote articles; do you think it will save me now, do you think that any of the things we do, any of the achievements we work toward are accumulated and preserved, do you think that anything on earth can save us from the wrath of the bull roaring in the bowels of the earth? Come with me to Thera and see how life turned to stone in a single moment, staircases cut in half, carpenters and blacksmiths dropping their tools and never picking them up again, food left in pots because people fled from their houses, taking nothing with them, and not far from there, in Crete, in a temple with collapsed walls, you will see an altar with a bound boy on it and a sword through his heart, a last, desperate attempt to appease the gods; so I'll go with you and return with you, but on my broken island no human foot will tread, and no one will rebuild its ruins and my life will not be returned to me.

Purple vapors mist the windows of the car in which I drove tensely on my urgent mission not long ago, a straw hat on my head and foolish hope on my face, winter has come early this year and only I know how long it will last, for it will be seven years before the sun shines on Jerusalem. Dina drives in silence, threading our way through the traffic, her eyes narrowed, her face proclaiming self-importance, as if she had succeeded in catching a dangerous criminal and was in a hurry to hand him over to the law. Occasionally she glances at me as if to make sure that I have no intention of escaping, undoing my seatbelt and jumping out of the car, how ridiculous she is, doesn't she understand that it no longer makes any difference to me where I am, who I'll meet, what he'll say to me, what medication I take, for, in the meantime, I've discovered something, perhaps the last secret the Minoans discovered in their panicky flight while the figures they left behind them on the walls of the palace in Knossos and on the walls of the houses in Akrotiri watched them with haughty surprise, those bright, stylish frescos testifying to a complex and sophisticated culture of the highest order that was obliterated in the earthquake that destroyed Thera and only came to light thousands of years later. When they fled their homes, watched by their own marvelous creations, did they pause for a moment to consider how dull and unclaimed reality is compared to its imitations, to its scrupulous documentation, were they consoled by this or were they filled with rage, terribly envious of the painted figures, of the letters fated to be slowly and laboriously deciphered.

When we get out of the car she holds on to my arm, leads me firmly along the noisy street, between the cars baring their teeth at each other with muffled roars, in the waiting room she sits next to me, the scent of the flowers on her balcony rising from her hair, her hand tensely gripping my shoulder, like a mother with her daughter on her first visit to a gynecologist. Don't hide anything from him, tell him exactly what you feel, she warns me; I know you, you're capable of persuading him that there's nothing wrong, promise me you won't put on an act, this isn't funny, Ella, you have to get help, and I nod wearily, even if I wanted to put on an act I wouldn't be able to. On the opposite wall I recognize a familiar poster from a museum I had visited more than once, a photograph of the famous Rosetta Stone, carved with three languages, which helped decipher the secrets of ancient Egypt, like a stone at the entrance to a magic cave it lay, hiding dead wonders behind it, and I stare in silence at the oval stone until a door opens and Dina leads me firmly down the passage, leaves me at the entrance to the room and immediately returns to her place.

He indicates the waiting armchair and sits down opposite me, and I sink into it, surprised, an ancient female instinct sending my hand to my wild hair, pulling my sweater tighter around my body, but he won't recognize me anyway, I wouldn't recognize myself, does he even remember the woman who once stood in the doorway of his elegant apartment, voraciously devouring a wine red pear, watching him in amusement as he stood and urinated, do I remember her myself, and suddenly it seems to me that the memory of that morning is igniting a feeble spark of life in me, like a beacon on a distant mountain top, the last morning of my old existence, free, bold, full of expectation.

Do we know each other? he asks, staring at me with a preoccupied air, just like then, and, like then, I answer, not really, and the lips that licked the crumbling chocolate stars spread into a smile, his hand strays unconsciously to his zipper, to make sure that this time he is dressed, it's you, he points an accusing finger at me, I remember you, you were in our house, you're Gili's mother, and I smile miserably, I was Gili's mother, now I'm not a mother anymore, I don't exist anymore, a stream of cold tears bathes my smile and I wipe them away with the sleeve of my sweater, ignoring the box of tissues standing between us, on a cold, elegant glass table. I understand, he says, Dina described your situation to me, naturally I recommend psychotherapy, but I think we should try medication as well; I'm afraid I won't be able to treat you myself, but in the meantime I'll write you a prescription as first aid and refer you to someone else for continuation of the treatment, okay? And he looks at me compassionately and hesitantly, as if he has seen a cat dying on the roadside and he is wondering if the animal can still be saved.

Do you cry a lot? he asks, his deep-set black eyes wandering over my face, as if seeking traces of blood? Do you feel relief after crying or is it inconsolable weeping, do you enjoy things you enjoyed in the past, do you enjoy anything at all, can you concentrate, do you have suicidal thoughts, do you suffer from guilt, have you lost weight recently, do you suffer from insomnia, are you allergic to any medication, when is the last time you felt good? And I answer weakly, the purple chiffon curtains send a soft dawn light through the room and my eyes slowly close, it seems to me that here of all places I could fall asleep at last, opposite him, on the comfortable leather armchair, and only the last question makes me pause, as the answer that will not be given becomes clear to me, in your house, on that Saturday morning, at the beginning of autumn, that was the last time I felt good.

The relief won't be immediate, he says, quickly scribbling the name of the drug on a piece of paper, and there may be side-effects at first, but within three weeks I estimate that your condition will improve, this drug takes the edge off emotions, I believe it will help you, and he hands me the prescription, start taking it today, he recommends, why suffer needlessly, and if there are any problems get in touch with me, you have my number at home, and he quickly adds the number at the clinic, for continuation of therapy I'll refer you to someone else, but let's try chemistry first, sometimes there's no alternative. Let's, he says, in the plural, as if we're talking about a shared problem here, and when I stand up and take the slip of paper from his hand it seems to me that I am passing something to him in return, that my hands aren't empty, I am laying my superfluous soul, that impossible hybrid creature, in his arms, and he stands before me rocking it in his arms until it falls silent and its sobbing has been soothed.

Chapter nine

I buy the pills that same evening, ask the pharmacist to gift-wrap the bottle and her eyes widen in surprise, appraising me and the pills and the doctor's signature with a doubtful expression on her face, looking as if she, if anyone had asked her, would have recommended something entirely different. Gift-wrap? We don't do that here, she snaps, but in the end she finds gold paper and a red ribbon and reluctantly bundles up the vial of pills, and I put the tempting little package on my bedside table, where I leave it unopened, the last thing I look at before sleep and first thing in the morning, glad to encounter it by chance, as if I had been given a rare gift waiting patiently to be unwrapped. Its presence next to my bed comforts me, a narrow, dainty package, looking as if it might contain a pair of gold earrings or a pendant, prepared to lie and wait for thousands of years, like the jewels of Troy glittering deep in the earth of Asia Minor while the entire Western World believes the story to be a legend with no basis in fact.

I didn't know those pills worked so fast, Dina marvels when she drops in a few days later, a pot of soup in one hand and a cake in the other, I thought it was supposed to take three weeks, no? I don a gloomy expression in order to avoid having to provide explanations, to myself as well as to her, as to the meaning of the sudden signs of relief in the air, faint and vague but definitely present, and perhaps it's the very knowledge that a cure exists and is within reach, that the grief can be tamed, that the howling jackal can be turned into an obedient puppy, or perhaps without knowing it I have already reached rock bottom, the place from which you can only go up, or perhaps it is the memory of that morning awakening within me, confronting me once more with the forgotten possibility of another life, which, even if it will never erase the loss, will be able to survive alongside it, and if that possibility exists, then the mistake cannot be final, nor the sorrow, and it seems that into the absolute darkness of the room in which I have imprisoned myself for all these weeks slants a glint of light that, while not yet strong enough to illuminate the entire room, is capable at least of distinguishing between one darkness and another, between the darkness of dawn and the darkness of noon and the darkness of night, and in this meager shaft of light, I squint, trying to recognize inanimate objects, nuances of sound and facial features, existing.

To exist within the contradictions flying around me like migrating birds, a flock making its way to the warmer lands, with a few worried birds on the fringe, trailing behind, looking back. I am the flock and I am also the straying fringe of the flock, for even if things are bad now, it doesn't mean that they were better before, or that they won't be better in the future, for sorrow is not necessarily evidence of regret, and regret is not necessarily evidence of error, and error does not necessarily bear witness to the future, and the future, even if it will not justify the act, does not bear witness to the past, just like the present, for my loneliness now is not evidence of the fact that I wasn't lonely in my marriage, the guilt that drives me to my knees is not evidence of sin, and the great rift does not bear witness to the whole. It seems that the murderous black certainty that buried me for all these weeks is beginning to loosen its grip, allowing me other moments, far from the radiant freedom I imagined but sometimes giving rise nevertheless to the modest satisfaction of lessening regret, like a shrinking tumor, which, while not wiping out the memory and terror of the disease, gives rise to the faint hope of recovery, even if temporary, a lull in the intensity of the torments of the mind.

All that remains now of the satanic certainty of error under which

I collapsed is a question, sometimes asked in malice and sometimes in trepidation and sometimes in sorrow, and I understand that this question will be asked until my dying day, even if its lips move and its voice is unheard, and when I die I will bequeath it to my only son; did I do the right thing when I got up one day and tore our family to shreds, was the deed worthy, was it right, should I have wished for more than I had, will I ever have more than I had; if I even know what I had, all this will take years to answer, to really know if our marriage was as hopeless and flawed as I thought before the separation, or as wonderful and rare as it seemed to me after it, whether it was folly or necessity, only at the end of my life will I be able to tally the days of sorrow and frustration and the days of happiness, though from this point on, it seems, my life will be stripped of its inalienable right to contain both good and bad, and will be narrowed down to an endless collection of data, to an almost mathematical exercise, every moment of contentment chalked up in one column, every moment of dejection in the other, and these tables will shimmer before me, challenging and oppressive, for the complexity of the calculations is becoming clearer to me all the time because right before my eyes the past is changing shape, far livelier than the present, full of twists and turns, and I try to hold it still, to direct a beam of light on to it, to see it as it was, our marriage, our family, before they were sanctified by the potency of the loss.

How capricious is the past. Like a person you repeatedly bump into on the street, one day he snubs you, and the next he greets you warmly, one day he is well groomed and attractive, and the next he is dirty and repulsive, but the more he denies me, the happier I am, the more muck I succeed in throwing at him, the better I feel. It seems that only by removing him completely from my path will I find peace of mind, but how can I get rid of him. This house is the past, this child is the past, I myself still belong to the past. This man who drops in from time to time is the past, and I watch him alertly, sometimes it seems that he has the key, that the answer resides with him, and if his face or his voice or his gestures repel me, I breathe easy, in the happy relief of doubts resolved, but if his beautiful eyes are shining in his face and his smile is pleasant, I fill with rage, and the more friendly he is, the more hostile I become, and the more hostile he is, the friendlier I become, for in the complex and oppressive process of collecting data and passing sentence there is no room for ordinary gestures, for simple feelings, every word is destined for classification, every gesture is a fact of weighty significance in the prosecution or defense's case, to which I will devote the rest of my life. Even Gili is unwillingly recruited to play a part in this mission, in him, too, I search for signs, every characteristic inherited from his father, every expression, must be classified, and in a most unnatural way I pounce triumphantly on his weaknesses because they may prove that, in fact, the deed had to be done.

Gingerly, I walk around the house, afraid to move anything, to disturb the evidence, as if it were an ancient site that has been destroyed and abandoned by its inhabitants and it is up to me to offer an interpretation as to the cause, was it fire, war, invasion, earthquake, the drying up of a water source, a change in the climate; was the destruction due to a natural disaster or can it be traced to the hand of man. I try to reconstruct the sequence of events in reverse order to the accumulation of the layers in the mound, to make inanimate objects speak, like the bronze coin covered with green oxidation or the potshards, to draw out of them our family history. Throughout, I fear that I am too late, for a site can be excavated only once, and I have acted rashly, hastily casting aside dirt of inestimable importance, without sieving, without documenting, rendering it impossible for any future excavator to verify or refute the data or their meaning, and neither can I, for the remains have been removed forever. Is it still even possible to cut a section from the sloping mound of our abandoned love, I wonder, and I remember how Amnon would assemble us all at the end of the day, standing in front of a long narrow table, his upper body bare, his jeans cut off carelessly, long white threads dangling from them like ritual fringes, and we would climb out of the excavation squares that were small as a child's room, the dirt making us all look alike, and set aside our tools and sit at his feet, and he would rapidly analyze the findings, put the most important ones away in a drawer and throw the rest into a pail, and in the end he would always say, pointing to the small mounds alongside the squares, where the accumulated layers can be seen, look how thin this layer is, it represents an entire civilization, look how little we leave behind us, and in the dark afternoon hours of this winter, while Gili plays with one of his friends in his room, I sit in front of the computer, with papers and photographs and maps and articles on my knees, how little you have left behind you, Amnon, I write, how little our ten-year-old family has left behind it, and from time to time I go and stand at the window, where the thick, muscular branches of the fast-growing ivy cling stubbornly to the walls, and marvel at the past spreading through the house, mournful and drawn out as the warbling of the cantor's voice as he practices for the High Holidays again, *me'yom kippurim ze ad yom kippurim haba,* from this Day of Atonement to the next.

From time to time the recollections are interrupted by the ringing of the telephone, the sound of knuckles on the door, all kinds of acquaintances taking the liberty to just drop in; finally we can come over, they say, when Amnon was here we always felt we were in the way, and I point apologetically to the flickering computer screen to show that I am not free to chat because most of the conversations don't even come close to the core of the matter, they are but an unnecessary burden on the brittle soul, and along with the visits comes the matchmaking, Ella, there's someone I want you to meet, you didn't leave Amnon to be alone, it's a shame to sit and rot at home in front of the computer, go out a bit, meet people, what do you have to lose? And I decline, I don't feel like it now, I'm not looking for someone now, the notion of the effort involved in getting to know someone summons waves of nausea.

You're just punishing yourself, they say, your suffering won't bring him back, but since that night I have made no such attempts, neither overt nor covert, neither one of us mentioning that night, as if it were the rotten fruit of our imaginations. When he brings Gili home, we cut our conversation short, like two unwilling partners in the running of a business, dependant on each other for the success of their common enterprise, but jealously guarding their privacy, and I show no interest in his new life and, to my surprise, the lack of interest is genuine. Only the past preoccupies me, and whatever he does in the present concerns me only insofar as it reflects on the past, with the consequential and the inconsequential of equal importance, his clothes, his gestures, his smell, his fathering, his decency, his generosity, with a warped and tortuous gaze I examine him, finding myself hoping that he will disappoint me simply in order to shed a sickly light on the years of our life together, but beyond this my interest in him has become dry and limited, almost scientific, as if he is no longer a living, breathing human being, but a valuable and ambulatory finding, a walking piece of data capable of shedding light on the research I am now conducting, research financed with my marrow and my blood.

Tensely I follow his movements, afraid to miss a scrap of information; is he alone in the lovely apartment overlooking the monastery, does he cook for himself, burning the bottom of the pot as usual, what does he do on his free days, does he meet women, does he still shower in cold water, does he get dressed without drying himself, has he finished the article on the Canaanite water system that we started writing together, whom does he tell his huffy stories of the mundane to, does he sleep alone on the bed covered with the embroidered cloth, does his hand stray over it at night in search of my body. It seems that all these questions have lost any relevance to my present life, and it is only to the past that they owe a reckoning because it is only the past I am examining, and it alone will sentence me.

And from those layers I emerge now and again, as from the depths of a dig, robed in dust, setting a hesitant foot on the thresholds of the homes opening up to me, the lives that have always taken place around me without my noticing, the lives without families, clusters of strangers, without ties of blood, without a shared child, without a shared home, who create substitute families for themselves, loneliness meets loneliness and redoubles itself, and this is what my new life has to offer, this is what Dina has to offer, this is what the rainy weekends have to offer, and this is what I find it hard to accept. Instead of the nearly impermeable triangle, familiar in every detail, mother, father and child, which, from time to time, annexes an appendage or two for a few hours and immediately casts them off with an inaudible sigh of relief, I am offered a motley crew of men and women, some younger than me and some older, some who have never established a family and some who have already dismantled one, and they busy themselves preparing Friday night and holiday meals, trying to part the loneliness, which for some is temporary and for others eternal, and when I come into their company I usually cling to Dina, examining her and her friends with dreary eyes, what a poor substitute for the family I had, for the honeyed comfort of husband and child, for the natural, self-sustaining habitat, that scarcely requires an external source of nourishment.

Come tomorrow, she says in her brisk voice, they say it's going to snow, I'm making *hamin*, and I ask anxiously, are you sure, is it definitely going to snow? And she says, that's what I heard, so, will you come? And I complain, why does it have to snow tomorrow when Gili's with Amnon? One snowfall a year and it has to be on the Saturday when he's not with me, we've been waiting for this for a whole year. What's wrong with that, she says, be happy for him, he'll enjoy the snow, and I have a hard time explaining myself, but I won't see him enjoying it, I say, I'll miss it, and she chuckles, he exists when you don't see him, you know, why do you think that without you he doesn't exist? And I say, I'm the one who doesn't exist, the snow doesn't exist.

Let him enjoy himself without you, she says, his enjoyment is valid even when you're not there, don't be so domineering, you want to control the weather now, too? So, are you coming tomorrow? And I ask, did they say how long it will last? It has to last one more day, but in truth the second day is less exciting, the snow is already dirty, I say, talking to myself out loud, and she says, I'm waiting for an answer, Ella, and I tell her, I'll let you know tomorrow, how can I commit myself now, maybe Amnon will let me come over so we can play in the snow together, and she says, you have to tell me now because if you're coming, I'll invite someone you should meet.

You're also matchmaking! I say in surprise, it doesn't suit you, you should know I'm not ready to meet anyone yet, and she says, maybe not, but you can be made ready, and I ask, who is he? And she says, he's the brother of a friend of mine, a pilot, divorced, interested in archeology, that's why I thought of you, and I say, but I'm not interested in archeology anymore, I'm just pretending, and she says, enough, Ella, stop being so negative, tomorrow, one o'clock.

Every few minutes I go out to the balcony and inspect the sky with inquisitive hostility, is it really harboring the pure, longed for snowflakes that have suddenly turned into a threat to my peace of mind, to the reality of my existence, wait one more night, I beg, restrain yourselves until Saturday evening, give me the pleasure of seating him on the window sill and looking at your magical powder drifting between his fingers, going down with him to the utterly transformed yard, together we'll make our way between the broken branches, as if we're walking toward an enchanted castle, on paths never trodden before, his curls wrapped up in a thick woolen hat, his face radiant with excitement, his voice soaring like a bell, and even at night I sit up in bed and look at the window, like a sentry on his watch, and when ordinary darkness greets my eyes, I calm down and go back to sleep feeling that my prayers have been answered, but when I wake up late the next morning to a suspect, startled stillness, like the silence after a crime has been committed, the sky flaunts a dazzling light at me from between the slats of the blinds, and I realize that in spite of my just and sincere efforts, I have not succeeded in keeping the snow at bay.

Don't come, it will confuse him, Amnon's voice is polite but firm, we're going outside in a minute to play soccer in the snow, he's in a great mood, it doesn't make sense to confuse him, and I don't argue, laying the phone down, my skin chilled by the clear words, and I pull up the blind with offended fingers, recoiling at the intensity of the beauty, the treacherous radiance suffusing the pale lips of the city as it spreads an icy smile.

When I was a child I had no child. Alone I was cast from season to season, as if they were stations in an enchanted amusement park, the colors of the autumn leaves chasing the fragrance of the flowers, clouds puffing dense smoke at the eye of the sun, hot scented vapors rising from the bowels of the earth, winds clutching at the tree trunks, every winter overshadowing the one before, every summer stinging the one before, riveted, I would watch the play of the seasons, like four kittens they would pounce on each other, flee from each other, with me in the middle, imagining that their games were meant for me, to ease my loneliness.

Down in the street merry little dwarfs cavort, round as balls in their puffy coats, hats and gloves, sitting down with a thud on plastic bags and sliding with their legs stretched out in front of them, and I look away, Gili's absence weighing on me, how I would love to slide down the steep hill with him, to hear him scream with delight, the realization of a dream he's been cultivating for a full year. Resentfully I pace the house, inspecting the view from all the windows, how thrilling the familiar sight looks in its new, deceitful apparel, but the more spectacular the view, the more it distresses me; if he were here he would run from window to window, his exclamations drawing clouds of vapors on the panes, look, look, he would shout, it's more beautiful than anything in the world, he would declare knowledgeably, as if he had already seen everything there was to see, and I go back to bed to nurse my disappointment, above my head, on the wall, our photograph still hangs, the three of us crowding together under a black umbrella while the previous year's snowflakes did their muted dance, a dance of farewell is what it was, though no one knew.

It seems to me that somebody is calling my name with a soft sigh at the window and I sit up startled, can it be the creaking of the dead cypress tree, its crown straining toward the wall of the house, and for a moment it seems that the tree is in bloom, snow flowers white as jasmine festooning its dry branches, within the space of a few hours it has become radiant as an almond tree, sparkling as a Christmas tree, and I am riveted by the astonishing sight, the resurrection of the tree, and even if it is temporary, even if it is imaginary, it arouses in me a vague forgotten desire, not the desire for a man, but the desire for life itself, and I watch the flight of the shining blossoms, drunkenly they spin around the tree, some trapped in its branches and some falling to its roots, bearing a secret blessing sent from the heavens, and this pure beauty is knocking at my window, it demands nothing of me and I demand nothing of it in return. Yes, why shouldn't I blossom for a few hours too, and suddenly I am flooded by the primal craving for pleasure that obeys no one, frightening in its egoism, bold in its power. Standing at the window, I giggle like an excited girl conjuring up again and again the magic of the first words of love, the delight of the moment when she realized that there was an answer to her yearnings, and I lean against the window sill, the air spirals thickly around me, stars cascade onto to my head, millions of down comforters have been torn in the sky and their feathers cover me, like the deciduous trees draping themselves in thin royal robes in memory of their leaves, and I take the gift awaiting me on the bedside table, the packet of pills wrapped in gold paper, tied up with a red ribbon, and I throw it into the arms of the cypress tree, like the bouquet thrown by the bride before she sets out on her new journey, bestowing my precious gift on the tree blooming after its death, a gift for a gift.

Years ago he bought me a white sweater that earned him a crooked smile, why white, I'm too pale to wear white, but now after a long hot shower I look for it in the closet, wearing the color of snow like camouflage, and I paint my lips a bright red, shake out my shining shampooed hair; I had not noticed how it had grown in the past months, reaching almost to my hips, and excited as a child seeing snow for the first time in her life, I go out into the glittering town, into the short-lived beauty of this wonder, like the beauty of a new love. My steps scar the still soft skin of snow, and when I look back I am surprised to see how quickly the scars have healed, freshly covered with white, and I continue on my way, passing a young mother dragging a wailing child behind her, I'm cold, he whines, my fingers are frozen, and she scolds him, of course you're cold, I told you to wear gloves, why didn't you wear gloves, her distracted look takes me in and it seems that she envies me for being so unencumbered, concentrated on my own enjoyment, yes, it's allowed, it's even possible, Gili is enjoying himself there and I am enjoying myself here, white flames reaching from me to him like torches signaling from mountaintop to mountaintop.

When I arrive, wild-haired and flushed from the walk, the meal is already in progress, the rich meaty smell of *hamin* cooked all night on a low flame greets me, together with the fumes of the wine-filled glasses, and body odors and perfume and aftershave all melded together in the warmth of the closed, heated house. Dina, in a black sweater dress, embraces me, her brown eyes examining me in surprise, tiny blood capillaries on her cheeks like the veins on a leaf, how beautiful you are today, she says, and immediately adds apologetically, he hasn't arrived yet, he should be here any minute, and I don't really know what she's talking about, never mind, I've already forgotten all about it, I say, it's much easier for me like this, to sit among disinterested strangers, who aren't testing me, to eat from the flaming hot dish, to calmly sip the wine.

It's incredible, they put pesto in the *hamin*, someone complains to Dina, a man no longer young whose paunch comes up against the table and whose eyes dart restlessly, seeking support, people have lost their minds, they ruin everything, what's wrong with classic traditional *hamin*, why add pesto, he cries, why? as if someone has made an attempt on his life, and the woman sitting next to him, presumably his wife, makes haste to disassociate herself from him. I actually like pesto, she declares sincerely, he's so conservative, she adds, and he immediately upbraids her, but you don't understand anything, I like pesto too, but not in *hamin*, not with everything.

The emotional intensity invested in the pesto debate tickles my nostrils, and I cover my mouth with my hand to hide my laughter while Dina does her best to change the subject, but Mr. Pesto has no intention of letting go, we are all obliged to judge between him and his wife, and it seems that he will not rest until she herself realizes her terrible mistake. What's wrong with a bit of conservatism? he cries, she thinks that if she runs after every fad she'll grow younger, she wants to impress the younger generation, I, as opposed to you, judge everything on its merits, I like pesto with pasta, not with *hamin*, he declares, and I get up and run to the bathroom where I choke on my laughter, Mrs. Pesto trailing me with her eyes, an ancient insult dwells there, the kind that nourishes a nagging discontent. Later she'll say to him, it was insulting, the way you spoke to me, and he'll say, you were insulted? I was insulted, you always contradict me, you'd rather die than agree with me about anything. How familiar this exchange is to me, as if I have been conducting it all my life, and now I am suddenly absolved of it.

When I return to the large table, they're talking about Jerusalem, with far less enthusiasm; she wants to leave the city, the man complains, after I finally got used to living here, she suddenly wants to move to Tel Aviv, and the woman sitting next to me, an old friend of Dina's I've already met on several occasions, says, it's not so simple, I've tried to leave Jerusalem a few times and failed, I always come back, it's the most interesting city in the world, and Dina says, maybe for you because you look at it through the eyes of a photographer, for ordinary people it can be oppressive, what do we have here? poverty, terror, increasing piety.

What do we have here? the man sitting opposite me moans, the whole history of the Jewish People is encapsulated here under our feet, King David ruled the whole of Israel from here, Solomon built the first temple here, and I remark quietly, that's not accurate, and again he raises his voice, not accurate? It's written in the Bible! And I snigger, what kind of an argument is that? The Bible isn't exactly an historical document, all the excavations in Jerusalem haven't succeeded in proving the existence of a great kingdom here in the period of David and

Solomon, on the contrary, even simple potshards were only found in relatively small amounts.

So what are you trying to say, that David and Solomon didn't exist? he upbraids me, and I say, apparently they did exist, the House of David is mentioned in an inscription from Tel Dan, but their mythological kingdom did not exist, Jerusalem in their period was not a magnificent city of palaces, but a small, remote mountain village. So why did the myth of the great kingdom come into being? Dina asks, and I say, the way myths usually come into being, in order to satisfy psychological needs, to cultivate hopes of a legendary golden age, which already existed in the past, or to serve later visions. He fills his glass sullenly, that's all bullshit, he grumbles, since when does lack of proof prove anything? You archeologists haven't got any imagination, tomorrow you'll find David's palace and you'll take back all these new theories, perhaps the proof you're looking for is right underneath this house, and I smile at him forgivingly, his stubbornness is touching, it reminds me of my stubbornness about Thera.

In any case, I'm finished with this city, says his wife, it's a city of masochists. Duh, Dina says, this whole country is a country of masochists, and he protests, do we have an alternative, tell me, what alternative do you have, have you got anywhere to go? And his wife looks at him glumly again, apparently not, apparently we don't have anywhere to go, and I feel like saying to her, even if you don't have anywhere to go, you can get up and leave him right this minute, the question isn't where you can go but if you can stay. The persistent ringing of the telephone interrupts the conversation. He's stuck, Dina says, still holding the phone in her hand, her eyes on me, as if it's my bridegroom she's talking about, the road to Jerusalem is blocked, and I shrug my shoulders, it's for the best, I'll be able to leave soon, apparently I have become accustomed to solitude and their pointless small talk is getting on my nerves. I try to ignore them, to listen only to the snowflakes falling softly from the sky, and when Dina pours boiling mint tea into glasses, I stand up, even if you have nowhere to go, you can go right now.

Can I give him your number? Dina asks as she sees me to the door, it isn't going to go on snowing forever, and I say, all right, if it's so important to you, as long as you let me go now, and, by the way, where did you find that couple? She smiles, together they really are intolerable, but each of them on their own is fine, it's a good idea to invite a married couple from time to time so we'll see how lucky we are, she whispers, and I have to agree with her for a sweet liberating moment, skipping lightly down the stairs, emerging into the slandered city, which greets me with frigid indifference, as if to say, you didn't defend me as you should have, but I don't need your protection anyway. When I look at the solitary spires of the churches, at the curves of the hills whose contours are being increasingly blurred by the crudity of the new buildings, I remember how foreign I felt in this city; it seems that I still hold a grudge against it, eager to take part in excavations that expose its disgrace, careful to relate to it as a subject of research, as a complex and misleading collection of data, without any real affection.

Inside the heated houses people are filling their bellies, resting from the newness that will soon become burdensome. A few cars make their way along streets that have changed beyond recognition, and alone I cross a playground where the swings and seesaws have paled, it's the playground opposite their house, I suddenly recognize it, and look up at the imposing building, the balcony on the top floor is empty now, no child is hurling plastic bags swollen with water. On a number of occasions I have suggested to Gili in a tempting voice, what about Yotam, why don't you invite him over? And he has grunted, no, I'm not friends with him anymore, and added confidentially, our gang is against their gang, we wipe the floor with them, and I tried to hide my disappointment, I had hoped to make friends with them through him, and again I think of that morning, the sight of the embarrassed man in his crimson polka-dot underpants, looking at me with an angry, exposed look, softening, growing resigned to my presence, far more vivid in my memory than the well-dressed, confident, professional figure he presented in his clinic, and I stand opposite his house, it must be warm and cozy there now, with the treetops whitening outside the windows, the pears replaced by citrus fruits in the pottery bowl. Is he sitting on the tall bar stool now, dunking cookies in his coffee, or perhaps on the rocking chair, a blanket on his knees, reading the newspaper, or a book, or has he gone out for a walk by himself in the snow, perhaps I'll bump into him now, making his way back home, and again he'll look at me and ask, do we know each other? And I'll reply, not really, but I'll walk silently by his side, and both of us will see other cities in our minds' eye, other lives. Is that him there at the end of the street, a scarf hiding his face, no, he's only a figment of my imagination, just like the commiserating look I saw in his eyes, and, even though my feet are already stinging with the cold, I go on standing next to his house, straining my ears, is the sound of stifled weeping still wandering through the rooms, was it the sigh of a strange family's obscure pain I heard then, or was it perchance my own.

Chapter ten

Ella, hi, he says, his tone urgent, demanding, it's Rami Regev, I'm sorry I didn't make it to lunch on Saturday, the road was closed, but as far as I'm concerned we can meet tomorrow, and I wonder to myself, what's so urgent, he's existed without me until now, why pounce on me as if I'm the last available woman in the world, and I hesitate, feeling as if the minute I agree to meet him I'll find myself tagged, even in my own eyes, with the worn, shabby label of a woman in search of a husband, an object looking for a buyer.

I can't tomorrow, I say at last, maybe the day after tomorrow, and he immediately returns the favor, the day after tomorrow is no good for me, only the day after that, and it seems as if we can go on like this forever, with him sticking to the even numbers and me the odd ones, but now he tries another tack, I just finished reading an article you published in that journal of yours, it's interesting, but it hasn't got a leg to stand on, he says, I completely disagree with you.

Who are you to disagree with me, what do you know, I protest in silence, but the sting has the desired effect, for a woman who publishes articles that haven't got a leg to stand on can hardly afford to turn down a man who is willing to meet her, despite disagreeing with her completely, and we arrange to meet in three days' time, in the cafe next to my house, and the closer the hour comes, the more pronounced my angst. Is this just the beginning of a futile, pathetic round of disappointments and humiliations, is this what I got myself into when I left Amnon, and I try to cheer myself up, better to go through the motions when I'm not really interested, the worst that can happen is that I'll be bored and leave early, and yet when I get dressed to go out, my frail tranquility abandons me. I frown at the mirror and wonder why I need this, but am forced to admit that I am reluctant to forgo the faint chance of falling in love with the divorced pilot who is also an amateur archeologist, of arousing his love, of finding, through him, the final proof that I was right to leave Amnon, the same proof that will abolish the doubts and make me whole, even if I remain forever broken, the shard that represents the entire pot, and is it really true, as was drilled into us, that every human artifact is of equal scientific importance, whether whole or fragmented?

Suppose Amnon Miller was sitting in front of me now, would I want him, would my shuttered heart awaken to him, allow him to wander through its chambers, is he, too, going on dates like this, how does he present himself, how does he describe the end of our marriage, does he say, my wife lost interest in me after the child was born, she took me for granted, as pair upon pair of made-up eyes widen opposite him in surprise. Really? How could anyone lose interest in you, what's so hard about being a mother and a wife at the same time? We'll never take you for granted, their sedulous eyes promise him, and maybe he offers a completely different version, maybe he says it was he who lost interest in our marriage, so as not to give rise to the least hint of a doubt in the heart of the woman sitting opposite him. Ten years is enough, he'll say, I couldn't see myself growing old with her, and for this, too, he will win sympathetic looks, tender invitations to grow old with them, and he will sing the praises of his professional achievements, invite the chosen amongst them to accompany him in the field, to put on work clothes and take up hammers and picks, and at the end of the meeting he will take them to his attractive apartment, and through the bead curtain he will lead them to the bed covered with the embroidered cloth.

Could I have been one of them if I met him today and not ten years ago, thrilled by the interest he showed in me, half blind, the very sightlessness needed for falling in love, am I still capable of this blindness, for without it how would it be possible to fall in love with this rough, clumsy, foul tempered man who was, at the same time, captivating in that lively, excitable eagerness that never lets him rest, is he superior or inferior to all the men I will meet in the future in cafes across Jerusalem, is he superior or inferior to the pilot walking toward me now, glancing at his watch, whom I recognize by the sign he gave me: I always wear shorts, he boasted; and this leaves no room for doubt because he must be the only person in the city walking around in a blue aviator's jacket and shorts that reveal slender, muscular legs and heavy hiking boots, and I decide to ignore this eccentricity, and not to ask him in wide-eyed wonder, aren't you cold? pretending instead that everyone I know walks around similarly dressed in the heart of Jerusalem's winter.

The sight of his declaratively naked legs makes me feel uncomfortable, as if I have been forced to watch a physical act to which I had no intention of exposing myself, and I inspect them dubiously, apparently he is one of the chosen few who feel at home in the world, and already I know that he opens the fridge without asking permission in every apartment he enters, takes a book from the shelf and looks into it, and with women, too, he is surely direct and blunt. Hey, Ella, I'm starving, he announces as he removes his jacket, as if I were his mother and therefore have an unquenchably avid interest in his nutritional well being, and only then do I look at his face, is it superior to Amnon's? I'm forced to admit that Amnon looks younger than he does, and his face is more handsome in my eyes than this one, which is unpleasantly thin, with sharp, tense features that twitch restlessly, without proper coordination between the eyes, lips and nostrils, like an orchestra without a conductor.

Have you been here long? he inquires, but before I have a chance to say that I have only just arrived, a more urgent question follows, do you smell something? And I say, nothing special, why? Immediately suspecting that my last shower left something to be desired, he says, there's a strange smell here, let's move to another table, and I get up reluctantly, my choice of this cafe is already being subjected to a strict review, and I follow him to a secluded corner table, my coat and bag in my hands. The door beckons, calling me to freedom, but I sit down opposite him obediently, watching the movements of his nostrils. This is a bit better, he pronounces, not yet completely satisfied, and only then he takes the time to inspect me, and I lower my eyes to the menu, who knows who I am being measured against now, who the woman I am unwillingly being forced to compete with is, my lips against her lips, my eyes against her eyes, my breasts against her breasts, and I order only a glass of red wine, despite my hunger. How will I be able to chew comfortably in the face of his twitching nostrils, his probing eyes. Better to cut the meeting short and eat at home, I decide, but it appears that his plans differ from mine, and he is ready to order every dish on the menu, whether to satisfy his ravenous hunger or to lengthen the meeting, his will trumps mine, and it seems that I will have to remain hungry and watch him eating for hours, soup and salad and bloody steak, raw, I like it raw, he shouts at the waitress's receding backside, exposing his sharp canine teeth as if he himself is about to rip the bleeding piece of meat from the animal's flanks.

After finishing with the menu he returns his tiny pupils to me, so what's your story? he says, trying a friendly smile at last, but he doesn't wait for an answer, I thought you would look different, he shares his secret expectations with me, I've met a few female archeologists before, they all had a tough, weathered look, you look more delicate, he remarks almost resentfully, in a second he, too, will say to me, you're a fresco, and I ask coldly, so what are you actually interested in, archeology or archeologists?

Both, he laughs in enjoyment as if I have paid him a compliment, I like the combination, digging is a very erotic activity, don't you think? And I say, digging is a destructive activity, you can only tell after the fact if it was justified, I would hope that the erotic is less destructive, but maybe it's the other way around with you, I sip my wine condescendingly, looking around me with ostentatious boredom. That article you wrote, he tries again, and I cut him short, I've written a lot of articles, which one do you mean? And he says, the one about the exodus from Egypt, I don't understand you, how can you ignore the fact that not a single shred of evidence of that whole story has ever been found? And I say, I know all those arguments by heart, I don't imagine that we're talking about an absolute historical truth here, all I'm saying is that you can't ignore Egyptian evidence of a huge natural disaster, which fits in with phenomena mentioned in our own sources.

I wasn't convinced by that evidence, he says grumpily, what's the linkage? Archeology isn't an exact science, I say, there's a lot of room for interpretation, the easiest thing today is to say that everything's a fairytale, but it's difficult for me to believe that the memory of such a dramatic historical event is purely a figment of the imagination. The arrival of the soup interrupts the conversation, to my relief, and he attacks it eagerly only to find that it, too, does not live up to his expectations, they overcooked the broccoli, he complains, if you overcook broccoli it turns into mush, he says severely to the waitress, and she apologizes, really? Nobody's complained before. I have a perceptive palate, he announces, and she is at a loss, would you like to order something else? she suggests, and he asks, what's your specialty? And she says, we have an excellent chef, or at least we thought so until now, and he snorts contemptuously, I'll wait for the steak and salad. She gives me a sympathetic look and escapes from the troublesome customer, if only I could do the same, I would gladly wait on each table if she would take my place opposite him, and I maintain a disapproving silence, taking small, nervous sips of wine.

So you're newly divorced? he asks, as if I, too, am a dish on the menu and he needs to check on its freshness, and I answer coldly, I'm not even divorced yet, I only separated from my husband a few months ago, and he says, your husband's that archeologist, Amnon Miller, right? I've heard of him, what's it like living with another archeologist? And I keep it short, it has advantages and disadvantages. Apparently the disadvantages outweighed the advantages, he says, pleased with his wit, and I nod, maybe, and how about you, how long have you been divorced? And he says, a long time now, I married young, we weren't ready for it, and ever since then I've been searching, and I nod silently, how will you ever find what you're looking for, if every dish disappoints you and every smell disgusts you.

At long last the steak joins us at our silent table, and he digs into it voraciously, not rare enough, but definitely okay, he informs me happily as if I am in need of reassurance, on the kibbutz we were forced to eat everything on our plates, he goes on apologetically, the food was terrible, ever since then I am very particular about what I put in my mouth, and I stare at him exhaustedly, how will I fall in love, how is it possible to fall in love at my age when one's eyes are wide open and one's heart keeps ledgers like a diligent accountant. It seems that falling in love, like sleeping, becomes more elusive the more you think about it, how can I fall asleep, I asked in my youth, how can I fall in love, I ask now, as a noisy group sits down behind my back, I can't see them but their loud merriment engulfs our table, a family birthday party, it appears, and he makes a face, what's that noise, maybe we should move to another table, I can't hear myself, he complains, and I look around me, the cafe is already full, where exactly can we move, only by the door, next to the security guard, one table remains unoccupied, and everyone is afraid to sit there, including the valiant pilot seated opposite me.

What can I do, he says, I'll have to ask them not to make so much noise, they've got a lot nerve, somebody's birthday, big deal, what's there to celebrate anyway, and to my chagrin I see him get briskly to his feet, straighten his ridiculous shorts, go up to the next table and say, excuse me, we're in the middle of a very important meeting here, would you mind not making so much noise? And I hear a low voice answering him with mocking politeness, we'll do our best, but it's a little difficult with the children, the voice is familiar, a voice I've heard before, more than once, do we know each other, he asked, do we know each other? And I turn my face discreetly, to steal a look at the family, two parents and two children, happy birthday to the Sheffer family, the woman's mango curls, held up with a gilt clasp, the serious face of the little boy, who always reminds me of Gili, the little girl's doll-like prettiness, and he himself, with his fleshy lips greedily swallowing the cookies, his black eyes magnified by dark rings, and shadowed by thick brows, he himself who gave me the most precious of gifts without even knowing it, no, we don't know each other, we will never know each other, is there anything I might want more than knowing you.

There's that smell again, my companion complains in an aggrieved whisper, as if it's the two of us against the rest of the world, before it was okay, apparently it's coming from them, and I bow my head, please don't let them notice me, I try to eavesdrop on their conversation, to discover whose birthday it is, their voices reach me, relaxed and enviable. Daddy, I want to sit on your lap, I hear Yotam announce, and Michal says, but how will Daddy eat, you'll get in his way, you're not a baby anymore, you're six years old today, and his father says, it's all right, come on, buddy, and

I don't dare look at them but in my mind's eye I see the full, dark lips straying over the high forehead of the child who reminds me so much of Gili, but how different the circumstances of their lives. How will our torn family celebrate his next birthday, all the birthdays to come, will there be two separate parties, a double, or rather divided celebration, or perhaps we will succeed in reuniting for one tense evening, as if huddled around the flame of our last match, one evening that, even if it goes well, will leave a long trail of gloom behind it.

Grandma and Grandpa will be here in a minute, says Michal, let's wait for them before we order, and Yotam shouts happily, I can order whatever I want because it's my birthday today, and you can't, he teases his sister, and she immediately retorts, you're just a baby, what are you bragging about, I've had more birthdays than you anyway, and again their father's calm voice defuses the budding argument. I order another glass of wine, and all this time my companion goes on telling me in minute detail about his travels in the world. We have a lot to learn from those Japanese, he enthuses, it seems that he has just returned from Japan, their aesthetic sense is unbelievable, it's a real religion with them, you should see how they prune trees, ten gardeners per tree, and I nod indifferently, listening only to them, not daring to turn my head so as not to be exposed in my humiliation, it's so easy to pick out couples on a blind date, Talia and I used to amuse ourselves by spotting them, but soon enough I hear a merry shout, presumably accompanied by a rudely pointing finger, look, there's Gili's mother, and I am forced to turn my ostensibly surprised face to them, and I even go so far as to approach them, hello, I didn't recognize you, I say, my head spinning from the wine, my fingers gripping their table like talons.

It's my birthday today, Yotam announces, and I pretend to be surprised again, really? That's wonderful, happy birthday, and he goes on to ask, why isn't Gili friends with me anymore? And I babble without thinking, of course he's friends with you, only yesterday he told me he wants you to come over, and Michal says, great, I'll call you this week and we'll make a date, and immediately she apologizes for her lack of manners, sorry, Ella, this is my husband, Oded, you haven't met, and we shake hands silently, smiling politely, neither of us bothering to bring our companions up to date, silent partners in transgression. His eyes turn to me with an obscure question, and I stand rooted to the spot, gripping the back of his chair, longing to join them, to be adopted for one evening, but then the commotion is renewed because Grandma and Grandpa reach the table, which swells with kisses and good wishes, and I mumble a feeble goodbye and return swaying to my place.

My temporary partner's plate is almost empty, dotted with little puddles of grilled blood, and he hesitates over dessert, cheesecake or chocolate cake, or perhaps both together, why not have it both ways, and I interrupt the fateful musing, I think we should get out of here, I warn him in a whisper, they're just beginning their birthday party, the noise will be unbearable, they've invited a lot of other people. Is that so? He is surprised and flattered by this consideration for his special needs, then let's go somewhere else, he suggests, is there a good pub around here? And I glance deliberately at my watch, I can't believe how late it is, I cry in alarm, the time passed so fast, I have to get back to the babysitter, and he looks at me suspiciously, but we arranged to meet today because your son is with his father, and I am surprised that he remembered, we had to change days, I lie, and his face darkens, it seems he has not been rewarded for his efforts, the time it took him to get here is still more than the time we have spent together, and he racks his brain for a way to get the most out of his voyage, to change the course of the evening.

The bill comes quickly, as I requested, but it is presented for some reason to me, even though I only ordered wine, and I examine it in embarrassment, waiting for the person sitting opposite me to reach out his hand and take responsibility for his deeds, ten years of married life have made me forget the accepted rules, which may also have changed since then, and I take my purse out slowly, waiting for him to follow suit, but he fails to do so. Did they charge me for the soup? he demands, as if that was all he ordered, and I nod, taking a large bill out of my purse, and he allows me to part from my money, as if he expects me to compensate him for his trouble. He lets the waitress take the little tray and she brings back a smattering of change that will immediately be returned to her, and I am astonished, are these really the new rules, that women pay for what they don't eat as well, it looks as if I won't be able to afford many dates like this, but my most urgent need is to get rid of him, at any price, I'd pay double to see him go, but does he intend on leaving; like a married couple we stand up together, filling the air with long held resentments, and walk quickly past the celebrating family busy eating and talking, none of them seeming to notice the faint goodbye smile I've left behind me.

Do you live around here? I'll give you a lift, he offers, as we emerge into the foggy, slippery night, but I immediately decline, thank you, I prefer to walk, I say dryly, I had a nice time, we'll talk, and he grabs my arm, wait a minute, he protests, stop treating me like the class idiot, I know you didn't have a nice time, I know we won't talk, stop pretending, and I pull my arm away in surprise, for the first time since we met I look straight into his eyes, listen, it really has nothing to do with you, I'm simply not built for blind dates now, it's too soon for me, I told Dina but she insisted, I'm really sorry. I'm sorry too, he says, his face next to mine, it's a pity you won't give it a chance, you don't take part in what's happening, you don't dare put your toe in the water, you don't eat, you don't talk, you don't contribute anything real to the meeting, you think that this makes you win the game but you're mistaken, you don't even play the game, and I look at him in embarrassment, what exactly did you expect, what real thing do I have to say to you?

For instance, that I should pay for the steak I ate, he says, it was easier for you to pay yourself than to say one straightforward thing to me, don't think I didn't notice, here, he says, taking a bill out of his wallet and handing it to me, I open myself up to you as I am, for better or worse, and you lock yourself up, what are you hiding? Tell me; apparently you have so much to hide that you don't open even a crack, and I immediately defend myself, I'm not hiding anything, these blind dates just aren't for me. Oh please, you think I like them? he says, you think anyone likes them? It's torture for everyone, but still we go on, unwilling to give up on the small chance that maybe this time it will work and make up for everything we've been through. You're not right for me, Ella, and nevertheless I care about you, and I'm telling you, you're just at the beginning of the road, and the road gets more and more unpleasant. You should know what's ahead of you, you have to play the game because it's your only chance of finding somebody. I know you didn't like me, but maybe everyone you meet from now on will be worse than me; I, for instance, always long for my previous date, so anyway, that's it, he shrugs, goodnight, and he hurries off on his skinny legs and disappears into a black jeep parked on the pavement, almost blocking the entrance to the cafe.

Embarrassed and surprised I watch him, unconsciously crumpling the bill he thrust into my hand, should I call him back, try to start again from the beginning, no, that's not what this evening was meant for, and I sit down on the wet stone wall on the other side of the road, opposite the cafe, exactly opposite the birthday table, watching them like a silent movie, Yotam's triumphant procession from his father's lap to the laps of his grandfather and grandmother, his sister's face turning green with envy, the words just addressed to me fall to my feet, irritating like an itch, which I try to ignore, shoving my hands into my coat pockets, determined to take full advantage of the melancholy opportunity that has come my way, to observe the behavior of a family intact, like on a good day at the zoo when the animals make an appearance instead of hiding away in their caves unseen, it isn't potshards I'm examining now, but human beings, who will decompose long before the dishes from which they are eating their meal.

The well-groomed grandmother with her silvery bob, the slightly clumsy grandfather with the relaxed expression on his face, judging by their complexions they must be Michal's parents; where are his parents, is he an orphan; and mainly I keep my eyes on him, his hard yet fragile looking profile, now he notices his daughter's frustration and offers her his lap, how proudly and defiantly she beams as she sits there with his arms around her, as if she has been crowned, his dark lips on the honey colored hair swept into a bun on her head, now she whispers something in his ear and they both smile, the secrets of a pretty little girl in a purple sweater. Let me hear too, a childish jealousy grips me as if I am her age, and to my embarrassment it is not his wife I envy, but his daughter, for as I watch this free and easy scene, in which little girls naturally embrace their fathers, I am suddenly struck by a feeling of loss as powerful as a blow, overshadowing the pain of the separation, the pain of Gili's future birthdays. My private pain from the days before I had a child opens a great pit before me, as if this is what I need now, not a mate, not a complete family, but a father who will offer me his lap, and I stand up and wander down the pavement on legs stiff with cold, between piles of snow that have turned to slippery patches of filth, looking for new angles of approach. My eyes focus now on Michal, the way her hair is brushed back emphasizes her shapely features, which have grown heavier of late, she looks a little older than her husband, his thinness emphasizes her fullness, her hands are busy with Yotam's plate, no doubt cutting the schnitzel into squares, like all the other mothers, now she speaks to her husband; what is she saying to him, why doesn't he answer her; they are sitting opposite each other, the chair vacated by the little girl stands between them and nobody moves to sit there, but now he answers her and she smiles briefly, pouts her lips, a fork loaded with food I can't identify makes its way from his plate to her mouth, and she chews carefully, nods her head, apparently in confirmation of the quality of the dish, and what do you think of pesto with *hamin*, ladies and gentlemen, would you, too, be outraged to suddenly encounter pesto in your *hamin*?

One of them is apparently not satisfied, for their plates are changing hands. All night long she will digest his dish and he will digest hers, together in the same bed, is this the sign of a successful marriage; how much pride there was in her voice when she introduced her husband to me, you haven't met, she stated, you'd be surprised, there are things you don't know. This mesmerizing spectacle I'm watching gives rise to a sudden hostility, as mysterious and incomprehensible to me as if I were a visitor from far away, examining the ways of the natives, and here is an astonishing discovery, it appears that they are arranged by families, and I, who up until a few months ago was exactly like them, stare in amazement at the phenomenon. What is it that connects two strangers to each other until they turn into a family, what keeps them together, what do they know about each other and what will they never know, what dies between them and what flourishes, what prevents him from leaving the laden table now and joining me, sitting here next to me on the wet wall like a pair of penniless hobos, what can the stranger peeping through the window learn about them, would anyone seeing us in this same cafe only a few months ago, when I came back from the last conference and the fridge was empty and we decided to eat out, and Gili brought the present I had just taken out of my suitcase, would it have occurred to this stranger that the family entering the cafe, the tall clumsy father and the mother whose head barely reached his shoulder and the delicate child hugging a red racing car in his arms, that this family was about to perish? No, no one would have guessed that the little woman with the black hair and white face and red-painted lips was at this very moment informing the father sitting opposite her that she had made up her mind to leave him, a decision she had come to when she was far away from them both, a grave and final, dire and harrowing decision, which she would regret before long, while the child played with his new car, pressing the buttons of the remote control, intoxicated by his total power over its movements.

You're joking, he said, you can't be serious, accompanying his words with a dry cough, and I said, why, why can't I be, because it isn't convenient for you? Well let me tell you it's convenient for me, you have no idea how happy I was without you over there, I didn't miss you for a single second, I want to be free, Amnon, free from you, and he said, tell me something, are you out of your mind? You go away for a week and, because you don't miss me, you decide to break up? You don't make a decision like that from one day to the next, what exactly happened there, tell me, did you fall in love with someone?

Fall in love? I sneered, I don't need to be in love in order to leave you, I don't need to have some man waiting for me, you don't get it, I'm unhappy enough with you to want to leave you, I'm simply sick of you, sick of our fights, I have no desire to go on living like this, and he shook his head in stunned disbelief that could surely be seen through the window, you're out of your mind, Ella, I won't do it, I won't let you ruin our lives, and what about Gili, huh, have you thought about him at all? He asked, looking at the child driving his car around the cafe, his joyful shrieks snaking like flames between the tables, and I said, what about Gili? I'm glad you mentioned Gili, you think it's healthy for him to hear us fighting, healthy for him to absorb our hostility? It's poison, we're poisoning ourselves and our child, and it's time to put an end to it, I want my child to breathe healthy air, I don't want him to live in fear of the next fight like I did, so if the only way is to separate between us, that's what we'll do, don't you see that we have no choice?

You don't know what you're talking about, he said, I went through it with my parents, as opposed to you, I know what divorce means, and I'm telling you that people have to exhaust all options before deciding to separate, and I snap, I don't know what I'm talking about? Sure, that's what you always say, when I started my research on Thera, too, you said I didn't know what I was talking about, and now I'm being invited to conferences all over the world to lecture on my research, and he made a face, that still doesn't mean that your ridiculous thesis is worth anything, I still think it's nonsense, but I haven't got a problem with it, go on developing your fairytales if it gives you pleasure and brings you fame, but as far as your plans for divorce are concerned, I suggest you forget about them. All of a sudden she has to get divorced, he appeals to an imaginary audience, perhaps to someone sitting like I am now on this wall, which gave off the dry heat of the beginning of summer, suddenly the spoiled little girl has to get a divorce, she's bored with her life, she doesn't like being criticized, so she decided to get herself a little divorce and all her problems will be solved.

Lower your voice, I whisper, you want Gili to hear? And he says mockingly, oh, so you intend to do it without him knowing? Very clever, Ella, that's really a brilliant move, and I said, thank you very much, really, after we've settled things between us we'll tell him, let him enjoy his present now, and he slammed his full cup of coffee on the table, could anyone sitting outside have heard the thud, seen the boiling coffee splash onto his bare arm, seen him waving his thick, sickening finger at me, thrusting it into my face, I'm warning you that this step is irreversible, just like an archeological excavation, if you still remember what that is, you see more airports than excavations now. If you break up our family, you'll never be able to put it back together again, even if there's nothing in the world you want more, and even though I was sitting next to him then it seemed that I couldn't hear his words, just as I can't hear the sounds of the dying birthday party now. Through a glass wall I contemplated him, staring in bemusement at his finger waving at me, and nevertheless we still appeared to behave like a family, because when the bill arrived we didn't hesitate, looking at each other to see who would take out his wallet first, and when we left, we didn't wonder who would accompany whom, but went home together, and on the way, exactly where I'm standing now, the new racing car slipped from Gili's hands and started rolling proudly down the hill, as if it was a real car like all the others on the road, and Amnon yelled, what's the matter with you, can't you take care of the presents we buy you? You'll never get another present! And Gili began to bawl, his mouth wide open and his baby teeth wobbling in his gums. Hovering on the edge of the pavement we watched in suspense as the red toy car careened down the hill, its plastic driver sitting at the wheel with a helmet on his head and a determined smile on his face, waiting for the moment when the road was clear of traffic and we could rescue it, almost ready to risk our lives in the attempt, while Gili kicked and screamed, my present, my present, I want my present, as it raced downhill, oblivious of the bus advancing toward it, throwing itself gaily against its wheels, the driver's crushed plastic smile, my overwhelming grief, Amnon's scolding, Gili's weeping, the way he clung to the remote control still in his hand, pressing its buttons again and again as if trying to regain the intoxication of power, the pleasure of absolute control he had experienced only a few moments before, his snippet of joy.

Chapter eleven

The wing of an airplane, embedded in the ground like a fearsome spade, glitters in the radiance of the prematurely setting sun, sharpening the primal fear of being airborne. Next to the wing lays a long line of deformed planes, dejected as though they had never sailed the skies. If he were next to me now, I would say to him, look, an airplane hospital, and the words would submerge into his eyes, embed themselves in the brownish green, we've got the same eyes, he boasts, our only likeness. We're still on the same plot of earth, he and I, but only for a moment, his small silhouette will shrink before me like the pupils of a cat, were he here at the foot of the plane, waving goodbye during takeoff, I would no longer see his hand, or him, I'm skyward bound and he's planted on the ground I have left behind, his little feet in last year's sneakers, his wild nails poking into the fabric of his socks, the distance growing, stretching and gaping.

The coastal plain is spread out beneath me like a narrow quilt blanket, awaiting a blow, and its city, leaning on the sea, suddenly seems neat and tidy, cut into geometrical shapes that can only be distinguished from above, a methodical procession of cars moves below me, threatening in its orderliness, the hooting, the curses, the loud music and the snatches of conversation are all inaudible, the miniature cars advance in the silence of an unending funeral procession, look, a dark cloud devours the city lights, leading the heavy silver bird out to sea, how brief are our partings.

Under my booted feet the engine roars, powerful and terrifying, a beast of prey imprisoned in the belly of the plane, and all the time at my side the silver wing reminds me of its twin, the one planted in the ground. The tune of the wind smashes against its cold body, if he were here he would say, look, a ship of clouds sailing in the sky, let's jump out of the plane and sail in the ship, as long as we stay together, he would say. Look, everything's upside down, I'm taller than the clouds, and his delicate voice would tremble with the burden of the onerous and unnecessary victory.

Are you feeling all right? A young flight attendant bends over me, her black hair combed back, her eyes heavily made up, and I raise my head, could I have a glass of water? Nausea gathers around my throat like a constricting collar, and she hovers over me, offers me a slice of lemon, a can of Coke, I have turned into their baby, the flight attendants are at least ten years younger than I am, and their light, official concern touches my heart as if it were personal. I was their age when I married Amnon, so proud of my achievement, capturing this confirmed bachelor, no longer young, who walked the corridors of the university with a gaggle of eager young students, was I more proud than in love? He's a difficult man, my mother would say occasionally, shaking her head, much like your father, and I would protest indignantly, how can you compare them, Amnon is much warmer, much less selfish, and she would say, really? shaking her head back and forth in disbelief.

Soft teddy bears made of whipped cream storm the sides of the plane, little whipped cream elephants, whipped cream bunnies turning pink, their flesh ripped by the plane's advance, blurring the difference between country and country, between mountain and cloud, between sleep and wakefulness, between childhood and adulthood, and it seems that the cord connecting me to the life I left behind, a bloody twisted fleshy cord, is being stretched across the length of the sky, soon to snap as I enter the no man's land where I detach from my life and my life detaches from me, separated as the sea is from the land.

The young man at my side chews his dinner, his face as smooth as a boy's, his hair long and flowing, we haven't exchanged a word, and yet it seems that there is a kind of intimacy between us as we eat the same food, salami, smoked salmon, a sweet roll, the same tastes mingling in our mouths, and even the knowledge that this uncertain intimacy is shared by dozens of other passengers does nothing to defuse the feeling. When he sips his wine he raises his glass to me in a little gesture and I respond with a surprised blink. Once, when I was the age of the flight attendants, a gesture of that kind would have been enough to ignite the miraculous process in which the galloping horses of the imagination overtake reality, anointing the long-haired youth with all the necessary charm, but now, supposing he spoke to me, what would I say, am I available, who is it that shackles me with this belated, superfluous loyalty, is it the child, is it the past, is there any way back to that old existence. I wanted to be a girl again, that's what I wanted, a bitter mocking smile crosses my lips and he sees it and smiles at me over the black, mysterious land crouching beneath us, panting like an animal.

This trip is a gift from heaven, Dina said, go, refresh yourself, meet people, and I had forgotten all about it, the dates had been set so long ago, the schedule printed, the hotel booked. I will always be amazed by the course of time, like a giant plough it advances, grinding rocks on its way, swallowing mountains, spewing out continents, the heaviest sorrow will not stop it, the wildest joy will not block its path, and I remember that I told Amnon then, why don't we go, the three of us, and he replied, why don't we go, the two of us, and now I am going alone, as it will always be from now on. Like the soft, furry clouds crashing into the windows, my longings have changed shape, no longer the yearning for the fawning infant whose presence filled me with complete serenity, but for the child who, in any case, is not as close as he used to be, whose new room I hardly know, whose new toys I have never seen, whose life has been cut in half, and the unknown half hovers around his head like a jagged halo that I have to shoo away every time I bend down to kiss his head, like a fly or a wasp, and even when he is asleep in his bed, as in days gone by, or sitting in the bath surrounded by mounds of foam, or playing on the carpet in the living room, he is accompanied by this existence over which I have no control, which will always be alien to me, where I will always be unwanted, and perhaps this is why the longings attack me so fiercely over the empty dinner tray, because it is suddenly clear to me that what I really miss will not be restored to me upon return, for I will always miss him, the child he was before our separation, softer, more angelic, more innocent, more protected, more happy.

We race behind the evening sun like horsemen who will never tire, accompanying a sunset that will never end, thousands of sheep drowning in the sea beneath our feet, trembling, turning blue, their curly fleece slowly soaking up the color and salinity of the sea. Look, I would have said to him, the desert of the sky is on fire, and only the moon that suddenly pops up at the window, surprising in its solidity, looks exactly as it does on earth, from our balcony in Jerusalem, and I know that the pale blue fleece of the clouds is hiding Thera from me now, the hollow island, shaped like a crescent moon, which erupted in an explosion that shocked the ancient world, its reverberations reaching all the way to distant Egypt, flooding cities and islands, burying beneath it the magical kingdom in the heart of the Mediterranean Sea, a palace dizzying in its splendor, with its hundreds of rooms, its spectacular frescoes, its seashell drawings of octopuses and dolphins, winged cherubs, painted figures escorting the guests from room to room, and among them the Parisian, with her cold, haughty gaze, as if she knew she would endure for thousands of years.

Come with me to Thera, he said, I have to show you Akrotiri, and have you seen the palace at Knossus? And right then and there I knew that as soon as we got married we would go there, to the new Pompeii, but I couldn't know that while he wandered the black rocks, thrilled by the eerie beauty of the island, I would be horrified by the prints of nature's cruel hand, by the signs of disaster everywhere, by the sight of the island's pieces scattered over the sea like a dismembered body, with what was gone far more present than what remained. The crater of a volcano that had completely disappeared, flooded by the water of the sea, the gray shadows of the rivers of lava, the great sheets of basalt covering the layers of tuff, the sulfurous fumes bursting to the surface and coloring the ground yellow, and more than all these I was horrified by the dour determination of life clinging to the remains of the land, the hovels dug into the soft volcanic ash, and the village of Akrotiri in the southern part of the island, site of the ancient Minoan city that froze on the day of the disaster, without a single human skeleton inside it. Could they have sensed the danger and fled for their lives? When I stood there in front of the grave of the Greek archeologist who unearthed the remains of the city and was buried inside it, I felt a grief as profound as if he had been my father, but my new husband shook his head grimly, stunned and insulted by this bewildering outburst of grief, now of all times.

At night, airports look like cavernous garages, astonishingly similar to each other, grim, gray labyrinths, peering dourly at the throngs of people clasping their luggage as if it contains all the treasures of the deep blue sea. I, too, am dragging a light suitcase behind me, an official expression on my face, when I see a short man waving a sign with my name on it, a kind of silent one-man demonstration, and for a moment I am tempted to ignore him and the oppressive name he is brandishing, which is no longer my name, Ella Miller, to walk past him indifferently, to go into the town on my own, without an escort to whom I will have to be cordial. Thankfully, he, too, shows no interest in making conversation, satisfying himself with a slight smile and the usual ritual of divesting me of my suitcase, and already we are in the car collecting people coming from all over the world, all heading toward the conference in order to discuss an event that has no effect whatsoever on our lives today, which took place thousands of miles from here, and perhaps never took place at all.

I would always hurry to call him, to inform him of my safe arrival, describe the trip, ask about Gili, what he ate, when he went to bed, retying the slackened rope, gathering the three of us together again, but now there is nobody waiting for my report, and I put my clothes in the closet, inspect the small room, paneled with golden pine. Have you opened the blinds already? Amnon would ask me, open them and tell me what you see. His curiosity is always inflamed by new places, while she, he would say to his friends, pointing to me scornfully, she once went to a conference in Italy and for three days she didn't open the blinds in her room, she wasn't in the least bit interested in what you could see from the window, so now I'm opening the iron green shutters and I'll tell you what I see.

In the square opposite the Gothic cathedral there is constant commotion, despite the lateness of the hour, so different from the gloomy atmosphere in the streets of Jerusalem. Is it a holiday, a celebration?

Apparently not, it's life. A white-winged angel whose long robe hides the stilts that double his height walks around the square, so tall that the top of his head almost reaches my window, his face painted white, his eyes calm, radiating serenity and contentment. It seems that he truly and sincerely believes that he is an angel, and accordingly he wishes to transmit this belief to the tourists clustering around him, taking photographs of each other under his wings. If Gili were here he would run round him like a puppy, touch him, ask him for a wish, ask him to fly up to heaven right away and set things up from there; would he ask for his red racing car back, would he ask for his old life back.

In the middle of the square there are two dark-skinned statues seated on a bench, a man and a woman with wide eyes and frozen expressions, as soon as they are given a coin they come miraculously to life, stretch out their hands, make a deep, grateful bow, part their lips in a smile, but look how short the life granted by the coin is, again they take up their poses, their faces frozen, their eyes fixed. Behind them the cathedral stands in all its nocturnal beauty, its arches illuminated like exquisite embroidery worked over hundreds of years. How can stone be so soft, soft as cloth, like a royal velvet cape draped over the shoulders of the town, sending its spires up to the sky, and the pigeons, look at the pigeons gliding radiantly between the crosses, the electric light trapped in their bodies, and they cast it over the dark sky as if they were winged light bulbs, slowly and dreamily they float, as if sunk in a deep sleep, it seems as if they are about to fall, as if whoever's head they fall on will be forever blessed.

In the morning I stand opposite the wild, rounded homes, supple as the waves of the nearby sea, in constant motion, and it seems as if I am made of stone and they are soft as featherbeds, I am rooted to the spot and they are mobile, it seems that anything is possible, is this the secret the city is trying to whisper in my ear, do I love this whisper, do I love Barcelona, does Barcelona love me, and it seems that for these few days the answer is yes, this city and I love each other, for now.

When everybody goes to see the Sagrada Familia I stay in the room, preparing for my lecture, but when they return I make my way there almost stealthily, to the unfinished temple of expiation, which will probably not be finished during my lifetime, nor perhaps even during

Gili's lifetime, craning my neck along the stone flowing like waterfalls from the sky, growing like trees from the ground, and toward the pictures of the holy family – the mother and child in the middle, the child and his mother, the simplest of traditions, which requires no further evidence. Gaudi detested straight lines, the guide at my side explains in a tired voice, there are no straight lines in nature, he based himself only on forms that existed in nature, and she immediately goes on to talk about the death of the architect, who was run over by a tram right here as he stepped backwards, holding his plans for the building that, within a few days, would become his tomb, looking up at its spires, an anonymous old man, shabbily dressed, only two days later was he identified. He is buried here, in a crypt in the depths of the church, just like that Greek archeologist in Thera, the unearthing of a building is actually not so different from the construction of it, and, as I did then, I sigh at the sight, only this time it isn't Amnon shaking his head at my side, but hundreds of noisy tourists. Why are they putting so much effort into completing the building, says someone behind me in Hebrew, they should have left it unfinished, like a symbol of everything we leave unfinished in our lives, and I look around for the speaker, who has disappeared into the crowd, holding a small child by the hand. If Gili were here, perhaps he would say, Gaudi is still building this palace from heaven, at night, when nobody sees.

Only a few months ago we met at another conference, in another city, on the banks of a gray river, like a traveling circus we circulate with our wares, which are hardly ever renewed, and it seems that a lifetime lies between these two journeys, from embryo to old age and back again. I wonder about my colleagues, they have not changed at all, calmly they crack the shells of their eggs at breakfast in the yellow painted underground hall, or stand in line for omelets with various additions, calmly they ask about Amnon, most of them know him well, for in the past he was a frequent participant in academic conferences, but lately the invitations have diminished, the publications no longer forthcoming. At first they were surprised to see my name on the program and not his, to see me and not him, their eyes sought him at my side, and their surprise seemed to echo my own; how had this reversal come about, when we met he was at his peak and I just starting out, was it there, in Thera, that our lives began to lurch off course; and I say nothing about our separation, taking advantage of the decorous, weather-appropriate behavior, where no one hurries to tighten the bonds of tenuous acquaintanceships, and only on the last day, after the lecture, when suitcases are already packed, is the distance between people shortened, the pleasantries turning into a true reluctance to part, and we set out to sail in the rain, receding from the colorful city whose back grays when you see it from the sea. Back out on the wide elegant avenues, making our way between the street musicians, the beggars, the flower vendors selling cheap romance, I feel a recurring sorrow for my own city, whose stones have not yet learned the secret of softness, whose soul is incapable of enjoying such carefree contentment.

On the flight home I miss Thera again, its narrow, broken smile, abruptly waking to the sound of snores from all sides, scores of people slumped in their seats at this afternoon hour as if they have never desired anything, leaning against each other as we pass over the glowing golden sea. A thin, dark girl is dozing at my side, her face pointed intently at me but her eyes closed, the short-haired head of a man resting in her lap, as if they have made a pact to drink together from the poisoned cup, in love to the death, will they come to life if I offer them a coin. We, too, would return from our trips like this, enjoying at least the intimacy that permits us to use each other's bodies as a pillow, a mattress, a support, the body that no longer tempts or surprises is at least convenient, and yet in recent years our return was accompanied by the sourness of disappointment, annoyance and resentment, a chronic failure, unable to fan the cold embers heaped between us, unable to bring down the wall; was it for this that we left our child at home, wasted time and money, in order to fight in Istanbul, in Berlin, in Rome.

With the same suddenness that it disappeared, it appears, the narrow, checkered coastal plain, illuminated in a glaring summer light, which seems strange even for this part of the world, unless three months and not three days have passed since I left, and the seasons have changed, and the sun has already seared the fields and torn away their emerald suits. Looking with a strange excitement at the approaching view, it seems to me that it is still possible to choose, that it is still possible to set my foot in a completely different way on the ground, for the return is always accompanied by an illusion of transformation, of calm, confidence and trust, planes taking off on time and landing safely, missions accomplished, new acquaintances added to my life, and it seems that the sky is no longer frightening and therefore the ground, supine beneath it,is less threatening too.

A feeling of relief coupled with a mild indifference and a few notes of excitement, all these accompanied me then too, when I returned from my previous trip a few months ago, the tidings of separation already climbing up my throat, and now I am coming back without any tidings, only a fresh curiosity sprouting among the gloomy folds of these last months, what actually lies in store for me, for my life? Drowsily we stumble from the plane, swaying a little, the tremor of the engine still in our feet, accompanying us on the familiar route, and to my surprise I am actually pleased that this time there is no one waiting for me outside the arrivals hall. They would always be standing there, exhausted by the effort to get here in time, Gili frighteningly high on his father's shoulders, waving to me, multi-limbed as an octopus, the joy of meeting quickly dissolving and the tension immediately rising, as both of them try to attract my attention and I am already exhausted, trying to compensate Gili for my absence, to compensate Amnon for being invited to a conference again when he was not invited, to minimize the importance of the event, to hide my wholehearted delight at the sight of the child as opposed to my reservations about him.

It suits me this time to adjust myself at my leisure, to soften the longings, which are no longer oppressive, no, this isn't loneliness, it's freedom, and in the taxi I call Amnon, his voice reserved and formal since the separation, and he says in mild surprise, Ella, you're back, as if I've gone somewhere you don't come back from, and this time he doesn't ask me how the lecture went and who I met and what I saw from the window, both of us sparing with words as though they cost more than we could afford.

Will you bring Gili to me or should I pick him up at your place? I ask, I'll be home in an hour, I bought him a racing car with a remote control like the one that got run over, I add proudly, as if I have discovered a magic formula for restoring the past, and he says, but he isn't here now, he's at Yotam's, I thought you would be back later, and you know I teach today, he adds, they live near you, you can pick him up there, and

I interrupt him, surprised, yes I know where they live, I'll pick him up there in a little while. If you get there too early he won't want to leave, Amnon says, pick him up in the evening, as usual, and I ignore the advice, and ask carefully, did you guys get along, the two of you? as if they were still my two men, and he replies, we always get along, omitting the words, without you, and I fill in the blanks, without you, and bring the conversation quickly to a close. I give the driver the new address as if I have moved in the interim, and I live there, in the grand, restored building opposite the playground, where I will get out of the taxi with my light, wheeled suitcase with the gleaming red racing car, the twin of the one that rushed so gaily to its death, as if sacrificing itself in a noble cause.

Strange, I tried so hard to coax him to go back and play with Yotam, and he refused, and now it happens precisely when I'm not there, and the thought of the straight backed man with the rigidly carved face and the sunken eyes, who is at this moment under the same roof as my child, gives rise in me to an agreeable excitement, which merges with the joy of coming home to Gili, and the vivid sights of the trip, and mainly with the overwhelming relief, as if I have just been rescued from captivity, mourning and regret and sorrow were my captors, and I have taken advantage of a moment's distraction on their part to escape, adopting a false identity, a convincing disguise, in the hope that they will never manage to track me down.

These hills will never be truly verdant, their green will always be a fraudulent shade of pale, faltering, every winter the vegetation is commanded to cover the scars of the summer fires, and the moment they fulfill their task the fires start to burn again. I open the window, the warm darkness is confusing, a hot desert wind blows into my surprised face, if it is summer why has the sun set so early, and if it is already dark why is it so hot, something seems to have disrupted the familiar laws, and the disruption is actually exhilarating, turning the drive on the hilly road into an adventure. How remote Jerusalem was, the access road eternally preserving its seclusion, did all those who swore by its name realize how modest it was in dimension if not in ambition, an impoverished oriental market town steeped in illusions of grandeur, secluded behind walls and gates, surrounded by the sparse habitations of nomadic shepherds, steep rocky hills, secretly cultivating its tales of heroism and exclusivity.

Next to the playground I step out of the taxi, dressed in the formal suit I wore last night for my lecture, a short brown skirt and a white silk blouse under a matching jacket. We sat till morning in a pub on the beach and from there I hurried to the airport without having time to change my clothes, like an elegant foreign tourist I cross the road, a passing visitor from a distant land, who has left a precious deposit here that she will collect and then immediately depart. As I climb the wide marble stairs, trying to catch my breath, fix my hair, the wish grows more defined, to see him, to see the dark eyes blooming under the thick brows, the expressive lips, to be seen by him as I am now.

Discordant voices leap into the posh stairwell, growing louder as I approach their door, are they really coming from there, I find it hard to believe, from that stylish apartment with the golden parquet floor and the leather sofa and the bowl of red pears. I approach quietly, a tall steel door separates me from them, and I knock loudly but they don't hear, how can they hear while they spray each other with bile, a thunderstorm rages inside the house, and I knock again, then try the doorbell, and again there is no answer. A cold prickly suspense climbs from my feet, gripping my body like barbed wire, as if I were a child and these people were my parents fighting early in the morning, would they separate forever this time, and I wait in dread for the moment that always comes, a final yell is hurled and my father leaves the house slamming the door behind him, and then she runs to me, a wild-haired invader in my bed, weeping in my arms.

As if I were their child, trapped in a terrible impotence, mine and theirs, I try to catch isolated words, bloody hunks of insult and anger, I don't believe you, I hear Michal's voice, as loud as if she is shouting into my ear, surprisingly coarse, I know you're lying, I don't believe a single word you say, and then his voice, restrained yet cold and venomous, I'm sick of your pathological suspicion, you hear? I'm sick of it, I'm not prepared to live like this, you're suffocating me, and she screams, so get out of here if you're sick of me, I don't want to see you ever again, you promised me it wouldn't happen, you promised me, and he snaps, I kept all my promises, what more do you want from me? I'm not responsible for everything in your twisted head. Aha, so it's all in my head? Are you trying to say I'm crazy? Is that what you want? Then let me tell you that this time it isn't going to work, I have proof, and suddenly I blush as if I have been accused, my cheeks aflame, I stand opposite the gray painted steel door and wonder what to do, afraid the door will suddenly be flung open in a rage and I will be discovered, a lowly spy, an expression of embarrassing satisfaction on my face, gloating over the downfall of all the couples who seem so happy behind the cafe windows, like we ourselves once did. I go quietly downstairs, holding the suitcase in the air so as not to make a noise, leaning on the hedge at the entrance to the building, considering my next step.

What should I do, perhaps I should wait here for a few minutes and then call them, they're bound to hear the phone ring, and while I go upstairs they'll have time to compose themselves; I have to get Gili out of there, from the moment they failed to open the door my longings for him flared up, and, with them, my anger at these near strangers preventing my reunion with my son. What is he doing now, is he sitting miserably in Yotam's room, the two of them listening tensely, or perhaps they gave them a noisy video to watch, like we used to do, bewitching the child in front of the screen so that we could argue to our heart's content. For a moment the anger gives way to gleeful pity, so he's cheating on her, poor thing, and she's suffocating him, which is too general an accusation for me to identify with at the moment, her side is more compelling, more credible, and mainly I feel comfortable on my own family-less side. Who needs the commotion of a shared life, I contemplate with a new feeling of superiority, a garbage dump of veiled and unveiled insults, a collection of petty crimes against humanity. I take my cell phone out of my bag, Oded and Michal Sheffer, I say into the phone, tasting on my tongue the solid and respectable names, what have they to do with the abuse being hurled at this moment in the elegant apartment, so loudly that it silences the ringing of the telephone, which nobody answers.

An unexpected obstacle has risen between us, my son; when will I finally see you, are you frightened, are you sad, are you surprised to discover that failure festers in other houses too, not only in ours, and I dial again, I won't stop until they answer me, but then a door slams with a loud bang, and I drag the suitcase behind me into the bushes and wait there in silence until I see his slender figure hurrying out of the building, as if he is being pursued, but in the street he pauses, stares into space, his eyes enlarged by the rings surrounding them, his lips clenched, dressed in a gray wool sweater and light corduroy pants, a big backpack on his back. I look at him and hear myself saying, Oded, and at the same moment I realize that this is the first time I have called him by his name.

His distracted, straying gaze focuses on my stumbling steps as I extricate myself from my hiding place, a few thorny twigs are stuck to my hair, and I pull them off in embarrassment. I just went up to your place to get Gili, I try to explain, you didn't hear me but I heard you, and he makes a face, wipes the sweat off his brow, are his hands really shaking? I can't stand it anymore, he says in a rush, blurting out the words as if afraid he might regret them, it's getting worse every day, and I draw closer to him, surprised by his frankness, where are you going? I ask, and he says, I haven't decided yet, and I surprise myself too, still excited by the exotic strangeness of the city, his strangeness, my own strangeness in my life, you want to get something to drink? I ask, and to my surprise he says, yes, why not?

Why not? I could give you a number of reasons why not, I think to myself, but, at the moment, all that exists between us is the yes, and so we set out side by side like a couple embarking on a long journey, after hours of careful packing, she dragging a suitcase and he carrying a backpack, and nobody would have believed that we barely knew each other, that my suitcase had never before met his backpack.

Let's go to the Cancan, I suggest as we stand by the busy road, and he says yes again, why not? It seems that in one chance moment he has put his life in my hands, and even if I said, let's go to India, or let's make love, or let's get married, he would have said, yes, why not, and if not to me he would have said the same thing to somebody else, but I was the one lying in wait for him downstairs, my face was the first face he saw when he came out of his house, and we cross the road and enter the neighborhood cafe we both know well. Here through the window I watched you on the night of the birthday party, here my envy burned along the wet street, between the heaps of grimy snow, leapt on the curb like a flame, and I lead him to the corner table where they sat then, the complete family, like you sometimes see on a good day at the zoo, a lion, a lioness and their two cubs, exposed to everyone's inquisitiveness. He sits opposite me, embarrassed and upset with the hump of a pack on his back. I stand up and remove it from his shoulders like the schoolbag from Gili's narrow back, pull it down his arms and set it down beside my suitcase, and to my surprise it is hard and heavy, and I ask, what do you have in there, stones? And he says, albums, and I begin to laugh, that's what you took with you, albums? Not a change of clothes and a toothbrush? And to my delight he joins in my laughter, it was a spontaneous decision, I didn't have a clue what you take when you're leaving home, I looked around and thought what do I love here, what would I save from a fire.

Show them to me, I say, and he asks, are you really interested, or are you afraid we won't have anything to talk about? And I admit, both, and he reaches for the backpack and takes out five thick volumes, like the five books of the Pentateuch, and stacks them on the table between us, and when the waitress arrives we glance at the menu, under her scrutiny, and like her I wait to hear what he orders, for this will dictate the nature of the meeting, and when he orders a double whiskey and a plate of toast and spreads, I breathe a sigh of relief, it isn't the business meal recommended for all hours of the day, which would have promised a longer meeting, but it isn't a single shot of espresso either. Will you share the toast with me, he asks when I order only a drink, and I nod immediately, as if I have never had such a generous offer, to share the toast with him, the cold water with lemon, the double whiskey and the triple sorrow, the fear, the shock, the loss, to share them with him! To be part of him, part of his life, to dissect my life before his eyes, to slice it into pieces, even if you had ordered a bloody steak I would have shared it with you, even if you had ordered nothing I would have shared the nothingness with you. The rich light shining on our faces traps two people, virtual strangers, in its radiant hoop, refining their movements, smoothing their skin, softening their hair, spiking their blood with an elixir of yearning, transforming every ordinary word that comes out of their mouths into a code that has the power to reveal the most exquisite of feelings, and when I look at him, at the lean man sitting opposite me in the gray sweater, his hair covering his forehead, his face pale and agitated, I know that this is the short precious time when the most terrible confessions will sound like an invitation to happiness, the harshest of blows will seem like pure pleasure, this is the short time when imagination slips past the sharp elbows of reality, the time when a single hour in a shabby cafe seems like the finger of God, and only these times are worth longing for because only they will bestow the faint glow of holiness on our lives, because if the miracle happened once it can happen again, lucid, staggering, accurate as a direct hit, bearing our full measure of grace.

Hesitantly he opens the first album, its stiff leather cover almost comes apart in his hands, and points with a slender finger to a picture of a bride and groom on their wedding day, the bride's face is plain and naïve. In spite of her obvious efforts she is neither pretty nor captivating, while the man is fair, handsome, the mocking smile crossing his face in an unpleasant diagonal, the gap between them so glaring that a child could see it. Your parents? I ask, and he nods silently, and I ask, are they still alive? He says, alive? They were never alive, and I look at him in surprise, afraid to cross the line from interest to prying, watching his expression as he studies the picture as if he hasn't come across it for many years. Look, they're so young here, he says at last, they haven't got a clue about what's in store for them.

What was in store for them? I ask, and he says, hell, he expected her to take care of him, she didn't even know that he was ill, and I ask, ill how? And he says, mentally, and I press, really ill? Was he institutionalized? And he says, yes, sure, in and out, and I go on looking wonderingly at their miserable pictures, on the face of it what did I have to do with them, he himself was still a complete stranger to me, and nevertheless I am drawn to their story as if it were capable of shedding light on my own.

Here's the father at a family affair, glittering in his cold complexion, a beautiful child in a white shirt and dark pants leaning on his knees and crying, and I ask, is this you? Why were you crying? and he smiles, that was my main occupation in those days, crying, and I look at the delicate face, the little fist hiding the eye, the mouth turned down in a wail I can almost hear. Why? I ask, and he repeats, why? glances at the picture again, as if expecting the little boy to provide the answer, but then says in a monotonous voice, as if he has already told the story dozens of times, what else could I do, my father didn't function at all, my mother more or less looked after our physical needs but emotionally she wasn't available, I think she was afraid that we weren't normal either, my sister and I, she was suspicious because we had his blood running through our veins.

What does that mean, I press him, didn't she take care of you? and he says, barely, she was afraid of growing attached to us, as far as she was concerned we were tainted, we were part of the trap that he and his family had set for her, a simple Moroccan girl who had no idea of what she was getting into. I don't blame her anymore, he makes haste to add, today I can understand how much she suffered, but then it was hard, we had nothing to hold onto, you see, here he's already after a number of hospitalizations, he's unrecognizable, and I look at the heavy jaw, the dull gaze, through the shirt you can see a sagging stomach, there's nothing left of his good looks, and here's his son again, a few years older, looking at him with concern, dry-eyed this time, focused only on him, dark like his mother, handsome like his father.

Look at the way you look at him, as if you're his doctor, and he says, yes, I had no choice, I learned to recognize his mental state, when to keep my distance from him, when to sleep with my eyes open, at his best, there was no one as charming, but when he broke down he was treacherous. It was hell on earth, he sighs, his hand on his brow, as if it was from there he had just escaped, with his bag on his back, not from his own house, where he lived with his wife and children. Look, he says urgently, as if pointing out some passing sight, a bird on the window sill, a baby's smile, this is his last picture, and I look sadly at the ravaged face in the final picture, which actually shows surprising signs of animation, reminiscent of the first. What did he die of? I ask, and he says, of a disease normal people get, cancer, and he was so proud when he was diagnosed, as if it was proof that he was the same as everybody else, when he discovered that insanity was no protection from death, he was ready to give up the insanity, but by then it was already too late.

So it's because of him that you look for traces of blood, I remark, seeing him crouching, his back arched like a cat's about to drink from the water in the toilet bowl, and he says, apparently, and it's because of him I became a therapist too, even though I didn't manage to help him, and all this time we're drinking whiskey on the rocks, and nibbling toast with assorted spreads, over a single ceramic plate, our greasy, spicy fingers touching the old pages and almost touching each other, and I listen to his calm, measured voice, every now and then his tongue gets entangled in his teeth in an appealing speech impediment, his lips form the words slowly, as though he's painting with a brush held in his mouth, drawing out the last letters as if loathe to part from the words. This is not Amnon's torrent of words but a different flow, soft and painterly, in which I join without any hesitation, asking a brief question from time to time and obtaining a long answer, and I understand that it is only about that family he wants to talk, and only its pictures he will show me, not his present family, not about what happened within earshot only an hour ago, but I'm not fussy, because this time it's clear to me how precious and brief the time is, brief and precious, I repeat to myself when he gets up to go to the bathroom and I wait impatiently for his return; what do I care what we talk about as long as we're here, together, illuminated by the rich light glowing on our faces, refining our movements, smoothing our skin, diffusing our blood with an addictive drug of yearning, desire, transforming every word that comes out of our mouths into a code containing the most exquisite of feelings; and when he returns and sits down opposite me, the sheet of transparent plastic stretched over the cafe courtyard suddenly groans because all of a sudden the rain comes pelting down, the unusual winter *hamsin* has broken over our heads, and Oded raises his face from the albums, looks around him in surprise; I didn't take a coat, he remembers, I wonder what that means, that I left home in the middle of winter without a coat.

Perhaps it means that you left in order to return, I suggest, and he looks at me intently as if seeking the answer on my face. No, he sighs, and his sigh draws out the short word until it spreads over his lips like a wine stain on a tablecloth, I'm not going back, and I move closer to him, my hand almost touches the gray sleeve, a poignant domestic smell of laundry detergent rises from it, listen, Oded, I say quickly, it's really absurd for me to give you advice, we don't even know each other, and you're the psychiatrist here, but I have to warn you, perhaps the only reason I'm here is to warn you, you have no idea how hard it is to break up a family, until you go through it yourself you don't understand anything, it shakes the foundations, it leaves you stunned with sorrow, believe me, I've just been through it, I don't recommend it to anyone, unless you've got really good reason. He nods his head and goes on nodding even after

I fall silent, what in your opinion are really justified reasons, he asks with interest, and I wonder if he wants to test me or himself.

If the relations are so bad that it harms the children, I say, if it's clear to you that you've made every effort to save the relationship, if you're miserable together and you haven't had a good moment for years, or if you have a meaningful relationship with another woman, and you're convinced that with her it will be different, these are issues that have to be examined over time; okay, now I'm being ridiculous, I say, falling silent in embarrassment, look at me, handing out advice to psychiatrists. He smiles carefully, don't make any mistake about it, Ella, you're not the ridiculous one here, I am, and then he brings the glass to his lips, takes a slow sip and lets the alcohol linger in his mouth, as if measuring its concentration, good, he says, I'm under the impression that I have justified reasons, according to your criteria too, and I immediately lower my eyes, apparently it's the last reason I listed, he's got someone else and he's leaving for her, Michal's right, he's cheating on her, and for a moment I feel as if he's betraying me too, the flame that burned between us on the corner table, the sweet frisson tingling the skin. Soon he'll return his five ancient albums to his backpack and go to her and start a new family with her, and perhaps I'll even get to see her at his side at the first grade end-of-the-year party, if not before then, at the class Passover *seder,* and he watches my withdrawal with interest, where are you coming back from? he asks, and I say, a conference in Barcelona, and he asks, an archeological conference? What was the subject? and I am surprised that he knows more about me that I happened to tell him. The exodus from Egypt, I say, and he quotes from the Passover *Haggada,* you will narrate the exodus from Egypt until the recitation of the morning prayers, and I giggle, something like that. My face burns with the sting of the lost opportunity and I can't look at him, I lower my eyes to the blue ceramic plate, a few red pimento flowers decorate it, emphasizing its emptiness, the uncertainty torments me, how am I going to attain a clearer understanding of his situation.

Do these kinds of things happen a lot, fights? I try indirectly, and he surprises me again with his frankness, much too often she keeps getting suspicious, she makes up her mind I'm seeing someone and makes terrible scenes, in front of the children too, you don't want to know, he sighs, and I can't restrain myself any longer, even though I am afraid of the clear answer emerging from his lips. So, are you seeing someone? I ask in a weak, almost inaudible voice, and he says, is that your phone ringing all the time or is it coming from the next table? And I rummage in my bag where the cell phone is shrieking its bird-ring chirp, ten unanswered calls, it announces dryly, and immediately shrieks again, and I hear Amnon's voice, where are you? Do you know what time it is? Gili's been waiting for you at Yotam's for hours, and I stammer, but you told me not to go there right away, and he says, right, but it's already ten at night, and you're not at home and not answering the phone and he's waiting, I thought you were dying to see him, he says, happily sticking a pin into the provocative maternal balloon I've been inflating in his face for years.

Of course I'm dying to see him, I say quickly, but something urgent came up and I forgot to look at my watch, I'm going there now, I add and switch off the phone, looking disconsolately at Oded. I completely forgot that Gili's still at your place, I tell him, I didn't notice how late it was, I have to run to get him, look what's happening here, I'm sitting with you instead of with him, and he's in your house instead of you, and I get up reluctantly, the disheveled remains of our families on the blue ceramic plate makes my heart contract, my feet are heavy and useless, how do I walk? I ask, and he replies seriously, you put one foot in front of the other, and I pick up my suitcase, should I give them a message? I ask, and he says, give Yotam a kiss for me.

How can I kiss him for you, I say, without you having kissed me first, and he gets up and pulls me to him, pushes the hair off my forehead and presses his warm lips to me in a gesture I already know, as if branding me with a stamp, the tattoo of a brief and precious time, and it feels as if my whole body is being swallowed up in his kiss, and I cling to his back, longing to stay with him until the lights go out, until the cafe closes, the slap of the lost opportunity makes my head spin, how brief and precious this evening was, never to be duplicated. Soon he will gather up his gloomy albums and go on his way and the magic will fade and disappear, never again will he be so confused and vulnerable, never will he be in such need of a stranger's ear, if only I could pretend that I hadn't come back yet, that the flight was postponed, if only I could stay with him tonight, before he starts his new life without me, and I stare at him as he sits down and takes a last sip of his drink, aren't you going back there? I ask, and he says, no, and his mouth remains provocatively open, exposing a patch of fleshy tongue.

Where will you go? I ask, and he says, I'll manage, don't worry, and I almost confess, it's myself I'm worrying about, not you, tightening my fist around the handle of my suitcase, my stiff joints creaking in protest, good night, I try to say in a steady voice, and he looks at me from below and nods in silence, how handsome he is with his clear cut features, the black rings around his eyes like the hollows in the earth that encircle flowers, and then I detach myself from him and go out into the roaring night without an umbrella or a coat, the rain pelting me, soaking me, and along with the cold rain, disappointment and frustration seep into my clothes, why couldn't I have spent the evening with him, only a few more hours. The suitcase dragging behind me fills with water, it seems to have doubled its weight, it's a wet present I'll bring my little boy tonight, a used present, dozens of raindrops have already played with it before him, and I try to stop a taxi, despite the shortness of the distance, but the taxis ignore my outstretched hand, the rain whips their white roofs and they flee from it like a herd of giant beasts, their yellow eyes blind.

When I reach the tall building, my teeth chattering from the sudden drop in the temperature, and climb the marble stairs again, there is an oppressive silence in the stairwell and my knocks are answered immediately, the door opening quickly this time, and Michal's face appears, bitter and downcast, her eyelids swollen and her skin patchy. Despite my curiosity I don't dwell on her appearance, for behind her on the leather sofa sits a long-limbed child, his arms crossed, his face as delicate and melancholy as that of an exiled prince, the insult on his face like the younger brother of the insult on hers, two victims of a meeting that lasted too long, that should never have taken place. When I hurry over to embrace him, he lowers his eyes, tears roll slowly down his cheeks, and Michal says in a loaded voice, as if trying to explain, he was terribly worried, we couldn't get hold of you, Yotam fell asleep long ago, she adds for some reason, and I fold him into my arms, I can't even say in my defense that I was already here before, a few hours ago, straight off the plane.

Forgive me, I'm really sorry, I say to them, I had an urgent meeting about work and I didn't notice the time, I missed you so much Gilili, I declare, but they both look at me skeptically, and I make haste to take my leave of her and go downstairs with him, his schoolbag dangling from my wet shoulder, and all the way home I ask him to forgive me, tell him how much I missed him, sing the praises of the red racing car I brought him, even bigger that its predecessor, but he refuses to take my outstretched hand. Down the stormy streets we walk, the gray waterlogged roads like old mattresses, each sunk in his own resentment, from time to time the sky is sliced in half by a blade of lightning, illuminating his face, the face of an exiled prince, which has suddenly lengthened, lost its boyish charm, and rain puddles lurk everywhere, but he takes no notice of my warnings, stepping into them, deliberately it seems, with his little feet in last year's sneakers.

I want to go to sleep now, Mommy, he says when we get home, refusing to wash, refusing even to open his present, in spite of my pleas, and I help him take off his damp clothes, my stiffly cold fingers mark his skin, my resentment at the missed opportunity swelling, its dimensions overshadowing his, and when he is already tucked in bed with the blanket up to his neck, he sends me his accusing look again and says quietly, as if resigned to his fate, I thought you decided to leave me too, just like you left Daddy.

Chapter twelve

What on earth gave you the idea that you, of all women, would be the one to offer him a home to replace his home, love to replace his wife's love, a child to replace his own children, you, half a woman, you, who wrecked your home and gained nothing in return, you, who were led to him weak and sick, what have you got to offer him, with his black eyes flowering in his face in the dim, calm light of dusk. Our aborted evening, when the temperature suddenly fell, our shared plate, a blue ceramic plate, the slices of toasted bread with assorted spreads, eggplant, mozzarella and tahini, he preferred the eggplant, you have to try it, he said. Our table, our rain, which collected on the sheet of plastic stretched above our heads and almost touched our hair, as if we were under the sea, our time, that little time we shared together, one single evening, which did not end as it should have ended, accompanies me, glowing and crumbling, like a gift given me and immediately taken away, like Gili's red car run over in front of him the day he received it, and this is all I wish to reclaim now, the continuation of that evening, and what I had within reach. I see us sitting there until the cafe closes, the plastic sheeting heavy with rain, groaning above our heads, I see us leaving together, a little drunk, free of all ties, would I have invited him to come home with me, would I have told him about the reservoir of sorrow inside me, accompanying me wherever I go, drowning the book of my life in its depths, obliterating its letters one by one, and as I speak everything vanishes, everything is made worthwhile, my suffering is not in vain, and as you listen to me you will know that your listening is the epitome of understanding, and your understanding encapsulates the amnesty and absolution I longed for, even though it was not you I sinned against, it seems that you have the power to pardon.

All night long he would sit on the armchair and I on the sofa, covered with a woolen blanket, a night not intended for sleep and not for kissing and not for lovemaking, but for words, and the howl of this night that never was, that was nipped in the bud, that waited for us till morning like an illuminated palace in the dark, that left only an elusive magic in my hands, accompanies me when I lie down and when I rise. I try to uncover its lost remains, to perceive its effect on the pale, agitated face opposite me. Every morning when I take Gili to school and every afternoon when I pick him up I step tensely into the schoolyard, searching for his face among the faces of the parents clustering at the gates in defiance of the security instructions, begrudging Amnon's days in case he gets to see him, he who has no need of it and no appreciation of the privilege. I look for her curls too, ready to make do with them for want of anything better, to learn from the expression on her face what's happening in his life. But neither she nor the boy make an appearance, as if they've all been wiped from the face of the earth, as if I made them up. Where are they, where have the three of them disappeared to, have they left town in the dead of night, did they go off the very next day on a sudden vacation in a desperate attempt to repair their relationship, or perhaps it's me who keeps on missing them. When I go into the classroom I look for Yotam first, my eyes brush past the face of my son, searching in vain for the child who looks like him, and only then they return to him in disappointment, a weak smile attempting to cover it up, how are you, my child, how was your day.

What's with Yotam, I haven't seen him in ages, I ask in a seemingly casual tone a few days later, and Gili says, Yotam? he's sick, and I seize on the new information, trying to interpret its meaning. Maybe you should call and ask him how he is, I suggest, and he says, later, and doesn't call, and I wonder how long a child's winter cold lasts, when will he be better, why don't they take better care of him, and I keep on searching, every morning and every afternoon, and it's a week before I see the two of them on the swings in the schoolyard, raucously swinging back and forth, steam coming out of their mouths, and I am happier to see Yotam than I am to see my son, he is the only piece I have succeeded in unearthing, and the value of the shard is equal to that of the pot it represents.

Excited, I go up to them and scan his face, seeking his father's face, seeking to understand the situation at home, has he returned to them, is he living with another woman, in a certain sense I am unbiased, for I lack even a clear desire, both possibilities are equally bad from my point of view, but not from his. I look at him thirstily, his father's black eyes are set in his face, underscoring its pallor, and I ask, how are you, sweetie, are you better? And he says, yes, but now Mommy's sick, and I drink in the news, hmmm, if Mommy's sick, Daddy will be here in a moment, walking through the green gate with the flowers painted on it, advancing toward us, next to the swings we will be reunited, and to be on the safe side I make haste to inquire, and how's Daddy? Is he okay? And Yotam says, yes, Daddy's okay, and I quickly say, do you want to come home with us? And to my relief Gili repeats the invitation, yes, come to me, you haven't been to me at Mommy's house yet, as if he was born in two houses and he has already mastered the terminology, and Yotam is easily infected with his enthusiasm, yay, I'm coming over to you.

When we enter the classroom I cover the foxy smile on my lips with my scarf, hoist the two schoolbags onto my shoulders, hold out my hands to the two children skipping around me, chewing the chocolate spread sandwich the teacher hands out at the end of the day, their lips turning brown, their cheeks covered with crumbs. We stand and wait for him next to the gate, to obtain his permission, maybe even to invite him to join us, I'll take you home with me, the children will play in Gili's room and we'll sit in the kitchen, mother and father in all respects, two broken parts forming a whole, for one afternoon. Come on, what's taking you so long, I urge him in silence, I've prepared a family for you, what more do you need, a heavy expectancy stops the breath of the street, the black asphalt awaits his feet, and I stare at the passersby, which of them will morph into him; and now a silver car stops next to us and I stare in suspense at the opening door, but it's a woman, an elderly woman with her hair dyed exactly the same color as her car, she looks faintly familiar but I ignore her because she isn't him, and the fact that she's here doesn't mean that he won't be, but then she goes up to Yotam, to my deep disappointment, and I hear him complain, Granny, why did you come, I'm going to Gili's. I, too, look resentfully at her well-groomed face, which I remember vaguely from the birthday party in the cafe, and she turns to me, is he going home with you? she asks, relieved, evidently pleased that her afternoon has been freed, and I say yes, is that okay?

That's fine, she says, and she even volunteers unnecessary information, Michal's sick, and I'm dying to ask about Oded but I don't know how to formulate the question in a way that will sound natural, maybe I'll try to find out who'll come to get Yotam in the evening, and I ask politely, should I explain where we live? And she says, I don't know yet if I'll be able to pick him up, give me your phone number, and she writes it down quickly on the back of her check book, and drops contentedly back into her car. Do you need a ride? she suddenly remembers to ask, and I say, yes, why not, even though the house is nearby, perhaps I'll be able to glean some information on the short ride, and we squeeze into the car, like we squeezed into her daughter's car at the beginning of the year. She drives calmly but her eyes blink nervously, she chews gum clenching her jaws, she's definitely worried, but what about.

So what does Michal have, the flu? I inquire, and she replies, something like that, she probably got it from Yotam, and she sighs, obscurely, and turns up the volume on the radio because the news is on, and I listen absentmindedly to the somber reports. To my regret the drive has produced nothing, and we're home already, and I point to our balcony, which overlooks the street, look, that's where we live, hoping to hear her say, never mind, his father will pick him up, but she writes down the number of the building obediently, parts from us with undisguised relief, and continues on her way. I hurry them inside, help them to take off their coats and boots, and offer them hot chocolate. I like looking after both of them as if they're my sons, twin brothers, and as we sit and sip the sweet drink, I look at Yotam, his closeness makes my longing for his father concrete, gives it a form, for it was from his seed that he was created, in his arms he grew, and it seems that a physical intimacy is coming into being between us behind his back, without his knowledge, since I am hosting his child, feeding him, stroking his hair to Gili's astonishment, trying to draw more information from him.

How's your sister, I probe, is she sick too? And he says, no, she's fine, and I ask, and your father, what about your father? deliberately not focusing the question, and he says, Daddy's okay. Apparently I'm not going to get anything more out of him, his tongue licks his chapped lips from which bits of dry skin are hanging, a slightly comical expression of profound seriousness on his face, and Gili urges him, come on, let's go and play, Mommy bought me a car with a remote control, and soon they're racing it all over the apartment, piling obstacles in its way, laughing maliciously at its difficulties, and I follow the blind efforts of the little car, the chilling plastic smile of its driver, the laughter ringing through the rooms. The presence of the new child dominates the house, my own son seems to me ordinary and predictable in comparison to his son, whose every movement is filled with meaning, derived from his father's slightly stiff, inhibited movements, and I stand in front of the big window, opposite the last light as it flees from the darkness, listening to an inner music becoming ever more tremulous; why doesn't he come, I'm almost his wife now, taking care of his son as if he were my own, why doesn't he take advantage of the opportunity. Is he still there, sitting in his comfortable armchair across from the purple chiffon curtains drifting over the windows, nodding sympathetically with his lips slightly parted, as if he's listening with them and not his ears, dishing out prescriptions to tortured souls and ignoring mine. I decide to call him there, didn't he give me the number himself, scribbling it hastily on the prescription; I'll tell him I have something of his here, and he should come and get it himself. I dial quickly before I can change my mind, but I'm greeted by the frosty voice of a receptionist, Dr. Sheffer's busy right now, may I take a message, and I hang up, maybe later he'll answer himself. If I leave my name I'll have to wait for him to call, and I don't want to do that, what I want to do is change reality, not wait around for it to take its course.

The fact that his son is here in my house, even though he himself is so inaccessible, gives me an immediate advantage, for he is like a hostage in my hands, captive in my home. If he falls now and hurts himself or if his temperature suddenly rises, or even if the boys start to fight and Yotam asks to go home, I'd have the right to interrupt his father in the middle of a consultation, and I go into Gili's room, where they sit opposite each other on the carpet, playing with the little Playmobil figures, dude, dude, the figures squeak to each other in their voices, and I ask, Yotam, does your father have a cell phone? And he says, sure he does, and I say, great, do you remember the number?

Sure I do, he boasts, no problem, and I hurry to get pen and paper, but then he gets confused and he mumbles the digits hesitantly, with a question mark after them, as if I actually know the number and I'm only testing him, I get a bit mixed up with the number of the phone at home, he admits in embarrassment, and in vain I try to coax the straying numbers from his mouth, until I give up, trying to conceal my disappointment.

What do you need the number for, Mommy? Gili shoots me a sharp look, and I say, for when Yotam wants to go home, we don't want to disturb his mother, right? And Yotam protests, but I'm not going yet, and I say quickly, of course not, I only asked to be on the safe side, and I leave them to go back to their plastic figurines, returning to the waiting keyboard, but the feeling of festive urgency refuses to depart, expectation piling up all around me. What pretext can I invent to summon him, perhaps a sudden change of plans; sorry, we have to go out now, can you come and pick Yotam up, and since you're already here maybe stay a while, maybe we can make a date for tomorrow. The darkening window covered with vapors interests me more than the computer screen, and I gaze at it through a fog, the radiator warmth enveloping my limbs. I lay my head on the desk and close my eyes, listening to the muffled voices behind the wall, I feel as if someone is stuffing my mouth with berries and I'm chewing them slowly, raspberries and cherries and blueberries, the smell of cool woods, wicker baskets, fairytales, the sweetness spreads through my increasingly full mouth, how will I answer the cries rising around me, I have to swallow the sticky mess, but my constricted throat has forgotten how to accomplish the simplest of acts, and then I wake up, raise my head and see them standing in front of me and I mumble, what's the matter, is everything all right?

We want to have a bath together, Gili announces, and I look at my watch, it's already after seven, I must have fallen asleep, strange that neither of the parents have come or called, have they forgotten they brought a child into the world; but, in the meantime, I am entitled to make the most of the situation. I fill the bathtub and help them to get undressed, secretly examining the reserved, tense nakedness of the strange child, his protruding ribs, his physical closeness to me amplifies the longing, everywhere in the house I am stabbed by a biting desire, come now, each one will dry his child, each will stroke his child and behind their backs we will steal completely new touches, utterly different from all those I have known up to now, because they will have come after a great rupture, and so they will bring solace.

Come now, don't keep yourself from me, our truncated evening searches every night for its end, it walks on tiptoe, peeps through the windows, trying to bring us together, and now that I am wrapping a towel around your son's shoulders in the dense vision-blurring steam, it seems that you are here by my side, your fingers meeting mine, because it is we who are wrapping ourselves in soft towels, and we sink up to our necks in the warm water, the rain murmuring on the ceiling above us, singing its mysterious song while we immerse ourselves in the water as in a healing spring. We haven't even slept together yet, we haven't even kissed, we've merely sailed words between the islands of foam, because I want to hear your voice saying all the words to me, not leaving out a single one, the controlled, measured voice, the charming speech impediment, the last letters drawn out as if loathe to part, and only after all the words are said will you ask me if I am ready, and when you go to bed with me I will weep with regret for all the years you did not go to bed with me and with joy for all the years you will still go to bed with me, and throughout our children will sleep bed to bed like identical twins.

What's wrong, why are you crying? Gili asks in a panic, and I come to my senses, it's nothing, I remembered something, and he asks, something sad? I wipe my eyes with his towel, no, actually something happy, and he says in astonishment, so why are you crying if it's happy? I am dying to include him, both of them, in the new joy I have imagined, as I shepherd them from the bathroom to the room. Sometimes your eyes water with excitement, with happiness, hasn't that ever happened to you? And Gili declares, not to me, and his friend echoes him, not to me either, and then he adds, his narrow chest swelling with pride, my father cried with happiness when I was born, and Gili is immediately jealous, how do you know? he asks, and Yotam says, he told me, and I remember too.

It's impossible to remember something like that, the pedantic Gili says, right, Mommy? And I say, sometimes people tell you things so vividly that it feels as if you remember them, and in my heart I turn to Yotam and add, I want to see your father weep for joy too, that's what I want, if you don't mind. The excitement swells in the house, he'll come soon, it's already late, this is the time to take children home, in a minute there'll be a knock at the door, in the middle of supper he'll come in, he'll see how well I'm taking care of his child, how good the omelet I made him smells, how fresh the salad is, he'll wait for him to finish his supper, he'll promise me to come back later, but I'm already clearing the dishes and he still hasn't come and I decide to call the clinic again, it's already after eight, I'll tell the receptionist it's urgent, that's it concerns the doctor's son, I'm not just some nagging patient, I'm in charge of the doctor's small son, the one whose birth he cried at, but to my disappointment there's no reply, the receptionist's recorded voice politely suggests leaving a message on the answering machine, and my dejection mounts, he won't come, this evening will close like all the others, in slack disappointment.

A muffled sound sends me rushing to the door and indeed a figure wrapped in a coat and hat appears in the spy-hole and for a moment I don't recognize it in all its wrappings and it seems that it could be anyone, any mother, any father, any grandmother, and I fling the door open in excitement and instead of his unique longed-for voice I hear a wet cough, and I cry, Michal, why did you come out? You're sick! There is so much disappointment and indignation in my voice that she smiles at me in embarrassment, surprised at the force of my emotions. I didn't have a choice, she says, and I go on scolding her, my rage swelling, it isn't right, I could have brought him home, you shouldn't have gone out like this, and apparently my concern touches her heart and brings tears to her eyes, presumably not tears of joy, and she says, you know how it is, once you become a mother you don't have the option of being sick.

That what fathers are for, no? I try my luck again, this time with her, and she sighs, Oded's at work, and this routine phrase slaps me sharply in the face, Oded's at work, how much security and order there is in the familiar combination, my husband's at work, my father's at work, and all at once I am seized with animosity toward him, you didn't do it, you weak-kneed coward, I succeeded in stopping you; why didn't somebody stop me; and yet I look her over with incredulity, what is she hiding under those words, a lack of appreciation for her situation or a real rupture. Now she's taking off her woolen hat and her curls, which have lost their bounce, falling like ropes around her face, her eyes are narrowed and her nose is red, from a cold or from continuous crying, who was it crying there that Saturday morning, was it her, in a previous fit of jealousy, was he running away from her crying then too, gloomily peeing in the guest toilet, while I lay in wait to ambush him unwittingly. No, this is not her familiar face, its expression is completely different, and I say, come and sit down for a bit, if you've already come all the way here, I'll make you lemon tea, and, in the meantime, you'll tell me what's really going on in your life, I add silently, but she is reluctant; thank you, Ella, another time, I have to get back to bed. Come along, Yotami, she urges him wearily, in the same maternal depression I know so well, for this is exactly how I plucked Gili from his friends' houses on the evenings after the separation, declaiming the familiar words to him without feeling a thing, hollow and lifeless as a scarecrow, and I hand her her son's schoolbag, and offer to help her until she recovers. I'll be happy to take him tomorrow too, they get along great together, I say, reluctant to let go of the bait, and she sighs, thank you, we'll see what happens tomorrow. Her priorities clearly differ from mine, and I stroke Yotam's head, trying to hang onto the contact, goodnight sweetie, I say, and when the door closes behind them Gili gives me a penetrating look and remarks, I see you really like Yotam. Yes, I say innocently, he's a nice boy, it's a pleasure to have him as a guest, and he says, yeah, but Gili's look lingers, and I put him on my knees, my arms around his waist in an instant the house has emptied of the expectation that filled it with such pungent life, in his going the new child took with him all the hopes I pinned on his presence here, and now the two of us are left alone, a fragment of a family, a wing stuck in the ground.

How I waited once for the moment when the door would shut

behind foreign elements invading our territory, a little friend and one of his parents, how I loved to seat him on my knees with his precious face opposite mine, to listen to his shrill accounts of the events of his day, to accompany them with kisses on his eyebrows, his eyelids, his eyelashes, was it all a mirage, a grace stemming from a deprivation that had nothing to do with him. Now it is all directed toward someone else, and this child sitting on my knees is no longer the object of that radiant, brimming stream of heartfelt emotion, but of that combination I once knew only by hearsay, of tired duty and laborious devotion, rising above itself on special occasions, such as illness, God forbid, or a rare moment of intimacy. Was it my son's fate in his first years to unwittingly fill the void, to compensate and console, with everything I found lacking in his father realized in him, and now that foreign elements have invaded the uninhabited terrain of my soul, a new order is coming into being and the truth is emerging, for he is a child, after all, not a heavenly salvation, not a radiant reflection, not a reliable address for the forces of unsatisfied love. He clings to me, lays his head on my shoulder, I miss Daddy, he suddenly sobs, I'm tired of living in two houses, when I'm with you I miss Daddy, and when I'm with Daddy I miss you.

For a moment I can't breathe, I am stunned by his words, so many weeks have passed in silent resignation, without any protest on his part, that I mistakenly thought his adjustment was complete, and I hug his heaving back, he's fed up, and he's right, he is the one whose life has been cut in half, he is the one traipsing from house to house, while I remained here, he wakes up in the morning and doesn't know where he is, every few days he has to get used to another environment, and this is only the beginning, perhaps he will still have to get used to new spouses, stepbrothers, the helpless victim of a great enterprise, paid for by the most vulnerable, and I rest my head on his shoulder, my cheeks already wet, and he asks, are you crying for joy again? And I whisper, no, honey, I'm not crying for joy, and he says, I'm not either, and now our tears mingle, his tears steal into my eyes and my tears steal into his, and indeed our eyes are identical, you can't tell them apart. Now he climbs off my knees and stumbles to the telephone, I'm calling Daddy, he pipes, I want him to come now and say goodnight to me, and I watch his little fingers faltering over the keys, straining to produce the ring that is now being heard in his other house, dancing between the beads of the colorful curtain, floating over the pale furniture, where a new life is trying to be built from the wreckage of our family.

Daddy? I hear his high-pitched voice, breaking in order to demonstrate the full extent of his misery, I miss you and I want to see you, and apparently the voice on the other end does not make haste to agree, but sternly explains the way of the world. There are Mommy's days and Daddy's days, and we don't mix them up, but for his part Gili is in no hurry to let go, then just today, Daddy, just to say goodnight, no, not on the phone, I want to see you, I want you to kiss me goodnight, and I listen in agony to the argument between them, and again the mountain of grief and guilt rises before my eyes, and again it seems that only one thing can prevent the eruption, only if the proof is found, sprouting and blossoming and blooming from my new life, the proof that it isn't in vain that the little boy is weeping as he approaches me and holds out the telephone, Daddy wants to talk to you, he mumbles, chastened.

What's going on there, the scolding begins, can't you calm him down? It's about time you start putting him in his place, from the moment he was born I've been warning you about it, you have to stop giving in to his extortion, he senses your weakness and manipulates you, the fact is that it doesn't happen with me, you have to put a stop to it the minute it starts, above all it's for his sake that I have no intention of coming there now, Ella, try to gain control of the situation, stop feeling sorry for him, it only makes things worse, and I whisper, calm down, what did he ask? If it's not convenient for you then don't come, just stop covering up your laziness with belligerent theories, and for a moment it seems that nothing has changed, so familiar are these exchanges to me, so many times have I had to stand my ground with trembling knees against the barrage of his words. I put the phone down, there is a maddening commotion raging in the cavity of my ear, as if some tiny creature has infiltrated it without being able to find its way out, the sudden reminder is oppressive but also liberating in its faithful reflection of the past, and even if it holds no consolation for the child who is sobbing again in my arms, it reassures me that perhaps in the final analysis our separation was not just a whim, perhaps this is the first sign, the first part of my proof.

On the roof the rain collects like it did on the plastic sheeting, the cold drops leaping into each other's arms, and I lie beneath them, it seems that the ceiling is transparent, revealing the stormy sky, a war is being waged over my head tonight, sending its thunderbolts and lightning flashes like missiles from their bases, with dull-black clouds advancing heavily as tanks, nothing will stop them, like a celestial battlefield that will never stop raging, but only move from place to place, like a faithful reflection of events on the earth below. I cover my head with the pillow, Amnon's pillow that still holds the smell of his heavy nape, if he were here now by my side, would I feel more protected and what would the price for that protection be, and would it be real, no, it isn't him I want next to me now, my urgent longing is not aimed at him, like the sight of a gun it has suddenly turned its aim on another. Where is his backpack full of albums now, where are his eyes, the color of a heavy rain cloud, like a sign of life from an ancient grave desire rises from the depths, where is he now, is he lying by the side of his sneezing wife, or by the side of some other woman, or perhaps he, too, is alone, searching like me for the end of that night.

Happy is he who forgoes knowing, who does not pin all his hopes on flesh and blood, on another, for who is this other, if not a near figment of your imagination, from your paucity you created him, like you created your son, from paucity he arose and to paucity will he return, and he will not fill it, for this is your fate, so howl the evil winds of the night, crashing against the closed shutters like waves against a lonely pier, unrelenting, and perhaps I, too, am like them, trying my luck again and again, in no hurry to relent, to take precaution, the wind of a bitter night unleashing its fury against shutters and treetops, water tanks and telegraph poles, woe to him who crosses its path tonight.

Chapter thirteen

Yes, this is the place, above the busy intersection, where he doles out his seductive medications, his looks of reserved sympathy, where he nods at those sitting opposite him, his mouth slightly open as if he's listening with his lips and not his ears, here, above the fumes of the buses and the honking of the drivers, where it's impossible to linger, where the city bares its sharp teeth and people run like rabbits across the crowded crosswalks, this is where I'll find him, for I have no choice, the time has come to find out what remains of that magic night, of the enchanted hoop of light that wrapped itself around us, and I push open the door on which there are three gravely printed names, as if this were a factory for the saving of souls. Looking official, I go up to the receptionist who presides over the deserted waiting room, I have to see Dr. Sheffer, I announce in a firm, assertive voice, but she is not impressed, do you have an appointment? She looks down at her appointment log, and I say, no, but I lost the prescription he gave me, I need another one, and she expels a bored breath, as if this is what everybody says, and not the private excuse I labored over for hours.

Blond curls frame her face and for a moment it seems that she is a youthful version of Michal, fresh and doll like, perhaps she is his new woman, perhaps it was for her sake that he left home, she protects him from me as if he's her property, glancing at her watch she admits reluctantly, he'll be free in a few minutes, give me your name and I'll speak to him, and I dictate my name to her and retire to one of the armchairs next to the door. The certainty of his closeness agitates me, makes it hard for me to breathe, he's there, at the end of the hall, he's within grasp, up to now it was only coincidence that brought us together, a coincidence as coordinated as if it had been carefully planned, while all my endeavors, all my attempts to reconstruct it, have failed.

The excruciating sound of a dentist's drill invades the stairwell of the old building, which has become an office building in old age and is probably deserted and menacing at night, and I clench my lips and keep a hostile eye on the receptionist, who behaves like a queen in her palace, in a minute she'll sashay down the hall to his room, my name in her hand, Ella Miller needs a new prescription, she'll say to him. Will he recognize my name, will he understand my secret intention and come out to meet me, or tell her to call me in, and allow me to sweep past her, sit down opposite him, the leather armchair facing the mauve chiffon curtains, I can think of nothing but you, I'll say to him, my life is waiting for your life. I try to recall the layout of his room, I was incapable of noticing anything then, all I remember is a soothing, dim mauve light, and the way he looked, a look of pity and horror, as if standing before a cat run over in the street, a cat dear to his heart, even if it didn't belong to him. On the wall in front of me is the familiar photograph of the long, gray stone, the Rosetta Stone, the Egyptian hieroglyphic script next to the ancient Greek, for thousands of years it waited to be deciphered, an ancient civilization rich beyond measure peeping out from behind it; who hung it here, before the eyes of the people waiting, hoping for the obscure letters of the soul to be deciphered, searching for repeated signs; but in fact our souls are more like the tablets of the Minoan script, a code that was deciphered alone, from within.

A door at the end of the hall opens, but nobody comes out into the waiting room, there must be a hidden doorway to protect the privacy of the patients, and now she makes her way toward him, deliberately slow, in a tight skirt and a woolen top that emphasizes her heavy breasts, is that his voice I hear, is that his laughter, I think I hear my name being called and I get up, but no, the voices are coming from the stairwell, people sighing in relief as they emerge from the dental clinic. What's taking her so long in there, why doesn't he send her to call me, why doesn't he come out to me, and I lower my eyes, my body is stiff with suspense, as if I were waiting for the results of a fateful test. Finally, her pointy-toed boots draw near with an ominous tapping, and she is standing before me, holding out a slip of paper, and I ask weakly, what's that? And she says, the prescription you asked for, and I take the slip of paper from her hand, but that's not enough, I protest, I have to see him.

That's impossible at the moment, she says, you requested a prescription, if you'd like to meet with him, leave your name and telephone number and he'll get back to you. I try to shade the insult on my face and examine the slip of paper intently, perhaps he wrote a few words or numbers at the bottom, the number of his cellphone, for instance, but there is nothing there apart from my name and the name of the drug, side by side, in long letters leaning slightly sideways, as if they were meant for each other. Is this a misunderstanding or is it deliberate, a clear hint that he is not available, that he is not interested.

Did you tell him that I was here in the waiting room? I ask, and she answers cooly, of course, and hurries to pick up the ringing phone while I flee the building, the slip of paper in my hand, again I examine it, but I feel giddy and my vision is blurred and I lean against the trunk of a pine tree planted in the middle of the square like an arrow shot from the sky, my life, emptied anew, prancing before my eyes in its repulsive nakedness. Like an insulted child I curse out loud, hit the tree trunk with my fists, furiously rip off the dry scabs of its bark, immersed in my dejection and ignoring the footsteps hesitating beside me until a pair of hands take hold of my shoulders and a low, amused voice purrs in my ear, hey, watch your mouth.

Embarrassed, I let go of the tree and raise my face to him, my sap-stained fingers fondle his face wonderingly, his laughter swirls through my hair. I disappointed you, ah? And I, transparent as a raindrop, stare at him and at the slip of paper, which of them is real, they contradict each other, why did you do that to me? I ask, even though it's not important now, not important at all, and he whispers into my hair, in order to surprise you; how can we feel joy without sorrow? His breath makes my ear tingle, and I look at him, his skin is hard and rough as the bark of the tree, his face is narrower than I remembered, his lips are trembling slightly or perhaps they're my lips, pressed against each other we stand in the middle of the intersection, my hands wandering over his thin shirt as it's dotted with rain-drops.

You still don't have a jacket? I ask and he says, I have one, I only came out for a minute to see you, I have to get back to the office, I have an appointment in a minute, and I won't let him go, when will we meet? I ask, rushing ahead as if he is already mine, but his voice is as urgent and ardent as mine, I'm busy till seven, where are you this evening? And I reply, wherever you say, I can wait for you here, or in a cafe, or at home, wherever you say, and he asks, are you alone today? And I say, I'm not alone, I'm with you.

Then wait for me at home, he says, I'll come to you, he gives my hands a parting squeeze in his cold hands, and I say, but you haven't got my address, and he says, yes I do, I have everything I need to come to you, and then he's gone, disappearing into the same secret door from which he had emerged, leaving me dazed in the middle of the square. Never had my wishes been fulfilled so completely, never had my life worked out so perfectly, and I cling gratefully to the sticky tree trunk, trying to draw it toward me as if in a minute the two of us will step out in a wild dance, crossing the little square, skipping between the cars that wait at the traffic lights, tap on their windows and grin mockingly, we to whom the laws of reality no longer apply.

And then I think, maybe I'll stay right here till seven o'clock, next to the tree, the sole witness to the miracle. I'll wait for him in the rain as thin as pine needles to make sure that he doesn't forget his promise, I'll stay here because it happened here, and if I dare to move away the magic will be dispelled and the truth will be revealed, I invented it, I imagined it, does anything on earth really happen like that, leaping above the highest of your expectations, as if he were waiting like me day after day for this opportunity, and it turns out that he knows my address too. Just as I'd been surprised to learn that he knows what I do for a living, was I, too, in some way present in his life ever since that morning at the end of summer, and this possibility sends a pleasant tremor though me, and I press my face to the tree trunk, thousands of sticky sappy tongues lick my cheek, smearing it with a sharp, vital smell.

The movement of the traffic around the square suddenly seems full of splendor and ceremony, like the circling of the bride on her wedding day, the hooting of the horns as elated as cheers of joy, the traffic lights radiant as the colored lights in the wedding hall, the passersby excited as guests streaming to the party from all over town, the old pine leaning to one side as proud and festive as if it were my delighted bridesmaid, and I raise my eyes to its distant crown, the raindrops threaded on its needles glimmer in the dusk like dark pearls fished from the depths of the sea. In deep gulps I swallow the sooty air, as if it were a delicacy at my wedding feast, how powerful happiness is, banishing all my doubts in a single slashing stroke, and it seems to me that now, in the roar of this purple afternoon whose glorious twilight is quickly fading, for the first time in my life I am truly ready to embrace it.

But the further I go from the slanting tree trunk, from the scene of the supernatural event, the louder other voices sound in my ears, I skip from store to store on the main street, buying the whiskey we drank together then, in the cafe, chocolate cookies and rye bread, and onions and mushrooms and cream for the soup, I'll restrict myself to soup, so as not to reveal too great an effort, and the more the bags in my hands multiply, the harder it is to ignore the horde of suspicions howling at my heels, insistent and demanding as starving alley cats with the scent of food in their nostrils. How can it be so easy; something's fishy here, something doesn't make sense, and against my will I remember the hoarse yells that greeted me at the door of their house, you promised it wouldn't happen again, she yelled, I don't believe a word you say, I have proof, and I stand stock still, put my bags down on the pavement, in a minute they'll be trampled by the passersby, yes, it was apparently true, apparently he's one of those men who wants almost any woman for a night or two, and I fell into his hands so easily; why shouldn't he exploit the opportunity, I'm no worse than anyone else, and I grab my shopping bags angrily and stomp along, the bags unbearably heavy in my hands. I have everything I need to come to you, he whispered in my ear, what does he need exactly, a few free hours, a few free organs. While I'm ready to adopt his child, he's busy planning some night-time entertainment close to home, and as soon as it's over he'll go back to his fashionable apartment, and he'll even have time to give his son a kiss good night on his smooth forehead. I decide to try and get the scoop from Dina, it takes precedence over the soup, let his wife make him soup, let her drown her winter germs in the boiling pot. Until now I haven't dared confide in Dina and now to I'll have to do it carefully, in a seemingly casual way, Dina is in no rush to share her few assets, and before I unpack my purchases I'm already on the phone to her; how are things with you? I ask lightly, and she says, I just got back from work, I'm dead tired? And I make haste to tell my story, guess who I bumped into in the street, and without waiting for her to guess, I say, your psychiatrist.

He's not my psychiatrist, she corrects me, he's an acquaintance of mine and he's a psychiatrist, there's a difference, and I say, he was really nice to me, and she says, yeah, why not, he's a nice guy, not as conceited as most of his colleagues, and I try to put out feelers, tell me, do you think he's into women? And she answers coldly, what do you mean? He's definitely not into men, and I say, oh come on, I mean does he hit on everyone? And she hesitates for a minute, why, did he try to hit on you? And I say, no, not really, he was just nice to me, realizing that the conversation wasn't going to go anywhere, and that I wasn't the only one hiding something. Then she says, Ella, don't even think about it, not with him, I don't advise you to go anywhere near him, and I say but why, tell me why.

I can't go into details, she sighs, it's enough that he's married, just keep away from him, and it's clear to me that I won't get anything more out of her at this stage, and I already regret even the little I've heard, what did I need it for, I could have been happy now had I not involved her, I feel as if I've been served a king's banquet and just as I'm about to eat, someone says don't touch it, it's poisoned, but I want to feast even if I suffer later, I hate the person who kept the delicacies from me even if she saved my life, and already I turn my suspicions on her, since when is she against married men, ever since I've known her she's had a nearly exclusive diet of married men, maybe she's just jealous, she's always been jealous in these matters, and I veer between the two poles, doubting him and then doubting her, and in the meantime the garden of happiness that bloomed around me for a moment is trampled; I didn't fence it in, didn't safeguard it. Does happiness come only to those who believe in it and hide its face from those who doubt, is it like a jealous god, demanding perfect faith and complete devotion without any proof of its existence, a vengeful, grudging god, quick to rage, and I lie down on the sofa in my wet coat, worn out by the emotional upheaval. I close my eyes, in a minute I'll get up and make the soup, and bathe and dress and perfume myself. Then I'll see for myself, I won't give him up so soon, I won't give up so soon, I repeat, and it seems that the hand knocking on the door is repeating the syllables with me, stubbornly echoing me, won't give up so soon, until I start, glance in a panic at my watch, it's seven thirty, instead of getting ready for him I fell asleep, stuck to the sofa in a strange, swooning stupor, and already the knocking has faded out, I missed him, and how will I find him now, and I run downstairs, drowsy and disheveled, still in my damp coat, my eyes webbed with sleep, my cheek grooved with the rough upholstery of the sofa. I catch up with him at the entrance to the building, grab hold of his coat, and he turns to me, his face stony, blank, until it seems that it isn't him, I have accosted a total stranger, but his features soften immediately and I murmur, I didn't hear you, I must have fallen asleep, and I lay my cheek on his shoulder, ready to surrender again to the stubborn sleep, sticky as sap, to gather him into my sleep.

I thought you got scared, he whispers into my ear, and I ask, of what? And he says, of me, and I ask quickly, why, do I have a reason to be scared? And he smiles, I don't know, it depends who you ask, as if he can read my secret thoughts, and I take him by the arm, let's go upstairs. It seems as if I am still asleep, and the supple laws of sleep govern our steps, and when we go inside I point shamefaced at the groceries dotting the kitchen floor, I was going to make soup, I was going to take a bath, and suddenly I fell asleep, it's never happened to me before, it usually takes me hours to fall asleep. He looks around slowly, as if engraving the sight onto his memory, his eyes take in the chronicles of this afternoon, the chronicles of this house, and he says, go and take a bath, I'll make the soup, and I say wonderingly, really, are you sure? as though a more generous offer has never been made.

Imagine that, he laughs, mushroom soup, right? And I marvel, how did you know? looking at him admiringly as if he were the most amazing creature I had ever come across in my life, and he points to the little baskets covered with taut plastic wrap, it isn't hard to guess, is it just the two of us or did you invite other guests? he asks, and I say, just us, I have no desire to share you with anyone else, are you sure you can manage?

As I walk barefoot through the tediously familiar rooms it seems that a soft carpet has been spread over the tiles, warm as the fur of an animal whose heart still beats. Is this really my house, a magical breeze is blowing through it, when I open the faucet a hot wave pours over my hand, when I take off my clothes in the bedroom, my body seems clothed in a new skin, radiant and sensitive to the touch, my face, the old wall mural, has been brightly restored, the eyes of the Parisian are full of vitality, her cheeks are gleaming, and while the tub fills up with the trumpeted roar of good fortune, I go back to him in the kitchen, wrapped in a towel like an ancient toga, and watch as he pours himself a whiskey, raises his glass to me, will you have a drink with me? he asks, and I answer with a question, will you have a bath with me? And he smiles, shaking his head silently.

Why not? I ask, and he comes close to me, his eyes inspecting my bare shoulders, my fingers holding the towel, I won't join you, he says, because then you'll think that I came here to sleep with you, and that's not why I came, and I ask, then why did you come? And he says, to cook you soup, and turns his back on me to take the right pot from the right shelf, as if he knows the secrets of the house, more so than Amnon, who always got mixed up; where did you hide the frying pan, where did you put that blue bowl, he would complain, it's impossible to find anything here.

How strange it is to see him filling the pot with water as he stands in the long, narrow, windowless kitchen, his feet planted firmly among the groceries, and for a moment it seems that they are standing side by side, Amnon crossing his legs with demonstrative reluctance, stooping over the marble counter that's too low for him; which of them is more of a stranger to me, this man I hardly know, or Amnon who was so tediously familiar and who changed so much, and I leave him there and sink into the bath. My limbs scatter in the water, excited as toddlers engaged in a happy game, it seems that the joyful shouts of our little children are still splashing through the house, and I add my own silent shouts of joy, sail them around me like ducks, like soap bubbles, but when I remember Yotam, my mood suddenly darkens, this is his father standing in the narrow kitchen, his father who wept when he was born. What are you trying to do, make another child unhappy, wreck another family, haven't you done enough, I have to find out what his status is, if he's gone back home, I'll send him on his way, without tasting the soup, without tasting of his charms, and I say in a weak voice, Oded, come here a minute, and to my surprise he answers immediately, as if he were standing all this time by the bathroom door, and he steps inside, his figure covered with a gray net of vapors, the glass still in his hand. No way, he grins, I told you I'm not getting in, are you sure you're even here? I can't see you, and then he opens the window, the steam quickly clears and he looks at me and complains, too much foam, I can't see anything, do you have a body there or only a head?

Oded, I have to ask you something, I say, and he smiles, if you must, his voice still amused, just be quick because I'm a little busy, and I say, I'm afraid to ask, why don't you help me. What are you afraid of, the question or the answer, he inquires, and I say, the answer, of course. He looks at me with the dark eyes that always seem larger than they are, I can guess what's bothering you, he says, his tongue stretching the words, and the answer is no, I'm not living at home anymore, I left forever, that same night. I'm so relieved I dunk my head in the water and close my eyes, and when I open them he's gone. Cold, dry air blows onto me from the window, and I scold myself, how can you be happy about the unhappiness of another woman, a woman you know, a child you actually like, and, nevertheless, the very knowledge that the deed is done exhilarates me, and I dry myself quickly and put on a long, black-velvet dress, which in recent years has turned into a house dress because the mood has turned surprisingly domestic, the smell of frying wafting out of the kitchen, the sounds of chopping and mixing, the creaking of shoe soles on the tiles, the murmur of the presence of another man moving about the house, sounds whose existence I have forgotten, reassuring as a smile cast your way on a foreign street in a foreign city.

I come out of the bedroom with my hair wet and find him in the kitchen, stirring the bubbling pot, his coat draped over the back of the armchair next to my coat, his long, fragile profile turned to me, his lashes lowered over the pot, can you really fall in love like this without any preambles, a love that is completely new and yet as precise as a reconstruction, bursting ripe from the depths of the soul as if it had been hiding there forever, waiting only for him, and I go and stand next to him, his look sending a shiver through me, and he puts out his hand and takes a lock of dripping hair and puts it in his mouth and sucks it between his lips, his shirt is slightly open, revealing a tangle of hair, gray as smoke. Hungry? he asks, my hair falling from his mouth, should we eat? And I am enchanted by the naturalness with which he volunteers to play the host to me in my own house, as if he senses that I am not yet ready to entertain a strange man here, that I am used to rearing a child in this space, to feeding a small family, and I lower my grateful nose to the bubbling pot but a strange, sharp smell rises from it, different from the smell I expected, the subtle, slightly sweetish smell of mushrooms in cream, and I look in astonishment at the mushrooms floating whole on the water, their stems upturned, with something unidentifiable floating next to them.

What are you cooking here? I ask, and he says, what difference does it make, as long as it tastes good; I never cook according to a recipe, he boasts, I like inventing my own recipes, and he pours me a generous shot from the whiskey bottle that is already half empty, has he poured its contents into the pot or down his throat, and I drink it quickly, so as not to be the only sober person in the house this evening, looking at him with renewed suspicion as he goes back to stirring the soup, gazing at it as a father at his newborn baby, and I set the little table with some embarrassment, unaccustomed as I am to romantic dinners. We usually put down three plates and three spoons, not even a knife, no napkins, and now I look for candles, as required, but I can only find Sabbath candles, which I light and even bless piously, Blessed are You, Lord our God, King of the universe, Who has commanded us to kindle the Sabbath light, even though it's neither Sabbath nor a holiday.

When I take the butter out of the fridge I discover, to my astonishment, that a number of items that were on the shelves have disappeared, the remains of a tin of tuna fish I used to make a sandwich for Gili this morning, a tin of tehina, and already my stomach is turning over, and I ask, Oded, what did you put in the soup? And he says, I never tell, and lifts the ladle to his mouth and smacks his lips with relish, you've never tasted soup like this in your life, I promise you, and then we sit down at the table, less at ease than before, slightly stiff and ceremonious with the Sabbath candles between us casting a dim light on the almost empty table, and he ladles the soup into my bowl and waits in suspense for me to taste, and I take a cautious sip, an unbearable concoction runs riot on my palate, a taste like nothing on earth, and he asks, well, how is it? I make a face, interesting, I try to say, and immediately confess the truth, it's awful.

I didn't think you were so conservative, he says disappointedly, you should open yourself up to new combinations, and I say, but why should I, what's wrong with the old combinations, what's wrong with mushroom soup with onions and cream, and he says, it's boring, and I immediately try again, but this combination is impossible, and I look at him, raising the spoon to his mouth enthusiastically, his straight hair falling onto his forehead, his cheekbones thrown into relief by dark shadows, a strange man, maybe we, too, are an impossible combination. He sits in Amnon's old spot, where hundreds of dishes have been set over the years, for hundreds of different meals, quiches, salads, schnitzels, steaks, omelets, and I think of Gili and Amnon, sitting opposite each other right now and eating their supper in their little apartment, is he saying to him, I miss Mommy, when I'm with you I miss Mommy, and when I'm with Mommy I miss you, and when he says Mommy he means me, me of all the women in the world. The long narrow eyes of the Sabbath candles waver doubtfully, where is the proof, I urgently need proof that I haven't forced him to suffer in vain, and I fall bravely on the soup as if it's hidden there, as if this is the poison I have to drink in order to earn the soothing of my doubts, and he watches me with satisfaction, I told you that you'd like it, he melts, my mother never had time to cook for us, in the winter we would come home from school starving and freezing, we would throw the whole fridge into a pot, add water and cook. It always came out delicious, and all of a sudden I feel my heart go out to him, opening wide to his ancient distress, is this the only way that we can know the other, out of identification and pity, for Amnon, who grew up like a spoiled prince, never made me feel like this.

Moved by this absent-minded revelation I take another helping, and this time it's almost good. A sad little boy in a gloomy old kitchen looks out at me from my bowl, he's standing in front of a greasy stove where strange-smelling dishes are simmering because Mommy is too busy to cook, Mommy is looking after Daddy, and I look at him, trying to adjust myself to his presence, to his calm, quiet reserve, his erect posture, his clean-cut features, is everything okay? he asks, wiping his mouth on the napkin, and these words, the simplest of words, reach me gilded and rare. This is exactly what he said to me then, in his house, is everything okay, and I answer, yes, and with you? and he says, more or less, his eyes straying over the living room, resting on the gaps in the bookshelves, and I look with him as if I, too, am a stranger here, is he put off by the mess, by the random collection of furniture, so different from his fashionable home.

Where are you staying now? I ask, and he says for the time being I'm staying in the clinic, and I say in surprise, really, in the clinic? Isn't it depressing there? And he says, a little, but it apparently sits well with my masochism, and I say, I didn't think you were a masochist, and he says, I most certainly am, why else would I enjoy this soup so much? And I laugh, even if he'd said, I'm sadistic, or paranoid, I would have been beside myself with enthusiasm. There are so many more questions I want to ask him, but in the meantime I gaze at him in silence, studying his movements, and when we dip chocolate cookies in our coffee, he turns his into a thick sweet mess, and I remember how I sat opposite him then, on the tall bar stool, the skeleton of the red pear disintegrating in my hand while a desperate, hungry yearning rose from within like a coyote's howl, mingling with the sound of stifled crying coming from one of the rooms, and I ask him, who was crying that morning? And he asks, what morning? And I say, when I brought Gili to your place for the first time, you remember, when I surprised you in the bathroom? And he says, do I remember, how could I possibly forget? And I say, why?

Because it was then I actually decided to leave, he says, I realized I didn't have a choice, she drove me crazy with her suspicions all night long, and in the morning I understood that it was over, that I wasn't going to go on like this, and I ask, but why was she so suspicious, did you cheat on her all the time? And so marvelous is he to me with his long, chiseled face that even if he said yes, I did, I would justify him immediately, without any hesitation, but to my relief he answers no, not all the time, only once, but the amount isn't important, it seems that once can be all the time too, the affair went on playing in her head long after it was over and done, and I say, tell me, and he smiles with his lips closed, his hand pinching his chin, leaving a red mark on it, I'm not used to telling, you know, I'm used to others telling me, strange that with you, of all people, the roles are reversed.

Maybe because I'm used to talking with stones, I say, and he laughs, maybe, but I feel a little ridiculous, talking about myself, and I say again, tell me, drawing him to the sofa, where he sits erect and slightly tense. A few years ago I fell unintentionally in love with someone I worked with, he says, a psychologist in a psychiatric hospital, she was small like you, she had well drawn lips like yours, his finger tasting of chocolate and coffee slides over my lips, only her hair was different, it was red; when I saw you then, in my house, I thought for a moment that you were her, that she had just dyed her hair, I was shocked, didn't you notice? And I say, not really, I thought you were embarrassed to have someone looking at you while you went to the bathroom. No, that didn't bother me at all, he smiles, I even liked it, altogether I liked you a lot, and I place my hand on his, the same goes for me, I wanted you to kiss me, and he says, I know, do you want me to now too? And I say, very much, his finger moves over my lips again and again, as if redrawing them, it wanders inside my mouth, awakening a pang of sharp, impatient desire.

Then imagine that I'm kissing you, he says, can you do that? See how powerful something that doesn't materialize can be, and I say in surprise, but why should I imagine it when you're right here next to me, and he says, because I want you to, and I close my eyes, his sweetened finger passing over my lips like the lips of a baby moistened with wine before a circumcision, and I try to stroke his face but he holds my hands to the sofa, slowly, he whispers, we have plenty of time, more than you know; I like doing everything my way, not by the recipe, remember? His lips approach mine, brush them and immediately withdraw, leaving a soft suspense, my hands imprisoned in his in wondering surrender, why is he dragging it out like this, we're not children anymore, we've kissed and been kissed so often, and at the same time it suddenly seems that this is right, precisely this, all our lives we have been in too much of a hurry, pouncing on our desire, extinguishing it with our crude panting, and when he finally lays his lips on me it seems that I have never been kissed, my lips are torn from my face and seem to become part of him, it is not I who am moving them, but something outside me and beyond my control. The enigmatic taste of restrained, calculating masculinity enters my mouth, his hand brushes my breasts and I hear his voice, what do you want now, what do you want me to do to you? Don't answer, he admonishes me immediately, just imagine that it's happening, I want to see you imagining it, and I try to lead his hand to me, but it refuses, no touching, he says, show me that you really trust me, show me yourself, and it seems that his rich voice is pushing me up a steep hill, keeping me from stumbling with two strong hands behind my back, leading me forward step by step, until I reach the place most desired, from which there is no retreat, and no fear of tumbling backwards, and the pleasure is already certain, the inn within sight, a fire burning in the hearth, a hot meal, and on its threshold I collapse, panting, limp, whole as a healed pottery jug, my dress hitched up, my legs stretched out in front of me, my feet still trembling, and precisely then he strokes me, as if soothing a crying child, and perhaps I really am crying, with tears of profound wonder. My sweet, he whispers, it's obvious that you're never been loved as you really wanted to be, nobody understood how delicate you are, you should be swathed in cotton, and I open my eyes to him, see him sitting erect on the edge of the sofa, his eyes wandering over my face, his lips parted provocatively, his intimate words filling the room; he speaks as if we were already lovers, as if he is already committed to my happiness, to my needs that are hidden even from me and apparently plain to him. The ancient wish, which life had covered in soot, has surprisingly come true, to be loved and understood, understood and loved, both of them together, for one of them is not enough, and I reach out with a hesitant hand for his thigh, fingering the fine lines of the corduroy, how generous are the words that came out of his mouth, a completely different code seems to be at work here, not of concealment and power struggles but of an abundant stream of loving kindness and acceptance, and I pull down my dress and lay my head on his shoulder, the same pleasant smell of fresh laundry wafts from his shirt, does she still launder his clothes?

You didn't tell me what happened in the end, I remember, and he says, you were there at the end, you heard it all, and I say, no, with that psychologist, what happened between you, and he says, love that was suffocated, that's what happened, I strangled it with my own hands because Yotam had just been born, and I wanted him to grow up in a functioning family, and Maya was barely four, and I didn't want to be a weekend father. To cut a long story short, I chose fatherhood over love, and I say, how did Michal find out, and he says, apparently I wanted my great sacrifice to be acknowledged and I was stupid enough to confide in Michal, and ever since then she hasn't stopped doubting me.

Where is she today? I ask, and he says, she's married to a Canadian and taking care of the mental problems of Canadians in Toronto; why, are you starting to worry too? And I say, no, not at all, you're not mine enough yet for me to start being jealous, although I was a little worried by your receptionist, and he smirks, really? Me and her? And I peek at him, his sharp profile is still utterly strange to me, and what about you and I, apart from the fact that I happened to cross your path at an opportune moment, what have you to do with me, apart from the fact that our children look like brothers, that each of us is a broken piece carrying the whole on his back. Is that enough, is it too much, and again a dull dread seizes hold of me, from the soles of my feet that had quivered with pleasure, through my lips that were shaped by his fingers, to my hair that he stroked with a fatherly touch, fatherhood and love, he said, what about motherhood and dread, his narrow, rather ascetic beauty illuminates the room like the light of a dying candle, and I feel as if I should warn him, even if I lose him, perhaps that is why I crossed his path, to tell him what I have learned on my own flesh, and I ask, and what's going to happen now, are you ready now to be a weekend father? I told you already, it's an ache that never leaves your body, and he sighs, I know but I don't have a choice, I have to accept that there are irresolvable situations, she won't change, the situation won't change; I believe that in the final analysis it's the right thing for her too. I tried everything and there's nothing more I can do, as far as the children are concerned, it's time to put a clear end to it, I'll rent a small apartment close to them and try to see them every day, both possibilities are bad and I hope this is the lesser evil.

And what about Michal, I ask, isn't she trying to get you back? And he says, of course she, is but there's no chance, I can't do it, it isn't healthy for her either, I really believe that the separation will cure her, and I say in surprise, how will the separation cure her if she loves you? She'll break down completely, poor thing, and he says, sometimes when the thing you're so afraid of happens, it liberates you, I've seen a lot of cases like that. I find that hard to believe, I say, but even if it does happen, it doesn't liberate you, the minute you realize that it's irreversible everything changes, you stand before the ruins and then the real terror begins, and I find myself telling him in detail about that night, it was a Friday night, after the holidays, a few Sukkoth booths were still standing in the yards of the houses, how I marched to Amnon's place determined to bring him back to me, how I found myself hiding in the toilet from my son, how I heard his voice through the closed door and how I couldn't show myself, how I heard Amnon saying to him, someone, a woman you don't know, she's leaving in a minute, how I dragged myself home with the last of my strength, how Gabi showed up, how I was with him until morning, right here on this sofa, writhing like snakes biting each other, and it seems as if the humiliation dripping from the words is transformed by some miraculous process into the splendor of an ancient epic, look how heroic I was, look how I suffered, but my suffering was not in vain, it was for your sake, so that you would be warned. Suddenly I feel like a goddess who suffered for the sake of humanity, liberated them with her blood, healed them with her wounds, and he listens to me with his eyes closed, his mouth open, nodding his head from time to time, his face concentrated, as if trying to catch faint sounds. This must be how he listens all day to his patients, trying to hear the muffled echo of their words, which is completely different from the words themselves, and I am carried away by his attention, by the deliverance of speaking the words, which once spoken can be sent on their way. I tell him about my father's threats, about my love for Gili that was disrupted, and the more I speak the clearer it becomes to me that I have succeeded in preventing his disaster and magnifying mine, his loss materializes before my eyes and nevertheless I continue, faithful to my mission, determined to leave no stone unturned.

He goes on nodding even after I fall silent, embarrassed by my outpouring, as if I were an old hag accosting strangers in the street, insisting on telling them my life story, I begin to shiver, it seems that nothing remains of the heating that was switched off at midnight, and then he opens his eyes and studies me attentively as he studied the photographs in the old album. I heard another story entirely from you, Ella, he says eventually, his voice quiet and authoritative, not a story of humiliation and unhappiness but a joyful story, full of strength, which I'm sure you wouldn't give up at any price, and I stare at him wide-eyed, tell me, how do you treat people if you can't even understand something so simple, is that what you call strength, is that what you call joy? It was the most terrible night of my life.

It all depends on how you interpret it, he laughs, I try to illuminate hidden corners, not to accept things at face value, sometimes I'm right and sometimes I'm not, but it seems to me that on that night you didn't want to go back to your husband at all, on the contrary, you went there to get his final refusal, the real divorce that would enable you to be free, free of guilt, free of your father who cast a heavy shadow on your life, of excessive dependence on your child, actually you knew that as long as you were living with Amnon your relationship with the child would never be healthy, because he had a distinct role in your relations as a couple, and it was only when you split up that healthier air could flow between you. I get the impression that you knew very well what you were doing when you left your husband, this is the secret knowledge that guides us like a dog guiding a blind man, it wasn't an impulsive decision, it was a deliberate decision, and I'm sure that you would do it all over again, and I examine him doubtfully as if he has taken leave of his senses, and nevertheless his innovative interpretation of the drama of my life attracts me, and I ask, so why was I so miserable, why was it so hard?

The psyche produces dramas in order to feel its life, he says, the logic of the psyche is tortuous, its time is different to ours, its language is different to ours, it's often difficult for us to understand what it wants, just as it's difficult to understand a baby. Sometimes I hear a man talking, and his psyche stands next to him and says something completely different, and I try to mediate between them. You know, he smiles at me a little shyly, I have a kind of habit, when I'm sitting opposite a patient, a word I can't stand by the way, when I'm sitting opposite a person, I try to see his psyche inside him, like seeing a face in the moon or the sun, in the eyes of my colleagues this is pure nonsense of course, but sometimes it gives me a clue, and I listen to him, enchanted, what does my psyche look like, were you able to see it?

Of course, he says, otherwise I wouldn't be here, your psyche is in constant motion, like a curtain blowing in a strong wind, a velvet curtain hanging in a beautiful antique room, and I ask, is that good or bad? I was apparently expecting a more flattering image, and he says, I think it's enchanting, and I comment, but the curtain always stays in the same place, and he says, right, it's the combination that enchants me, movement and stability, and the more he talks the more I marvel at his rarity, as if by chance I have stumbled on a precious charm, a silver tablet bearing finely engraved verses in an ancient Hebrew script, like the amulets found on the south-western ridge of the valley of Gehenna not far from here, a rarity that I dimly sensed before, but that is growing clearer the longer he goes on talking. Every other conversation on earth seems an acerbic, exhausting battle of wits in comparison to this exchange, remote and at the same time familiar to me; were these the things that men said to their women in those far off days, were these the words that walked the corridors of my imagination when I was a girl, when I had no child. How much happiness his words bring me, how attractive happiness is, I never attributed such powers of attraction to it, seeking my freedom, I won happiness, and after tasting it I have no desire for freedom, all I want is to be enslaved to him, like a priestess in his temple, a bondmaid of happiness is what I want to be, chopping wood from morning to night to feed the flames of his fire so that it will never subside.

And then he stands up and gives me his hand, come, let me put you to bed, he says, it's late, and I protest, not yet, stay a little longer, just like Gili when he is told to go to bed, and he says, I have to go, I have a busy day tomorrow, and I still want to see the children in the morning, I go at half past six to wake them up, I can't give that moment up, to see them before they see me, and again I press him, Oded, how will you cope, you won't be able to cope with this separation, when Michal realizes that it's final she won't let you come in the morning, you won't even have a key to your children's home, I forced Amnon to give me back his key, Michal will do exactly the same; why am I insisting on weakening his resolve; and he sighs, okay, I understand, now let me see you go to sleep.

What's there to see, I wonder, I don't have any special rituals, and he smiles, I'm sure you do, just promise you'll ignore me completely, don't do anything in my honor, can you do that? And I say, ignore you? Not a chance, and I take off my dress and stand before him in my panties, my hair falling over my upper body, will he put out his hand and part my hair like a curtain, but his interest is absolutely passive, and at the same time extremely thorough, enriching my simple routine movements with splendor and significance just by watching them with a serious, slightly tense expression, as if it were a complicated dance whose steps he must learn. Is that how you sleep? he asks, and I say, no, not at all, and he says, so show me how you really go to bed, don't do anything in my honor, okay, try to ignore me, as if I wasn't here.

There are three brown felt teddy bears on my pajama top, and Gili would point to them and say, this is you and this is Daddy and this is me, even though all three are exactly the same size, and I put it on with some embarrassment, and brush my teeth, and wash my face and tie back my hair, trying to ignore him, but all the time I remember his presence, there he stands leaning on the door frame, the glass in his hand, riveted to my movements, there he waits for me next to the closed bathroom door like a father for his sick daughter, and when I come out, he accompanies me to the bedroom, let me see you fall asleep, he requests, and I get into bed a little bewildered by him, making room for him next to me, but he sits down carefully on the edge of the bed, let me see you sleeping, and I ask, what is this, an initiation ceremony into some secret sect? And he says, not at all, let me get to know you in my own way, and I look at him in indulgent wonder, the weariness is evident on his face, in a minute he'll go away, what is he looking for, and will he find it here, now this evening too is slipping out of my hands, and he will vanish from my life again.

When will I see you? I ask, and he says, go to sleep, honey, whatever has to happen will happen, and I protest, but if I go to sleep I'll miss you, and he says, on the contrary, but doesn't explain, and I stretch out in bed, it's hard for me to fall asleep when someone's looking at me, I say, and he whispers, do it for me, it's important to me to see you falling asleep, his hands stroke my hair until my eyes close, and I try to keep my mouth tight shut, so that it won't suddenly open in an embarrassing hole with an unpleasant smell, but he speaks to me warmly as if he were my father, stroking my clenched face, would I recoil from Gili's breath, is his smell unpleasant to me? Beloved as my child is how I feel, beloved precisely because of the smallest details, ones I would never have imagined possess the power to arouse love, and now leaves of tranquility drift softly down and collect on the covers, and I close my eyes, but,instead of darkness, a light flames under my eyelids, a blazing red light, a summer sun at noon in the middle of the night, and I open my eyes but the room is dark, and again the light blazes when I close them, a bouquet of ripe roses burns under my eyelids, my flower lips part for the kiss of the fire, their red petals quickly turn to ash poured into little jars, one jar contains a whole bouquet. Look, I murmur, one jar of ash is enough for a whole bouquet, but he is no longer on the edge of the bed, perhaps he's on the chair, next to the computer, is that him or a pile of clothes that has taken on the shape of his body in the darkness, and in fact what does it matter, even if he has left already he is present here, and the moment it makes no difference to me I fall asleep, sinking into the sleep of a beloved child, a child whose father likes to see her face in the morning before she sees his.

Chapter fourteen

The gleaming sides of the empty pot distort my face, lengthening and narrowing it as I thrust my nose deep inside, searching in vain for evidence of that smell, that strangest of smells; why did he abolish all traces of the night, pour the remains of the soup down the drain, scour and polish the pot like a mirror, wash the plates, clean the table, even take the garbage bag out with him, leaving a fresh one in the can, like changed sheets. I stand perplexed before the marble countertop; what makes a man obliterate all evidence of his presence, not leaving a trace, what is he afraid of, what is he trying to say; if the house were buried with ash now, no material evidence would remain of the last meal eaten at its table, only the evidence of the heart; is that what he was trying to tell me, only if you believe will you remember, only if you remember will you believe, and perhaps he really wanted to say, nothing happened, I never stood in your long narrow windowless kitchen and cooked soup, I never sat next to you on the sofa and listened to you talking, I never accompanied you on your way to sleep.

What makes a man expose without being exposed, caress without being caressed, pleasure without being pleasured, what is the meaning of these eccentricities that enchanted me last night but today swim inside me swollen as the mushrooms floating upside down in the soup among the lumps of melting tahini and disintegrating tuna, a collection of contradictory tastes: admiration and suspicion, excitement and repulsion, gratitude and resentment. I sit down in front of the computer, there are no clothes lying on the back of the chair, apparently it was him last night, watching me sleep. What is he looking for, a likeness to the woman he once loved, the way her face looked when she slept, is this the meaning of the quick, surprising intimacy, his love is poised and ready, that's why it pours out of him so easily, effortlessly, but on the other hand it is not addressed to me, my name isn't printed on it. By mistake I took a package belonging to someone else from the post office, by mistake I opened it and by mistake I enjoyed it, but it isn't mine and never will be mine. The mistake created an illusion of intimacy, but we are actually strangers; do we know each other, he asked; you don't know my husband, she said; no, I don't know your husband, is there anything I would like better than to know him, and again I am tossed from side to side like a curtain in a gale, sitting opposite the computer screen that is being covered with words.

As the island of Thera was shaken and torn to pieces, a huge wave rose to unfathomable heights and rolled through the Mediterranean Sea until it reached the distant shores of Egypt, where the eighteenth dynasty was shrouded in total darkness. Alas, the land is turning like the wheel of the creator, the cities are destroyed, Upper Egypt is in ruins, all is in ruins! The palace has been leveled, if the land ceased from its commotion it would no longer exist, Lower Egypt weeps, alas, all that was still visible yesterday has been utterly destroyed, the land lies desolate as after the cotton harvest, the beasts weep in their heart, the cattle groan, the sons of princes have been thrown into the streets, the land reverberates with wailing, wails of mourning and lamentation, the land is not light, it is not light but darkness, the land is the handmaiden of the God Aton, the god of the disk of the sun, who under the cover of the heavy volcanic darkness becomes a single, abstract god, without figure or form, for he is the sun itself, the disk of the sun itself as it passes across the sky, deemed the only god by the Pharoah Amenhotep who changed his name to Akhnaton, imposing a profound religious revolution upon his people, a cult difficult to understand and difficult to comply with. Blindly the priests of On would stand on the rock facing the rising sun, removing their shoes, trying to hide their eyes with their hands upraised in the familiar gesture of the priestly blessing, while the people were reluctant to give up a world full of gods, and went on secretly worshipping the old, familiar pantheon.

This route changes every day, not on account of the shifting weather but the colors of the psyche, which turn the same street into an agitated cloud, a steep obstacle course, a blooming garden. Even a single street is impossible to really know, it seems, not to mention a human being, and now at this midday hour it is as transparent and fragile as my happiness, a single crude step could crack it, an overly intent gaze could shake its foundations, and I walk carefully, slowing my steps, trying to come late today, to arrive after the other mothers, or to be more precise, after her. The curiosity that had hounded me in recent weeks has turned overnight into reluctance. I can't bump into her today, her nose red with crying, her defeated eyes, her curls that have lost their vitality, but my dawdling is insufficient, for next to the gate I see all three of them, an attractive woman in a long black coat, her hair the color of mango flesh, and two children, one of them wearing a woolen hat, and the other running toward me, as always there's a demanding request on the tip of his tongue, like the prey quivering in an animal's mouth. Mommy, can I stay here with Yotam? We're waiting for you, for your permission, I want us to have a picnic with them in the park, say yes, say yes, and I look at Michal questioningly, her almost transparent eyes are threaded with red, like a pond in which a murder has been committed, and she sends me a faint smile, it's such a lovely day, I thought we might sit in the park with Yotam for a while, why don't you join us? And I say, thank you, we're in a bit of a hurry, my parents are expecting us, but she looks at me doubtfully, she has already heard me make an excuse before, no less false and feeble.

Please, Mommy, Gili coaxes, we can go to Grandma and Grandpa later? I want to play with Yotam on the lawn, and I realize that I have no choice, that I am doomed to spend the next hour with the abandoned wife of the man I have suddenly fallen in love with. I feel tense as an escaped convict obliged to spend an allegedly relaxed afternoon with a policeman, every word he says and every move he makes is liable to give him away, but excessive caution will betray him too, and at the same time he has no choice in the matter, for backing out will endanger him even more, and I try to remind myself, it wasn't for me that he left her, I was there by chance, after the decision was made, I have no part in her tragedy, I even tried to persuade him to go back to her, what else could I have done, should I have given him up altogether; she wouldn't have gained anything and I certainly would have lost out, if it's even possible at this stage to talk in terms of profit and loss. Who knows, perhaps she'll profit from the separation in the end and I will be the one to lose, and I trail behind them through the park, the glass from the broken bottles glittering in the sun, the rocks huddled together in the grass, like pale animals sunk in sleep, and in the narrow stone canals rain water flows, and I remember the rain collecting above our heads, close together under the transparent plastic sheet; can I give him up, will she ask me to give him up.

She sits down under one of the olive trees, takes a checkered tablecloth out of the wicker basket in her hand, spreads it out, and sets a pile of stuffed pita bread and cut up vegetables in the middle, even a thermos of coffee and a bottle of juice and glasses together with the star-shaped chocolate cookies I know so well, and miraculously there is enough for everyone, the amount perfectly calculated. Did she plan a picnic for four in advance, did she plan to invite us in advance, I'm not the only schemer it seems, not for me alone was this park, teeming with ravens and dogs, transformed into a scene of stormy upheavals, and I look at her with growing unease, she must know, perhaps he himself confessed to her this morning, or perhaps she followed him yesterday like I followed Amnon, saw him going into my house, and this perfectly organized supposedly innocent picnic is immediately transformed into a menacing trap from which we must extricate ourselves as quickly as we can.

Maybe we should leave now, Gili, I wheedle him, Grandma and Grandpa are waiting, but he objects forcefully, attracted by the food piled on the tablecloth, stretching out his hand for a pita with a fat schnitzel peeping out of it, giving off a tempting smell of home, where she stood in front of the stove in the spacious kitchen, turning over schnitzels in the pan while he was moving about my long narrow windowless kitchen with a glass of whisky in his hand. Why don't you call your parents and tell them you'll be late? she suggests cunningly, and I evade the trap, no, it doesn't matter, we'll just make it short, and she asks, coffee? And immediately adds with touching sincerity, the truth is that I wanted to talk to you about something, but not when you're in a hurry, and I can hardly breathe with the suspense, and I murmur, that's all right, I'm not in such a hurry. Under her coat I can see a red and black striped sweater and black pants, her clothes show good taste and deliberate effort, is it directed at me; her hands tremble slightly as she pours coffee for both of us, and an aromatic brown stain spreads over the tablecloth.

I don't know what's happening to me, she sighs, my hands aren't steady, did you see what I did to Yotam yesterday? And I say, no, what did you do? And she pulls the woolen hat off his head, exposing an elongated skull with a cropped, uneven haircut. I always cut his hair, she says, I have good hands, but yesterday I don't know what happened to me, look what I did to his hair, poor thing, and I hardly listen to the content of her words, only to the tone, which is friendly and not aggressive, confiding and not accusing, and Yotam grabs the hat from her and quickly covers his head, only now I notice how upset he looks, his eyes, too, are suspiciously bloodshot. It's because you're a stupid mother, he shouts, because of you I'll have to wear a hat until summer, you're the most annoying mother in the world, and when I see the hurt spreading over her face like the coffee stain over the tablecloth I come quickly to her defense, Yotam, all mothers are annoying sometimes, you know how many times a day Gili gets mad at me? But he is not convinced, I didn't want to have my hair cut in the first place, he wails, she made me and she gave me the worst haircut, and Gili hurries to join the consolation campaign, it isn't the worst at all, he says generously, it looks good on you, and you'll see how fast it grows, I had a bad haircut once too, he adds, unwittingly contradicting his previous words and making up something that never happened, yes, yes, he stresses in the face of my doubtful looks, you don't know about it because I was at Daddy's, and by the time I came back to you my hair grew back again.

His valiant efforts to reassure his friend fill me with shamed admiration, and I say, really? I didn't notice, and I immediately add, there's no reason to feel bad about a haircut, hair grows so quickly, but it seems that it's clear to all of us, even the children who have just turned six, that it's not a haircut we're talking about on this fine sunny afternoon around the checkered tablecloth, and not the ruined locks of the little boy whose head is covered with a hat as if he's sick, and I go on talking to the children and not to her, it's clear to me that she's waiting for them to go away so that she can speak freely, but I fear her words and I want them to stay, to protect me from what looks like an awkward heart to heart at best, so I shower them with questions, show an interest in all their stuff, the kind of questions that Gili usually doesn't take the trouble to answer, but now, with Yotam at his side, they compete to give the fullest answers, which of their classmates they like and which of them they hate, and who is the nicest teacher, and which subject is the most interesting, and so on and so forth, taking quick bites as they speak, until Gili loses patience and pulls his friend after him to the rolling lawns, and in a moment they disappear, leaving half eaten pitas behind them, sticky juice stains, yelps of glee.

She watches them in miserable silence, just when I have readied myself for the onslaught she's silent, her fingers crushing the sprig of rosemary she picked from one of the bushes, until she sighs and says, I'm terribly worried about Yotam, and I ask, why? meticulously brushing the crumbs from my pants, and she answers in a rush, as if afraid of the words, it looks like my husband and I are separating, I wanted to ask you what it was like for you, how Gili took it, how long it took him to get over it, do you mind my asking? And I say, of course not, but the qualification she added gnaws at my ears, it looks like, she said, it looks like, and it seems that a long finger is reaching for us like a branch of the nearby olive tree, pointing at the two of us and saying, you, don't be in such a hurry to grieve, and you, don't be in such a hurry to rejoice.

The knowledge that, in a distorted way, my happiness depends on her calamity, even if it is my uncertain happiness and her uncertain calamity, makes my tongue cleave to the roof of my mouth, and I am struck dumb, look, we are like Hagar and Sarah the wives of Abraham, each clinging to her son, and today one of them will be banished to the wilderness, and there she will wander until she almost dies of hunger and thirst, but the finger pointing at us is still wavering, undecided as to which of us will be banished, and I look at our children skipping between the water canals, in the distance they look like two ravens in their dark coats, in a moment they will spread black wings and glide above us, cawing grimly, their wingspan casting a dark shadow on the checkered tablecloth, from their gaping mouths the cry will leap, the cry of the children whose families have split in two, the cry of the abandoned women, the men thrown out of their homes, the belongings moved from place to place, the cry of love eroded by the passing of the years. Ella, are you alright? she asks and I raise my hand to my forehead, I've got a splitting headache, I'm sorry, and then I say, don't worry about Yotam, he'll be okay, Gili got through it pretty easily, as soon as he realizes that he isn't losing either of his parents, he'll calm down.

My voice sounds grating and metallic in my own ears, how is it possible to reduce a complex process, which in truth has hardly begun, into a few words, but I am unable now to tell her everything I told her husband last night, I am unable to respond to her distress, I am a biased party in her life, my hands are not clean, and, throughout, I am aware of how this conversation will curdle in her stomach in the future when the truth comes out, and therefore I must be as brief as I can, not exploit the opportunity that has come my way for my own needs, not be tempted to ask her questions, not try to extract information from her or cross-reference it, and she looks at me with raised eyebrows as if taking in my words, were they said only in order to reassure her, can it really be so simple, unwittingly she twists the thick wedding band around her finger. How did you tell him you were separating? she asks, and I knit my brows as if trying to fish this detail from my memory, we made it short and simple, I say in the end, you know, the usual thing, we'll always love you, we'll always be your parents, even if we don't live together anymore, the most important thing is to radiate confidence, I declare, examining her suspiciously, perhaps she's feigning innocence, perhaps she really knows what happened between us yesterday, and she's trying in her roundabout way to distance me from him as she shares her distress with me, to awaken an ancient female solidarity in me, so that I will withdraw my hand from her husband.

It seems that my reassuring words have not even scratched the surface of her anxiety, and she takes a pack of cigarettes out of her bag and lights a cigarette with tense fingers, coughs slightly, how, how can he do this to us? she sighs, looking around to make sure the children are far away, you live with someone for almost fifteen years, you think you know him as well as you know yourself, and suddenly look what happens, she says, spreading her arms to encompass the park bathed in a brilliant wintry sun, suddenly he's the one who ruins your life. All these years you worry about your family, about illnesses, accidents, terror attacks, and in the end the catastrophe comes from inside the family, from him, the father of your children.

But why, why did he do it? I whisper, matching my voice to hers, and she shakes her head, as though trying to shake the tears from her eyes, why? For the most banal reason of all, he's got someone else, after all the years, after everything I did for him, encouraged him to study, supported him, took him off the streets, believe me, like the way you take in an alley cat, and this is how he rewards me, and I shake my head in scandalized incredulity, are you sure he has someone? And she turns to look resentfully at a familiar figure approaching us with a broad smile, the beautiful Keren, Ronen's mother, who drops down beside us as if on the point of collapse, I'm so glad you're here, she says, I'm waiting for Ronen to finish one of his activities, am I intruding? No, of course not, I say, overwhelmed by the venomous suspicion that has reared its head, like a scorpion that I'd thoroughly trampled brought back to life, advancing toward me with its stinger aloft. It's the double betrayal that stuns me, her heartbreak, which I can peer into like a burnt-out house, and the heartbreak that awaits me, and Michal wipes her eyes with a paper napkin, politely invites Keren to partake of the picnic fare, but she declines, I don't know what's the matter with me lately, she complains, I have no appetite, I can hardly eat a thing. Her long hair falls onto the tablecloth and she gathers it up with lean hands, her thinness suddenly looks severe, sickly, her complexion sallow. You have to have that checked out, Michal says, it's not something you should neglect, and Keren sighs, forget it, it will pass in the end, I hate doctors, and the conversation is immediately diverted to school affairs, and we talk about security: is the elderly guard really capable of protecting our children, is the fence around the schoolyard high and sturdy enough.

No amount of security will help, Michal says, if anyone really wants to get in we won't be able to stop it, we have to learn to live with the fear, we have no choice, and Keren says, still we have to do what we can, we have to pay for another guard or do guard duty ourselves, don't you think? She turns to me, and I say, yes, we have to have at least two guards, we're in the center of the city, and I let them continue their hollow conversation, who will guard our children from us, who will guard them from their fathers, if he really wants to leave, you won't be able to stop him, just as no one was able to stop me, no protection will help, and I see their lips moving but I can't hear their voices, for once more the scream invades the golden raven park, deep and deafening, racing like fire from the far reaches of the lawn, and I lower my eyes to the stained tablecloth, the remains of the picnic scattered over it like the remnants of our conversation. Which of them to believe, delusional attacks of jealousy, as he said, or a real mistress, as she claims, and I know that the way to the truth is barred, both contradictory versions lie before me and I have to choose one of them and pay the full price, even if I lack sufficient data, and I know that I have to get up and get my son and leave, the conversation between us is flawed and she'll figure that out soon enough and recoil from me, and still I wait for Keren to rise above us on her thin legs in their black leather pants, will she invite us again to come to a party at her house. Sorry for intruding, she'll apologize gracefully, and we will of course deny it, but as soon as she is out of earshot I will ask hesitantly, are you sure he has someone, did he admit it? And she will raise the napkin to her eyes again, her thin lips will tremble, I don't need him to admit it, they always deny it, why should they admit anything? Look at my mother, for years she suspected my father and he denied it, tried to persuade her that she was neurotic and she almost believed him, and even when she actually caught him, he said that she had driven him to it, because of her neurosis, and I listen in amazement to her feverish outpouring, which reminds me of the sounds of the fight I overheard behind the door. Michal, you have to distinguish between your father and your husband, I dare to say, rising to the defense of the cheating husband, maybe it's a completely different story, and immediately I fall silent because she reacts coldly, embarrassed by the frankness of her outpouring, after all, we're not friends, we hardly know each other, and we examine each other in suspicious silence until discordant voices rise in our ears, and our children come running toward us, a long stick clasped in all four of their hands.

I found it, Yotam yells, it's my stick, and Gili wails, I saw it before he did, I said to him, look what a big stick, and we try to reassemble ourselves, to suggest a solution to the problem, there must be another stick here, let's go and find another one, we'll help you, but they both refuse, each afraid to be the first to let go of the booty, and Michal threatens, if you don't find a compromise, I'll confiscate it, neither of you will have it, we'll leave it here and that'll be the end of it, and we split up to look, our eyes on the ground, but all we find are twigs, nothing to compare with the splendid staff. So maybe it can be both of ours, Gili suggests hesitantly when we return empty-handed to the checkered tablecloth, it will be a stick with two homes, part of the time with me and part of the time with you, as if its parents have split up, but Yotam stamps his feet, no way, it's just mine, it will only be in my house, he screams, his chapped lips almost splitting as they stretch, and I pull Gili aside, why don't you let him have it, I urge him, I'll tell you why later, let him have it and I'll buy you something on the way home, but, as expected, he refuses, waving his fists at me, no, I won't, I was the one who found it.

That's enough, I'm not asking you, I scold him, I'm deciding here, and I drag him away, smiling falsely at them, Yotam, Gili's letting you have the stick, I declare, in spite of the loud protests, and to Michal I say, I have to run, hang in there, we'll talk again, and she whispers, thank you, next time I'll see to it that Yotam gives in, and I answer her mutely, what are you talking about, how can there be a next time, when I'm full of love for your cheating husband, soaked in it like a sponge, and as we walk away I steal a backward glance and engrave the sight of them on my memory, standing helplessly next to the checkered tablecloth as if they are homeless, among the remains of the food and the feud, a big stick in their hands.

Gili's crying trails behind me in growing protest, it seems that the whole street is listening, blinds are raised, windows opened, an angry, gasping crying, hoarse and uninhibited, almost dying down and flaring up again. He didn't cry like this when we told him we were separating, or when he fell off the swing and cut his lip, or even when his new car was run over before his eyes, for some reason the loss of this random and unnecessary stick, which no doubt lost its charm as soon as the competition was over and will probably be forgotten on the lawn, has given rise to this overwhelming, unbearable grief, and I drag him behind me with such force that it seems my arm will be wrenched from its socket, stop crying, I can't stand it, I scold him, and he screams, and I can't stand your yelling, you're a bad mother, because of you I lost my stick, you care about Yotam more than me.

Nonsense, I say, it's just that today you have to let Yotam have his way, I can't tell you why, and he sobs, I know why, I know better than you, so what if his father left home, my father left home, too, and nobody let me have anything. I take in this surprising new information, how do you know that his father left home? I ask, and he says, Yotam said so, he said his parents are splitting up, like you, and a new mystery emerges, Yotam already knows, they've already told him, so why did she take the trouble to consult me about how to tell him, and I try to remember how exactly the question was put, what was actually the nature of the conversation that took place between us, was it an unexceptional conversation between two women about their common fate, or a well planned plot, was she deliberately sowing seeds of suspicion, already trying to infect me with the curse that separated them.

We walk into the dwindling sun, its cool rays touch my skin in farewell and their touch is false and chilly. His exacerbated voice is on my heels, he didn't give in to me so why should I give in to him, remember you said you'd buy me a present, you promised, I'll take that stick away from him, who does he think he is, I was the one who found it, what an idiot that Yotam is, I'm not friends with him anymore, I hate him and his father, and I stop dead in my tracks, what, what did you say? And he repeats, I said I hate Yotam's father.

How can you hate a person you don't know, I say, what has he ever done to you? Of course I know him, I know him more than you, once I was over there and he yelled and Yotam's mother cried, and it's not nice for him to leave his child either, and I say, he's not leaving his child, parents who get divorced don't leave their children, like Daddy and I didn't leave you, right? And he delays his answer deliberately until the question dissolves, his eyes peeled to the curb, searching for a new stick.

What will become of the stem of our love, too soft to be broken, only crushed in silence, oozing a greenish liquid under every foot, even the little foot of a child in last year's sneakers. A stem thin as a thread, which has not yet sprouted so much as a bud, dwarfed even by the grass we sat on, and nevertheless planted in my heart, fertilizing the desolate country, alleviating its sadness, spreading a soft glow of hope. What hope, our love will never be a strong, sturdy staff to lean on, but a sticky mess, trampled by my own child, his own children, our previous spouses, and mainly by the calloused feet of guilt. What is the power of love at all in the face of the demanding creatures of reality, in the face of the hungry ravens, the love of a man and a woman who are almost strangers, who drag a backpack and a suitcase behind them through the wet streets, the shards of hostile families.

Chapter fifteen

But then he speaks to me, his voice melodious as a blessing, he looks at me, his eyes radiant as a promise, he touches my shoulder and it seems that these hands will wisely, patiently dismantle the barbed wire fence I have laid before him, the razor-wired fence that stands before both of us, if indeed there is such a thing as both of us, and it seems that in fact there is, for immediately after the light goes off in Gili's room there's a knock at the door. He stands there in his black coat, with his tired, planed face, with his reserved smile, with his tense, stiff-backed stance, all of him there for me, from tip to toe, as if his presence is self-evident in my house this evening, and the evenings to come, and he says, I thought the light would never go off, what do you read to him before he goes to sleep, *War and Peace*? He's holding two well-wrapped silver packages in his hands, I brought some take out from the cafe, have you eaten yet? And I say, no, I was waiting for you, for even if I didn't dare wait, I waited, even if I didn't dare hope, I hoped, and we sit side by side on the sofa, the remains of last night's whiskey in our glasses, bending over the aluminum trays, still warm, with the plastic forks he brought with him, as if this, too, were a picnic in the heart of nature, a reflection of the previous picnic in the company of his wife and child. Is he being careful again not to leave a trace, and therefore came equipped with disposable cutlery, do these details have any importance at all, or only what exists beyond them, the beaming certainty hovering above our heads, above our encounter as it gropes along, a joyful certainty that clashes with its surroundings, like a person walking amid ruins and humming a merry tune, a giddy smile on his face. All the time I try to remind myself we have no chance, there are too many difficulties, the bricks piled on our bodies are too heavy: his children, his wife, my child, the proximity of us all in one neighborhood, one class, but this knowledge does not align itself into a true sensation, it simply clashes with the sensation that has followed him into the room, a calm, enlivening ease, the feeling of a well-paved road marked out for us by the gods, and all we have to do is trod upon it, step by step, one foot after the other.

It takes me by surprise every time, he says, wiping his lips on a paper napkin, how attached people are to their problems, the girl who was just with me was lightly wounded a year ago in a terror attack, and since then she hardly leaves the house, she avoids almost everything life has to offer, but when I recommend medication, she refuses, I'm afraid to change, she says, I'm afraid the medication will turn me into somebody else, and I ask, how long has she been coming to you? But I can hardly hear his reply because of a loud muttering from Gili's room, and I hurry over to his door, nervous, maybe he hasn't even fallen asleep yet, now how will I hide my guest from him, should I hide him in the bathroom, but Gili's eyes are closed, his lips are sullenly pursed, there is an expression of immeasurable exhaustion on his face, as if he has tired of living, he must have been mumbling in his sleep, the words have evaporated, but their foul breath still hangs in the air, maybe he said, I hate Yotam's father, I hate Yotam's father. How can you hate someone you don't know, how can I love someone I don't know; riveted to my son's face I am suddenly reluctant to return to the living room where a strange man is sitting, who is not his father, but the father of another child, with whom he may have been fighting in his dream, trying to pull the stick from his hands; what do we have in common, I can't succumb to that false glow, I have to see the whole picture, its sharp angles, at least for the time being I should keep my distance, everything is too fresh and painful in my home, and in his, I'll tell him right now, this very minute, when I return to the living room.

Before he notices me I see him wiping his mouth again and again with the paper napkin he brought with him, but his lips still have the sheen of the oily pasta sauce, and when I sit beside him on the couch he issues me a look I have come to know, practiced, unsurprised, and asks, are you having doubts, Ella? Straight to the point, as usual, and I sigh, I don't have any doubts about you, every minute I want you more, but it's clear to me that it's impossible for the time being, it's too fast, things are too complicated, and he takes hold of my chin and raises my face to his, his lips cover my mouth in a sudden movement as if trying to draw the doubting words from it, sucking my lips to prevent them from saying anything else, the touch of his mouth bitter and muscular, and when he lets me go my head falls onto the back of the sofa, my eyes are damp, don't believe me, I want to say, please don't believe me, and then he gets up and puts the disposable dishes back into the bag they came in, his lips pursed, puts on his coat in silence, and I watch him, see him slipping out of my life, this isn't what I meant, I wanted him to persuade me, convince me that it was possible, and I beat him to the door, lean against it, Oded, don't go, I didn't mean for you to go, we have to talk.

There's nothing for us to talk about, he says quietly, I heard what you said, if it's impossible for you then there's nothing for me here. I'm alarmed by his reaction, but I want to talk to you, I want to hear what you think, and he raises my face to his again, lingering on every pore in my skin, every sun spot, listen, he says, his voice colorless, the speech impediment becoming more prominent, the syllables entangled in his teeth, I don't have time for games, I want you and I have no problem showing you that, I'm not afraid of the difficulties because they're everywhere anyway, if you want to give up, then go ahead, I'll respect your decision, but don't start bouncing me around on your emotional seesaw.

It's not a seesaw, I protest, I want you too, if we were single without any children it would be completely different, but I can't keep on playing this double game with Michal, seeing how hard it is for her, hearing how you've got somebody else, and not even knowing if it's me or some other woman, then our kids start fighting about some miserable stick, and then you come over and I so want you to stay, but I have a child here who can't so much as see you, and we hardly know each other and already we're saddled with all this, and he comes closer to me, reaches for the door handle; let's take a few things off the table, he says, I left Michal for myself, not for any other woman, even if I never see you again I'm not going home, so she won't benefit if you decide to take yourself out of the picture. I know it will be hard for her and the children, but if something's right then it's right, period. I'm not prepared to reopen every question every minute, I can only function if I have some base that's clear to me, otherwise I go crazy, do you understand? I'm not going home, if you want us to see what we can have together in spite of the difficulties, I'll be glad, and if not, I'll be sorry, but that will be the end of the story, so think about it and let me know, and he opens the door with a sharp movement. A gust of cold, black air hits my back and I say, wait, don't go, I'm sorry, all I wanted was to talk to you, and to my surprise he's immediately pacified, all right, I'll be back in a minute.

Where are you going? I ask, and he says, to throw out the garbage, and I say, now, why? And he says, never mind, it's an eccentricity of mine, I can't relax if there's any garbage in the house. Only at night, I ask, or in the daytime, too? trying to assess the extent of his weirdness, but he doesn't answer, goes downstairs with the plastic bag, and I wait for him at the open door, my fingers on the light switch, exactly like Gili who waits for me at the top of the stairs, afraid to be in the house without me, counting up to fifty out loud until I return, out of breath. But I don't count, only pray silently that I haven't done any harm, and when he comes back he looks at me and smiles, I frightened you, huh? And when I confess with an ingratiating nod, he says, you frightened me too, please don't say things you don't mean, I attach great significance to words, and I nod obediently, but at the same time I wonder, where does this impatience with the vacillations of the mind come from, in him of all people. I watch perplexedly as he washes his hands in the kitchen sink, soaping and lathering every finger. Do you want me to stay, are you sure? he asks again, and I say, yes, I'm sure, and he says, then come to bed, okay? Slowly drying his hands on the kitchen towel, his lips moist, his nostrils slightly flaring, is it okay tonight, he asks, the child won't wake up? The child, he says, as if he doesn't remember his name, and I say, not at this hour, and draw him down the hall to the bedroom, on the way we pass Gili's room, where three night lamps are glowing softly like three stars in the sky, and I take a quick peek at his face that is still angry, as if the stick he found is being confiscated again and again.

Perhaps you should lock the door, he suggests, and I examine the key suspiciously, in fact we never used it, Amnon and I, we always relied on the cover of darkness and the way his voice preceded his steps, but now the threat is far more disturbing, and I lock the bedroom door with the surprised key, the lock tumbling noisily, stiffly, giving rise to the momentary fear that it will not be able tumble back again, but that fear submerges and disappears in the trembling ocean of desire, in the tugging tide of limbs about to be loved. The blue light of the computer illuminates the room in which two people slept for nearly seven years, thousands of nights, but these people seem as strange to me as they are to my guest, an unknown couple, Amnon and Ella, who left here long ago, in a hurry, apparently, for they've left behind furniture, dishes, clothes, pictures, and even a child, a real child, sleeping in his room, unaware that the inhabitants have changed, and when he wakes up he will come into my arms as if I am his real mother, even though I am utterly estranged from her, the woman who slept in this bed night after night for almost seven years, somehow I've managed to leap over her in a kind of spectacular pole vault from my girlhood to today, and I thank her for permitting me to use her comfortable bed, her spacious room, her computer, in front of which now sits a man who has made my lips tingle, and asks, may I read?

Lower Egypt weeps... Alas, that has perished which yesterday was seen. The land is desolate like after the scything of the flax ... All the animals weep in their hearts. Cattle moan... the children of princes are cast out in the street... he reads aloud in a surprised voice, what is this, it doesn't seem academic, did you write it? And I say, of course not, it's from an old papyrus document that was found in Egypt. It was written by a sage called Ipuwer, it's not clear if he was describing the past or prophesying the future. When did he live, he asks, and I say, like everything in archeology, there's a difference of opinion, I'm trying to show a connection between the phenomena he describes and the Ten Plagues, but most researchers believe that the plagues never happened at all, that they're fictional.

What difference does it make if it really happened or not, he says, in my field that's immaterial, it hardly matters to me if someone's telling a true story or a fictitious one, from his point of view it's the truth, and I say, in our profession we ostensibly try to reach the objective truth, but in many cases the line remains blurred, I seem to be trying to prove something that can't be proved, and he says, you know that Freud compares the mind to an archeological mound, he saw himself as the archeologist of the mind, today they say that the human brain is built like a mound, with its levels arranged in the reverse order, from the newest up to the most ancient, and he passes his hand over his skull, as if to indicate the different levels, and I lie down on the bed opposite him, parting my legs, putting my hand between them, as if I were naked, because his eyes are wandering from the computer screen to the covert intersection of the body, and he says, you always have some kind of secret down there, it's charming the way you take that secret with you wherever you go.

Come here already, I hold out my arms to him, but he remains sitting erect on the chair opposite the screen, wait, he says, don't let just anyone touch your secret, and I say, you're not anyone, and he says, but you don't know me, you don't even know yet if I have someone else, and I say, at the moment I really don't care, come already, and he strokes the keyboard with his fingers; you know, we used to have a candy drawer in our house, when my father was hospitalized, my mother would fill the drawer up for us, and I wait in silence for the rest of the story, but he pauses, his eyes lingering between my legs, when I was a child I thought that's what you had there, a candy drawer. His slow measured speech plays in my ears, the elongation of the words, it's a secret waiting to be deciphered, he says, at first it waits gladly, and then sorrowfully and in the end it stops waiting, and then he stands up and comes toward me, sits down on the edge of the bed, pulls down my pants, looks at my naked thighs, his brows knitted, the lines between his eyes deepening, like a lost tourist examining a complex map.

The locked room with its blinds drawn and its blue light fills with heavy breathing, it seems that every limb is breathing separately, each in its own way given over to expectation, even the restless mind, used to straying between fragments of thought sharp as glass, is now focused on the yearning rising from below deck, and when his fingertip touches the sole of my feet, I shiver, a redolent pleasure passed from his hands, his gentleness, so potent and calculating, is threatening, his restraint attractive. Slowly, he whispers, you know I'm not a rusher, talk to me, tell me what you like, and I breathe, you know better than I do, and he whispers, but I want to hear you say it, and I hesitate, touching his face, his skin rough, firm to the touch, contradicting the softness of his speech, and the words flee my head, beating their wings like birds from a dead treetop.

Tell me what your body likes, he says, tell me your secrets, and still I am silent, how hard it is to be precise about desire, how hard it is to believe that you can be truly loved. A recurrent distress wells up in my throat, I see myself among the trees, rapidly digging in the ground with worn fingernails, my clothes and hair covered with earth: I am digging myself a den, a place to hide and never come out. Don't be shy, he whispers, I want to hear you, I've already told you, words are important to me, and I hear myself speaking as I've never spoken before, in a voice that is not my voice, telling the story of a body about to be returned to the earth, a deceptive body whose growth was arrested, wizened before it ever ripened, and the intense solace of the forgotten grace of youth spreads through me, as though the illusions of the past have come to fruition long after they've lost their vitality, and it seems that I can hear the peel of my ancient loneliness splitting, the protective barrier, from those I loved too, from their presence and their absence, splitting and keeling like a wall, the city-palace is exposed, a visiting stranger walks through the innermost chambers, looking at the wall paintings, seashells, octopuses and dolphins, winged cherubs, bare-breasted goddesses and muscular gymnasts, and I accompany him with fretful delight, how scary it is to part from loneliness, how loud, its voice carrying from one end of the earth to the other.

For a long time he rests his ear on my thigh as if listening, his hand stroking my skin, I hope you're patient, he whispers at last, a coiled silence filling the air, because I don't intend to go to bed with you tonight, and before I can ask why, he says, it wouldn't be right, we're not alone, reminding me of the child forgotten behind the wall, he has no part in our love, in our pleasures, in the plot thickening under the cover of his cantankerous sleep.

When will you be alone? he asks, and I say, over the weekend, it sounds so promising, the weekend, but it's also far away, at the end of an eroded road. For a moment it seems too tall an order, and he is still fully dressed, smelling of detergent, as if his clothes are being washed at home along with his children's clothes, for the exact same smell comes from the clothes of his son, and I try to undo the buttons of his shirt, he recoils but then allows me to expose his narrow, unassuming chest, and even in the poor light cast by the computer screen I can see the big scar bisecting the length of his chest. What's that? I ask, and he says, never mind, it doesn't matter now, and I persist, my fingers on the taut skin, what's that? I ask again, and he says, my father attacked me once when I was a small child, I can barely remember it, and I look at the scar in horror, how did he do it, with a knife? And he pushes my hand away, what difference does it make, my father did it with a knife, your father did it with words, the main thing is that we won't do it to our children, and I think of them, of our three children, as if the three of them were sleeping now in the next room, the fair little girl who sat on his lap as proudly as though she'd been crowned, and next to her the two boys; haven't we done it to them already, in our own manner.

His increasingly exposed body is surprisingly dark in contrast with his complexion, as if everything said to him during the day drains the color from his face, and I look at the lean, damaged chest, the face too big for the shoulders, the same disproportion between his head and his body, which for some reason gives me a strange sense of relief, his hands rest on my breasts, with one movement I will be aroused again, and this knowledge is enough to keep the fire burning in the far regions of my body, the lower half of his body is still clad, belted with a leather belt, who knows what scars are hiding there. He falls silent, stretches out on his back next to me and closes his eyes, felled by sudden exhaustion, absolute as a loss of consciousness, and with his shirt removed his body is open to my gaze and I try to attack it with my eyes, as I've been trained, utilizing the lull to amass data for the coming battle. His words have tremendous power, but when his hypnotic speech runs dry, he is like anyone else, his assertive face folds into its creases when his eyes are closed, and I list his flaws to myself with satisfaction, is this really the only way to feel a sense of worth, instead of being ennobled by his charms, I ensure my own security by heaping defects and shortcomings on him, for instance the sharp snore whistling through the parted lips that swallowed my lips, and I examine him in disappointment; it appears that he is just like Amnon, like all those other men who fall asleep immediately while women toss and turn, nurturing a primeval bruise, and although I am alarmed by the force of the hostility toward a man who has done me nothing but good, I find it difficult to staunch the bitter flow.

Yes, the moment he falls asleep his strangeness is awakened, and with it alienation and suspicion, a strange man is in your bed, the bed your child climbs into early in the morning, and again I hear Gili's voice, I hate Yotam's father, I hate Yotam's father, is that him murmuring something through the cracks of his sleep, is he calling me, and I drag myself out of bed and hurry to the door, but the door of course was locked hours ago, so as to spare all parties from embarrassment, and now I have to turn the key, the simplest of actions, just as I locked it I'll open it, and I grip it firmly and try to turn it, but the lock sticks, refusing to retrace its steps and refusing to reach its destination, as if a pin has been inserted in the keyhole and is preventing the key from completing its revolution, and I kneel down before it, pressing my eye to the narrow hole, straining my ears to hear what's happening on the other side of the wall. Is he awake, is he calling me; in the small hours his sleep crumbles and he tries to invade the fortress of my bed like a small bold knight, what will I do if he really has woken up, how will I be able to see to his needs through the locked door, be his mother through the keyhole, and I look around and try to find a solution, there isn't even a telephone in the room, there are no useful appliances here besides a sleeping man, who has upset the order of my life with his outlandish proposal, to lock a door that has never been locked, with a key that has never been tried, a man who doesn't belong to the house and who doesn't know its ways, which have now been thrown into nightmarish disarray, setting an insurmountable obstacle between me and my son.

What will I do if he calls me now, if he needs some water, to be tucked back in, taken to the bathroom, what will I do if he knocks at the door, what will I say when he discovers that it's locked, perhaps I'll tell him to call his father, but Amnon no longer has the key, and anyway the front door is locked from inside, a locksmith will have to be called in to open it, and the same goes for the bedroom door, and then the two of us will be discovered here to our great chagrin, and I throw myself onto the cold floor, stunned by my inability to reach my son, who cannot imagine that his call will not be answered on this night. Is motherhood at odds with love, is maternal love, the oldest and strongest of loves, unable to tolerate competition. Tonight I attempted an impossible combination, to love a strange man with my child in the next room, and the bill has already been presented and I have no idea how I'll pay it, and I implore him in silence, sleep, my darling, don't wake up, seeing his head shining in the dark between the teddy bears like a fourth light, and I raise trembling fingers to the key, swearing it to obedience in a whisper, and again it refuses, and I try lubricating the keyhole with the hand cream lying on the table but the key stays stuck, taunting me with its obstinacy. Why didn't I insist when he suggested locking the door, and why is he sleeping so calmly as if the problem isn't his responsibility, who's ever heard of such a thing, that a mother can't go to her son when he calls her in the middle of the night, and I curse his tranquil sleep, he lies there undefended, exposed to my hostility, bereft of the words that cast a smokescreen as sweet and fragrant as incense, should I wake him up now so that he can kick the door to pieces, and Gili, who will of course be awakened by the noise, will be astonished to see Yotam's hated father rising from the ruins, and then the voice I was so afraid of hearing comes clearly to my ears, his nocturnal baby voice, when he forgets to pretend to be a grownup. Mommy, is it morning? he pipes, is the night over? He is haunted by the fear that one day he will be faced with a night that is not capped by a morning, and I answer quickly, pressing my lips to the door, go back to sleep, Gilili, it will be morning soon. My heart is beating so hard that it shakes my body, like a reed in a storm, and I collapse onto the bed, go to sleep, go to sleep, I murmur, wake up, wake up, I murmur into Oded's ear, and he sits up immediately, his expression reserved. What's wrong? he asks, his voice sharp, and I whisper, Gili called me and I can't open the door, and he jumps out of bed, sits on the chair opposite the computer, like at the beginning of the evening, rapidly buttoning his shirt, like someone practiced in the art of survival he wakes up, suspicious and alert, so different from Amnon who would groan indulgently and sink into a prolonged slumber of parting from his previous sleep.

His eyes scan the room, lingering on my face, on the shuttered windows, taking in the radically altered atmosphere. Complaint hangs between us where yearning intimacy formerly resided, and I whisper, what should we do? He's already woken up once, in a minute he'll call me again. To my surprise he gets dressed quickly, as if he hasn't understood my words, as if the child is about to charge into the room, but this is not the danger, no one will enter the room and no one will leave it, the room is sealed, cut off from the cycle of life in this house, like a railway car detached from the rest of the train, and now a small child has been left alone on that train, a child of six, whose mother lusted after love, and the word itself produces a wave of revulsion, there is no love for mothers, can any love in the world, however great and passionate, justify the dread of this child when he realizes that he has been left alone in the train, and my skin feels as if it is opening its pores to vomit out the pleasure it has enjoyed, and my hair bristles in furious denial, and I moan, what are we going to do, looking hostilely at the shriveled man by the computer, it seems that the scar is drawing his shoulders together like folded wings, and his chest is sinking and vanishing, disappearing.

Calm down, he says, there is a solution, we just have to find it, and he re-examines the room in which there is no telephone and no sharp instrument, and no possibility of getting out through a window or a balcony, only a bed and a computer and a closet, a transparent shadow of intimacy, a faint echo of moans of pleasure, and in the end he focuses on the key stuck in the keyhole, approaches it warily, warms it a little between his hands as if to allay its suspicions, and with a rapid, casual movement, tilts it sideways and turns it, with his hand completing the movement and the surprised key following suit before it manages to object.

The door is open, Ella, he states, pointing to it with a theatrical flourish, and I burst out before it locks again, go to Gili's bed and kiss his forehead, his face, which has relaxed in the meantime, soothed by the magic wand of sleep, a few stuffed animals have fallen on the floor and I pick them up carefully as if they, too, might wake up, and arrange them next to him, turning their heads to face him, like body guards, sleep, my sweet, I murmur, but he is sleeping, and I look at the door, Oded is standing on the threshold, blocking the light from the hall, beckoning me to come out, as if this room is out of bounds to him, and I go to him, thank you, I whisper, slightly embarrassed, that was scary, I was really scared.

Yes, he nods, you told yourself a scary story, and I stiffen; what do you mean I told myself, it was real, the door wouldn't open, it was stuck, you don't believe me? And he chuckles, of course I believe you, apparently it was a bit jammed, the question is, what's behind it? And I'm already on the defensive, what do you mean, it's a lock that's never been used, and he says, yes, but the fact is that I was able to open it without a problem.

What exactly are you getting at, I ask, and he says, it's obvious, you didn't want to open the door, you didn't want to go to your child, the sticking place wasn't in the keyhole it was inside you, and I protest, inside me, what garbage, the fact is that I tried to open the door, the fact is I was terrified, and he says, yes, our deepest fears are of ourselves, isn't that clear to you? And I listen to him in astonishment and indignation, what garbage, Oded, I'm not prepared to accept that baseless interpretation, I didn't want to take care of my child? How do you know what I want and what I don't want, how well do you know me at all? And he chuckles, his fingers brushing my face, calm down, you don't have to accept any interpretation, I don't usually analyze the people close to me like that, and even if I do, I don't share my conclusions with them, but this time I had no choice, it was too transparent, and you were too blind. Okay, he says, forgive me for the harebrained analysis, I'm leaving before you throw me out, a thin, reserved smile dawns on his lips as he opens the door in his black coat, which covers the buttoned corduroy shirt, which covers the large scar, whose shape is the shape of a trident.

Chapter sixteen

Keep away from him, my mother would say, everyone knows that he's sick, and I would protest, what do you mean, sick, he looks perfectly healthy, and she says, you're so naive, it's only in remission, who knows how long it will last, you're new in the class and you don't know yet, everyone knows except you, he won't live to see seventeen, and I refuse to believe it, he looks so strapping in his white tennis clothes, he's always pre- or post-practice, he always looks relaxed, not worried about anything, all the girls flock to him, and he was the first to take any notice of me in the new class, of my face, ravaged by sleeplessness, offering me access, a gesture of inestimable value that I didn't recognize until, one after another, they all followed his lead, till the strange, alienating city turned its warm face to me, and one Friday he called, my parents are gone for the weekend, he said, I'm alone at home, come over, tell your parents you're sleeping over at Dorit's, and I set it up with Dorit, who lived across the street from him; then, too, it was the heart of winter, the sky erupted overhead as I left the house, accompanied by her suspicious indignation, I hope you're not going to Gilad, she said, she always insisted on calling him Gilad even though everybody called him Gili, I know you're flattered by his attention, but believe me, it's only because he's sick.

What do you want from me, I'm going to Dorit, I growled at her, and in a few minutes I parted from the blue-blooded streets and arrived at the apartment blocks of the housing project, so similar to each other that I always mixed them up, it was easier to distinguish between the trees in the orange grove next to our old house. Long empty sleeves leered at me like living creatures hanging upside down on the laundry lines, the thin concrete walls black as basalt in the storm, and he opened the door without a shirt, in his tennis shorts, as though all his clothes had been forgotten outside in the storm, his teenage chest was smooth and golden, his hair touched his shoulders, dripping water from the shower onto his skin, his eyes gleaming like leaves after the rain. How lovely he was, as if he wanted to stop the breath of the world before he abandoned it, to leave an indelible stamp of youth behind him, and he made us thick hot chocolate, and read me a story he had written, how beautifully he writes, and he's at the top of the class too, and the best at sports, and the most charming, and everybody loves him and nobody knows who he really loves, and even I don't know if we're a couple, there is always something ambiguous between us, and when I look at him I am filled with yearning for his glorious youth, which reflects indirectly on my own clouded, insubstantial one. He notices my look and smiles at me, you're special, Ella, he says, you're not like everyone else, your life won't be ordinary, you'll do something valuable, and I say, why me, you're the one destined for greatness, you'll probably write a novel that everyone will admire, and I'll read it and call you, but you won't remember me at all, and he waves his hand dismissively, what does this gesture mean, in spite of myself I look for signs, did you know that you wouldn't live to see seventeen, what did you mean when you said, only the earth will read what I write.

His little sister has gone away with his parents, and when night falls he offers me her bed, you're about the same size as she is, he laughs, only she's in third grade, and I tell him about my breasts that are afraid to grow, that night in the dark I tell him everything, filling the space between the two beds, about how lonely I am in the face of the scolding, the prohibitions, the threats, how I dream of having a sister or brother at my side, maybe then I'll be able to grow; I wish I could stay here forever, in your sister's bed, and when he suddenly gets out of bed I ask where to, and he says to you, his golden body glowing in the dark like a big candle, luminescent, comforting me with eager hands, is this the taste of youth, tangy and feverish, antecedently disappointing. We writhe on his nine year-old sister's bed, have you made love with anyone before, he asks, his language lofty as always, and I say, no, have you? And he says, not really, and I don't know what that really means, is it the burning between my thighs, and I draw back, not yet, Gili, it's too soon for me, for in my ears I hear my father's ceaseless warnings, a person needs brakes, or else he'll crash, like a car, sowing destruction all around.

But I don't have time, he whispers, I have no time, and I ask why, a sticky dread pressing my limbs together, but he evades the question, it doesn't matter, it doesn't matter now, what a sweet sister I have, he says, and his fragrant hair tickles my face, his skin is smooth and tight, as if it's about to tear, and I'm frightened by the unfamiliar closeness, let's go to sleep, my beautiful brother, and he says, absolutely not, it's forbidden to sleep, and then I know that it will happen tonight, even if it is too soon, because he whose will is clear will always trump the vacillator, and I wait for words, but I hear only breathing, he pants as if he is alone, silently, fervently, disappointingly, give me the words that will bestow meaning on our breathing, that will allay our loneliness, say that I am your beloved, am I destined to search for signs forever.

One of us is sobbing or perhaps both of us are, on the coldest night of that winter, clinging to each other as if hiding from a stalker, until we fall asleep in his sister's narrow bed, and early in the morning a sharp ring of the doorbell wakes us, and my mother is standing there, and she hisses, it's lucky for you your father doesn't know, looking furiously at my body draped in his tee-shirt, which is as long as my nightgown; if your father finds out you're finished, come home immediately, and like an inanimate object I am snatched away, with no time to say goodbye, and all the way home she drives with gritted teeth, breaking the only alliance between us, the alliance against my father. If this doesn't stop right away I'll tell him, she threatens, you know I'm not like him, I have no problem with you going out with boys, but not with him, believe me it's for your own good, that boy is sick, and I scream, what are you doing, what are you doing? For that very reason I have to live with him as much as possible, take me back right now, and the temptation to jump out of the driving car is strong, to return to him and hear the words of love.

I'm not willing to see you get attached to him, she says through gritted teeth, believe me I know what I'm talking about, I'm not prepared to see you become a widow at the age of sixteen, and the next morning I waited for him at the gate, but he didn't come to school, and the teacher told us that on Saturday there had been a sudden deterioration in his condition and he had been flown to a hospital in Switzerland, and everyone who could should donate money, we should all tell our parents, and write letters, and my mother contributed generously, as if this was the opportunity she had been waiting for, and the money was collected and the letters were written, but the beautiful gifted boy, the pride of his little family, the pride of the poor neighborhood he came from, the pride of the school and the class, did not return from the hospital in Switzerland and did not live to celebrate his seventeenth birthday, and I, who was not given the chance to become his widow, swore that if I ever had a son I would call him Gilad, and if my husband refused I would leave him immediately, but Amnon didn't refuse, and yet I left him later, for entirely different reasons.

Your mother was right, he says, totally right, wouldn't you have done the same thing? Would you have allowed your daughter to get involved in that type of relationship? I understand your attraction to sex and death, we all dream of making love and dying, or making love and living forever, which is more or less the same thing, but there is no doubt that your mother fulfilled her maternal role, she had no choice, and I say, you're absolutely wrong, she had no right to snatch me away like that, without giving me a chance to say goodbye, everything was cut off so tragically, not only his great tragedy, but my insignificant one too, I wasted my entire youth on it, on trying to understand if he loved me. He asked for his stories to be buried with him, and I would dream of digging up the ground and finding the stories, and reading, at last, that he loved me, for years afterwards I couldn't make love, perhaps that was what killed him, it was such a cold night and he sweated, the sweat gave him chills, perhaps if I hadn't been with him it wouldn't have happened.

Yes, he says, anger can definitely kill, and I ask, what anger, at my mother? And he says, no, anger at him, he forced himself on you, you wanted a brother not a lover, and he slept with you and abandoned you, without even satisfying your narcissistic need, no wonder you punished him, and I repeat in horror, I punished him? What are you talking about? And he smirks, calm down, I'm speaking symbolically, you're always amazed to discover the existence of the subconscious, I'm beginning to think that people who deal with stones don't understand human beings. Really? Well, I'm beginning to think that you impose your weird interpretations on reality without taking the facts into account; how can you say such baseless things? I say in a fit of outrage that melts in the face of his smile, and he says, by the way, I wouldn't have agreed to that kind of memorial gesture, I wouldn't have let you name our son after that boy, and I ask in surprise, really? Why not? It didn't bother Amnon at all, and he says, it would have bothered me, choosing the past, the unsurpassable, there's something taunting about a lover who died young, it doesn't seem healthy to me, not for you, and not for your son and certainly not for your husband, and I scowl at him again, reluctant to admit Amnon's advantage over him, if it really is an advantage, did my choice of the past dictate our future?

Do you have any more dead lovers in stock? he inquires, and I say, no, that's the only one, and he grins in relief, good, then at least we won't have to argue about that if we have a child, and I hold my breath, looking through the arched window toward the Old City walls, David's Citadel covered with black storm clouds, is that what you see in me, a new, united family, while I see youthful fantasies; it wasn't a child I wanted when I left Amnon, and yet I can imagine for a moment that on the floor at the foot of the table there is a baby in a portable car seat, and he is rocking himself gleefully as Gili once did, propelling himself around the house with back arches and leg movements, and although the child is far from reality, it is impossible to ignore him once the word has been spoken, even if his voice never reaches my ears and his smell never reaches my nose. Will we ever sit like that, surrounded by new and old children, will that be our consolation, will that be what defeats us, and I laugh, you're talking about a child already? We haven't even slept together yet, and he says, you're right and that's a glaring oversight that will be corrected within the next few hours, I assure you; why don't you finish what's on your plate already and we can get out of here? And I contemplate the colorful remains of the fish and salad and sweet potato, and sigh, why don't you finish it, I'm not hungry anymore.

I hope your sexual appetite is more voracious, he grins, drawing my face toward his and planting quick kisses on my lips, as if the restaurant is empty, as if the Old City walls are not watching us now with oppressive stone eyes, and it feels as if my bones are growing soft, doors are opening with a supple, inviting whisper; this time I won't say it's too soon for me, for right now his wish is mine and my wish is his, and when we rush out, leaving the money on the table without waiting for change, I look pityingly at the faces of the few customers, how miserable they seem, how weak and worried, and I feel as if I have a consoling message for them, a message that has taken long months to reach me. Don't be afraid, don't be afraid of change for you will be born again and again, your story will be written again and again, and the new life will overshadow the old, look at me, you wouldn't believe where I was only a short time ago, and look where I am now, wearing a new suit of love instead of the rags and tatters that barely covered my nakedness, a new love that was written inside me line after line in mysterious ancient letters, and it seems that now, with his face beaming at me like a flattering mirror, the letters are coming together, on this Friday afternoon, opposite the walls as the mustard rays of the sun pierce the curtain of clouds, hinting at the existence of other seasons sitting in the storerooms of the sky, waiting their turn, hiding in their bosom all that is in store for us.

In the parking lot he is greeted by a young woman with her hair so severely combed back it looks as if the teeth of the comb are still dug into her scalp. She flashes him a meaningful smile and follows us with her big, made-up eyes. Who's that? I ask and he replies, no comment, and I go on, a patient of yours? And he says, no comment, and I tug at his arm, all right, just say that she's not your lover, and he moans, no, she's not my lover, what's the matter with you? In the end you'll be like Michal, would you like me to suspect every man you say hello to in the street, and I say, certainly not, believe me I was never suspicious of Amnon at all, but I don't know you well enough, and Michal's jealousy might be contagious, and again I remember our conversation over the checkered tablecloth, yes, it was deliberate, she was trying to spread the germs of her jealousy around me, and I try not to think about her when I get into the car, about the bleak weekend awaiting her, alone with the two children, has she invited her parents over for dinner in order to blur his absence, to enlarge the shrunken family.

He drives carelessly, a little preoccupied, promise me not to ask questions like that anymore, he says, I don't want you being like Michal, and I say, all right, I'll try, but I'll definitely be a little like Michal sometimes and you'll definitely be a little like Amnon, it's inevitable, and he says, maybe, but this is something I'm very sensitive about, and I examine his profile, what are you not sensitive about, but for now all this just sparks my curiosity, as if I am holding an ancient figurine, a human-like figure, in my hands, and I nestle up to him until his face softens, how frosty he was this morning when he said, Ella? I didn't think you would call, and I said, we made a date for the weekend, didn't we? And he sighed, what will I do with you, you're not prepared to pay a price, how will you have a country if you're not prepared to pay taxes, and I say, I pay taxes all the time, I just don't want to sacrifice my child.

Are you out of your mind? he said; who asked you to sacrifice your child? And when he said your child his tone was unpleasant, but I ignored it; let's meet for lunch, do you know the new restaurant opposite the Old City walls? And now I say, this isn't the right direction, you have to turn left here, and he smiles, puts his hand on my knee, the question is where we want to go, and I say, home, no? And he says, whose home? We don't have a single home, come and let me show you my house.

I thought you lived in the clinic, I say, and he grins, you're not up to date, and I say, you're not keeping me up to date, the dust of a dull insult burns my eyes, he's been making a life, signing leases, transferring funds, committing himself to dates, dipping his feet in the churning river of life while I was busy praying that I didn't chase him away for good, waiting in suspense for the end of the week; it seems that the road to the end of this week is too long for me, the destination too far, the path littered with obstacles, and great happiness is promised to those who walk it's length, but how monumental is the effort. When exactly will the happiness begin, when he enters my house, when he enters my body, when I imagine all this is truly happening, but where is my private happiness to be found, happiness not tucked away in the pocket of a man, arriving with him and leaving with him, perhaps it is this I should be seeking on this weekend, for when I was a child I had no husband, I had no child, I slept alone in a narrow single bed, I woke alone, the sky changed before my eyes, with its blue light quenching the fire of the sunrise blazing between the covers.

At the end of an avenue of bony carob trees, their limbs distorted with age, their unwanted fruits surrounding them like a decaying shadow, he parks his car, not far from my home, not far from the home he's abandoned. I know the street, but not the narrow lane splitting off from it like a broken branch from a tree trunk, I have never walked down this steep slope, never stepped on the gray patches of asphalt, which give rise to a feeling of neglect, as if this lane is nothing but the back yard of a superior street, and not fit for habitation, only for hurrying down, with the steep slope quickening your steps like a tailwind.

The start of a smile appears at the corners of his lips as he flings open the door to the stairwell of the old concrete building, then the door to the apartment, on which his name does not yet appear, leading into a white and almost hollow space, where the smell of fresh paint lingers, making it hard to breathe. I haven't had a chance to buy furniture yet, he says, I just saw this place yesterday and I took it right away, it's the first apartment I saw, do you like it? His voice echoes between the spotless walls, lending his words a celebratory tone, a bit forced, as if he's delivering a speech for my benefit, and I walk through the rooms, their number multiplies, it seems as if each room gives birth to another room. It's enormous, I say with wary admiration; what do you need so many rooms for? And he says, better too many than too few, no? And I say, yes, if it's possible, and, nevertheless, I wonder what kind of life he's imagining for himself, he's at the clinic all day, the children will be here once or twice a week, is he trying to hint at something, to signal that he has already taken us into account, me and Gili, am I now walking through the apartment that is to be my home, like a person unwittingly treading the paths of her future?

Whose room will this be? I point to a completely empty space, square and spacious, with a little porch stuck to it like a drawer that's been left open, and he says, Maya chose that one, and Yotam the one next to it, and I'm happy to say they managed not to fight over the rooms, and again the insult like grains of sand in the corners of my eyes, they were here before me, his children; actually why not, it's supposed to be their home after all, and yet, who is the extra room meant for, next to the bedroom, which has been outfitted with a queen-size bed and a mirrored closet into which I glance in surprise, not used to seeing myself next to him surrounded by white air. The room isn't big, but a big mystery surrounds it, and when he inspects it at my side, an unformed smile shimmering on his lips again, he seems to be studying my face, expecting a question, but I quickly put an end to the half-guided tour and fall onto the lonely sofa in the living room, examining the view from the windows, pine trees too tall for their slender trunks, bare-boned Persian Lilacs, in the spring their branches will be covered with tender green shoots, they will be transformed, like a house filling with the gleeful shouts of children, and it seems that there is nothing I want more than to be here with him in the spring, to see the trees change their mood as if by command.

Congratulations, I say, and he nods absent-mindedly, sitting down next to me on the sofa, he, too, seems ill at ease with the emptiness, is he, too, thinking now about the home he left, about the armchairs and sofas and carpets and paintings and bowl of red pears and notes on the fridge and children's voices and the muffled weeping from one of the rooms. It's still a little sudden for me, he says apologetically, I did it all in a hurry, before I had second thoughts, this month at the clinic was too long, I needed something domestic to make up for the home I had. And a wife in exchange for a wife? I suggest, and he repeats after me, drawing the words out as he does, a wife in exchange for a wife, perhaps, does that bother you? And I reply, not really, as long as it's me, and he says, yes, it's you, I believe it's you, but his eyes stray restlessly over the empty walls, as if he has just noticed that his creditors have confiscated all his belongings in the night, and I whisper, then why don't you make love to me? And he turns to me as if rousing himself from a daydream, but I do make love to you, I make love to you all the time, can't you feel it? And he slowly unbuttons my thin orange sweater, smiling at the exposed chest, like someone happy to meet an old acquaintance.

The daylight becomes you, he whispers, you look softer in the daytime, and it seems that the jeans slide off me of their own accord, willed by the flattered body eager to expose itself, like the bodies of infants restricted by their garments, and even he parts from his clothes with surprising ease, and when he gets up to pee I follow him with my eyes, the way he stands sunk in thought in front of the toilet, and it seems as if I am watching him like then, from the threshold of his house on that Saturday morning, with our children playing in the next room, and he is a complete stranger to me, and here he comes back to me, pale and ardent, draws my face to his and licks my lips, this is what should have happened that morning and look, it's happening now, even if the summer has turned to winter, and not a single leaf is left on the trees. A rare grace has befallen us, a second chance, the permitting of the forbidden, and a high, white wave of gratitude lifts me in its arms and flings me into the depths of this weekend, as if it is a place and not a time, the name of a distant island, Weekend Island, which is in contrast to Children's Island where the children have been left without their parents, on our island the parents have been left without their children, for an albeit limited time, to recall the indulgent, self-centered existence, and even Gili's words, I hate Yotam's father, are stripped of their power because this exceptional man whose hair falls gracefully onto his forehead and whose eyes are moist isn't anybody's father on this weekend, he belongs to my body, abandoning itself to his movements, to my ears falling in love with his voice, to my lips clinging to his lips, to my fingers speaking to his fingers, he belongs to my body, which denies the knowledge that it has ever held another, my vagina has erased the knowledge that a baby passed through it with gargantuan effort, my nipples, stiffening to his tongue, have forgotten that they were ever sucked by toothless gums, that sweetish milk dripped from them, it is only pleasure these organs seek to produce, vapors of hot, bubbling pleasure, vibrations of the ancient yearning howling inside them, the tolling of swaying breasts, the whisper of sighing skin and the growl of desire.

Is it too soon for you, you trust me enough already? he whispers, and I shudder toward his outstretched organ, slide myself around him like a ring, consecrating each of us to the other with rhythmic movements that strive onward toward a point that's vanished like a dream upon awakening, yes, I trust you, even if only because you asked, and when the pleasure arrives, it will knock on the door like a dear, basket-laden guest, slow and heavy, golden as a honeycomb melting in the sun, and we'll be soft and sticky as hot dough, steaming human dolls fresh from the oven, we'll roll over, locked in an embrace, my hair in his mouth, his hands on my shoulders, my face in the hollow of his neck, sinking into a slumber that is neither sleep nor wakefulness but the trickling memory of the body's own glee seeping back in. The remembering doubles and triples the pleasure until it seems that the body can no longer contain it, and the apartment can no longer contain it, nor the steep narrow lane, the street, the entire city, groaning under the weight of the pleasure. The Sabbath siren wails at the windows, and although it is produced by a machine, it seems to burst forth from the heavens themselves, joining in the consecration, adding its blessing to the blessing of the wet stones, the bare branches, and I know that every Friday evening, when I hear the Sabbath siren, I will remember this moment, and this moment will remember me, and even if it never returns again the knowledge that it once happened will accompany me like a prayer whose words have been forgotten. I lean on my elbows and look at his face, and it seems to have acquired a subtle note that only we can see, as if we have suddenly discovered a secret blood bond, a secret childhood experience, his face becomes familiar, as if he had been hiding next to me there, digging a tunnel in the ground of the orange grove, a tunnel that would hide us both.

A chilly winter gloom covers the stones of the homes, the heavy, darkening treetops, and it seems that the radiators set in the wall are trying in vain to heat the big empty apartment, still devoid of real life, and when I reach out for the sweater lying at the foot of the couch he grips my arm, wait, don't get dressed yet, he gets up and brings a blanket from the bedroom, a light, airy blanket, but the air sewn into it seems blazing hot, and he tucks it around my body with little pats, as though he's covering my body with sea sand, silently stroking my hair and spreading it over the cushion, and nothing has yet been said, and it seems that both of us are afraid, and even the words themselves are afraid of stumbling, of marring the magic of the evening, which covers the windows with darkening purple drapes.

In silence I listen to his bare footsteps as he turns on the faucet and fills the kettle with water, opens the wrapping on a cake, draws a knife from the drawer, a plate from the cabinet, and every movement appears more wonderful than the one that preceded it, and I, it seems that my limbs have forgotten how to move, strewn around me, paralyzed by surprise, surprised by joy, a voluntary lameness has come over me, as if I have moved enough, and now I have no more interest in doing so, all I want to do is lie here on the sofa, in the regal pose in which he sculpted me, and see how good everything can be. How rich the cake will be, how aromatic the coffee, how lovely this man is who is taking care of me so naturally, how deep the satisfaction of doing nothing, new laws seem to have descended upon the world, and there is no more need to make an effort, the offerings arrive one after the other, in a ceaseless parade of delight, and when he lays the tray down on the sofa next to me he says, now what will you do, you can't complain that we haven't made love yet, and I laugh, I don't think I'll ever complain about anything again, I'll have to do something else with my life, and he chuckles, why, did you complain a lot? And I say, endlessly.

About what, for instance? he asks, handing me the hot coffee, and I sip quickly, a few drops escape from the cup, trickle down my chin, and fall onto my chest. He bends down and collects them on his tongue, and I sigh, what difference does it make, what's the point of trying to remember my former life, which seems to me now like a dark narrow path, full of pits and potholes, a path whose sole purpose was to bring me to this moment, to this apartment, to this man, and with typical rashness I dismiss all my years with a wave of my hand, as if there wasn't a single worthwhile moment in them, as if no thread will stretch from my former life to my new life, no connection, no similarity, and with the arrogance of someone saved from a disaster who imagines that his happiness is now guaranteed, I repeat, what difference does it make, from now on I'll never complain about anything again, and he looks at me in amusement, promises made in bed have a limited warranty, you know, his hands play with my hair, like a child stroking a cat's fur again and again, waiting for the soothing purr.

The muffled squawk of a startled bird emerges from the depths of my bag, surprising me in its familiarity, and I rummage around in the bag, I'll just see if it's Gili, but even when it turns out to be another number on the screen I answer and hear her grating, perpetually anxious voice, Elinka, where are you, you haven't been home all day, my mother complains, and I say, I'm with friends, and she asks, friends of Gili's? as if I no longer have any existence of my own, and for some reason I say, yes, and she asks, you remember you're having dinner with us this evening, you and him? And of course I've forgotten, I must have agreed without thinking, forgetting that Gili wasn't even spending the weekend with me. So be here at seven, she says, I made his favorite pudding, and I say alright, without pointing out her mistake and filling her in on the latest developments, as if the invitation is dragging me toward them with an irresistible pull, as though it were decreed, for more and more I feel inclined to surprise them this evening, to flaunt my new and unexpected happiness before them, to set the blessing I received here against the curse issued there.

Oded, I have plans for us this evening, I nestle up to him, I hope you don't mind, and he's surprised, really? I hope they don't include other people, and I say, not many, just two, a couple, and he protests, Ella, you have to consult me before you make plans, I see so many people during the week, over the weekend I have to be alone, and I say, it's something I forgot about, and it's too late to cancel now. Well, who are they? He sways, raising my chin, which is already lowered in insult, and I say, my parents, I want us to go to my parents for dinner, and he recoils, don't you think it's too soon, taking me to your parents for Shabbat dinner like a prospective groom? But I insist, if it's not too soon to sleep with me, it's not too soon to go to my parents.

What's one got to do with the other, he grumbles, where did you get these old fashioned ideas from, who are you trying to punish, do they know you're not coming alone? And I say, of course they know, and he sits up reluctantly, let me think about it, I'm going to take a shower, his narrow body moves stiffly as if a careless movement might undo the ancient stitches in his chest, and I wrap myself in a blanket and stand in front of the window, the wind sways the treetops as if they were a vast herd of animals, coming to life at night, advancing slowly in the dark, tomorrow they will already be in another place, and I turn my face from the window to the room where a single sofa stands clinging to the wall, trying to transport my furniture here in my imagination, weightless the pieces float through the air, a sofa, two armchairs and an orange cotton rug, and bookshelves with sad gaps in them like eye-sockets, and in their wake floats a child, his eyes autumnal, his hands full of little toys dropping from his fingers as he flies, and I, when I was a child I had no home, I loved the orange grove next to our house as if it were my home, only there did I feel protected, as the sunbeams sewed the golden tips of the branches together above my head.

I admit it's hard for me to say no to you, he says upon return, his fragile chest exposed, pink from the shower, smelling faintly of lavender, the lower half of his body clad in black pants, his hands fastening his belt, but this is really not right for me now, don't be offended, let me be your lover, don't turn me into your bridegroom yet, and I say, okay, no problem, I'll go by myself, jumping up as if the floor is burning beneath my feet. I shower rapidly in the bathroom with its pale blue tiles, the vapors that touched his body have not yet evaporated and they float around me, around the insult swelling even though I know that justice is with him. Who needs it at all, where does it come from, this drive to provoke my parents, to let them feel the new baby of my happiness, to pinch its cheeks with their chilly fingers, and I decide to let it go, but when I return to the living room wrapped in a towel, he is waiting for me at the door dressed in a white cotton shirt and a dark jacket, his damp hair combed back, as if it were an official event. I've grown used to the idea in the meantime, he says, if you insist you must have your reasons.

Give me instructions, he says as we set out, do you want me to make a good impression or a bad one? And I say, a bad one, obviously, and he nods seriously, good, I'll do my best, and he goes on nodding as if a heavy responsibility has been laid on his shoulders, walking by my side in streets as still and dark as an old photograph. The sounds of the evening, its colors and smells, are imprisoned behind windows closed against the cold, life has evaporated from the streets like mist, and suddenly there is no one around; does everyone know something we don't, does mortal danger roam the streets tonight, and again I berate myself for the pointless, nonsensical idea, unnecessary to everyone concerned, both present and absent, already longing to be back in the empty apartment where I knew complete happiness. From time to time he glances at me, calm and amused, his pace measured, and only when we climb the red-tiled steps does the expression on his face change, after I say, they'll probably be surprised to see you, they think I'm coming with Gili.

That's wrong, Ella, he protests, you said they knew, and I smirk, I said they knew I wasn't coming alone, that's exactly how you phrased the question, I attach great significance to words too, you're not the only one, and he sighs, I hope you know what you're doing, to me it seems unnecessary, going out in this cold in order to embarrass your parents, and I press myself to him and kiss his cheek, and before I ring the bell the door opens and my father steps into the dark hall, his eyes lowered to the spot where Gili's little head is supposed to be, and he opens his arms and says, who's coming to Grandpa? Who's coming to play chess with Grandpa?

Me, Oded replies in his low voice, and my father straightens up in surprise, his hand hurriedly seeking the light switch, his handsome features in disarray, Ella, he says sternly, we thought you were coming with Gili, completely ignoring the man standing next to me, even though his eyes are fixed on him, and I announce gaily, there was a last minute change of plan, this is Oded, as if I had given birth to a new child in the meantime, and my father blinks at him disapprovingly, stretching his lips with an effort in a smile too wide, exposing his graying teeth. Please come inside, he recovers, making a sweeping flourish, as if permitting us entry into a magnificent palace, and my mother comes out of the kitchen, wearing a shabby flannel dressing gown, her feet in old slippers, which look completely out of place on the elegant floor tiles. Ellinka, you didn't say anything, she announces for my father's benefit, to make it clear that she had no part in the conspiracy, looking at him timidly, and as she stands opposite him I wonder again how she always manages to look shorter than he is, even though she is actually the taller of the two.

Excuse me for a minute, she makes for the bedroom at a hurried waddle to change her clothes, and my father repeats his invitation, come inside, come inside, even though we're already inside, please sit down, and I sit down in my usual place at the round kitchen table, offering Oded Gili's chair next to me, which is permanently raised with an embroidered cushion, and he sits down obediently on the cushion, in front of Gili's empty plate, that has two colorful monsters printed on it, a plastic glass with a straw to the right of the plate, and colorful miniature cutlery to its left, and nobody takes the trouble to change the place setting, and neither do I, already regretting my inexplicable impulse. Oy, what are we going to do, my mother hurries back to the kitchen wearing a faded sweater the same color as the discarded robe, her steps accompanied by a steady lament, I made him his favorite food, chicken soup and sweet noodles with raisins, as if the child's absence on this occasion is a sign of things to come, eternal and absolute, as though he will be replaced forever by a pale, thin man in a formal jacket with chilly black eyes.

With uncivil speed, without any preamble, she places a small plastic bowl containing lukewarm soup on the uninvited guest's plate, as if adamantly refusing to acknowledge his adulthood, and my father irritably holds out his plate, and I follow suit, like needy souls in a soup kitchen, and to my surprise it seems that the only person at the table who feels comfortable is Oded, who calmly picks up the toy-like spoon and silently sips his soup, looking around the kitchen, which is disproportionately small for the size of the apartment, revealing the owners' disinterest in the body and its needs. Under the table I put my hand on his knee but he takes no notice, who knows what he's thinking, he is suddenly a stranger, not only to them, as if I have just picked him up in the street, fulfilling the obligation of guests on Sukkoth. Is he remembering Friday night dinners with his wife and children and in-laws, is he about to lay down his miniature spoon, say goodbye and go join them?

We usually eat in the living room when we have guests, my father tries to correct the impression, we thought we would just be family, and Oded says, it's perfectly all right, it's very comfortable here, and my mother continues in her tearful voice, so where is Gili? And I answer impatiently, with his father, he's with his father every second weekend, and she says, yes, I know, I just thought that he was there last week too, are you sure you didn't get the weeks mixed up? She gives Oded an aggrieved look, as if he were to blame for the mix up, I think you got confused, and my father interrupts her and finally addresses the guest, remind me of your name, and I hurry to answer for him like an overprotective mother, his name is Oded, but this isn't enough for him, it seems that he is determined to find out exactly who the stranger is, and above all what the nature of our relationship is, and he puts down his spoon and asks, do you work together? Are you also an archeologist? And Oded answers briefly, so to speak, yes.

What exactly is your field? My father goes on to ask, and Oded replies, the human field, you could say, and my father declares, aha, you mean DNA, right? Forensic archeology, that's very interesting, and to be on the safe side he inquires, so you know Amnon too? And Oded replies, yes, more or less, to my father's great relief, and I see his face relax as soon as he gains the impression that the man is a professional colleague, a kind of family friend, and not a lover or a mate, for even though he knows very well that my marriage is over, it seems that he is not willing, and neither is she, to accept me in the company of a new partner. In their opinion I should atone for my sins by growing old alone, devoting my life to the child I have harmed, and I have no right to a life of my own, and I can hear this in the metal of their spoons across the bowls, and in fact I have been hearing it all my life, the appearance of a boyfriend always involved a sense of oppression and guilt, as if it constituted an unforgivable treachery, a betrayal of a secret obligation toward them, of the role to which they had consigned me, and now, also, of the child with whom they are suddenly so identified. But for the moment my father is apparently satisfied, for his curiosity is limited, and his main concern is the impression he himself makes on others. A vague response suffices for him to drape his own needs on it like a hanger, for every scrap of life provided by another is only a faint echo of his own life, and every accomplishment a diminished reflection of his own accomplishments, and he is already holding court in a loud voice, the presence of a guest spurring him on.

I returned this week from a conference in Mexico City, he announces, about the new anti-Semitism, you wouldn't believe the things that were said there, outrageous things, that Jews are to blame for the hatred they inspire because on the one hand they are too different, and on the other hand they are too similar, both too strong and too weak, too alive and too dead, and in any case they are always responsible. The image of the Jew already has an existence of its own, just as Sartre said, the anti-Semite created the Jew in order to project his own fears of himself onto him, it is not the Jew he fears but himself, his freedom, his loneliness, and I said to them, go and examine yourselves honestly, gentlemen, perhaps you, too, are afraid of yourselves, perhaps you, too, are afraid of change, he raises his voice, turning to us aggressively, as if it were our opinions that are the target of his horror and disgust.

David, you're not eating, she complains, I want to serve the fish, and he interrupts his lecture for a moment, rapidly swallowing the cooling soup, not enough salt again, he pronounces, smacking his lips with a disapproving expression, and she protests, but last time you said the soup was too salty, you remember that's what he said, Ellinka? And for a moment both of them fix their eyes on me in suspense, whose side will I be on this time, the only function of the only daughter, who herself borders on the superfluous, since her father is occupied with his own affairs and her mother is occupied with her father. What does it matter, I complain, why should I bother to remember it, even though I remember very well that she is right, and he says, what nonsense, you never salt the soup enough, and he immediately remembers that we have a guest and bursts into loud, affected laughter, distancing the argument from himself. She snatches up the bowl, which is still half full, with an offended expression, and sets before him a portion of juicy looking pink salmon spotted with black peppercorns.

There are hardly any bones, she announces, as if she herself cunningly cast the net and carefully caught the chosen fish, and immediately sets a slightly smaller portion of fish on my plate, and one on hers, and then she picks up the guest's plate and puts a round noodle kugel on it, oy, there isn't enough fish to go around, she claps her hands, sorry, Ohad, Gili doesn't like fish so I made him noodles instead, and I correct her, Oded, and immediately offer him my fish, I'm not really hungry, and he looks at us in amusement, no problem, I'll be happy to eat a sweet noodle kugel, my mother used to make exactly the same thing. Mickey Mouse is smiling beneath his hands on the baby plate, but he chews in enjoyment, and praises the dish, are you sure it's sweet enough, my mother inquires before she begins to eat, and he says, it's just fine, graciously ignoring the ritual humiliation ceremony to which he has been invited.

The new anti-Semitism disguises itself as anti-nationalism, my father continues to hold court, they present us as a reactionary remnant of the past, as a fossilized nation isolating itself behind bars and walls, without taking the danger that threatens us into account. What is your opinion of the matter, he turns unexpectedly to Oded, not out of a sincere desire to find out what he thinks, but in order to embarrass him, stealing a glance in my direction as if to remind me that he will always gain the upper hand over any man I bring to this table, and indeed there is no room for anyone else at the table and there never was, only for a silent and admiring audience. How I feared those meals, evening after evening, the suffocation I felt facing him, for if I ever tried to express an opinion that differed from his he would dismiss my words angrily, ready to acknowledge me only as his own reflection, it seems that only with Gili I could sit calmly at their table, holding him in front of me like a soft human shield, but the uninvited guest, unlike me, is neither anxious about his worth, nor, it seems, is he argumentative. I think that what we're talking about here is the relation between stimulus and response, he says calmly, and the responding side suffers from a sickly sensitivity to the stimulus, rendering the disease incurable, and he resumes his concentration on the disappearing noodle kugel on his plate, where the monsters' true faces are being revealed, their beaks, their jaws. Is he trying to obey my instructions or is he always like this with strangers, withdrawn, reserved, non-committal, uninvolved.

Nevertheless we can no longer ignore the most dangerous element in the new anti-Semitism, prevalent as it is in academic circles, even in Israel, my father insists, I have even had a few arguments with Amnon and Ella in this regard, and when he says Amnon and Ella the flow of his words is interrupted and he clears his throat and takes a sip of water, I think I swallowed a bone, he says accusingly to my mother, didn't you say that there were no bones in this fish? And she immediately defends herself, I said there were hardly any bones, I can't be responsible for every single bone, and I say, if you've already swallowed the bone it doesn't matter, forget it, and he sips the water anxiously, his Adam's apple bobbing up and down, I think it's stuck there, he announces in a melancholy tone, as if he's doomed, and he is shaken by a violent fit of coughing, but when she gets up and hits him with all her strength on his back he recoils and protests in a tone of outrage, what are you doing, Sara.

Take a piece of bread, Oded volunteers, speaking of his own initiative for the first time, it might help, and my mother hurriedly breaks off a piece of challah and hands it to him, and we all watch him chew until the bread turns into a pale mush in his mouth and he finally swallows it, a slow, agonizing swallow, and again he coughs until his eyes water and his smooth leaden face takes on a bluish tinge, and she circles around him in alarm, what should we do, David, try another piece of bread, and he grumbles in a weak, impatient voice, I've already eaten half the loaf, it doesn't help, and the temporary loss of his loud, clear voice wipes the arrogant, self-satisfied expression from his face, his eyes are red and damp, his finger goes to his throat and shrinks in pain. Perhaps we should go to the emergency room, Davidi, my mother suggests, we have to get it out, and he says in a shrill squeak, don't call me Davidi, and I'm not going to the emergency room; from moment to moment his voice grows weaker as if the worn out vocal cords are snapping one after the other, and to my surprise I see Oded rising urgently from his heightened chair, let me try, he says, do you have a flashlight and a pair of tweezers? And my mother hastily removes the required items from a drawer and hands them to him, like an obedient dentist's assistant.

My father's eyes follow the proceedings anxiously, he is clearly not eager to entrust his throat to the stranger's hands, but he is even less eager to visit the emergency room, and he puts his head back obediently and opens his mouth wide, exposing his long gray teeth, his purple gums, his darting lizard tongue, and Oded directs the beam of the flashlight into his mouth, pressing his head firmly to his waist and squeezing his cheeks as if afraid of being bitten, while my mother and I watch in suspense. For a moment it seems that we are watching a cruel burglar trying to extract the gold teeth from the mouth of a helpless old man looking at him in outraged indignation, but then he says in a soothing voice, I think I can see it, try not to move. Take the flashlight, he says, putting me in charge of the lighting, and thrusts his fingers holding the tweezers into my father's mouth, and I look at them and remember that these fingers were inside my body not long ago, and the thought sends a shiver of pleasure through me, and it's reflected in the movements of the flashlight, just as he declares, I got it, as if he's talking about a living creature capable of fleeing for its life, and against the background of my father's groan of pain and relief the bone is extracted from his throat and displayed, surprising in its size, like a newly unearthed finding that sheds light on a long gone age.

Well done, Ohad, well done, my mother claps, stubbornly bastardizing his name, and my father hastens to steady his head on his neck, to fix his hair, to hide his mouth's dishonor, to restore his dignity, which is based among other things on disdain for bodily matters, and he clears his throat to make sure that the offending object has indeed been removed, and looks at the guest with new respect, as at a poor student who has done surprisingly well. Thank you very much, well done indeed, I am very grateful to you, and he adds admiringly, you did it as skillfully as if you were a doctor, and Oded admits, yes, I am a doctor too, and my father is beside himself, what do you say, an archeologist doctor? That's a rare combination, and Oded corrects him modestly, a psychiatrist doctor, significantly less rare.

Didn't you say you were an archeologist? My father demands in astonishment, and Oded replies, not exactly, but apparently I gave that impression, and my father yells at the top of his voice, so why, why did you hide your true occupation? I take a great interest in psychiatry! He is already lamenting all the lost lectures he could have delivered to the silent guest, amazing him with his knowledge, his originality, and Oded smiles a sweet, shy smile, the truth is that I try to keep it under wraps, people who know there's a psychiatrist among them begin behaving strangely. In what way? my father inquires, immediately setting himself apart from the common herd, and Oded says, they stop acting naturally, as if I'm liable to have them committed if they're themselves, they're sure that every word they say is being analyzed, even though I really don't concern myself with such things in my leisure time, and my father bursts into his artificial laughter again, and for a change she joins in, pointing to the plastic plate, as if she has only just noticed it, oy, what will you think of us, giving you kid's food on a kid's plate?

I'll think that you love your grandson very much, he says gently, looking at her with his dark eyes, and then at me, come Ella, we have to go, and the way he says we, slowly and emphatically, thrills me with the promise of the fulfillment of that ancient yearning for the knight in shining armor who will rescue me from the incisors of this couple between whose teeth I was gnashed, wandering from mouth to mouth, it's a we that no longer includes them, only me and him, a new couple that has no family name in common and no apartment and no child and nevertheless is called we, and this ordinary word, presented to me by his lips, is a rare and precious gift.

You're going already? my father asks in disappointment, sincerely lamenting the early departure of his audience, and I say, yes, we're in a hurry, enjoying the repetition of the word, enjoying his disappointment. You see, nobody died, only you nearly did; Gili is alive and I'm alive, as I never was before because you never allowed me to be, you of all people who gave me life prevented me from living it, and then he gets up from his chair and shakes Oded's hand appreciatively, I must thank you again, he says, come and see me sometime, I'll be happy to discuss your profession with you, I have just read a fascinating article that casts doubt on people's ability to change, I will be happy to hear your position, he adds graciously, come and visit me, he persists in addressing him in the singular, as if refusing to acknowledge our we, and Oded smiles, thank you, I'll try.

The cold dark fist of night hits me in the face, taking me by surprise when we leave, the street lamps have gone out already despite the early hour, and the moon cuts a thin sliver of light in the sky, and I take Oded's arm, trying to tighten the we, a wild happiness makes me cling to him, as if thanks to him I have been saved, thanks to him the curse has been dispelled, for it was from that rheumy purple throat that it came, with his skillful hands he removed it for me, not only the curse aimed a few months ago at the head of my son, but a far earlier curse, issued with birth, by the very person who gave me life. Gratefully I snuggle up to him, kiss his cold neck, his lips still sticky with the taste of sweet noodles, and suddenly I am wild to surrender myself to him, to belong to him as absolutely as one of his limbs, ready to drag him into one of the back yards, take off my coat and lie down under the sky studded with pale stars, and he sighs with pleasure, why outside in the cold, he murmurs, let's go home, and this word, home, is presented to me as another gift. I walk beside him silently, my arm around his waist, a faint smell of lavender rises from his skin, hinting at the coming closeness of his body, for every step brings us closer to home, to that palace shining in the dark.

I'm glad you took me there, he says in the end, once I had already resigned myself to his silence, and I ask, why? And he says, because now I love you more, and I hang onto this dryly spoken sentence and break it up into two sentences, I love you, I love you more, and precisely the first, the more basic one, which has never been said, echoes alongside us, reassuring in its decisiveness, but the second, which is derived from it, sounds a little doubtful, for if it is possible to love more it is also possible to love less, and how frightening that could be, to love less, to be loved less, and this keeps me so busy that I don't ask why, or notice the direction, what do I care which way he chooses to take as long as we go home, to the new we waiting for us there; it seems that our common vocabulary is as small as a toddler's, we, home, I love you, more, but they are the most perfect words I have ever heard, I have no need for others.

Arm in arm we walk the dark streets, acquainting ourselves with each other's proportions, his shoulder is closer to me than Amnon's, which loomed above me heavy and hostile, his body is narrower, withdrawn into itself, careful, respecting the boundaries of space. His stride slows and he asks hesitantly, do you mind if we sit down here for a while? And I look around me in surprise, I hadn't noticed where his feet were leading me and all of a sudden we are standing in the little playground opposite his old house, and I ask, but how did we get here in the first place? And he says, my feet have gotten used to bringing me here, and I accept his explanation suspiciously, climbing after him onto the little merry-go-round that creaks beneath our weight, surprised to accommodate such grownup children on such a cold night, and, like him, I look at the building opposite us, the imposing renovated stone building, the shuttered windows, and the electric light from within the home that seeps through the slats like the blank lines of a golden notebook.

What are we doing here, Oded, I ask, looking at him uneasily, I thought we were going home, and he says, we'll go home in a little while, I have to stay here for a bit, and I ask, why, what are you waiting for? And he says, I'm waiting for the children to fall asleep, every Friday I sit here for a while, until they switch off the lights, he informs me casually, as if nothing could be more natural. I sit next to him embarrassed and sulky, an unwilling accomplice in an onerous and private ritual, which awakens my own hurt, and it, too, demands its pound of flesh. Perhaps when we're done here, we'll proceed to Amnon's street, sit on the bench opposite the two stout palms, and follow the progress of the stripes of light through the rooms of his house, and already the resentment climbs up my throat, why is he burdening our young time with his memorial rites, why doesn't he separate the fresh love from the fresh sorrow, and I lower my eyes to the rusty metal floor. Once I came here with Gili and a bigger boy spun the merry-go-round too fast and Gili, trapped inside, suddenly vomited, right here, at our feet, and we escaped as quickly as we could, and for months we never returned in case the cloud of his vomit still hung over the playground, his name etched in malodorous letters on the merry-go-round floor.

Ella, he says, putting his cold hand on my knee, don't worry, it doesn't take anything away from you, and I whisper, yes, I know, but still the moment of silence in front of his children's house elicits a surprisingly potent rage and resentment. Every Friday night I sit here for a while, he explains again, I thought of letting it go this time but there's no reason why I should, right? he asks with surprising urgency, tell me that you can take it, and I ask, take what, and he says, my sorrow, and the words leap from his throat like Gili's vomit, threatening to cover the transparent body of the newborn we, and I can't hold back, entrenching myself in demanding insult. I thought you were happy with me today, I thought it was good for you, I complain, and he takes his hand back in disappointment from my knee, of course it was good for me with you, he says in a tired voice, but there are a lot of feelings inhabiting this body of ours, on one floor the happiness and contentment, and on another the sorrow and the guilt, there's no way that you don't understand that. Of course I understand, I say quickly, but nevertheless I have to ask myself, is it right for our children to be the shattered glass under the wedding canopy, a memorial to the destruction of the temple, and I get up from the cold narrow seat, squeezing a creaky sigh from the merry-go-round tilting on its axis. Let's go, Oded, I'm freezing, and even though I know I should sit by his side in noble resignation and prove my ability to empathize with him, I'm incapable, just as one's feet sometimes freeze in the face of certain danger so a surprising hardness paralyses my feelings, and he looks at me in disappointment, but they haven't gone to sleep yet, he protests, and I raise my eyes to the high balcony, to the transparent glass balustrade, to the shutters sealed on a Friday night without daddy.

So what, I retort, you can't tuck them in from down here, read them a bedtime story from down here, they don't even know you're here, your presence doesn't help them, don't you see how pointless it is? And he says, I do it for me, not for them, I always wait here until they switch off the light, and I lecture him with suppressed impatience, Oded, you can compensate them on the days when they're with you, but on the days when they're with Michal you have to detach yourself, to rebuild your life, is that what you left home for, so you could stand outside and stare at it? What you're doing makes no sense.

I left Michal, not my children, he defends himself, I wish I could be with them all the time, and I say, of course you do, even though this, too, insults me, what am I for him then, a poor substitute for his children, a temporary substitute, would he have wanted to be with them this afternoon too, for example, instead of being in bed with me, and why don't I feel like him, not for one minute did I feel the lack of my son today until we came here, is he a better parent than I am? Oded, listen, I say, for the sake of your children, too, you have to build a life without them, they need you to be strong and stable, isn't that clear to you? And he sighs, do me a favor, you're parroting clichés, you aren't the least bit interested in what they need, you're only thinking of what you need, and I say, really? what garbage, I don't need anything from you; as far as I'm concerned you can put up a tent and live here on the grass and see exactly when they come and when they go, just don't expect me to live here with you, because I, as opposed to you, intend to make a life for myself, I have a small child, too, and nevertheless, I didn't go and live in Amnon's garden, and when I say the words 'small child' a high, tremulous wail comes out of my throat and I cover my mouth in increasing embarrassment, for it seems as if Gili's weeping is suddenly bursting from my lips, dangerous as a sudden hemorrhage, the weeping of Friday nights in a cleft family, the weeping of the wandering from home to home and parent to parent, the constant longing, the burdensome adjustment, the slight confusion in the morning, where am I, the times when he calls me Daddy, the missing toy, the picture he started to draw and left in the other house, all the small details that create constant discomfort stick like pins into my skin that's stiff with cold, the smaller they are the sharper they stab. The way I brought the toy knight he forgot at my place to Amnon's house yesterday, he wanted to play with it so badly, but by the time I arrived, he had already fallen asleep, tear tracks on his cheeks, the envious way he looks at the children being picked up by both their parents, the way he hesitates whenever he brings a picture home from school, where should he hang it, at Mommy's place or Daddy's, trying with all his might to maintain a righteous balance, when I'm with you I miss Daddy, when I'm with Daddy I miss you, and I sit down again on the narrow bench, and bury my head between my knees, ashamed of the tears contradicting everything I tried to say, the contemptible, selfish, pleading tears, love only me, console only me, compensate only me, show me that I didn't make a mistake.

He puts his hand on my shoulder slowly, with an effort, as if he isn't sure that he really wants to embrace me after I condemned his sorrow with crude arrogance, and then hurled myself headlong into mine, which suddenly becomes more urgent, more noisy, but by now there is no way back, neither from the arrogance, nor from the weeping, my only recourse is to amplify it, to let it careen through the city like a car without brakes, sowing destruction in its wake, and I do, and in fact I am no longer in control, for before my eyes the pictures pass like pages in a photo album, not pictures of sorrow but pictures of happiness, anxious, brittle happiness, quick to crumble. Amnon and I sitting next to Gili's feverish bed at dawn, the delirious visions rising from it like steam from an open pot, and now Amnon's hand reaches for me, over the shivering little body, lacing its fingers in mine, in a rare contact that has no demands, and here I am with my father standing in front of a brightly lit display window, and he points to a gold bracelet watch, would you like it? he asks, would you like me to buy it for you? And I am astonished by his offer, really? Will you really buy it for me? His presents are so rare, and he steps briskly into the shop, takes the money out of his pocket, and I walk by his side proud and erect as a queen on her coronation day, gracefully gesturing with my golden wrist, and the next day I drive down to the beach with a boyfriend, and when we return to the car in the evening, our sunburned arms entwined, it had been burglarized, and nothing had been stolen except for the bracelet watch as if my father had broken into the car himself to take back his gift, of which I was no longer worthy, and more pictures cover my eyes, pictures of anxious happiness, always threatened, always short-lived, cast in doubt, and like the little plastic driver whose smile was crushed under the wheels, I can't stop, I can't prevent the catastrophe, and all the time I know that the person at my side is no longer with me, that I have lost him, his heavy hand on my back, petrified as if it froze long ago, and for this, too, I grieve, and when I try to peek at him between my swollen lids, I see his eyes raised intently, devotedly, to the windows of his house, as if it were the east-facing wall of the synagogue to which he is directing his prayers, and when the crying, which is no longer mine but a kind of *dybbuk* that has taken possession of me, begins to die down, turning into breaths wild as an irregular pulse, I hear him whispering soft soothing words, enough, enough, my little girl, everything will be all right, go to sleep now, and it is clear that his words are not addressed to me but to his daughter who is going to bed now, for the light has been switched off, the golden lines have been erased. He waits a little longer and then gets up with a sigh from the merry-go-round, which responds with a stumbling turn, come, he says to me, they're asleep now, as if this news is supposed to comfort me too, as if this is why I was crying and now there is nothing to cry about, for they have gone to sleep at last, Maya and Yotam.

I'm staying here, the voice squeaks in my throat like the merry-go-round creaking on its axis, my hands gripping the wobbly little steering wheel, stressing my words, and he looks at me grimly, his eyes hardening against my eyes, his eyebrows approaching each other, the line between them deepening, too bad, he says, you're behaving like a child, grow up, get a grip, you have no choice, and I shake my head, I'm staying here, and I can see the decision hardening on his face, he isn't going to try to persuade me, he's going to leave me to my own devices. Okay, he snaps, as you wish, you know where to find me, and this time he doesn't bind me to him with a muscular kiss but gets off the merry-go-round and turns his back to me, making his way between the deserted swings and seesaws, walking past the rusty rocking horse, the stone slide covered with mud, walking stiffly, as though on prosthetics, his eyes fixed on the road, leaving me sitting hunched on the merry-go-round Gili stained with his vomit long ago. I take up his vigil opposite the home he left, most of its rooms in darkness, only the living room lit, or perhaps it's the kitchen. Is she washing the dishes now, three plates, three bowls, three glasses, her hands, used to four, shaking under the stream of water, and I know that I should get up and leave, but an inexplicable heaviness nails me to the seat, like the rusty rocking horse I am stuck to the spot on this dilapidated merry-go-round exposed to the wind and the rain and the sun and the tread of the children's feet, their vomit and their sweat. In the morning I'll be found here by the passersby, a new kind of homeless person, with an elegant coat and a bulging purse, covered with a layer of frost, the frost of dry resignation, because what difference does it make, between the old life whose door is closed to me and the new life I cannot enter, nothing exists but this hallucinatory emptiness, a deserted void of a playground sought by no one. No child would dream of stealing into this place at night to fill it with his gleeful shouts, no mother would sit on the damp grass now and revel in her child at play, and I cover my wet knees with my coat, my hands swelling and tingling in the narrow pockets, which are growing tighter from minute to minute, the petrifying of the limbs is as hard to achieve as the petrifying of the heart, and nevertheless the surrender, the wild dismissal of the chance for happiness, is almost consoling, who are you punishing? he asked, and I lie down on the narrow bench, a prickly sleep snatches hold of me, like when I was in high school at my desk, until a hand tousled my hair and I looked up into the shining eyes of Gili, but this time it seems that the nap will extend forever, for Gili will never come back. I won't open my eyes even when the light goes on in the stairwell and an elderly couple comes slowly and somberly out of the building, what will become of her, the woman will sob in a familiar voice, how will she cope, what will become of the children, how could he leave like that, and I won't open my eyes even when dazzling golden rays flood my face, is it really morning, has summer really arrived, leaping over the cycle of seasons and coming to save the playground, and I seem to hear children playing, and one of them shouts, Mommy, stop the merry-go-round, I feel nauseous, and I wake up with a start, the sun has not yet risen but the moon is directing concentrated beams of light at me, a strange, double moon, low twin lights rising from the earth as if the world is standing on its head, the sky below and the earth above, and I blink my eyes until I realize that the light is coming from the headlamps of a car, and the noise of the engine is buzzing in my ears, and even the fear isn't enough to make me get up and run away, and even when the door opens I stay where I am, and even when a dark shadow emerges from it and advances toward me, and even when I hear his voice, come home, Ella, and I lay my head on the little steering wheel in the middle of the merry-go-round, grasping with the remnants of my exhausted mind what is about to happen, how my body will be gathered up, a cold piece of meat deprived of sensation, and with it of reason and control, responsibility and maturity, logic and hope.

Through the fog of my shattered sleep I try to follow the direction of the journey, will he take me to my home or his, and the warm relief when I recognize his lane, is its name really Penitential Lane, with narrowed eyes I watch him, pretending to be asleep so as not to have to face him from the depths of my shame, trailing behind him with heavy steps, as if in a daze, following him into the apartment, letting him undress me with practiced hands, the coat and the sweater and the bra and the shoes and stockings and slacks and panties, so many wrappings and yet so cold. When I lie motionless in the full bath, my head aching from the crying and the uneasy sleep, from the feeling returning with the full force of remorse and regret, when I sip the hot tea he hands me, see the careful way he scrutinizes me, as if looking for a bone in my throat, and through the waves of pleasure at being suddenly cared for as I have never been cared for before, perfectly, painstakingly attended to, the price of my folly is slowly becoming apparent to me, for the movements that undressed me a little while ago were not the movements of a man undressing a woman, but those of a father undressing a child, or a doctor undressing a patient, and the looks directed at my nakedness, too, are matter-of-fact, devoid of intimacy.

When I step out of the water still shivering with cold he rubs me with a towel, dresses me in white flannel long underwear, and all this time he doesn't speak to me, all he has to offer are efficient movements, as if I were a mute foundling he picked up at the roadside in order to save her life, a stray cat he took pity on in a cold night, but who will be sent on its way when the sun comes up, and I, too, say nothing, absorbed by the bed with its hard new mattress, covering myself with the blanket, sipping the rest of the sweet tea, watching his measured movements, is this the way he took care of his father, his mother, his sister, in a sad, efficient silence, not daring to complain, to express his resentment. Do you want another cup of tea? he asks and I say, no, I want to talk to you, and I stretch out my arm, and he says evasively, you should drink some more, it seems that he is afraid of the moment when the necessary actions are finished, what will he do then, will he suggest another bath, undress me and dress me again, and I say to his receding back, talk to me, Oded, and he says, let's wait before we talk, and I ask, wait for what? And he comes back with a fresh cup of tea and sits on the edge of the bed, as if he is afraid of being infected with my disease. I don't want to be hasty, he says quietly, I don't want to say things I'll regret later, I need time to think, and I whisper, I disappointed you, I'm so sorry, and he says, yes, and I disappointed you, but let it be, we're not here to convene a court of emotions, you're entitled to yours and I'm entitled to mine, the question is if they're compatible.

The bed is cold and pristine, the walls around it glow with a pearly sheen, we are surrounded by white horizons, like soldiers that have lost a battle on a winter prairie, praying only for a quick death. A cold pillow under my head, a blanket of frost covering my body, even in the deserted playground I felt warmer than I do here in your bed, what should we do, Oded, a tiny stillborn fetus is lying here between us, a premature baby, a fallen star, a plant torn from its soil, what should we do? Go to sleep, he whispers, it's late, and I bury my face in the soft shivery snow; how can I sleep when I'm losing you? Carefully I cross the white border between us, press up against his back, which is turned to me, hard and unyielding as stone, make love to me, Oded, and he turns to me slowly, the tips of his fingernails brush my face, sketching the collapsing arch of my brows, the trembling of my lips, I can't, he says, his voice insulting in its gentleness, in its condoling waver, I can't rescue you and make love to you as well, the two things aren't compatible, and I try to stop the new torrent of grief already on its way to my throat, the grief of a premature parting, advancing toward me with a slow, mournful beat, like a hymn sung by people in a funeral procession. It was all so fleeting, doled out with such frugality, doomed to fail, what was I mourning there in the frost-stricken playground, I was mourning the past, and now the future, too, presents its throat for the slaughter; why couldn't I sit by his side in noble silence, after all, his sorrow wasn't aimed at me, it was a kind of test, and I failed it, I failed it miserably. All I needed was to show a little empathy, understanding, sympathy for his plight, compared to the parting to come it all seems so easy to me now, and already the desolation of the future without him stretches out before me, night after night I'll sit on the merry-go-round opposite his children's house, waiting for the lights to go out, from now on this will be the hidden bond between us, my dedication will surpass his, I won't miss a single evening as the days slowly stretch toward summer, I'll keep a record of the precise time the lights go out, and perhaps once in a while I'll bump into him, stealing into the dark playground with a new woman, testing her ability to cope with his sorrow, with his devotion to his children. They will sit by his side as if it were a movie premiere, their fragrant shampooed heads on his shoulder, watching the movement of the light with feigned interest, the test is so easy, how could I have failed it, no one but me could have failed it, but suddenly my anger at myself turns into anger at him, why couldn't he have given it up, on our first weekend together, why did he insist on dragging me to that private joy-stifling, guilt-ridden ritual of his, and between the two angers snarling at each other our chance is smothered, like a newborn baby crushed by its loving parents in their heavy, tired sleep before it's even taken into the covenant of Abraham.

I'm sorry, Oded, I whisper to the pillow, and to my surprise he hears me and says, so am I, or perhaps he didn't say anything because he's fast asleep, lying on his back, his beautiful eyes closed, his face slack, as if his features are only held together by force of will and now in his sleep his cheekbones have melted, his eyes spread farther apart, each turned on its side, covered by a drooping eyelid, while my own eyes are wide open in the strange apartment, in the strange bed, next to the man I won't see again, who will disappear from my life with the same sudden force as he entered it, and I chant softly into the pillow, when I was a child I had no lover.

The radiator wakes up before me, spreading a lazy Saturday morning warmth, and for a moment it seems to me that I am at home, and Gili is playing in the living room, and Amnon is making coffee, scolding him quietly, don't make noise, let Mommy sleep, this must be the kind of confusion Gili feels every morning, when he tries to make out where he is, and the moment I realize where I am, I remember that we are about to part, and I decide to accept my fate with proud resignation, not to complain and not to beg for my life, and when he comes into the room with a tray holding coffee and cake I give him a reserved smile, and try to comb my unruly hair with my fingers. He is already dressed as if getting ready to go out, in a black turtleneck sweater and blue jeans, his hair damp, his recomposed cheeks giving off a pleasant smell, their pallor underscored by his recent shave, the dark stains of his eyes. My heart goes out to him, this is what my new life could have looked like, and he hands me the cup, do you want to talk? He asks, and I sip silently and shrug my shoulders. Do you have anything to say to me? he presses me, as though coaxing a prisoner for his last wish so that the sentence could be executed, and when I maintain my silence he says, good, then listen to me, and raises my face to his, his hand under my chin, I want to propose something to you, I'm not sure that it's a good idea, but it's the only one I've got, I think we should try it.

Birds crossing the window etch a leaden gray line in the clear sky, and I follow their flight, what are you going to propose, a melancholy farewell party in bed, a short stilted walk on this surprisingly lovely day, both of us marching behind the empty coffin. Come and live with me, he says, and I whisper, live with you, here? And he says, yes, there's plenty of room, gesturing toward the white walls that testify on his behalf, and I breathe a sigh of doubtful relief, for a moment it seems that his surprising proposal does not possess the power to cancel the inevitable parting, but only to postpone it, until it's more excruciating, more heartbreaking.

You're confusing me, I say carefully, full of doubt, I thought I'd lost you, a note of complaint in my voice, for my prediction that failed to come true, and he says, I know, so did I. So what changed? I ask, and he says, I understood that you need more reassurance from me, and I need more from you and perhaps a clearer framework will make that possible, and I take a deep breath, but it's too fast, we don't know each other yet, and he smiles, do you know a better way of getting to know each other?

But what about the children? I demand, it's too soon for them, we can't experiment at their expense, and he says, nonetheless, we'll do it gradually, if we're wholehearted, they'll adjust, and I try out the first half of the word, whole, if we're whole, if we were ever whole, and it seems to me that all kinds of distant rumors about love and happiness are coming closer to me, and I am not even surprised at how long it's taken them to come but how soon they've arrived, for it's possible after all to depart this life without ever having tasted this taste, your happiness is my happiness, my happiness is your happiness; yes, why shouldn't we be whole as a loaf of bread, as a picture in an album, as a restored pot. Whole is what we will be when we try to stick the fragments of our families together, whole when we gather up the remains of our wishes, whole when we lie down and whole when we rise, whole in our transient existence that we think is eternal, whole in our sorrow and our guilt, in our ruin and our restoration.

Chapter seventeen

In a minute the traffic will stop, the pedestrians will stiffen as though a wailing memorial siren has severed the morning, the advancing waitress, our coffees balanced on her tray, will stop in her tracks like a wax doll, and he himself will freeze, his lips robbed of their will, his polished light blue eyes fixed on me as I make my announcement, Amnon, I have a new partner, I'm moving in with him, and even though our separation is many months old it seems that only now is it becoming real, that only now a booming voice from heaven has declared, so-and-so, daughter of so-and-so, is not intended for this one but for that one, and she must take everything she possesses, her furniture and her dishes, her clothes and her books, and her only son, to his house in Penitential Lane, never to return to her home.

He runs his broad, meaty hands over his head in a nervous gesture, his cheeks swell like sponges gathering water, his body surges before me, filling with the remains of ancient anger, jealousy and frustration, his eyes widen in an expression of astonishment so familiar to me from the face of our son. I don't believe it, Ella, only a few weeks ago you wanted to come back to me, you were prepared to do anything for us to get back together again, and now you're telling me that not only do you have someone else but you're already moving in with him? What's going on?

A screen falls from the ceiling, crossing our table like a dark shade, distancing me from him, alone I face him, but it's as though I'm sitting on my new love's lap, peeping from within his arms at the bristling man with his crude movements, new love draped all over me like jewels, declarations of my new lover's love, heralded before one and all, and to no one more than to Amnon Miller, who's sitting opposite me now, waving his arms, his mouth bubbling with coarse syllables.

It wasn't a few weeks, Amnon, it was a few months, I say quickly, and you were quite clear about it being all over between us, and everything that's happened since then is none of your business, I'm only filling you in now because of Gili, and also so that we can finally go to the Rabbinate and make it official. As always, I find myself on the defensive when arguing with Amnon, and we're so well versed in argument, we've tasted them all, the ones that flare up in an instant and the ones that take shape at their leisure, the ones that end in reconciliation and the ones that trail behind us unfinished, reeking like stagnant water in a vase, is there enough closeness left between us to feed an argument, between me and this clumsy man in the plaid flannel shirt, whose eyes evade mine but whose big teeth, with the fine cracks running down them, are bared before me; ah, so that's what's so urgent now, he pounces on the information, to get things over with between us, to finally get rid of me, that's why you wanted to meet; and I say, obviously, what did you expect, that I was going to beg you to come back to me like then so that you could humiliate me again, maybe shut me up in the bathroom again, can't you see that I'm already in a different place?

Do you have any idea what I went through that night, do you know how hard it was for me to turn you down? He bursts into rapid, feverish speech, I did it for you, for both of us, I knew that if we got back together so quickly nothing would change, and that I had to give you time, I wanted to make sure that you really meant it, that I could rely on what you said; and I shake my head doubtfully at him, I really don't understand what you're trying to tell me, you didn't leave me even the shadow of a doubt, we've been living apart for months now, each of us is free to make a life for himself, what are you saying now, that you've been waiting for me?

I've been waiting a long time now to see if you were serious that night, he says; yesterday, when you called, I was sure that you were going to ask me to come back, but this time not out of panic, but out of love, please excuse the expression; now I realize that I was naive, as usual, I gave you too much credit, you haven't grown up, you haven't learned anything, not if you can throw yourself so quickly at the first man who shows an interest in you, without even thinking about your son. I breathe heavily, trying not to let the words fired from his mouth pierce the screen between us; Amnon, listen to me, it's true that at first I thought the separation was a mistake, but you didn't want to come back and now it's clear to me that you were right, we would have had exactly the same problems, I don't understand what you want from me, you turned me down, what right do you have to complain.

I didn't turn you down, he growls, leaning forward, his arms folded on the table, the tips of the hairs sprouting from his head making cloudy patches on his scalp, I told you that we needed time, in all this time I haven't touched another woman, and you're already moving in with someone? And I say in a hoarse voice, but I didn't expect you to stay faithful to me, I thought that you were with Ofra, what do you want, what are you saying?

I'm saying that if you suggested getting back together again now I would consider it seriously, but if you're really moving in with someone else then I'm done with you for good, this is your last chance; and I mutter, I thought you were done with me a long time ago, I don't believe a word you say, all you want to do is spoil things for me, Amnon, don't do this to me. Why did you ask me to come here for in the first place, he says sullenly, a little mustache of sweat collecting on his trembling upper lip, we're not part of a coffee klatch, what did you want, for us to plan together how to tell Gili that you're bringing him a new father? And I say, not a new father, you're his father and nobody's going to compete with you, if that's what's bothering you then you've got nothing to worry about, and he wipes the sweat from his face with his hand, leaving a red mark at the bottom of his chin; the whole thing bothers me, how would you feel if I invited you to breakfast and you were sure that I was going to ask you to get back together and then I told you that I had someone else and I was moving in with her, wouldn't it bother you? And as his lips move before me and my lips before him, repeating the same sounds over and over again, it seems to me that I am seeing us over the years, planted opposite each other with our mouths open, our necks extended, making discordant sounds, in various different places, in nature, in hotels, in the homes of friends, in our own changing apartments, growing old as we argue, crashing against each other's contrasts, is this our past or is it our future.

I've had enough of your manipulations, I whisper, because two elderly women are sitting down at the table next to us, looking at us curiously, you had no reason to think that I wanted to come back to you, and I'm sure that it didn't even occur to you until five minutes ago, you just want to make things difficult for me, but you won't succeed, I'm so sure of this relationship that even you won't be able to undermine me, and he says, really? You've found the perfect guy, the flawless man? For his sake I hope he is because he doesn't know what he's in for the minute you discover that he isn't perfect, he won't be able to recognize you anymore, will he? You thought I was perfect, too, at the beginning, I had a few months of grace until you started nagging, you're not so different from your father, don't kid yourself, you don't know how to love, your love's an annual plant, at best.

A sharp ray of sunlight flits across our table, between the cups of coffee that have gone cold while we argued, wavering between us as if seeking the guilty party, feeling his face like a blind man, darting nervously from eye to eye, from cheek to cheek, was this the piece of skin you loved, would you like to see this eye every day for the rest of your life, highlighting the alienation that now towers over our years of intimacy, is this my husband, it seems as if I have crossed the lines and from my new position he is strange and repulsive, my ears, having grown accustomed to Oded's mild manner of speech, are astounded at the crude outburst. Protected by the stacked sandbags of my new life, I eye him through the slits as if I'm watching a battle that has already been decided, but is still dangerous, the possibility of a final, stray bullet still hovering in the air.

Amnon, I've heard enough, I didn't ask you to wait for me, I thought that all that was already behind us, try to calm down, we have to keep on reasonably good terms for Gili; and he repeats in a loud, resentful voice, for Gili, for Gili, I'm sick of that pair of hypocritical words, you care so much about Gili that you break up his family, you care so much about him that you move in with a strange man, as if he didn't have enough to deal with, and all this at lightning speed so you don't regret it, do you have any idea what you're doing? Sometimes I think you're just out of your mind, you need a psychiatrist's full time attention, I'm telling you; and before I have time to tell him that he can relax, I have a psychiatrist full time, he gets to his feet, shoves the chair back, and says, you know what, leave me out of you compulsive messes, deal with them on your own, don't expect any help from me, not with Gili, not with the Rabbinate and not with anything else, let your new boyfriend help you, and he storms out, colliding with the waitress and the breakfast for two we ordered, scrambled eggs and a green salad, hot rolls, a platter of cheeses.

Troubled, I watch the waitress as she sets the table for two, laying the scrambled eggs in front of the empty chair, the glass of freshly squeezed orange juice, the silverware on a folded napkin, as if the orderliness will ensure his return, and I, too, pretend to be waiting, nervously drinking the cold coffee while I look out the window. A heavy shadow has fallen over the gleam of my new life, a worm has been discovered in the apple, ants in the cake, and I try to reassure myself, it's just talk, he'll calm down, when we split up he ranted and raved and in the end everything worked out, what can he possibly do, he won't take the child away from me, or disappear simply in order to punish me, and even if he delays the divorce I'll manage, but above and beyond the explicit threats, the greatest, most agonizing fear of all is gradually exposed, as if with his brutal words he has opened a forgotten musical box and turned the key, and sure enough it begins to play its somber, agitating tune of doubt and uncertainty.

Are these eggs taken? I hear a smiling voice ask, and look up happily; they were my husband's but he didn't want them, they're all yours, I say, standing up and embracing her. Talia, how good to see you, I missed you; and she says in a tone of playful, exaggerated grievance, I'm not friends with you anymore, not after not returning my calls for months, if you don't mind I'll polish off Amnon's omelet and be on my way; and I say, believe me, I wasn't capable of talking to anybody, you have no idea what I've been through; and she gives me a penetrating look over her preoccupied mouth, judging by the way you look, only good things.

You're wrong, I say, the good things are recent, and she devotes her attention to the cream cheese on her roll; don't tell me, you're in love? And I giggle in embarrassment, you have no idea, it's too good to be true; and she says, you worry me Ella, it sounds bad; and I complain, stop it, do you want to spoil things for me too, like Amnon? What's wrong with everybody this morning, you see a happy woman and first thing you do is get jealous.

You didn't expect Amnon to revel in the news, did you, she says; and I sigh, I thought it wouldn't make any difference to him by now; and she sniggers, watch out, I'm on his side now, when you didn't return my calls I talked to him whenever Yoav wanted to see Gili, we went to his place a few times, didn't Gili tell you? And I say, no, you know what they're like at that age, they don't tell you anything, quickly covering up my embarrassment, trying to keep her from realizing the extent of the distance yawning between me and my son. Half his life is hidden from me, and even if he had tried to clue me in I wouldn't have been able to close the gap, certainly not with a child who refuses to reveal even the smallest detail to me.

Actually we had a nice time, she says, direct and matter-of-fact as always, you have no idea how much better Amnon is now without you; and I say, yeah, I had that impression, too, until this morning, I told him that I'm moving in with someone and it was too much for him, he went right back to being his old self; and she abandons her roll, and swallows hard, Ella, you're going to live with a man? And I giggle, who do you want me to live with, a cat? And she says, at the moment that would definitely be better, how long have you known each other? And I say, not long, but since when is time so important?

You're running too fast again, she says, her voice agitated, it's great you've fallen in love, but why live together, why drag Gili into it? Does he have children, too? And I say, two, but they have a mother, I don't think they'll actually live with us; and she says, you have no idea what you're getting into, it's much more complicated than you think, I have a girlfriend who's going through hell now with a divorced man who has three kids she can't stand, and they can't stand her, you have to wait before you get the children involved.

But I'm sure I'll get along with his children, I protest weakly, I already know the boy and he's great, and the little girl seems sweet too, how bad can it be? And she says, who knows, with children on both sides it's impossible to know. How is he with Gili, for example? And I say, he hardly knows him but I'm sure it'll be fine, I've seen how he is with his son, he's a wonderful father.

He's a wonderful father to his own children, not yours, that's the difference, she takes a hurried sip of Amnon's coffee and makes a face, listen, as opposed to Amnon I do want things to work out for you, but you have to take it slow, why not get professional advice? And I say, I have, he's a psychiatrist, I'm sure he's given it a lot of thought; and she says, the fact that he's a psychiatrist is irrelevant, in their private lives they're just as bad as anyone else, worse, actually, because they think they know everything. Don't rely on him, think for yourself, think about what it will do to Gili to suddenly get a step-brother and sister; and I say, but Gili and his son are best friends, that's how we got to know each other in the first place; and still she isn't impressed, so what? Gili was once Yoav's best friend, do you think that if I moved in with Amnon tomorrow it would be easy for them? I don't think so.

So that's the thing, you've fallen in love with Amnon? I snicker, and she gets up quickly, I have to run, take care, she kisses me, her luxuriant black hair spilling onto my cheek, we have to continue this talk later, why don't you come by with Gili this afternoon? It's been six months since you've been to our place, and I say, some other time, today we're planning to bring the children together, we're trying to stage a falling in love; and she grimaces again, to stage a falling in love? This doesn't sound good, Ella, you worry me, promise me that you'll think about what I said, even though I know you well enough to know it's already a lost cause.

Our role is to stage falling in love, I tell the chair opposite me, empty again, a love that grows gradually, naturally, within a family framework. We have a limited audience, only three people, all minors, ostensibly sympathetic but also perched on the brink of hostility, they are seemingly inattentive but focused, trusting but wary, at ease but afraid, their young eyes notice the faintest hint of falsity, the jarring notes, the stolen glances, the effort and the tension, and unlike an ordinary audience they are alert, hardly breathing, like soldiers before battle, for the play that we are putting on for them this afternoon is the story of their lives, the story of their rocky, uncertain childhood, and its plot will determine their fate.

Here they are sitting opposite each other on the tire swing in the yard, rising and falling like a pendulum, accompanying the movement with shrieking delight, the cold rays of the sun playing on their muddy coats, their cheeks flushed with a strange, blue-tinged color, as if they have been made up. Mommy, not yet, Gili shouts, let us swing a little longer, and Yotam echoes him, not yet, a little longer, and my heart goes out to them as if they were both my children, twins I gave birth to, and in an overexcited voice, as if I have never collected a strange child from the schoolyard before, I announce, Yotam, you're coming to our house, your father asked me to pick you up today, and already, even as he pumps his legs on the swing, Gili's eyes wander across my face and it is clear to me that my enthusiastic voice has not gone unnoticed, he notes every detail. Really? Yotam says in surprise, my mom didn't said anything this morning, and I say reassuringly, don't worry, your father just called and asked me to take you to our place, he'll come later, after he picks up Maya from her class, that's what he told me, I add quickly, trying to cover the tracks of my intimate knowledge of his schedule.

Together they slip off the swing, collect their schoolbags from where they threw them down in the yard, and we make our way through the commotion of the stifling corridors, weaving through the corporeal smells, elbow-like in their presence, chocolate spread, white bread and carefree farts, damp socks and the sweat of little people fighting for their place in the hierarchy every minute of the day, without pause. I'm taking Yotam, I tell the teacher; and she strokes their mute heads, great, they're best friends, these two, just like brothers; and I agree, yes, just like brothers, every casual word seems to take on great significance, heavy, pregnant words surround me lately, issued from the mouths of strangers.

On the way home I walk behind them, trying to overhear their conversation, together they stride, showing each other creased cards that they take out of their coat pockets, this one's worth the most, where did you get it, this one I've got doubles, why don't we make a deal, they chirp like tender, innocent chicks, a new family is being built for you and you don't know it, twigs and leaves and threads and scraps of cloth are being gathered around you, binding you to each other and before you know it you'll be linked. I bought six more packs, I tell Gili, three each, and he announces, you hear that, she bought us cards, and immediately he inquires, did you buy them before or after Yotam's father called? Making sure that all six packs weren't originally meant for him and that now on account of Yotam he has lost out in the deal, and I say, after, of course; and he stops to think for a moment, weighing my words, smoothing the card in his hand, I don't even know your father, he says to Yotam in a mildly reproachful tone; and Yotam is quick to defend himself, that's because he's always working, he almost never comes to school, I don't see him that much either, he admits, but now I'll get to see him more, he tries to encourage himself and his audience, because he moved into a new house, and we'll be with him half of the time.

What's that supposed to mean, half the time, I silently digest this new information, hearing Gili hurry to even the score between them, I'm with my dad half the time too, right Mommy? They've found themselves something to be proud of, the pathetic achievements of the children of divorce, and I say, yes, more or less, careful not to contradict him, but the rumor of the new arrangement that has accidentally come my way preoccupies me far more. Half of the time? What about our time? I try to imagine the nature of our day-to-day life in the future, will he cut down on his working hours to be with the children, or will he rely on my help, will we spend half our time with all three children, or will we separate between them, half the time with his children and half the time with mine, and never on our own, and the sound of Talia's voice comes back to me, it's a lot more complicated than you think, but I silence her, so what if Yotam said so, it isn't up to him, and even if it's true, and even if there are difficulties, our love will overcome, and when I think of our love, of this surprising new we, it seems as if warm healing sunlight is bathing the chambers of my heart, which have been shuttered like a sickroom, why trouble myself with details when I want him so much, when in fact I have no choice.

Take your shoes off outside so you don't bring mud into the house, guys, I remind them as we climb the stairs, happy to use the plural form once more, and Gili who goes in first remarks, you cleaned the house, Mommy, what for? And I hug him, for you boys, to make it nice for you, and although he is not satisfied he lets it go, pounces on the new packs of cards, presents three of them to Yotam with a generous flourish, and soon they are busy comparing and trading. I hurry to the bedroom, wondering what to wear, something simple and homely but at the same time flattering, not too sloppy, but not trying too hard either, finally selecting a red sweater and faded jeans, still not satisfied, should I tie my hair back or leave it loose, it seems I have never taken so much trouble over a meeting with him, most of the times we met it was by chance, and this time everything is planned, staged, should I put on new makeup or be content with what's left of this morning's, and when I try gathering my hair into a red velvet elastic band and immediately change my mind, I wonder who all these preparations are really meant for, for this man who has already seen me sleeping and naked, or for his pretty ten year old daughter, am I trying make an impression on her, or trying to compete with her in front of her father, to overshadow her.

Again and again they hit the carpet with their little hands, raising clouds of dust in their attempts to turn over the cards, which lie obediently on their backs like dead cockroaches, and perhaps this is why I fail to hear the doorbell ring, and when I look up from the sofa I'm reclining on, the door is already creaking open and they appear behind it, the father and his daughter, arm in arm, and I immediately regret not having tied my hair back, for her fair hair is perfectly braided, lending an air of maturity and nobility to her porcelain face, which looks at me with overt displeasure.

Good afternoon everybody, he announces ceremoniously, his low voice suddenly sounding a little ridiculous, affected; and I leap up to greet them, hi, how wonderful to see you, as if it's a big surprise, and the two of us would no doubt have laughed at each other if we weren't so tense, almost desperate; and he tries to make his voice casual as he says, do you know Maya? For some reason he points at her, and I wave at her even though she's standing next to me, hi, I'm Ella; and she sulkily cuts the stilted ceremony short, I know who you are, I saw you once in a cafe; and I say quickly, give me your coats, and he tries to take off his coat but her hand clutches his arm, makes it impossible. Daddy, I want to go home, she says sullenly, I have homework; and he says, let's stay for a while, you can do your homework later, I'm sure Yotam doesn't want to leave yet; and only then Yotam takes them in, abandons the cards and bounds over to his father, Daddy! he roars as if they haven't met for weeks, Gili's mom bought me cards! And Oded shouts, that's wonderful, congratulations! As if these cards were some amazing, unprecedented acquisition, while at the same time trying to extricate himself from his coat, shaking her hand, her slender, delicate, insulted hand off his arm in order to do so, and I note a first small, satisfying victory to my credit, snatch his coat quickly from his hands, and hang it up carefully in the coat closet, as if he isn't going to need it any time in the foreseeable future.

Give me your coat too, you'll be hot like that, I say, and she removes her coat with an audible sigh, revealing the splendid ensemble underneath it, shiny blue lycra tights and over them a long-sleeved blue leotard hugging her slender body, what a gorgeous outfit, I say; and she smiles cautiously, Daddy got it for me in America. Really? I examine it appreciatively, what fun to have a girl, not like these boys who won't let you dress them up, I rant, trying to create the illusion of feminine solidarity, sacrificing to this end my own son who gets up from the floor and stations himself at my side, keeping a suspicious eye on the proceedings, and so we stand at the entrance to the apartment, me and my little child, and opposite us Oded and his little children, like two camps silently taking the measure of each other's might.

Are you hungry? There's a chocolate cake, and vegetable soup, and we can order pizza, I say, as if I were the owner of an out-of-the-way restaurant pouncing on rare customers, and to my relief the two boys cheer, pizza! psyching each other up, blurring the sharp line dividing us, and I busy myself taking their orders. What toppings do you want? Olives? Mushrooms? How about you Maya? And she answers coldly, I'm not hungry. She likes corn, Oded says, and I ask, and you? embarrassed for a moment by the question, do we know each other at all, I know the taste of your skin but not your taste in pizza; and he says, I don't care; and Gili shouts, olives for me, as if afraid that I'll forget his preference; and Yotam shouts after him, mushrooms for me. So maybe I'll take mushrooms too, so I won't be jealous, Gili wavers, his confidence fading, and I say in surprise, why should you be jealous if you prefer something else? And he mutters, don't tell me what to feel, and suddenly his eyes fill with tears and he wails, I don't know what kind of pizza to order.

Order what you like best, olives, I say firmly, but he can't make up his mind; I'll be jealous of Yotam, I want Yotam to have olives too, and I sigh, is there anything more complicated on earth than ordering pizza for five people trying to become a family. What's wrong, Gili, I say, what does it matter to you what he eats; and he clings to me sobbing, it does matter, it does matter, the snot peeping out of his nostrils coming alive, picking up steam and trickling down his lips, the tears streaming down his cheeks and collecting black dust on their way, his eyelids hooding his eyes, and his open mouth, without the two front teeth, reveals the sharp incisors of a vampire. I have never seen him like this, disheveled and unattractive, as if a stranger's eyes have been planted in my head, and perhaps they are not a stranger's but the eyes of the man who sits down quietly on the sofa, his beautiful fingers that I kissed and fondled only yesterday trapped between the fingers of an arrogant, glamorous little girl, looking with undisguised disgust at the brat weeping in my arms as if the sky had just fallen on his world.

I have an idea, I say with forced gaiety, we'll order you both kinds, and you'll taste and decide, I come up with an extravagant, clearly anti-educational suggestion, which fails to satisfy him, and only causes Yotam to protest; if he gets two then I want two too; and I declare, fine, problem solved. I pick up the phone, order the biggest pizza with the most toppings, to satisfy the wishes of all those present, although it's clear to me that none of us is particularly hungry yet, and the leftover slices will outnumber the eaten ones.

Gili, go and wash your face and blow your nose, I say once I've placed the order, and he trails shamefaced to the bathroom, returning immediately with his face dripping, as dirty as it was before, with dark stains running down the sides of his cheeks like dust swept under the bed, and I shake my head at him, but I don't accompany him back to the bathroom to help him empty his nose, afraid to abandon the living room to their meaningful looks, allowing them to exchange signals agreed upon in advance, and take the opportunity to disappear, for they are an almost-whole family, a whole family not in need of any additions, certainly not a demanding, headstrong, spoiled crybaby, but suddenly Yotam goes up to him, don't worry, Gili, I'll eat what you do, he offers, with sweet generosity, I'll eat the pizza with olives too, so you won't be jealous; and Gili sobs happily, so what will we do with the mushrooms they got for us, and Yotam comes closer and whispers in his ear, and the two of them burst into mischievous laughter, like a pair of scheming fox cubs, and I look gratefully at Yotam, the dear child, almost my only ally, far superior to his father, because despite my joy at seeing him on my sofa, observing the proceedings with dark eyes, I have to admit that he has done nothing to better the situation and has refrained from exchanging a single word with Gili.

What would you like to drink, Oded? I ask, and he says, something strong, and I pour him a shot of vodka from the freezer. Would you like chocolate milk, Maya? I raise my voice from the kitchen and to my delight she consents, perhaps withdrawing her vehement objections to this visit. I hand the chocolate milk to him and the vodka to her and burst into nervous laughter. Where's our love gone, Oded, can you see it, do you feel it, is it hiding like a nervous cat, but these strangers are our children, our flesh and blood, and it seems that our love is no longer tangible to me either, and what I really want is for you to go, to leave me alone with the sniveling spoiled brat, because only when you've gone will I find beauty in him again, and when, I wonder, will the animal we've bred show the tip of its tail, when will it sound a muffled howl so that I can breathe a sigh of relief, so that I can believe in its existence again. Ramrod straight he sits in the corner of the sofa, in a white cashmere sweater I have never seen before, one that accentuates his finely chiseled face, the lines running down his cheeks like grooves on a tree trunk, an outside observer silently gathering data, his expression as cold and supercilious as his daughter's; have I, too, become uglier in his eyes as Gili became in mine, does he see me now covered in black tears and green snot, how quick I am to doubt him, his loving, promising words, as if they were tiny beads I'd carried in a mesh basket, nothing kept, nothing saved.

Maya, you want to play a computer game with the boys, or can I find you something to play with? I ask when they disappear into Gili's room, dying to be alone with Oded; Gili has a couple of Barbie dolls he sometimes plays with, betraying his secret without hesitation to get her to occupy herself with something, to get her to let go of her father's hand; but she refuses, no, I don't like Barbie dolls anymore, and to my horror, she climbs onto his lap, wraps her arm around his neck, Daddy, let's go,

I have homework. I'll go and get your schoolbag from the car, he offers; and she says, but I can't concentrate here, I want to go home; and he promises, we'll go soon, sweetheart, his hands gently stroking her honey colored hair, and his tenderness toward her stokes a mean, murky anger in me, only a few minutes ago I gave in to my son's demands, but facing them I am full of indignation; why doesn't he shut her up, why doesn't he say, we're staying here and that's that, I'm the one who decides here not you. Their presence in my living room is oppressive and condescending, in two-headed silence they inspect my simple furniture, the picture of the Parisian hanging on the wall, it seems that even the thousand-year survivor on the wall of the palace in Knossos is obliterated under their gaze, and I stand up quickly and go into the bedroom, the clothes I tried on lie on the bed in a colorful, superfluous heap; what was I thinking, could the most glamorous garment overshadow the ties of blood, she's his daughter, she'll always be his daughter, while I'm transitory as the rented apartment, and I take the red velvet elastic band and stand in front of the mirror, trying to gather all my hair into it, without letting a single hair escape, and just when it seems that I've done it, I hear him approaching; Ella, are you there? And he closes the door and leans against it, looking at me in astonishment. What are you doing? he asks, and I drop the hair band and quickly remove my sweater; I suddenly felt hot, I'm changing my clothes, I say, and in order to verify my words I take a short sleeved tee-shirt out of the closet, but I don't put it on, I stand facing him with bare, challenging breasts, like someone clinging to a weapon of last resort in the battle for their honor.

Come here, he says, holding out his arms to me; and I sigh into his mouth, come to me tonight, Oded, how I need his closeness, urgent as a drug, essential as proof; and he says, that's impossible, the children are sleeping at my place; and I plead with him, but Maya's a big girl, she can stay with Yotam for a while; and he says, but it's the fist night they're sleeping over at my place, I don't want to make it any harder than it needs to be.

Then maybe I'll come to you, I insist, my mother can stay with Gili; and he says, it won't work out tonight, they'll probably go to bed late; but I persevere, then come tomorrow before work; and he says, I start work at eight, it's not going to happen, let's wait for a better time;

and I turn my back on him, staring at the dead treetop, the yellow street lamp falling on its dry, bonelike branches, you don't want me enough, you don't want me anymore, the feeling of rejection blankets my bare skin like leprosy, the greater the insult the greater the need. What's the matter with you, he asks; and I turn to him, I'm not going to wait for a better time, I say, if you really want something then you find the time, and then I kneel down in front of him and hastily unzip his pants, ignoring the existence of the children on the other side of the wall, my mouth takes hold of his flesh and I hear him sigh; stop it, Ella, this isn't the right time, but the sigh ends in a groan of pleasure, and when it seems that his doubts have been resolved, I stop abruptly and stand up, now let's see you wait for a better time, and he pants, mouth agape; really, Ella, I'm surprised at you, he says in hoarse rebuke, the lowest kind of feminine manipulation; and I am already heavy with dread, overcome by the weight of the day's events, you simply don't know me, I whisper in his ear, I have another manipulation for you, even lower, if you don't come tonight then don't come at all, and I throw my tee-shirt on and leave the room, and with the insult immediately giving way to remorse I sit down on the armchair in the living room, and only then I become aware of her light, slightly slanting eyes, like her mother's, examining me nervously, where's my father?

I'm here honey, I hear his voice, calm and steady again, carrying no trace of the hoarse panting of before, we're leaving soon. What's going on with the pizza? he addresses me in a scolding tone, as if I'm responsible for the speed of the delivery, and I glance at my watch; it'll be here any minute, it's been less than half an hour; I try to catch his eye, to signal a shamefaced apology, but he avoids my eyes, looking expectantly at the door, as if his salvation will come from there, and indeed it does, a hot aromatic pizza covering the coffee table, drawing us around, uniting us for a while just as it divided us at the beginning of the evening, for Gili and Yotam are perfectly in sync, chewing their olive-covered slices, and even Maya succumbs to the tempting smell and takes her corn-covered slice, while Oded meditatively chews his plain slice. Now that the children have calmed down he, too, looks more at ease, and I pour myself a vodka and fill his glass too. Like a clan of famished cats around a plate of food we surround the table, and for a moment it seems that everything is all right, and perhaps it was before too, only as usual I panicked prematurely, mistook a shadow for a mountain, and in my haste to lament our demise, I hastened it, and to my relief I see Maya sitting on the carpet with Gili and Yotam, gradually thawing, joining almost in spite of herself in their mysterious project, as they take scissors out of their schoolbags and with clumsy fingers try to cut up the remaining slices of pizza, we're making food for the birds, they explain to her in a loud whisper, we'll throw the crumbs on the balcony and watch them come.

What are you doing, wasting food like that, Oded scolds them; and I coax him, never mind, let them enjoy themselves, and both of us seem surprised by this exchange, as if we were the mother and father in a normal family, having a mild disagreement about how to raise the children, and I mouth at him, come here for a minute, and I return to the bedroom, but he fails to join me, and I call him in an official tone, Oded, can you come here for a minute, since he can hardly ignore an open request in the presence of the children.

What now, he asks, giving me a tired look, have you got any more threats for me? And this time I am the one who leans against the door, I'm sorry, I didn't mean it seriously, I understand that you can't come today, I'll wait for you as long as it takes; and he sighs, regarding me with narrowed eyes, you know, Ella, maybe I don't really know you, maybe I don't really want to know you either, but his hand strokes my flaming cheek in a rough caress, I'm prepared to forget what happened here, but I'm warning you, those tricks don't work on me; and I murmur, I'm sorry, forgive me; and then he asks, so, where were we? And it seems to me that I hear a spark of lust in his voice, and I kneel down before him, like a supplicant, if this is the way to you let it be my way, his hands push down on my head, guiding it, my forehead bumping into his hard stomach, steam seemingly rising from my throat as I gather like a bird the crumbs his children have left me.

This time he leaves the room before me and I hurry to the bathroom, wash my face and spray myself with perfume, and when I return to the living room they are all sitting on the carpet around the Monopoly board, and Gili is beside himself with delight, come on, Mommy, we're just waiting for you; and Maya, who has forgotten that she has homework, is explaining the rules, you hardly know how to read so the parents will help you, Gili with his mother, and Yotam with Daddy, and me on my own; and we settle into the game, throwing the dice, marching around the board, accumulating imaginary property, streets and entire towns, houses and hotels, buying and selling, and already a feeling of joy embraces me, yes, it's possible, every evening we will sit like this and play together, and whenever I look at him I will shiver as if a breeze has crept under my clothes, and when he hands me the dice his hand lingers on mine, arousing a surprisingly powerful desire in the middle of the family bliss, and it seems that I have received a double gift this evening, because I get to kiss the nape of Gili's neck as he sits with my arms around him, thrilled by the game, while a provocative and pungent gaze tracks my every move.

Long before the game is over he says, it's late, we'll play again another time; and Gili, who has amassed the greatest fortune, begs, a little longer, just a little longer; and I try to compromise, why don't we leave everything as it is and continue next time? But Maya, who has been left with hardly any property, pronounces, next time we'll start again from the beginning, and these words have suddenly become self-evident, even to her, yes, there will be another time, another game, another pizza, another meeting, even though she dons her former, chilly indifference upon departure. She takes her coat from my hands and I try to smile at him over the heads of the three children, good night to you, and he replies, good night to you too, blowing me a kiss with his beautiful lips; and all of a sudden the house is empty and Gili clings to me and hugs my waist, finally the two of us are by ourselves, just me and you.

I thought you had a good time with them, I try to hide my disappointment; and he says, I had fun with Yotam, even his sister's kind of nice, but now it's fun to be alone with you, he adds, completely ignoring their father; and I say, for me too, Gilili, his innocence makes my heart quake, he has no idea how rare these moments will be, soon they will be transformed into a distant memory, and as we tread softly along the paths of our daily routine, warm bath, goodnight story, bedtime chat, and I seem to hear the tolling of the bells of separation. Another separation is being wielded above your head, my child, a separation from this routine, from just the two of us, which has been laboriously brought into being here over the past six months, the routine of survivors trying to build a new settlement on the ruins of their old one, making mud bricks from the beds of nearby rivers, quarrying stones from the rock, collecting broken beams and hacked reeds, forever their modest achievements will pale in the face of the glories of the past, and nevertheless a kind of order has been established here, brittle and strained, yet familiar.

With a heavy heart I sit beside his bed, he kicks the blanket aside, spreads his arms, the pajama top stretched across his chest exposes the thinness of his waist, his taut belly button, his protruding ribs, the beauty spots strewn over his skin like stars in the night sky. His face is luminescent in the light of his three night lamps, his luxuriant curls fall alongside his cheeks, his beauty has been restored; you tell me, son, must I give up my chance of happiness, of a new family, for your sake, and when he falls asleep I call Talia, surprised that I still remember her number by heart. You claim that I have to wait, I upbraid her, but how long exactly, until Gili goes to the army, perhaps? Who knows when the time is right for such changes, now he's still young enough to adjust, and if I wait too long this new relationship may fade away. I have a real chance at a new life now, Talia, I'm afraid to lose it, maybe it's my last chance, who knows, you think it's good for him to grow up alone with his mother, without a family? Perhaps precisely this change will do him good, but even as I listen to her reply the door opens and Oded is standing there, in his white sweater, again without a coat, and his presence softens her sharp sentences, defangs them. Am I disturbing you? he asks quietly; and I pull him to me, his hands already under my clothes; in my opinion you have to wait, she goes on talking, it's not a question of age but of circumstances, first let him get used to your separation from Amnon, don't burden him with a new family so soon, you won't lose anything by waiting, on the contrary, if you lose your new boyfriend because you want to wait it's a sign it wasn't serious in the first place, and you should examine your relationship with him more thoroughly before you expose Gili to new people in his life, think about it, if it doesn't work out you'll have to go through another separation with him, what do you need it for, why is it so hard for you to wait a year, and he hears all this together with me, until I cut her short, Talia, I have to hang up, I have guests, we'll talk tomorrow, and he takes the black receiver from me and contemplates it gravely. Ostensibly she's right about every word she says, that friend of yours, he says at last, but I don't believe in that kind of advice, nobody knows better than you do what's right for you, try to listen to your heart, your inner voice; and I ask, what are you doing here anyway, I thought it was impossible tonight? And he smiles, I have fifty minutes for you, will that be enough?

Why fifty precisely? I wonder, looking at my watch; and he replies, because I told Maya I have an emergency meeting with a client who needs first aid; and I am filled with the magnanimous pride of the victorious, I really do need first aid, I whisper in his ear, but I thought you weren't attracted to women you have to take care of? And he smirks, those rules evidently don't apply to you, just as your girlfriend's rules don't apply to us, at least I hope not; and I snuggle up to him, so you came to give me emergency treatment; and he says, yes, what exactly is troubling you? And I switch off the light and pull him down to the carpet, I have a small local problem, as soon as you make love to me I believe it will go away, and he says, that sounds symptomatic of a graver problem, but I believe that I can solve it too, if you give me the chance.

The Monopoly pieces I haven't had time to pick up stab my back, the houses we built and the hotels we put up in the streets we acquired, the fake bank notes stick to my backside as he slides through the narrow path that is his and his alone, as if paving it again and again, and when he withdraws I beg him to return, pulling him in with my hands and knees, with my tongue and hair; promise me you'll trust me, he whispers, I need you to trust me, and I promise and promise, following the movement of his organ through my body like the movement of light, igniting a flame and moving on, awakening hidden nexuses of desire, for wherever he isn't I crave him, how will you put this fire out, many waters cannot quench it, and when I quiver beneath him on the Monopoly board he jumps up and fastens his fly in the dark; I hope I was able to help, he whispers, and I giggle, not really, to my regret, it seem the problem has only grown more acute, and he laughs, that was precisely my intention.

Chapter eighteen

Not on the walls of the Egyptian temples, not on tomb inscriptions, nor on the papyrus scrolls, neither above the ground nor beneath it, is the name of Israel mentioned in the New Kingdom, neither as friend nor foe, neighbor or enslaved people, and although the exodus of Israel from Egypt is without a doubt the historical event most present in the scriptures, in law and story and song, in the words of the prophets and the verse of the Psalms, as of yet no proof has been found of the great saga of suffering and salvation, of a new beginning and a second chance.

Excavations and archeological surveys have repeatedly failed to prove anything besides what did not happen, all along the eastern delta, the shores of northern Sinai, in Kadesh Barnea and Etzion Geber, no proof has been found of slavery, or of redemption, or of wanderings in the desert, apart from the stormy and indirect testimony regarding natural disasters: I show thee the land upside down, the sun is veiled and shines not in the eyes of men, he is in the sky like the moon, the river of Egypt is dry, barren, the south wind shall blow against the north wind.

Is history once more ignoring the awesome role of the natural world in the course of events, since it seems that the elements shook the ancient world to its foundations, not the hand of man but the repeated upheavals of nature, utterly dwarfing the exploits of conquerors and machinations of politicians, Forsooth, the land turns like a potter's wheel, the House of Royalty is instantly overturned, behold, the flames have risen to the heavens!

Did Thera's natural disaster shake the mightiest of powers to its foundations, were its shores visited by a great and terrible wave, water high as a mountain, moving at the speed of lightning, pillars of cloud and fire, blood and darkness, blow after blow, plague after plague, did parents sacrifice their firstborn to appease the gods? To this day a layer of volcanic ash rests on the bed of the Nile – and still proof is required that nature's destruction of Thera triggered man's destruction of Egypt, the miraculous victory of Israel at the hand of its God, is the attempt to verify the miracle tantamount to denying the miracle? It seems that all this belongs to my former life and has nothing to do with the new life coming into view, golden and glowing, like the radiance in the east before sunrise, when its light is already visible on the horizon and nobody can deny its advance, nobody can doubt its promise.

With arrogant indifference I try to reconstruct the story of Thera, as if it were a painful childhood memory I have dwelt on *ad nauseam*, trying to bring the sad affair to an end because I am sick of these mornings in front of the computer, of the dry excavation reports, longing for the well marked squares of earth lined with sandbags like trenches in wartime, for that concrete but strangely abstract labor, for the reassuring tools, for the endless dust and the tapping of the picks and the noise of the bulldozers and the smell of the mold rising from the earth toward the fresh air falling from the sky. All this year I have been afraid of being called out on a salvage operation and now I wait impatiently, as the winter grows weaker, eradicated little by little from the face of the earth, torn into scraps through which the hesitant, clandestine buds of the deciduous trees sprout.

A feverish alertness accompanies me in the last weeks of winter, with the certainty of change rapidly approaching, a change I have no way of escaping, nor have I any wish to escape it, since the dull, gnawing hunger, the inevitable shadow of all loves, is gradually taking on the clear shape of a life together, of an official connection that cannot be doubted, of brief leisure hours that need not be divided between two houses, commuting like the child of divorced parents, synchronizing myself to the wanderings of Gili, Maya and Yotam, the migrant tribes of the modern age, the children of divorced parents, herding their toys in the afternoon from house to house, from father to mother and mother to father. I am forced inside on the increasingly rare off days too, for Amnon is suddenly extremely busy, emphatically busy, and Michal, even the letters of her name make me feel uneasy, Michal suffers from migraines almost daily, avoids her children, and it seems as if the two additional supports on which our children's lives are based have joined forces against us, and between our tasks we grope hurriedly for closeness, complaining in advance of the need to part, and it seems that every day climbs toward the twinkling point of the brief reunion and immediately recedes from view, and the wish to string these twinkling moments together grows ever more urgent.

Our simple, comfortable apartment now looks like a transit camp, the living room shutter is stuck and I make no effort to repair it, the faucet leaks, the halogen lamp has burned out, and it seems to me that these are no longer my concerns, but those of whoever lives here after me, when Gili and I move at last into the spacious apartment waiting for us, and there we can string the twinkling moments together, and there I will not have to part from him after the greatest intimacy, and there I will not have to choose between time with him and time with Gili, my two loves will dwell under the same roof, at ease and relaxed, and so the wish, which in contrast to most wishes seems easy to realize, comes into being, all it requires is that the deed whose presence is already reverberating in the air be done, to call in the movers, to load the sofa and armchairs, the clothes and dishes and books, and Gili's bed and closet, and even his lampshade, his room transported in its entirety, down to the last toy, as if he fell asleep at home and woke up elsewhere, without even noticing the difference, but still I hesitate, like the key that got stuck halfway, unable to return or to complete its rotation.

Come on already, you're wearing us out with your doubts, he says, when each of us is in his own apartment, next to his sleeping children, and despite the short distance between us his voice over the phone sounds faint and muffled, we could be together now, what's the point in having duplicate lives? Don't worry so much, he says, I'm not afraid of the pitfalls, the only thing that scares me is your hesitation, what exactly are you waiting for? And I don't know myself what I'm waiting for, for it is clear to me that the deed will be done, and nevertheless the thought of the moving truck parked outside the house prompts a deep, throbbing grief, as if it were an unspeakably sad sight.

The children aren't ready yet, I say, and he casts that aside, they'll get ready as it happens, all this playacting is getting on my nerves, we're both bad actors, you have to jump into the water, he says, all these hesitations are only harmful, you're undermining my confidence, in the end you'll convince me that it won't work, is that what you want, for me to change my mind? And I say, of course not, just give me time, walking around the house like a bride excited by the new life awaiting her, but afraid of parting from her childhood, from her virginity, from the narrow confines of my life with Gili, as if he were my nuclear family and I have to climb a swaying rope ladder into a more extended family.

I send ahead of me a sweater and a scarf and a few books, shampoo and stockings, and it seems that they, possessing a clear will of their own, already know the way there and not the way back, like the raven that failed to return to Noah's Ark and was, therefore, painted black. One after the other they migrate, well hidden among his things, but we two, Gili and I, still belong here, to the apartment we moved into a few months before he was born, overlooking a bright, protected inner courtyard, with pomegranate trees now standing starkly bare, but soon to put out leaves and after them crimson blooms like goblets of wine, which will turn into fruits that will ripen in autumn, illuminating the yard like red lanterns, tempting flocks of migrating birds, which will peck them until they are hollow inside although from the outside they'll look whole, much to the disappointment of the child wishing to dig his teeth into the abundant seeds, and as winter approaches they will drop like bodies without souls onto the narrow paved paths and stain them with dark juice, and we will not be here, and between the tree trunks the first wood sorrel will appear, and we will not be here, and the *hush-hash* tree will flaunt its unnecessary fruit, and we will not be here, we will not come down to the balding lawn with a ball and a blanket and some snacks, we will not stroke the friendly cats that frequent the yard, we will not admire the kittens emerging from the undergrowth, a jumble of tails and ears as they play among the bushes, and when I look at the yard from the living room sofa, I place a proud and apprehensive hand on my stomach, as if the deed I must do already exists, present as an embryo, and it will ripen regardless, and in any case there is no way back, just as there is no way back from an advanced pregnancy, and in any case there is nothing to be done except to hope that the world will look favorably on it, and perhaps my sorrow is only the feeling of loss that accompanies any change, for I am being led to a new family, which will overshadow the previous one precisely because of its complexity, because it cannot be taken for granted, and it will stand as a miracle and a wonder, a holy family, and in comparison my lonely life with my only son will seem dreary and slow.

And yet I hesitate, there is no doubt that it is too soon, too sudden, it won't be easy for him to adjust to two additional children in the house, to the presence of a new man, almost a stranger, for in spite of our frequent meetings, no bond has yet been forged between him and Oded, and when I complain to Oded he immediately grows defensive, it's hard for me like this, when we live together it will be more natural for all of us, and this seems to be the only answer he can come up with at the moment, when we live together everything will work out, stop fattening your fears, they only grow hungrier, sitting opposite me pale and tired after long hours of work, looking at me in growing doubt, don't wear us down, Ella, don't spoil things, trust me, and when he is by my side I am almost persuaded that there is no reason to wait, but without him I vacillate again, facing Gili with my knees trembling, like a woman who's trying to tell her husband about her love for another man but does not dare.

The secret I am hiding from him nails me to the floor, frozen and guilty I stand before him, keeping some distance on account of my pity, and sensing the change he suddenly clings to me, forcing me to reconstruct our crystalline afternoon hours, our chiming chatter, the innocent bleating of an ewe and a lamb, what's the matter, Mommy, he asks anxiously, are you sad? Are you mad at me? And it seems that in my concern not to harm him I am hurting him in another way, and perhaps for his sake, too, it's preferable that the deed be done, that the change be exposed to the light of day, rather than remaining veiled behind my every step, my every look, threatening us when we sit in the living room with the broken shutter, the burnt-out halogen bulb peering down at us from the heights of the ceiling, the poor, focused light of the table lamp drawing a vinegary circle around us, and it seems that the apartment is unrecognizable, as are we.

Sometimes I'm aghast at how easily I informed him of our separation, reconstructing over and over that succinct conversation, Amnon beside me but not saying a word, Daddy and I are splitting up, but we'll always love you, and set beside it the new, up-to-date announcement: Yotam's daddy and I love each other, and we're all going to live together in their house; it seems that this news may shake him up a lot more than that laconic announcement, what a pity I can't send him a telegram, ask him a riddle, draw him a picture, act it out for him with the help of smiling little plastic dolls, this is me and this is Yotam's daddy, this is you and this is Maya and this Yotam, and this is the house we're going to live in together, or perhaps it would be better to use his beloved stuffed animals, to pair up the lioness and the tiger, teddy bears and lion cubs, build a mixed family before his astonished eyes.

Listen, Oded says, sometimes in the course of a treatment I have to take drastic measures, if I'm sure that it's for the good of the patient, I have to take an unequivocal stand, even exert pressure, I don't like it but sometimes there's no choice; and I look at him anxiously, the light from the table lamp lends his face a lifeless gray hue, what are you trying to say, what's that got to do with me? And he sighs, you know exactly what I'm trying to say, I made you a serious offer, I gave it a lot of thought and realized that it was the best thing for us to do. The difficulties you make so much of don't deter me, and I have difficulties of my own if you don't mind, the day you tell your kid is the day I'll tell my kids too, you don't have a monopoly on difficulties, you know; and I say, but it's not the same thing, your children are staying in their own home with their mother, your house is just a home away from home, for Gili it means parting from his real home, his main base, it's far more traumatic; and he says, let's not get into a competition, my children are coping with a mother who has almost ceased to function, and despite his mild manner, it seems to me that I can sense the glint of a metallic hardness behind his words.

There comes a time when talking isn't enough, he says, when action is needed, and I think that moment has come, and if you're still hesitating, permit me to come to my own conclusions; and I say in alarm, what conclusions, what do you mean? And he says, about your ability to trust, your ability to pay a price, and above all your ability to cope with the situation; and I protest, what do you want from me, did you expect that the minute you invited me to come and live with you I would pack a suitcase and come running? And he says, that's not exactly the case, two months have passed already; and I burst out, so what if two months have passed, why's it so urgent? Why can't you wait for the right time, do you need someone to cook for you? To raise your children for you? Is there some biological clock threatening you? I simply don't understand this urgency, and he says, I'm sorry, Ella, I'm not prepared to put up with that tone, don't talk to me the way you talked to your husband, the habits you brought from your previous marriage don't suit me.

And where exactly did you come from, I say resentfully, I heard the way she screamed at you the day you left home, I was standing outside the door and I heard every word, it wasn't exactly a cultured conversation, and when I recall that day, the clear, mesmerizing serendipity of it shines before my eyes, so different from this murky conversation, how we walked down the street, complete strangers, he carrying a backpack and me rolling a suitcase, and nevertheless we were light, full of excitement, the strange hot wind breathing around us, hurrying our steps, is this how I should approach him now. I come closer to him, please, Oded, don't push me, how can you not understand that it's complicated? It's not something you do from one day to the next; and he says, if you're not sure you want to do it, that's one thing, but if you're sure and all that's worrying you is the timing, believe me that putting it off will only make the problem worse.

Of course I'm sure, I say, can't you see? And he says, no, I can't see, and it's your right, but I, too, have the right to draw my own conclusions, why don't you take a few days to yourself and decide what to do, I'm not the right person to advise you about this, or perhaps about anything else; maybe we were in too much of a hurry, but now I feel that we're stuck in the same place and I don't like it, take as much time as you need, but when you decide I expect you to act on your decision, okay? And I take his hand, surrendering immediately, unable to bear the slightest threat, the faintest hint of loss, you know I've decided, I decided long ago, I'll tell Gili tomorrow, and he rises wearily to his feet, his face loses the lamplight and is dark and narrow, the lines running down his cheeks deep as gashes, take your time, don't do it for me, when you're ready let me know.

He strokes my hair with a limp hand and turns to the door and I stare at the lemony shaft of light, at the hollow bookshelves, like a mouth with several teeth pulled, trying to imagine the life awaiting me without him, sealed as the broken shutter; when Gili grows older, needing me less as I need him more, would he expect me to make such a sacrifice for his sake, to forgo a partner, a new family, and really for what; Gili, sweetheart, come here a minute, I have something to tell you, something good, I'm sure it will be good, even if it's a little hard in the beginning, not really hard, confusing perhaps, but I'll be with you all the time and I'll help you. Listen, me and Oded, Yotam's father, love each other like a husband and wife, no, we're not getting married, we're moving in to live together, you and I are going to move to their new house, they moved there first and now we're going to join them, from now on it'll be home to all of us, you'll have a really nice room there, just like here, and Maya and Yotam will be there when they're not with their mother, and it will take a little time but we'll all get used to it and we'll be happy because we'll have each other like before, but we'll also have a bigger family, and we'll all love each other and help each other and play together and go on trips together, and it'll be much more fun than being alone with me all the time or alone with Daddy, right, my little cub?

Last summer I had to tell him that he was starting school without his friends from kindergarten, who were going to other schools, and every day I would plan what to say in detail, and not be able to say it, until a few days before school started he said to me, Mommy, in my new school I won't have any friends, and I breathed a sigh of relief, how do you know? And he shrugged his shoulders, I just do, and I made haste to say, I'm sure that in a few days you'll make new friends, you're such a great kid everybody will want to be friends with you, and he said, maybe they will and maybe they won't, and his eyes looked soberly at me from his childish face, wiser than their years, and perhaps I was hoping for the same sort of miracle now, a perverted miracle, which would make my job easier, so that I would only have to confirm and reassure, not to announce, for there is never a convenient time for news like this, even if it isn't the worst of news, to be announced. In the morning before school, no, in the afternoon, he's tired and hungry, and afterwards he's busy playing with a friend, and when the friend leaves it's late, and before he goes to sleep is definitely wrong, and in the morning before school it's out of the question, and this weekend he's with Amnon; come here, sweetheart, come and sit next to me for a minute, I have something to tell you.

Is it my imagination or has his face turned white, a worrying pallor, barely perceptible beneath the flush, are his eyes closing, my own eyes are already misty; Mommy, why are you crying? Should I say that I'm crying for joy, I'm crying because I'm so happy; come, my darling, come and sit on my lap, his body stiffens in my arms, his muscles tighten, and still his face is full of trust when he asks, in his pure, innocent voice, but it's not for always, right, just a long visit, right?

And who, my child, will determine the length of the visit, me or you, or our hosts, their civility, their generosity, their patience; it isn't a visit, Gilili, I say, trying to steady my voice, it will be our home; and he protests, but this is our home, gesturing with his little arms toward the dark square room, and then he asks, and who'll live here, Daddy? And I say, no, we'll rent it to other people. And they'll sit on this sofa? he protests in bewilderment, and they'll eat our food? And I say, no, of course not, when people move they take their furniture with them, and their food, we'll take our things with us to the new house, we won't leave anything here; and he buries his head in my lap, his voice breaks, but I don't want to move, I want to stay here, and to my surprise he doesn't relate at all to the circumstances, to the new family we'll be joined to, in a kind of complex operation, without an anesthetic, vein to vein, artery to artery. I know, Gilili, it isn't easy, I say, I feel a little sad too, but we'll get used to it together, and we'll have a bigger house, I say, cunningly appealing to the competitive, materialistic element already emerging in his young personality, and I'll buy you a present for your new room, even a TV, I promise rashly, repelled by myself, but unable to stop, you'll be able to watch television in bed, I say, as if this constituted the very peak of happiness, and immediately retreat to a more educational track, change can be a positive thing, it may be a little scary at first, but it's interesting too, isn't it, would you really want to spend your whole life in the same place?

Yes, he replies simply, until I'm grown up; and I kiss his hair, a smell of wintry sweat rises from him, muddy, as if he has been fished up from the depths of the earth, you're growing up all the time, and changes happen all the time, sometimes big and sometimes small, changes help us to grow, they help to make us stronger, but in the limp light of the table lamp, drawing a dank circle around our two touching heads, we seem to be growing weaker, huddling together as if hiding from murderous pursuers, O my son Gilad, O Gilad, my son, my son!

Like a sick baby I cradle him in my arms, it seems as if I have informed him of his parents' separation, their final, tragic separation, and all the weeping he has accumulated since then is pouring from his mouth, long sobs, competing with each other in their volume, I don't want to move, it's bad enough that we split from Daddy, I don't want to split from our house too; and I say, you'll get used to the new house, you'll see, like you got used to the new school, like you got used to Daddy's house; and he hits my chest, I don't want to, I don't want to get used to it, I'm used to here, and suddenly he asks, will you be Yotam's mother?

Of course not, I cry in relief, this fear at least can be honestly, easily allayed, I'm only your mother, not Yotam's and not Maya's, they have a mother, you know her, and Oded won't be your father by any means because you have a father who loves you more than anything in the world; and he says, but Yotam's mother's dead, he told me she was dead; and I say, not at all, she's as alive as I am and she's a very good mother, and most of the time they'll be living with her, you'll be in the new house much more than they will, I say, trying to seed a sense of superiority, to make up for the fact that they arrived in the new house before him.

And Yotam's father will only be there a little too? he asks; and I say, he'll come there every day after work and he'll sleep there, it will be his house too, but I'll be there more because this year I'm working at home, I say, heaping the building blocks of the ridiculous, fake superiority around him; is it really worth it, Oded, I try to collect all our moments of happiness, those that have passed and those on the horizon, and weigh them against the sorrow of a little child; and then he says, but if we don't like it there we can come back home, right; and I can't bring myself to quench the hope in his voice, right, if we really hate it, but I really, really hope that that won't happen, I hope we'll be really happy.

I want chocolate milk, he bleats in a high, squeaky voice, and when I'm standing in the kitchen boiling the milk he asks, do they have chocolate milk in Yotam's house? And I say, if they don't we'll buy some, you'll have all your favorite things there, don't worry; and he picks up the brightly colored tin and hugs it to him, I want us to take this tin there and for it to be just mine, they won't be allowed to have any of it, okay? And I don't dare argue, okay, if it's important to you; and he adds quietly, as if whispering into the ear of the picture of the rabbit on the tin, when we come back here we'll take our chocolate back.

But that same evening, when he's sitting in the bathtub, surrounded by islands of quickly disappearing foam, I hurry to answer the phone, hoping that it's Oded who hasn't replied to my message yet, and I hear Amnon, in the official, hostile tone he has maintained since our last meeting, Ella, I've found buyers for the apartment, you remember the French couple that visited us once? And I am filled with dread, which apartment? I ask, and he says, our apartment, the apartment you'll soon be leaving, if I'm not mistaken.

What do you mean, buyers, I cry, I had no intention of selling, I wanted to rent it in the meantime, I'll share the rent with you, I offer hastily, but this isn't what he requires, it seems; the apartment belongs to both of us, he says, as long as you were living in it with Gili it never occurred to me to put it up for sale, in order not to uproot him, but if you're moving out anyway, there's no point in hanging on to common property, it only complicates things.

We have a child in common, I remind him, what difference does the apartment make? And he says, it makes a difference to me, I need the money, there's no reason why I should wait; and I say, you can't sell it without my consent; and he points out dryly, you can't rent it without my consent; and I sigh, all right, then the apartment will stand empty, and we'll both lose out. Ella, I'm warning you, he says, I need the money and I have buyers, the market's in very bad shape now, I'm not prepared to lose these buyers, if you make problems for me I'll do the same to you, you know how happy they'll be in the Rabbinate to hear that you're living with someone when you're not yet divorced? And I put the phone down without a word, Mommy, take me out, the water's cold already, Gili shouts from the bathroom, but I drop into the armchair next to the telephone, unable to move my feet in his direction; get out by yourself, I mumble, overcome by a debilitating, swooning weakness, and when I open my eyes he is standing in front of me naked and silent and dripping with water, holding two silvery rubber sharks in his hands and shivering with cold.

Why didn't you dry yourself? I ask, and he says, there was no towel in the bathroom, and I get up heavily and stumble to the closet, wrap him in a big, dark towel like a cloak, rub his delicate, fragrant body with stiff hands; Mommy, you're hurting me, he squirms, squeezing the bellies of the sharks whose gaping jaws wheeze with a whistling noise, we'll take these sharks with us and we'll leave the others behind, he pronounces, putting them down on the carpet, and heaping additional, carefully chosen toys next to them, the towel slips from his shoulders and he scampers naked between the baskets of toys like a beautiful cherub, absorbed in his judicious packing, as if he is leaving home for a few days, soon to return.

Chapter nineteen

Only now, one day before the move, I notice that his new room overlooks the dreary back of the building next door, with its exposed pipes, shabbily enclosed back porches, soot stains, and I grip the windowsill tensely, Oded, come here a minute, and he advances slowly toward me from the kitchen, glass in hand, what's the problem? he asks; and I point to the ugly, inferior view, can't you see for yourself?

He comes up to the window and looks down, did you drop something? And I say, look how ugly it is, why does it have to be my child who gets the ugliest view? And he looks at me in surprise, it's an ordinary city view, what's so ugly about it, what do you think they see from the other windows, the Dead Sea? And I say, no, but you can see trees and sky, not this squalor, and he says, you're exaggerating, Ella, children don't notice such things, you know what I saw from my window when I was a child, the neighborhood garbage dump; and I interrupt him, I don't care what you saw, I want to change his room.

You know that's impossible, he lowers his eyes, I understand your sensitivity, but you're doing damage, the child will feel good here if there's a good feeling, if you're sure of yourself, not if there is or isn't a tree outside his window, and I look into his children's rooms, examining them resentfully, the natural, easygoing life thrives there opposite the treetops wreathed in the violet dusk. It's a fact that you looked out for your own children, I say accusingly; and he says, it turned out like that, they chose those rooms, don't forget that we didn't move in together, but that's really not what's important, if it bothers you so much buy a pretty curtain; and I say bitterly, I should buy it? You go buy a curtain, I've been packing for a week already, I don't have the time to go shopping.

I won't buy a curtain because I don't believe in artificial solutions, he says, it's clear to me that if this works out something else will bother you, perhaps you'll begin measuring the size of the rooms, who knows, you might discover that his is a couple of millimeters smaller; and I am already almost shouting, I'm sure his is smaller, why didn't you wait for me before you moved in, you were in a hurry to get here before us on purpose so you could establish facts on the ground, so that we would always feel inferior here; and he gives me a quick, angry look and turns away again, as if he can't stand the sight of me, slams his empty glass down on the windowsill, and says coldly, I moved in here because I couldn't go on living in the clinic and you know it, I had no bad intentions, on the contrary, I took an apartment that would be big enough in case you decided to join me, if you don't take back what you just said, then I think you should leave right now, and without waiting he strides to the front door and flings it open, go, he says, I don't want you here; and I scream, you go, this is my house too.

It isn't your house yet and it won't be your house either, he says coldly, I don't want you here; and I rush out and slam the door behind me, but after descending five steps I stop, drop to the floor and burst into stifled weeping, Oded, I'm sorry, I didn't mean to hurt you, I know you didn't mean any harm, I know it's impossible to change the rooms, I'm just so worried about Gili, I'm afraid he won't be happy here, that he'll feel inferior. Standing on the sill of the long, narrow window in the stairwell is a solitary potted plant, a spindly plant with milky white leaves, which I address as if it's the plant's forgiveness I am begging, mumbling hoarsely, I'm so worried about Gili, how he'll cope, he's losing his home, and this house is already occupied, he's used to being the only child and suddenly there'll be competition from all sides, I'm afraid he won't be able to cope, he's a weak, sensitive child, I'm afraid of a disaster.

Again and again the light goes on in the chilly stairwell and I huddle against the wall, but the all movement is on the lower floors, nobody comes up here, so easily people return to their homes at this time of day, so easily I lost my home. Only after I fall silent and close my swollen, throbbing eyes does he open the door and come out to me, sitting down beside me on the fifth step, okay, shhh, calm down, everything will be all right, he whispers laboriously, handing me his glass that has been refilled, have a drink, cheer up; his arm goes around my shoulder and I murmur into his ear, I'm sorry for pouncing on you like that, I don't know what's happening to me, I didn't think it would be so hard for me to part from the apartment, I feel as if I've lost my home, that I don't have a home anymore. But you have love, he says quietly, you have me, you are so preoccupied with details that you don't pay attention to the larger picture, it's a happy story, our story, I won't let you turn it into a tragedy, we're trying to build something new together; and I whisper, but in order to build it we've destroyed so much; and he says, we did exactly what we had to do, stop dwelling on the past, you have to pull yourself out of this regression, you were so brave at the beginning, I remember how I admired your courage when we first met.

It wasn't courage, it was stupidity, I say, I didn't understand what I was doing, I believed everything was for the best; and he says, you don't understand now either, when you believe that everything is for the worst, come on, get up, he coaxes me, wash your face, we're going; and I ask, where to? I can't go anywhere, I haven't finished packing yet; and he says, we're going to buy a curtain, hurry up, the shops are closing soon; and I get up heavily, my head giddy and aching, gripped in a cold vice, I thought you didn't believe in artificial solutions, I remind him; and he says, that's true, but at the moment I'm not looking for solutions, I'm looking for a curtain.

And the next day, the first of the month of Adar, at half past eight in the morning, the heavy truck parks on the pavement under the poplar trees, and I point with a waving hand at the items to be moved, the sofa and the armchairs, the computers and the desks, bed and chest of drawers, closet and shelves, carpets and pictures, and the clothes crammed into pillowcases, and the boxes of books, kitchenware, toys and electrical appliances. For the time being the fridge and stove are staying here, until the apartment is sold, and so is the double bed, and I look silently at the rapidly emptying rooms, exposing walls as gray and sharp as sickly teeth, the axe has fallen on this chapter of our lives, nearly seven years, what are seven years on the thick trunks of our lives, but for the child it's his entire history and it's being uprooted, transported to far looser soil, laced with strangeness and competition, and devoid of the blood relationships that smooth sharp edges, that sweeten bitter pills.

It's a happy story, I try to remind myself, it's a happy story, but it seems that happiness has not been packed in the cardboard boxes laden with books, not wrapped in newspaper among the dishes, not loaded onto the truck next to the washing machine and the dryer, like the things nobody wants, it lies on the pile next to the garbage cans, like the remains of toys that once gave rise to thrilled delight and are now swept into a corner of the living room, a dinosaur's tail, an elephant's trunk, the skeleton of a motor car, and as the movers go up and down the stairs, in and out of the door, exuding the bitter smell of winter sweat, it seems to me that with every box removed from the apartment a certain truth is exposed, a supremely ugly and repellant truth, which from the moment that it has been revealed to me I can no longer ignore.

Our fingerprints on the walls move like shadows, painting dim pictures; what is this script that has not yet been deciphered, and perhaps the person who succeeds in deciphering it will prefer not to reveal his findings, for the inscription tells not of victory but of defeat, not just the private defeat of the family that lived here for nearly seven years, but also of those that will live here after it, above it and below it, for it tells of our futile efforts, and of the nakedness of life, and of the pointlessness hidden like a venomous insect under every rock, and of the misery wandering from place to place, with the possessions enthusiastically acquired, signaling stability and security, and I go into Gili's empty room, pale surfaces outline the contours of the objects that stood there until a few minutes ago, the bed, the chest of drawers, the closet, and here are the marks registering his height regularly measured at his request, here next to the doorframe he would stand, stretching his little body, and I would draw a straight line and write Gili at two, three, four, five, six. Look how tall I've grown! he would exult, I'll be as tall as Daddy, and I stroke the lines as if his head is still there, the downy hair that grew thicker, darker, and then I stand up straight next to the doorframe and draw a line at the top of my head, Ella at thirty-six, I write, the whitewash will cover all our traces anyway.

His window looms up in front of me like a picture on the wall, and I study the view as if this is the apartment I am about to move into, thickly growing ivy clutches at the trunk of the tree next to the window, bejeweled with purple bougainvillea, and I think heatedly of the view from the window of his new room; am I moving from the country to the city again, like then, in my girlhood, losing a home for a place that will never be my home, and I want to stop the movers, to tell them to bring back the boxes, and the child's bed and his closet and carpet, for this is his room and this is his home, and he will never have another home, just as I never had one. Leaning on the windowsill I sigh, above the heads of the passersby obliged to make a detour around the truck filling up with boxes, should I call them to come to my aid, for thieves are emptying out my house, leaving me with nothing, how carefree they look, will we, too, walk down this street like them one day, engaged in animated conversation, and I'll point to the big window and say, once you and I and Daddy lived here, and he'll glance up at the balcony and say, really? I barely remember.

The movers' hands are quicker than my thoughts and already they are standing at the doorway, anything else, they ask, and I shake my head silently, and I almost cry on their shoulders, you are the last witnesses to the life lived in this house, in a minute not a trace of it will remain, you tell me what really happened here on these tile floors, between the bedroom and the living room, between the kitchen and the balcony, and when I follow the last box downstairs, carefully locking the door behind me even though the house is nearly empty, to my horror I see the narrow winding street dotted with the remains of our lives, spilling out of the overflowing garbage bin. Pictures painted by Gili whose colors have faded, pages of my rough drafts, receipts and accounts, a single sock, an elastic hair band, a shopping list, insignificant details steeped in a heart-breaking intimacy, lying on the pavement, drifting in the breeze, sticking to the shoe soles of the passersby, scattering with frightening speed, and I kneel down and try to gather them up, encountering a hastily scribbled note, I'll be late, don't worry, simple words based on rock-solid assumptions, the assumption that the other is expecting you and thinking of you, the assumption that you have somewhere to return to, a trivial note, written in pencil, without a date, dozens like it have already been swallowed into the belly of the trash can. When I sorted out the papers I attached no importance to it but here in the street it breaks my heart in its innocence, and I thrust it into my pocket, suddenly noticing photographs that have apparently fallen out of one of the boxes, the last photos of us together, of Gili's sixth birthday party, which we had no time to stick into the album because we were so busy separating, here we are lifting him on his chair, his expression princely, dreamy, his smile reserved, the garland almost slipping off his head, the lawn was decorated with balloons, the children played tag, nobody noticed that we didn't exchange a word.

Like a swarm of locusts, the remains of our life spill out of the overflowing trash can and move through the city, soon they will reach every house, penetrate every window, and I rummage with bare hands in the can that vomits our family's private affairs into the public domain, fishing out photos that are covered with a damp, stinking film that sticks to my fingers, and here comes one of the women from the building with a bag of her own trash and sets it down next to the can. Are you leaving? she asks in surprise, and I twist my face into a forced smile, yes, we found a bigger place, but the smile dissolves even before I can complete it, and I wipe my eyes with filthy fingers, my lips twitch, and she stares at me in embarrassment, never mind, she mumbles, don't be so sorry, these buildings are falling apart anyway.

Like sheep to the slaughter the cardboard boxes are led, in the belly of the truck, marked with red letters, Gili's room, bedroom, living room, kitchen, bathroom, with me in the cabin next to the driver, looking down from on high at the familiar streets, from this height there is hardly any importance to human life, so miniscule are the creatures crossing the road, and their vehicles are tiny, their preoccupations, their wishes, their motives; what sent masses of displaced people over land and sea in search of a new home, was it the invasion of violent groups, the peoples of the sea who arrived from the west and destroyed everything that stood in their way, or a sudden climate change, or perhaps the earthquakes that shook the ancient East to its foundations and broke the continuity of history, annihilated civilizations, drove entire populations to migrate. In front of the white door I stand, the key ready in my hand, I have never used it, will it open both locks or will they require another key that I don't have, and I try to stick it into the upper lock, without success, and it doesn't fit the lower one either, and one of the movers pants behind me, the washing machine strapped to his bent back, what's wrong, open the door already, and I apologize nervously, just a minute, there's a problem here, and I call Oded but he doesn't answer, did he give me the wrong key on purpose, so that I would wander forever with the contents of the apartment, trying to open door after door throughout the city.

Are you sure that's the key? the driver asks me, crowding onto the landing with us, taking it from me and trying his luck, maybe there's another one? I rummage in my bag and to my relief I come up with another ring of keys, sorry, that was the key to the old apartment, I mumble and hand him the keys, and in a few minutes the half empty apartment fills with boxes and pieces of furniture. My gray sofa is at home opposite his black leather one, the carpet is spread and paints the room in orange and crimson stripes, and in Gili's room the bed is placed next to the window, the closet along the other wall and between them the rug, and on it the present I bought for him, a splendid knights' castle surrounded by walls, and as I direct the operation, sending this box to the bedroom, that one to the kitchen, like an authoritative traffic cop, I slowly regain a sense of control, replacing the tremulous anxiety, and it seems that my existence, gone adrift with wavering hesitation, has been somewhat steadied by the act I dreaded so much, and for a moment I take pleasure in being this woman who will live here with her new partner and their children, in a spacious apartment, generously kneading and molding a new family from two broken ones, a whole family that transcends the sum of its parts, and perhaps it need not necessarily mean a total amputation from the past, but a kind of continuation, involving assimilation and merging, just like my carpet merged with his sofa.

How simple it is after all, to move things from one apartment to another, for when the movers finish their work it is not yet noon, and I unpack the boxes in Gili's room, returning his familiar clothes to his familiar chest of drawers, his toys to the shelves we bought before he was born, and soon the new room is hardly distinguishable from the old one. I gaze with satisfaction at the collection of items that have arrived here in their entirety, like the stage set of a traveling production, and then I hurry to the bedroom, shake out the pillowcases full of clothes, empty the boxes, put my carelessly folded clothes into the empty drawers, not resting for a moment despite my tiredness, as if I am in a hurry to establish facts on the ground, once the last garment is laid in the closet will this house become my house, this room my room.

How does a small girl like you fill such a big closet? You haven't left me room for a pair of socks, I hear a low voice behind me, and I turn around immediately to face him, my joy at seeing him surprises me with its intensity, all morning I was hoping for him to come, even though I knew he was busy, I hoped he would be with me when I parted from my old home, that he would welcome me to his home, but now I know that the time is right, a patient cancelled an appointment, he says, I brought you something to eat, and he produces a warm chocolate croissant from a paper bag and hands it to me, examining the contents of the closet admiringly. Do you think I'll have a chance to see you in all these clothes? he chuckles, it seems to me that an entire lifetime wouldn't be enough, and I smile in embarrassment; most of them are really old, don't forget I stopped growing when I was twelve; and he fingers the summer dresses on their hangers with obvious enjoyment, I can't wait for summer, he says; and I laugh, greedily biting into the croissant, seeing him stretch out on the made bed in his clothes and shoes, and immediately stretching out beside him, scattering crumbs around me, am I allowed to eat in bed in this house?

Everything is allowed in bed, he says, his fingers collecting chocolate crumbs from my lips, and quickly my pants come down and the room fills with thirsty afternoon breathing, and for a moment I don't remember where I am and who I'm with, surrounded by familiar objects but still in a strange house, next to his still ambiguous body, testifying indirectly to my own body, give me the words that will bestow meaning on our breath, that will alleviate our loneliness, will I search for signs forever.

Who are you going to see now? I ask, as he washes his face, combs his hair back in the mirror, and he says, a person, why? A male or female person? I ask, and he grins, stop it, Ella, that's enough, I see about eight patients a day, at least half of them women, if you start worrying about it you'll go crazy; and I say quickly, I don't have a problem with it, I just want you to stay with me; and he says, I'll come back at three, will you be here? Of course, I say, this is my house, and he chuckles; judging by the amount of boxes, I'm not sure there'll be any room left for me.

Be good, he bends down and kisses my forehead, okay? And I nod obediently, what do you mean, exactly? Whatever you think I mean, he says, and when I hear him leave I pull up the blanket, even though my clothes are dusty, and it feels as if his tongue is still lapping at the secret pleasure box, and I sigh like a bride anticipating her wedding night, be good, he said, what exactly did he mean, good to myself, perhaps, is it the same thing, be good and it'll be good for you, is that the way things work, for a moment I can believe it, in the comfortable bed, with the closet already full of familiar clothes, with the child's room almost ready, save for the curtain that will arrive tomorrow, the doubts seem to be receding like a disease that's suddenly taken a turn for the better, giving way to a wild exhilaration, and I turn onto my stomach and spread my arms out on either side like a bird gliding through the sky. What a mystery, to be loved, why am I loved, how much will I be loved, a delightful and troubling mystery, but the moment I am able to accept it, simply submitting to it the way one does to the dominance of nature, a liberating release follows, to the extent that I can fall asleep here in the middle of the day, establish my belonging to this house in a peaceful, untroubled sleep, after long nights when I hardly slept a wink, eaten up by worries and doubts, tossing and turning alone among the boxes.

A cool breeze blows on my face, and in spite of its chill, it seems to be trailed by the scent of spring, and its refreshing touch lulls me into a deep sleep, it feels as if I am sleeping under the open sky, I've run away from home again after a fight with my father, ran and ran until I reached a flowery field, and there I fell, burrowing into the butterweed and the chrysanthemums, the simple golden jewels of winter, and gradually the echoes of the fight recede, its curses retreat, all that is left is the empty and absolute sense of freedom in this field, no one will find me here, and I breathe in lungfuls of air, at home his presence is so oppressive that I can only snatch gasps of breath like a rabbit, and now in the field full of yellow oxygen I am healed. Tiny bells are tied to the necks of the grasses, and they chime in the wind, carefree, and I decide never to go back, I'll run away from home for good, I'll beg in the streets, in my mind's eye I see my parents walking past me, elegantly dressed, returning from the theatre, and my father casually throws a coin at me, but I won't touch his money, until one day a charming handsome man will stop next to me and take me home with him, he will wash the black dirt from my face and see that I come from a good home, that I am a king's daughter who ran away from the palace, and he will feed me and bathe me and put me to sleep in his bed, and stroke my hair in my sleep, sitting on the edge of the bed, and when I open my eyes he will say in a slightly surprised voice, I'm glad to find you here, and I wake up, you're back already, what's the time? I must have fallen asleep for a bit.

You slept for a long time, he says, I came home long ago, and I free myself from the chains of sleep; I dreamt that I ran away from home, I mumble; and he asks, from this home, already? No, I say, from my parents' home; and he says, you can never run away from your parents' home. Apparently not, I say, but you never stop trying; and he grins, at least you didn't escape empty handed, he points to the open closet; actually I dreamt that I was begging in the street, I tell him, that I was sitting on the pavement and my parents walked past, but I was so dirty that they didn't recognize me, and only then I notice that he isn't listening to me, his eyes are still fixed on the packed closet, his expression disapproving, and I say tensely, is something wrong? And he answers, no, nothing in particular.

Aren't you glad I'm here? I ask in a coy voice; and he says, I just told you I was, but he looks disturbed, you don't fold your clothes, he remarks; and I say in surprise, they don't look folded to you? They're rolled up, not folded, he says, didn't your mother teach you how to fold? Maybe you really do need to go back home for a few finishing lessons. And that bothers you? I ask; and he admits, yes, it's like white noise for the eyes, and despite myself I sink into the sticky affront, unable to find a foothold to stop the fall, just as it was on the top of the gate, you don't want me here; I mutter, is that all you can say to me on the day that I come to live with you here? But it doesn't sound like my voice, it sounds like the voice of the beggar in my dream.

What's the matter with you, he grumbles, what's wrong with

what I said, where did this chronic sensitivity come from? And I try to come back to my senses, it's true, Amnon also used to complain about my messiness and it never seemed this hurtful, it wasn't as if he was rejecting me, and I look at him, in the black clothes that accentuate his thinness, his hair growing thickly over his skull, his heavy brows linked to his eyes, his shadowed cheeks, an optical illusion in black and white, like a complex pencil drawing, and all this is, in some strange and exciting, slightly alarming way, at my disposal, a new man, his appearance still foreign to me, like my own in this house, which is far better lit than mine, exposing the first gray hairs, a slight asymmetry, a slackness in the neck, a temporary blurring of identity, and I get out of bed, for some reason holding onto the walls, the boxes bar my way and I barely make it to the kitchen.

To my relief he follows me and I turn to him, how was your day? trying for the first time to practice a domestic routine; and he says, reasonable, without going into detail, contemplating the boxes in a gloomy silence; and I say hurriedly, don't worry, soon there won't be a single box left, and I immediately cut the duct-tape with a kitchen knife, remove pots and pans with a faint feeling of embarrassment, looking for precisely the right place to put them, at least they don't have to be folded, a few cookbooks, and suddenly a pastel greeting card falls out of one of the books, and I open it, the date of our wedding is written on top, and beneath it in an elegant script, in flowery phrases: Dear Ella and Amnon, on your nuptial day, may you know only happiness. The name of our well wisher is not known to me, probably one of Amnon's students, and I stare at the card, an intruder from other days, what will I do with it, Dear Ella and Amnon, what shall I do with you, and I almost call him to come and read it, to wonder with me at the well-timed mocking reminder, but I immediately change my mind, bury the card between the pages of the cookbook, as if the strict excavation rules apply here too, and I have to return the finding to its place until the documentation is completed.

An edgy tension hinders my movements, strains me, gives me pause, as if I am being secretly observed by hostile eyes, it seems I felt more comfortable here before he arrived, where is he anyway, the living room looks empty, but then I see him in the corner of the sofa, his black clothes blending into the black leather, even though the room is getting dark he doesn't switch on the light, and I stick the knife into the boxes, suddenly they seem to have been packed many years ago, returning from an exhausting journey, like lost luggage that has wandered from airport to airport all across the world, and by the time it is returned there is no longer any need for its contents. For whom are these decorated ceramic plates intended, what meals will be served on them, what family will sit around them, and when I take the tin of chocolate with the smiling rabbit printed on it out of the crumpled newspaper I hug it to my heart, as if it were a precious object saved from the ruins, and hide it at the back of the cupboard, so that no foreign hands will touch it.

In the wide kitchen window, divided into steel and glass squares, the sun is starting to sink toward the top of the pine trees, staining the marble counter a reddish gold, and I glance at my watch, four thirty already, last year he stayed in kindergarten until the afternoon, and at exactly this time a solid male tread was heard on the stairs and behind them childish steps so light that they hardly seemed to touch the floor. Is it the soft angle of the sun that is giving rise to my longing, usually Amnon would come back from the university agitated, brimming with complaints and a coarse speculation that fermented the house, which, while trying, I now miss, as Oded answers my questions in a listless voice, and when I make myself coffee in the kitchen full of boxes of our things, I feel the drip of an acidic dread, as if I have been caught in an act of betrayal, not necessarily the betrayal of a man, but of a family, a mission, a homeland. Could it be that making coffee in this kitchen, in a cup I brought from home, constitutes a breach of trust far worse than making love on the black leather sofa, how mysterious is the book of laws. If you move in with somebody else, I'm through with you for good, he said, and I turn my back to the window, and look at the man melting silently into the corner of the sofa, his elbows on his knees, for a moment we seem like strangers, why and for what purpose did we come here, why and for what purpose did we bring our children here and ask them to turn into siblings while the gently slanting sun dips between the pines and ladles its sadness upon us, until it seems that the weightiness of the decision and the extent of the preparations, the words without end and the volume of the expectations piled upon it, have doomed the act to failure, too heavy to bear, even the rays of the sun bow beneath its weight.

Do you want coffee, Oded? I ask; and he says, no thank you; and I go up to him, the sharp knife in my hand, and I still believe that I have the power to banish these foul winds if only he stands beside me, but his face is as stiff and dry as cardboard, and I try to ask him with affected lightness, what's the matter, is something wrong? And he shrugs his shoulders, and says in a tone of dull rebuke, there's always something troubling us, no? But I insist, you look particularly troubled since you came home, tell me what happened.

Forget it, he says, I don't want to burden you with my difficulties, you have enough of your own, and I sit down next to him; what are you talking about, Oded, you have to confide in me, I have to know what's going on with you, and he looks at me doubtfully; I went to see Michal, he blurts out almost unwillingly, I told her that you moved in with me, it wasn't easy.

What did she say? I ask, shaken by gusts of anxiety and guilt, and he shrugs his shoulders; the content isn't important, and it isn't personal, she knows that it wasn't because of you that I left her, and that even without you I won't go back to her, but it's hard for her, and it's hard for me to see her like that, the truth is that I thought the children had told her, I was surprised that she didn't know anything, and again I find myself gasping like a rabbit for air. What will we do? I ask clumsily, and he says, there isn't much we can do, I can only try to bring the kids here as much as possible until she recovers, it isn't good for them to see her like that, and I nod tensely; just remember that we agreed that tomorrow Gili will be here alone, I want to give him a chance to adjust on his first day here, not to feel like a visitor; and he sighs, I hope it will work out.

It has to work out, I say, I'm not asking for much, just one day, but the look he gives me is rebuking and critical, as if I have no right to put my interests before hers, my child before her children, how quickly the former wife turns into a saint, while the new woman, even if she grinds her teeth down with the effort, will always appear petty. Why don't you prescribe something for her; and he says, she's been taking medication for years, and I say in astonishment, really? Michal? She always seemed so calm and balanced to me; and he says, she gives the wrong impression, she's neither calm nor balanced, and I try to display a mature interest in this news, not to show signs of panic, even though all this information is no longer detached from my life; and I ask, where did you meet in the first place? you never told me; and he snaps, there are a lot of things I haven't told you yet, and it almost sounds like a threat, and I shudder, stay away from him, my mother said, everyone knows he's sick.

We met in medical school, he answers reluctantly, we started studying together, and I say, really? She studied medicine? Why did she stop? She was looking for something more spiritual, he says, that was the official reason, but the truth is she stopped because of me; and I am taken aback, because of you? Why because of you? And he says, when one person runs ahead the other one lags behind, that's how it generally is with couples, she left in the fifth year, she wasted years searching for all kinds of things, in the end she became a biology teacher. When she realized she'd made a mistake it was already too late, Maya had already been born, and she was stuck, and perhaps she would have been content if she hadn't seen me getting ahead in a field she had intended as her own, I think that's what unsettled her.

Tense and stiff I sit beside him, how quickly I have lost the ability to listen to him calmly, sympathetically, to respond to his distress, every word he utters threatens me; Oded, it's really sad but it's not your fault, I announce urgently, you have to stop condemning yourself, I feel as if his guilt toward her endangers me and I try to defend myself against her, my knuckles whitening on the handle of the knife.

On the face of things you're right, he sighs, but I was so absorbed in myself that I hardly noticed what she was going through, when I was young I was crazy with ambition to succeed, to prove to the whole world that the son of a lunatic could treat other lunatics. In the course of time I realized that it didn't impress anyone, except for my mother who told all her disbelieving neighbors, but Michal was hurt by my ambition, and later on came the fits of jealousy, and the frustration, and the medication, and it was already into all this that the children were born, and having them wasn't easy either, in short, nothing went smoothly for her, and now I've delivered the final blow.

Wretchedly I pick my way between the boxes in the living room, as if I'm stepping between gravestones etched with red letters, for hours and hours I packed, emptying shelf after shelf, while Gili prowled around in the mess, not knowing what to do with himself, slowly and painfully the house was stripped, and for what, in order to double and triple the misery? His face disappears in the dark room, we are both lost, lost, lost as the two skeletons found above the aqueduct in Megiddo; I told you not to leave her, I squeak, my voice as high and thin as Gili's, I warned you she wouldn't be able to stand it, that you wouldn't be able to stand it, what are we going to do now? and I go to the kitchen, throw pots and pans with a hasty clatter into the boxes just emptied, I don't want to live here, Oded, I'm leaving.

Stop it, Ella, calm down, he scolds me impatiently, don't make things even more difficult for me, there are no practical implications to what I told you, I'm sorry I said anything, it was a mistake, and I switch on the light; tell me, of all the things we planned, initiated and carried out, what wasn't a mistake, and how will I bring my little boy tomorrow to a home set up by mistake, and how will I hide the immensity of the mistake from him, and as I lean on the cold marble counter it seems to me that the lament of the woman weeping for her life not far from here is coming through the squares of glass and steel, filling the house like gas seeping from the stovetop, until I no longer know if the weeping rises from my throat or hers.

Chapter twenty

It must be accurate and exact, weighed and measured, precise as a military campaign, resolute as a battle that cannot be lost, I've considered every detail, tried to foresee every mishap, anticipated every wish, I filled the fridge with his favorite foods, so that they'll float around, soft and consoling, in his little stomach, loaded the kitchen cupboards with candy, so they'll melt between his tongue and palate, spreading a sticky calm, I covered his window with a bright curtain, paying double to ensure it arrived this morning, again I go into his room to make sure that nothing is missing, the stuffed animals lying in exemplary order on his bed, family by family, lion, lioness and lion cub, tiger, tigress and tiger cub, their pupils dilated, indifferent, the calm of their world unruffled by the revolutionary winds. The computer sits on the desk, the books on the shelves, the toys in the wicker baskets, the brightly wrapped present on the rug, and I, too, am perfectly packaged, in a black pantsuit, hair washed and tied back, never before have I prepared so carefully for a meeting with him, my little son, as if my very being is on trial today, my love and my judgment, my intelligence and good taste, my devotion and loyalty.

I have even arranged for company, calling Talia this morning and inviting her to come over with Yoav, shamelessly asking her to bring him a present for his new room, I'll give you back the money, just bring something, so he'll feel like it's a celebration, and admire his room, too, okay? It's really important to me for him to have a friend over today, it will help him feel at home, and I can hear all the things she doesn't say skipping off the tip of her tongue, but she makes do with a long sigh; no problem, Ella, when do you want us to come? And I try to calculate exactly, best if they arrive after he's had time to eat, explore the apartment, open his present, and before he begins to feel sorry for himself, three thirty, I decide; and she says again, no problem, and obediently writes down the address.

Before I leave I check the room again, is it pleasant enough, big enough, for a moment it seems to me that it's a little smaller than his old room, and I peek again into Maya's and Yotam's rooms, no doubt about it, they're bigger and lighter, and above all they exude a comfortable, natural feeling of being lived in, a sweater hanging on the back of a chair, an open book on the bed, a mug on the window sill, while his room remains petrified, off-putting in its lifelessness, like a memorial room, and I try to untidy it a little and immediately change my mind, he might think some other child has been in his room, played with his toys, but if I carry on with these comparisons I'll be late, I promised him I'd come early, and I hurry to the school in my dark suit, as if I were on my way to an official appointment, in high heels and make-up, a business woman whose every move is calculated, trying to display confidence and control, even though I didn't sleep at all last night, striving half-heartedly to reach a tepid reconciliation, even an artificial one, anything to relieve the tension in the house to which my son is coming for the first time.

He's waiting for me at the classroom door, his schoolbag dwarfing his thin back, I don't know what's wrong with him today, his teacher says, he didn't concentrate in class or play at recess, and I make haste to say, we moved yesterday, didn't he tell you? No, she says, ruffling his hair, he didn't tell me anything, and I make a dialing motion with my hand, I'll call her this evening to explain, I probably should have called her a while ago, and she accompanies us, jabbering tactlessly, we moved a few months ago too, my kids took it very hard, they say it's a real trauma for a child, almost as bad as divorce; and I snap, thank you so much for the uplifting information, and get out of there in a hurry, waddling like a duck in my pinching high heels, the trauma-ridden child trailing behind me. Come on, sweetie, I made you a delicious lunch, and your room's ready, and there's a surprise you won't believe, something you really, really wanted, and you know who's coming over later? Talia and Yoav are coming to visit us, they're bringing you a present for your new room, and he silently absorbs the barrage of cheerful information I produce for his benefit, his lips sealed, but his hand clutching mine tightly. Don't worry so much, Gilili, it's fun to move, all your friends will come to see your new room, and you'll get lots of presents, you'll get used to it quickly, you'll see, but he shakes his head doubtfully, who's living in my old room? he asks in the end; and I say, nobody yet, but my answer doesn't satisfy him, Daddy said we can never go back to our old house because you're going to sell it to other people, he bleats, and I curse Amnon with clenched lips, why must the child be kept up to date on all the details.

That may happen, I say, but it's a long process, and for the time being the apartment is empty, you can go and see for yourself; and he asks, what's a process? And I announce, look at that, we've reached our little street already, it's much closer to school than the old apartment, and here's our building, isn't it nice? The word our seems to be coming out of my mouth *ad nauseum*, like sticky phlegm, like foam on my tense lips, and we go upstairs, the key is already in my hand, why don't you open our door, I suggest, and to my relief he responds with enthusiasm, lets go of my hand at last, and takes the key, but immediately it slips from his fingers, making a cold clatter in the stairwell, and he tries again, his unpracticed fingers turning it with an effort in the wrong direction, you locked it, Gilili, I say, and only when I put my hand on his and move it like a puppet, does the door open and he runs, curious and apprehensive into the alien apartment.

Where's my room, he asks at once, and I lead him to it tensely, his hands hurriedly stroke the teddy bears' fur, rummage in the wicker baskets, making sure that nothing is missing, here are my crayons, he announces like a merchant listing his wares, here is the playmobil, here are the cards, here are the marbles, amazed that every little item has succeeded in arriving safely, and only when he's satisfied, he turns his attention to the present, falling on it eagerly. A knights' castle! he shouts and kneels on the rug, and already the room fills with the torn pieces of bright wrapping paper, and the castle is revealed in all its grave splendor, and I leave him in his room and go to the kitchen, walking slowly down the hall, looking back to see him caught up in his games. How strange it is to stand in front of the stove in this house and to know that he is here with me, and to call him in the most routine way to come and eat, the food's ready, Gili; and he asks, where's the kitchen? Find it for yourself, I say, let's see if you can find me; and he enjoys the game, running in and hugging my waist, you brought my plate, he marvels; and I say, of course I did, I brought all your things, nothing's missing.

The chocolate too? he asks, as if it were his most precious possession, irreplaceable, and with a magician's flourish I produce the tin hidden at the back of the cupboard; of course the chocolate too; and he says, remember that it's only ours, and he eats the mashed potatoes and the schnitzel with relish, he even enjoys the salad, atypically asking for seconds. The food in the new apartment is delicious, he pronounces loudly, and I say, good, eat; but his voracious appetite worries me, is he making sure that there won't be anything left for the other children, is this his way of marking his territory, what a yummy salad, can I have some more? he asks, his voice particularly loud, almost yelling, as if he is far away from me, the two of us perched on two mountain tops, one opposite the other, shouting the message of our love.

It seems as if he is swallowing without chewing, sucking the food into his thin body, why don't you rest a while, so you don't get a stomach ache, I suggest, anxiously noting the crumbs surrounding him, a crescent under his chair, and when I hear a noise in the stairwell I bend down and quickly gather them up, as if we were guests on probation here, and he, too, looks uneasily at the door. Are they coming? he asks in a whisper, watchful and alert as a forest animal; and I say, not yet, Talia and Yoav are coming in an hour. No, what about Yotam and Maya? he asks; and I say, they're only coming tomorrow, does he breathe a sigh of relief, sitting tensely in front of his familiar empty plate, what should we do now, and before he can begin to dwell on memories and comparisons, I make haste to suggest a guided tour of the apartment, show him the bedroom and Maya and Yotam's rooms, and he looks around warily, his eyes darting, his nostrils quivering, he doesn't touch anything, and pulls me quickly away; he only wants to be in his own room, and when we go back to it he says, why do I have a curtain and they don't, I don't want that curtain, for some reason turning an advantage into a disadvantage, and when he pulls it aside he doesn't complain about the view from the window, and he seems a little more at ease, perhaps the rumor about children is right, how adaptable they are, how resilient, he voices no further complaint, only admiration, baseless and over the top, flying in the face of the facts.

Mommy, the room's huge, he spreads out his arms, it's much bigger than my old room, and I don't dare correct the obvious error. You think so? I ask carefully; and he says, sure, look how much space there is here, the old room was crowded, and I breathe a slightly suspicious sigh of relief, as if hearing news that seems too good to be true, and lie down on his bed while he plays with his knights, who gallantly defend their castle, go away or we'll kill you, he declares dramatically, this is our castle, not yours. One after the other they fall from the walls with a faint thud, their little bodies surrounding the castle, until only a single knight remains entrenched there, fighting the invaders to the bitter end, and I try to stop searching for significance in his every expression, every blink or gesture, looking through the window where the curtain has been drawn aside, dark gray crocodiles cross the sky, crawling on their short legs, their jaws gaping in wide smiles, the winter seemed to be over but now it's back again, and I cover myself with his blanket, breathing in the smell of the sheets, like him I cling to the familiar details, like him I marvel at how the smells moved too, like him I feel comfortable only in his room, a friendly enclave, an oasis in the desert.

Even while absorbed in his game he remains alert to every sound, his eyes raised apprehensively to the door, lest a foreign entity should suddenly emerge from one of the other rooms, his voice louder than usual but occasionally dropping to a whisper, and when I get up to wash the dishes he accompanies me, and demands that I accompany him to the bathroom, and thus we accompany each other all over the apartment, across the wide smooth tiles, he slides over them in his socks, yelling as he makes himself fall. At precisely three thirty the doorbell rings and I send Gili to the door to greet his first visitors, and he jumps for joy to see Yoav, come see what my mother bought me, he pulls his friend behind him, no longer in need of my company, and I hug Talia, who is holding her little girl in one hand and the present in the other; wait a minute, Gili, she shouts after them, we brought you a present for your new room; and I quickly say, really? You shouldn't have, and she make a face at me and holds out the wrapped present that is eagerly opened, a framed picture of three beautiful kittens; and Gili cries enthusiastically, aren't they sweet, this is me, he points to the white kitten in the middle of the picture, and this is Mommy and this is Daddy.

But all three of them are kittens, Yoav says, they're all exactly the same age; but Gili insists, no, it's a family, and he puts the picture down on his bed; and Talia says, what a beautiful room, and they start playing with the castle, and the plan seems to be working well, but nevertheless when I sit down in the kitchen with Talia I feel like a con-man, as if the whole things is a plot contrived for my own convenience, to pull the wool over his eyes, to confuse him with trivial, transient joys in order to prevent him from noticing the strangeness of the new situation, which is becoming clearer to me with every passing moment.

It's a huge apartment, Talia says, strange, kind of like a maze, no? It feels weird to see you here, I'm so used to your old apartment; and I say, yes, it's weird for me too, and she looks at me sharply; why are you dressed so formally, where were you, who were you meeting? My son, I reply,; and she says, that doesn't sound good, and I sigh; that's the way things are these days. What am I going to do with you, Ella, she laughs, you should have let me be in charge of your life, you do everything the wrong way around; and I ask, chastised, what do you mean? Before you do something, she says, you're too sure of yourself, and after you do it you're not sure enough, you should see how guilty you look, as if you're leading your child to the slaughter.

Really? I thought I was radiating confidence and control, I say in astonishment; and she says, right, confidence, you're not fooling anyone, definitely not Gili; and I sigh again, so what do you suggest? And she says, your suit and heels are not going to impress him, just try to be more at peace with the decision you made, you have a big apartment, a partner you love, a chance of building a new family with him, be happy, don't be so tense.

You're right as usual, I admit, the problem is that now that I'm here I can only see what's lacking; and she scolds me, stop it, get a grip, you're going to make this new relationship fail too, what's the matter with you, is that what you want? I'm warning you, not all men are as tolerant as Amnon, and I protest, Amnon, tolerant? What are you talking about? It's true that he loses his temper quickly, but in a deep sense he accepted you as you were, he resigned himself to your constant criticism; and I protest again, what criticism? I kept most of it to myself, or for you; and she says, maybe, but you made your discontent very plain, you think he never noticed? It isn't easy for them with their fragile egos; and I pour the coffee, examining her in astonishment, what are you talking about, Talia, don't you remember how he complained about everything I did, how he nagged me all the time, how he hurt my feelings? And she sweetens her coffee reflectively, stirs it slowly.

Maybe on the surface, she says, but you always knew that his love wasn't affected by anything you did or said, as opposed to Amnon, who felt that your love was conditional, that he couldn't rely on it, it's a fact that in the end it was you who left and not him, and I shrug, it seems she's mapping out a total stranger's marriage, not mine, and I stare out of the big kitchen window, the shadows of the pine trees etch their self-portraits in black charcoal on the stone walls of the opposing building, gray sparrows dive between their branches. It's going to rain soon, I say, I thought the winter was over and now it's all beginning again, and she examines my face; you look so worried, I don't understand you, if you're so concerned about Gili and so sensitive to every nuance, why did you go ahead with it anyway and break up his family? it doesn't make sense; and I sigh, it's a complicated process, it's hard to explain to anyone who hasn't been through it, I've gotten more sensitive since the separation, the more I realize the price he's paying, the more I worry about him. The trouble is that it isn't doing him any good, she says, you shouldn't make such an effort, be natural, you're allowed to show him that it's difficult for you too, you should let him see a credible picture of the situation, it'll be easier for him, believe me, that way he'll be less alone in his own troubles.

When will you make a mistake, I say, so that I can preach to you; and she giggles, I just made a mistake letting the little one wander around the apartment, who knows what she's up to, and we both jump up, and find her sitting on Maya's bed, drooling as she scribbles away on the books and notebooks she pulled off her desk. Yasmini, what are you doing, I say in a panic, what will I say to Maya? And Talia drags her away as she kicks her little legs and clings to a purple crayon, intent on continuing her drawing on the floor.

I'm sorry, Ella, she says, don't worry about it though, it happens all the time, all Yoav's notebooks are full of scribbles, you're an only child bringing up an only child, you have no idea what goes on in regular families, but I am not reassured, what will I say to Maya, I'll have to buy her new notebooks by tomorrow, and I hand the sobbing baby a smushed Oreo, hoping to cleave her tongue to the roof of her mouth for a while, and call Gili and Yoav too, and the living room fills with commotion as the three of them jump up and down on Oded's leather sofa, bearing the Oreos like torches and shedding crumbs of chocolate and dabs of sticky white filling onto the black leather before I can persuade them to move to my sofa, it seems that there is no our yet, and I watch them helplessly, realizing once more how far I am from feeling at home, we are guests here, trying not to leave any sign of our presence, not to inconvenience our hosts, who loom large even in their absence.

Do you want us to leave before he arrives? Talia asks as I glance absent-mindedly at my watch, and I say, no, of course not, but the thought of the man who will soon open the door, without his children, to encounter three strange, noisy children, makes me feel uneasy, and I hope he is delayed, that he has to deal with a couple of emergencies, and in the meantime I can clean up the living room a little. Outside, darkness has fallen and the rain is coming down hard, shadowing the wall of the opposing building, and I think of the apartment I vacated yesterday, I left the windows open and the rain is coming in, and in the bedroom, alongside the dead tree, the shutter is slamming in and out.

Sensibly Talia ignores my protestations, bundles her daughter in her coat, and calls her son, come, Yoav, come on, I shouldn't have to ask you a million times, while I offer, deliberately late, why don't you stay for supper? But she declines as expected, thanks, some other time, Yair is coming home early today and I want us to eat together, and for a moment I see them sitting around the table in their crowded kitchen, their heads almost touching, their movements natural, and they all have the ability to withstand crumbs on the floor, arguments and complaints, coughing and profuse vomiting. Their children have turned them into kin, bound them together with a bloody, fleshy cord, and they enjoy the wondrous feeling that wells up in us toward our own children, and is only rarely aroused by the children of others, and I try to imagine our dinners, will the three of us eat together, and what will we talk about, will I sit separately, first with Gili and later on with Oded, tensely chewing two dinners, and why am I so glad that he's late, wasn't it just so we could be together that this exhausting deed was done, why am I so apprehensive about his arrival this evening, the arrival of his children tomorrow, if to be alone with Gili is what I wanted I could have had that in the old house.

Bath time, I chime, careful to maintain the familiar routine, look, there are two bathrooms here, one for us and one for them; and he squeals, I want to have a bath in theirs; and I say, sure, sweetie, no problem, strewing his toys in the foreign bathtub, and he comes over naked, carefully counting the steps from his room to the bedroom leading into the bathroom, and suddenly he stops in embarrassment, hugging his ribs as if shy of the walls, and I hurry him into the water, enjoying the familiar sight. Just as at home, he splashes around, surrounded by sea creatures, octopuses, sharks and dolphins, but this time he refuses to let me go and clean up the living room, and I sit on the lid of the toilet seat next to him, listening absent-mindedly to the tales of his exploits, and I remember with amazement our own exploits, how we bathed here together, with no barriers between us, but now his presence has taken over the house, everything that happened here before him seems to have been abolished, the hours of love, the hours and hours of love.

Suddenly he stops playing, gives me a determined look, before I go to sleep I'm watching TV in bed, he announces; and I say, but I didn't get a chance to buy you a television yet, didn't you see that there wasn't one in your room? He kicks the water in frustration, but you promised, you promised I'd watch television in bed; and I say, right, I promised, and I'll keep my promise, just not right away, it'll take a few days; and he whines, but you promised, I'll never believe a word you say again, you get mad when I tell lies and then you lie yourself, and before I have a chance to reestablish my credibility with a mild rebuke, there is the sound of a cough and I turn and face Oded who is standing in the adjacent bedroom; hi, I'm so glad to see you, I announce with an effort, getting up and going toward him, and Gili protests at once, don't leave me alone, and I retrace my steps, trying to stand at an equal distance between them.

Gili, look who's here, Oded! I cry, as if this news will calm him down immediately, signaling to Oded to peek into the bathroom and say something nice to the sulking child, but he ignores my desperate, vigorous gestures, I'm absolutely soaked, he says, I walked around with the kids for hours in the pouring rain, I hope they didn't catch a cold, and indeed his pants are soaking wet to the edge of his coat, his hair is dripping, and he takes a towel out of the closet and diligently dries his hair. Why were you walking around outside? I ask, they have a home, no? One home was barred to them, as you know, he says, and Michal was in such a state that I couldn't take them there, her mother just arrived now to take care of them, and I return to my place on the lid of the toilet seat, here one kid paddles around like a coddled baby alligator in a warm bath, while there two children traipse around in the rain just because of me, already on day one I have turned, despite myself, into a wicked stepmother, and I hurry Gili up with sudden impatience; that's enough, come on, get out of the bath; and he whines, not yet, I'm still playing; and I say, then play by yourself, I have to talk to Oded, moving away before he can protest, I'm really sorry, Oded, I only wanted to give him one day to get used to the new house, I was sure the children would be at home with Michal, you could have called to tell me that they were with you and you had nowhere to go.

Oh, really? he retorts, and what would you have said? Come home, no problem? Don't pretend like you would have given up on your ambition to exercise complete control over the situation, and I am astounded by the amount of hostility soaked into his voice, like the water soaked up by his pants; Oded, what did I ask of you, one afternoon is all, one day of exclusivity, is that too much to ask? You're acting as if I exiled you from the house forever; and he says, because that's how I felt; and I protest, why do you exaggerate so much; I asked for one day to be here alone with Gili, I thought you were at work and they were with Michal anyway, I never meant any harm. I'm not so sure, he snaps, and I whistle an exhalation at him; I'm not so sure of your intentions either anymore, why didn't you take them to see a movie, or to the mall, or did you wander around with them in the rain just so you could blame me? You'd be surprised, there are other considerations, in times like these I don't take children to public places; and I say, that's ridiculous, they have security guards at the mall; and he says, no public place is safe. So why didn't you go with them to Michal's? You could have stayed with them there, I say; and he says, she wouldn't let me in; and I sigh, the whole thing doesn't make any sense, it's impossible that you couldn't find any solution, if you'd wanted to you would have found something, it's always possible to take them to some friend for a few hours, it's not so complicated.

Mommy, I want to come out, Gili shouts, overly loud, and I hurry to remove him warm and flushed from the bath, to rub his water-crinkled skin with a towel, an unpleasant feeling of triumph stealing into my heart, we defeated them this evening, we proved that this is our home no less than theirs, but I didn't think we would pay the price of our victory so soon, for when we go into the living room, Gili combed and fragrant in his pajamas, dragging the faithful Scotlag Bear behind him, Oded doesn't even look at him, unlike his father who would stretch out long arms to grab him and seat him on his lap after his bath, sniffing his clean sweet smell, hugging and kissing and tickling him until he squealed with delight. Are you hungry, Oded? I ask, trying to catch his eye; and he says, no, I ate with the children, and I coax him, but you'll sit with us, right? And he says in a formal tone, not at the moment, Ella, I have a few calls to return; and I turn to Gili in a voice I hardly recognize, the voice of a saleslady in a toyshop, a saleslady whose job is in danger, Gilili, why don't you show Oded your teddy bear? And he bobs over to him, his feet in blue socks, stepping trustingly, look, this is Scotlag Bear, he says; and Oded studies the teddy bear's face grimly, as if it belongs to a stranger to whom he is being introduced, and in the end he says abruptly, I don't like bears.

My daddy loves bears, Gili answers heroically, while my eyes burn, he brought him for me from Scotlag, and Mommy bought me a knights' castle, and tomorrow I'm getting a TV in my room, he tries to impress the reserved stranger; and Oded sets his jaw at him, looking at me sternly, a TV in your room? Yes, I say, why not? And he says, because then Maya and Yoav will want television in their rooms too, and I'm against it, it's impossible for him to have and not them, we have to be on the same page; and I say, then buy them one too; and he grumbles, I can't spend thousands of shekels on television sets now, I've already reduced my working hours so I can spend more time with the children. I can't take that into consideration, I say angrily, I promised him one and that's that, so there won't be a socialist regime here in the meantime, so what, and Gili withdraws from him in disappointment, turning his back to him and squeezing the teddy bear, while I try to signal to Oded with a circular gesture like the turning of a clock's hands that we'll talk about it later. Not in front of the child, I whisper; but he ignores my request, I don't think it's possible to buy a TV for your child only, you're trying to establish an artificial advantage here that won't do anyone any good; and I whisper again, we'll discuss it later, seeing Gili standing pale and tense in the middle of the living room, the teddy bear slipping from his hand; then I'll let them watch my television whenever they want to, he offers in a piping voice, surprising me with his maturity, as if he's been facilitating peace like this all his life.

Excellent idea, I say quickly, that's really nice of you, now come and eat, and I hurry him into the kitchen, rapidly make an omelet, cut up vegetables, slice bread, eat up, honey, I try to encourage him, stealing hostile looks at the man paging through the papers he takes out of his briefcase, the three of us won't sit around the table conversing at our ease, learning to adapt the pace of our chewing, alone I shall love him, alone, and again the longing hits me in the back, like a shutter hitting the wall in a gale, the longing for the natural fatherhood that he's now lost, or more accurately, I've lost, for he has not lost his father, only I have lost what once seemed so trite, the right to chew bread and eat salad alongside a man who loves my son as much as I do.

Do you want to come early tomorrow morning? Can you manage till then? You'd better take another Clonex, I hear him saying into the receiver, in the same attentive and sympathetic voice that was directed at me, only a few months ago, in his office, try to remind yourself how you pulled through before, it will help you get through the night, I'll see you tomorrow at seven thirty then, take care, and his voice continues to reverberate throughout the house, but it is not addressed to us, and I lead Gili to his bed, read him a story in feverish haste, intent on setting things straight with Oded. What will happen if I wake up in the night and I can't find your room? He is already worried, thick clouds gathering on his clear brow, and I show him the way again, count the steps with him, I'm sure you won't wake up, I encourage him; and he protests, but I'm not used to it here yet, I'm allowed to wake up, I'm allowed to come to you, you, in the singular he says, as if I'll lie there alone, in the room nine steps from his.

Of course you are, I say, kissing his forehead, I'm going now just for a minute, I'll be back right away to see if you're asleep, and I hurry to Oded who is still sitting in the armchair, go and say goodnight to him, I request, not noticing the telephone in his hand; and he whispers, but I'm in the middle of a conversation; I'm going to fax it to you now, he says into the receiver, rapidly filling in a couple of forms; and I urge him, say goodnight to him, so vital is my need to connect them for a minute, to conclude the day with a fatherly gesture, but when I lead him to Gili's room he is already asleep, snoring faintly, his fingers on his chin as if he is sunk in profound thought. Look, it's a good sign, I whisper, I was afraid it would take him hours to fall asleep, but Oded does not appear to be impressed by the achievement. How this pleasant ritual has changed, how many times have I found myself standing next to Amnon opposite the bed of the sleeping child, both of us brimming with the adoration aroused by the sleep of a beloved child, whereas now after a cursory glance he leaves me there and returns to the living room, where his voice is heard again; try to carry on with the medication for a few more days, the side effects usually disappear in a couple of days, let's wait a bit, try to stick with it, life has a strength of its own, call me tomorrow and we'll see if there's any improvement.

I go back to the living room and sit down on my old sofa and feel a dull pain in my bones, a rippling chill through my body, and when he puts the phone down and sits opposite me, fortressed in his black sofa, his pants still damp, his already dry hair slightly rumpled, his eyes cold, I ask him with chattering teeth, Oded, why did you tell Gili that you don't like bears? Because I don't like bears, he replies, I never have. What's wrong with that? What's wrong with that is you insulted him, I say, it was as if you told him that you don't like him.

Why, is he a bear? he asks; and I say, don't be a smartass, it's obvious that he identifies with his teddy bear; and he says, you hunt for insults everywhere, there's nothing wrong with telling a child what you feel, I would have said the same to my own children, but I'm not mollified; it's not the same thing, in their case you would have smoothed things out, mentioned something they do like, but with Gili that was the only thing you said to him today, it was totally insensitive, and he looks at me with dense resentment, doubled by his heavy brows; tell me, is this what you plan to do with me every evening, give me a grade at the end of the day?

You give me no choice, I say, for me it's crucial that Gili feels comfortable with you, and you seem to have no intention of making things easy for me, you promised that when we lived together it would happen and I don't see it happening; and he sighs, Ella, give me time, don't pressure me, hardly two hours have passed since I came home. I walked around with my kids in the pouring rain because you wouldn't let me bring them here, it's hard for me to be sensitive when you were so insensitive; and I say, oh, so this is just a form of revenge? Not at all, he says, it's not revenge, it's just a feeling dictated by the circumstances, and I look at the black window over his head, a few streets away from here the rain is coming into Gili's empty room, the iron shutter of the bedroom is banging against the outside wall in the strong wind, there is nobody there but still it seems that we're all getting wet.

Oded, you can't blame him for those circumstances, I say, I don't understand it, with your patients you're so gentle and tolerant and with him, a kid whose life has been turned upside down, you're so callous, would you like me to act that way with your kids? And he says, since I don't feel that I did anything wrong I'm not moved by your threat, if you traipsed around in the rain for hours with your son I would certainly understand if you were insensitive. Stop harping on that, I snap, you know it was a one-time thing; if only I knew that what you did was only going to happen once, he says, maybe, but it was a mistake on your part; and I get up and stand opposite him, a wild impulse takes hold of me, to leave at once, to go home, but in the next room my son is sleeping, and I have to stay with him; you know what, Oded, when you said to Gili that you didn't like bears I felt like I didn't love you, and he looks up at me; really? I'm sorry to hear that.

And yet when he gets into bed after me his fingers tap my back, be patient, he whispers, we dove in head first, it will take us all time to adjust, and I don't say anything, waiting for him to go on mollifying me, but he falls silent and only his hands fondle my backside, and for the first time my body shrinks from his touch, in thrall to a new, disconsolate anger, I am knocking on a closing gate, begging for mercy for my small son. Perhaps I should condition my response on his smiling at Gili tomorrow morning, I try to work out a simple, logical deal, my body in exchange for a smile, sexual passion in exchange for paternal warmth, like the barter in ancient times, the farmers of Canaan supplied the nomads with oil and wine in exchange for animal products, milk and meat, and perhaps this is what is required of me here, to behave like a businesswoman, not for nothing have I been walking around in a business suit all day, in high heels, but the circumstances are stacked against even this elementary deal; not tonight, I whisper, Gili will probably wake up soon, it's his first night here; and I hear his voice making an effort to smile, we can improvise something under the blanket, he suggests; and I say, not tonight, Oded, my first refusal.

It seems that his silhouette is hesitating at the door, his feet pattering to the bed, a fearless little knight, assailing the fortified castle again and again, and I strain my eyes in the dark, no, there's nobody there, alert and tense I listen to Oded's breathing, to the sounds of the strange house, the hum of the fridge, a motorcycle crossing the lane, heavy steps in the stairwell, everything that didn't bother me at all on the previous nights when I slept here, when my belongings were waiting for me at home, the light of the street lamp glowing through the pin-thin slits in the shutters, perhaps I should have responded to him, soothed, with a warm intimate touch, the bristling alienation that has pounced on us. Mommy, where are you? It seems that as soon as I manage to burrow into a brief sleep, feeling like a train swaying on loose rails, he drops down beside me, Mommy, are you here? He tries as usual to tunnel into the middle of the bed, between me and his father, but the thought of such physical intimacy being imposed on two strangers deters me, and I guide him to the edge of the bed, keeping him away from Oded with my body; go to sleep, sweetheart, it isn't morning yet, but he is wide awake, unfortunately, chattering in a loud, clear voice. I climbed up a tree, he tells me, the tree was full of children, and there weren't any grownups there, and suddenly I saw the white cat in the picture Yoav brought me, he was high up on the tree and I was afraid he would fall, is that a good dream or a bad dream? I hush him, we'll talk about it tomorrow, you have to sleep now or you'll be tired in the morning, but he snuggles up to me in tense, feverish wakefulness; but I've got lots of things to tell you, I didn't tell you yet what happened in school today, and what I did yesterday at Daddy's, he says, volunteering to provide full answers to all the questions he was asked during the day.

Tell me in the morning, I whisper, this isn't the right time; and he says, but in the morning I forget, today Yotam and Ronen were on the swing and when I wanted to get on, too, they called me a retard, it isn't nice to say retard, I'm not friends with them; and I say, but maybe tomorrow you'll be friends with them, these things change quickly; and he asks, what's a process; you forgot to explain to me; and I say, a process is something that takes time, that you build slowly. Move over a little, I don't have any room, he complains, and I try to press against the body sleeping at my side, it seems that a barbed wire fence marks the border on this wide bed, I can feel it on my back, sharp and cold, and he says, look, I brought Scotlag Bear, pushing the soft, dusty creature into my face, do you like Scotlag Bear? And I say, Scotland, of course I like him; and he remarks, I thought everybody liked bears, and I hear Oded turning over and snorting; Gili, you have to sleep now and so do we, I whisper in his ear; and he protests, but I'm not used to sleeping in this house.

Just close your eyes and stop talking and I'll hug you tight and sleep will come, I promise him, wrapping him in my arms, covering him with my body, hiding him from the spirits roaming the house, snatching children who get out of bed. Endless nights he curled up like a kitten between me and his father, how natural it was, to wake up and find the small creature between us, scolded but cheerful, a delightful nuisance, even you had no idea, Talia, how fractious the simplest moments were going to be, for when I try to reconstruct the events of a single day I feel suffocated, lying motionless between the man and the child who are strangers to each other, it is up to me to connect them, night and day, and the weight of the task and its complexity cast me into a mood of black despondence so deep that without noticing I let go of the sleeping Gili, who tries to flip onto his stomach and falls out of bed like a rolled log. He raises his head and immediately drops it to the bare floor and goes back to sleep, at our feet, as naturally as if this has always been his place, and I get out of the bed that has just tossed my son like a corpse onto the shore, bend over him and try to lift him, holding him by the waist and dragging him as if he were unconscious, wounded on the battlefield, and I have to rescue him before he is taken prisoner, dragging him nine steps over the slippery floor to his safe room, and there I lay him on his bed and lie down on the floor, awake and afraid of the future.

In the big bedroom Oded remains alone, his face slack in sleep, his eyes closed, not far from here his two children sleep, their mother's grief exuding from the walls at night, and at the other end of the neighborhood Amnon Miller lies on his back, next to a bead curtain swaying in the breeze, faintly clicking, and only our house remains still and empty tonight, no child will burst gleefully out of its door in the morning, his schoolbag on his shoulders, a plastic bag of chocolate milk in his hand. On the cold floor at Gili's feet I lie awake, while poor Scotlag Bear is obliged to spend the night next to a man who doesn't like bears, and it seems that, of all the changes and upheavals that we've known in recent months, Scotlag Bear's journey to Oded Sheffer's bed is the saddest and the most chilling, and it seems that it is for him I am weeping when I wake up in the morning with burning eyes and an aching back, for the innocent, genial Scotlag Bear whose life has been changed beyond recognition.

Chapter twenty-one

My back is still sore as I sit down opposite the two of them, a distortion of how we used to meet, with Amnon and I already there and Gabi joining us, or Gabi already there and us joining him, but now the two of them are already there when I arrive and, with mild condescension sift through the crumbs of their conversation. We never really liked being a threesome, but that was our life, that was what we were used to, habits provide security, make it difficult to distinguish between obligations and inclinations, and now it seems that each of us is ready to slip into his usual role, except that the official papers lying on the table between us remind us all of why we have assembled here, and once reminded we allow them to dictate the terms of the meeting. It is only thanks to them that I enjoy a friendly, almost fatherly reception, for these papers require my signature, in initials and in full, it is only thanks to them that I succeed for the time being in maintaining the old air of biting condescension, because I'm not going to sign, it's clear to me that I'm not going to sign.

The contract's ready, Amnon informs me, beaming, as if this is a particularly encouraging piece of news. Gabi worked all night, he says, pounding his friend on the back, and only then do I remember to marvel at the fact that their friendship has survived, the buyers are really eager to wrap this up, they're going back to France tomorrow and they need to seal the deal now, or else we'll lose them, he says, waving his finger near my face. The real estate market is weak these days, Ella, Gabi adds, it's hard to find buyers, certainly at this price, they're offering you a great deal, you won't forgive yourselves if you let them get away, his smooth tongue creates the illusion of partnership, of identical interests, as if we were still a couple with a common financial future ahead of us; and I interrupt him, but I don't want to sell, Gabi, I want to rent the apartment until I get my life straightened out, as far as I'm concerned it's not the right time, same goes for Gili, and as I address him I'm surprised to hear a sympathetic note creep into my voice, as if that night, which was the last time I saw him, left a vague trace of intimacy behind it, and when I remember the details, with Gabi's face so close on the other side of the table, it seems, much to my chagrin, that the night with him was ten times better than last night in my new home, that there was more tenderness in that bitter intertwining, more generosity.

We can't only consider your best interest, Amnon says, the apartment I'm living in is for sale at a bargain price, I want to buy it myself before someone else buys it, before I'm forced to move again, that's for Gili's benefit too, you can't put everyone's life on hold until you see what's happening with your life; and I turn to him animatedly, a brilliant idea has suddenly occurred to me, Amnon, why should you buy that apartment, why don't you move back into our house, that would be best for all of us? For a moment it seems to me that this will solve everything, Gili will get his home back, and even I'll be able to come by sometimes, on one pretense or another, and I look at him imploringly, enchanted by the vision of his return to the home from which he was banished six months ago, a first, seductive hint of the reversal of the whole process; but he shakes his head vigorously, definitely not, Ella, I want to move on, not back, that was our family's home, I won't start a new family there, I just want to get rid of it, and I absorb the disappointment in silence, hearing Gabi's voice addressing me in turn, how coordinated they are. I understand that you're starting a new life, he says, what do you need that appendage for, common property is always a source of friction, what do you know, maybe in six month's time you'll want to sell and then it won't suit Amnon, why should you be dependant on each other? This is precisely the time to make the break, and I can't explain to them, and obviously they aren't interested in hearing, how frightening and upsetting it is to give up eighty square meters plus a balcony, continuity, belonging, security, a chance, it seems that precisely this is the step that will put the seal on our separation, after which our family will turn into a chapter of a past receding into the distance, a closed story, irrevocable, completely dead, dead forever.

As soon as you sign the contract you'll be able to go ahead with the divorce, Gabi says, dangling the bait before me, if you're living with someone it's certainly in your interests, but this bait, too, now seems meaningless to me, our apartment is the only thing I cling to, the simple, comfortable apartment to which we brought the bare legged, two-day-old Gili, overlooking an inner courtyard where the pomegranate trees are just coming into leaf, and soon they will bear crimson fruit like goblets full of wine, illuminating the courtyard with their red glow, if only I could buy his share and keep it for myself, if only I could persuade them to wait, but they keep at me, proving how right this decision is from every point of view, morally, tactically, strategically, a decision that will enable us all to achieve economic security and emotional stability, happiness and prosperity in our divorce, and I stare at the clear streets, the sky is dry this morning and only at the sides of the road puddles glitter like miniature lakes, in memory of the heavy showers that soaked two children yesterday. Not far from here Oded Sheffer is sitting in his office shaded by purple chiffon curtains and speaking in a soft voice to his patients, perhaps I, too, should go to him, perhaps I should ask his advice; give me a few days to think about it, I request, I can't decide now.

We don't have a few days, Amnon says, they're leaving tomorrow, not everything moves according to your inner rhythm; and Gabi immediately adds, your refusal will have a price, you should take that into consideration; but Amnon silences him with a firmness that touches my heart, listen, Ella, I've tried to be considerate of your needs over the past months, I didn't make things difficult for you or take revenge on you even though you forced this separation on me, now it's your turn to be considerate, for me this step is crucial, and he falls silent and hands me the pen, all you have to do is sign, I'll take care of the rest, his face shines with a fleshy sheen, a simple face, innocent of sin and transgression, he's not to blame, he had nothing to do with it, he walked between the excavation squares and chanced upon an accident for which he was not responsible and for which he paid the price, he is what he is, maybe he was right for me, but it didn't help him, or me, and maybe he wasn't, but that makes no difference either, a powerful blast tore me from him, and I take the silver pen I bought him for his last birthday from his hand and, as if compelled by some external force, I fill in the blank spaces to which he points, Ella Miller, Ella Miller, Ella Miller.

As soon as they get what they want they become businesslike, preoccupied, exchanging rapid words with the buyers' lawyer over the phone, going over the contract again, and I, having done my bit, and am free to go, to leave my trembling signature behind me and to set out on my new path, but still I cling to the contract with its many paragraphs, refusing to part from my name emblazoned there beside his name, like on a marriage contract, the fatefulness of the moment counted out in trivial details, in banal paragraphs, there are so many aspects to parting, it turns out, and most of them are only revealed with the passing of time, when it seems that the great difficulty is already behind us.

Congratulations to you both, you did the right thing, Gabi announces, magnifying the moment and at the same time making it ridiculous by lending it such great, promising significance, it seems to me that he used the exact same words seven years ago, when we bought the apartment, how consoling this sentence could be if only it had come at the right time from the right lips, you did the right thing, what is it that makes a step the right one of all the steps that were taken and that could have been taken, and I give them both a hesitant smile, and to my surprise they look at me sympathetically, it seems that my distress arouses them, squeezes a drop of generosity from them, and Amnon orders another cup of coffee for me, without foam, showing that he remembers my whims and takes them into consideration, a whole cup of coffee for half an apartment, what a fantastic bargain, and I examine them admiringly, will every man now look more appealing to me than he to whom I have linked my new life like a bicycle to the rusty railing in a stairwell. How gentle they have suddenly become in the wake of my concession, radiating a tender chivalry, without a trace of gloating, like a pair of guardian angels, and I find it difficult to part from them, but when I swallow the last sip of my coffee they rise to their feet in unison, the contract locked in Gabi's briefcase, congratulations, he says again, emphatically, as if we have just announced our engagement, and Amnon bends down to me and asks, are you all right? And I nod, his body exudes a sense of family, as if he were a blood relative, and as I watch him walking away it seems to me that I can see Gili perched on his shoulders like a bird on a tree, what is he taking with him as he walks away, an entire tower on his shoulders, a tower reaching to the sky, an infant who has just learned to sit, a toddler with a pacifier in his mouth, a little child, his face lengthening from year to year, his hair darkening, everything that can be called ours.

Half familiar neighborhood figures pass me by, glancing at me as I stand in the cafe entrance, standing next to the security guard checking the bags of the people, like a mourner at the entrance to a hastily erected mourners' tent. In a moment the passersby will stand before me in a long silent line, they will shake my hand, speak words of condolence and encouragement, you have to go on, they will say to me, what's done is done, there's no point in bemoaning the past, think ahead, ahead, think of what there is, not of what there isn't, this is the anthem of life that rises strenuously from the streets, the anthem of those that move on, and all I have to do is add my voice to theirs, until we become a united choir, marching ahead, in unison, in spite of the sorrow, the disappointment, the regret, and the fear of abandonment, of disaster, of erring.

In all this big city there isn't even one home that is mine, a city so big that I have never set foot in some of its new neighborhoods, tens of thousands of crowded, densely populated stone buildings and not even one of them will open its doors to me when one day I leave the apartment in Penitent Lane, holding Gili who is holding Scotlag Bear by the hand, when I am ready to admit that the operation was not a success, the transplant did not take. Where will we go, it seems that the antiquities of the city are more familiar to me than its new buildings, will we go to The Burnt House in the Jewish Quarter, which was destroyed on the eighth day of the month of Elul, in the year 70 CE, like the rest of the houses of the upper city of Jerusalem, or to the burial caves carved in the rock of the Kidron River that surrounded the city like a belt, or to the valley of Hinom, the entrance to Gehenna, or to the Canaanite water system, shafts and tunnels covertly dug, circumventing the city walls, tricking the enemy who seeks to lay siege to the city's water.

This is the weight of the surrender, its stab, its grief, its depth, this is the final parting from the home that was my home, from the life that was my life, I came this morning determined not to give my consent, and now I find myself opening the door hesitantly, looking around me stealthily as a trespasser, for it is no longer mine, why did I give in to them, soon they will present me with more papers to sign, terrifying white papers, full of paragraphs, and them, too, I will sign, wearily, almost indifferently, and it will turn out that I have surrendered my only child as well.

How hard it is to adjust to the surrender, astounded I stand before the banal facts of life, like a cat seeing snow for the first time in its life, if you move into another apartment it goes without saying that you surrender the previous apartment, if you live with another man it goes without saying that you give up the previous man, that's the way things work in the real world, with cruel simplicity, like in nature, and I walk around the dark house where the blinds are closed and the electric current has been disconnected, examining it as if I have been sent by the Antiquities Authority on an urgent documentation mission, a detailed report I will have to present, documenting the train of events that led to the abandonment of this site, was it drought, famine, the presence of a foreign ruler, the intervention of the elements. A faint smell of burning comes from the bare walls, as if a tire smolders in a hidden corner, sending foul tongues of flame toward me. Is it the sign of fire I must seek, charred wood and ash, toppled stones and bricks, and I repeat simple truths to myself in the darkness, clinging to them as to the railing on the edge of a pit, remember, the contents of homes that have been abandoned are different to those of homes that have been destroyed, the objects trapped in the rubble of a building express a short period of time in its history, first you must learn from the findings about the routine life of the population before the site was abandoned or destroyed.

Remember, routine life is not completely static, but change is extremely slow, a little like biological developments in nature, sometimes it is possible to see a sudden, significant revolution in a short period of time, as a result of technical innovation, the invention of a new tool, the production of a new material, most changes took place as a result of the search for solutions to problems in the area of warfare and defense. Remember, as a rule excavation does not solve all the known problems, data discovered in excavation may solve old problems and at the same time present new questions, remember, you must not mix findings belonging to one complex with objects and data belonging to an adjacent complex, or you will end up with an inexplicable mass of data.

Remember, the explanation of human activity is not different in essence to the explanation of phenomena in the field of the natural sciences, remember, the excavator will never succeed in finding all the parts of the picture and he will have to complete it with the historical data according to the context and according to the dictates of logic, historical sources can be misleading too, intentionally or not, at any given moment the archeologist is in possession of a particular truth that exists until additional data comes to light and changes this truth and leads him forward.

Where did the sofa stand, I strain my eyes in the dark empty spaces, where did the picture of the Parisian hang, it seems that I have already forgotten, it seems that the house has been empty forever, a fit of giddiness glues me to the wall, how will I perform my task, the data has been removed too soon, before it was fully documented, the remains have been obliterated forever, the soil has not been sifted, an undocumented excavation might as well not have taken place, and it seems that this morning nothing remains for me but to cover the pit with its own excavated earth, remember, you must not leave the excavated site as it is, it must be covered up in order to enable future generations to continue from the place where the previous excavation left off, remember, the excavation pit is like an open wound in the body of the site and if it is not properly covered up it will wreak havoc on its environment.

A large expanse of mattress remains in our bedroom and I lie down on it, a naked exposed mattress, spotted with pale, secret semen stains, blood stains in warm earth colors, wide, continental urine stains whose smell has faded, a testament to Gili's nocturnal visits, this is the mute map of our brief family history. Through the swinging iron shutter I examine the view from the window for the last time, a dark, almost purple cloud, a sunset cloud in the middle of the morning, is caught between the drooping branches of the dead tree, and they digest it slowly, with the last of their strength, in the distance the tips of the cypress trees wave goodbye with green-black torches, as in a memorial procession, ten torches in total, for the number of our years together, the palm fronds wave beside them in sudden agitation, like the hands of a man trying to persuade another of the justice of his arguments, but to no avail, to no avail.

A damp mist blows in from the open window, it looks like it's going to rain again and I hurry to the balcony to take down the laundry that I hung up last night but the laundry line is empty, the rooms I pass through are empty, shaved clean, as if a thief has visited them, leaving only an abandoned mattress facing a dead tree, and I fall onto it again with creaking bones and springs, and it seems that the front door, too, is creaking, are guests arriving, guests I invited once, many long weeks ago, and now they are standing in the doorway, astonished by the hollow house, where will I seat them with no furniture, what will I feed them with when the cupboards bare, how will I talk to them with my parched throat.

New stains are spreading over the mattress, broken islands of tears, no, no guest will visit me again in this house with a bottle of wine or a fresh cake in his hand, not even the householder himself, carefully holding two disposable cups of coffee in his hands after taking our son to school, but when I raise my eyes from the mattress I see him, slightly stooped, surrounded by a dark light as if carrying a black cloud on his shoulders, his face crumbling, his eyes lowered, Amnon Miller, we met only an hour ago and how he has changed since then, I came to take a few things, he says, as if to apologize for disturbing me, but I know he has come to say goodbye, like me, and I hear him wandering through the rooms, the echo of his steps, how little we leave behind us. What is left of us, Amnon, of our shared body, when it splits into its separate parts, is there some secret place, in a celestial attic or the bowels of the earth, in which something of our family remains, where will its memory go, Gili is too young to remember, even though all his life he will yearn to do so, only the two of us, you and I, will be able to bear witness to what our family was, that body with three heads and three hearts, cut down in its prime.

When the mattress at my side emits its familiar sigh I know that his body is next to mine, as it was night after night, year after year, as it will never be again, we will never lie under this ceiling again listening to the nervous pecking of the rain, I will never unthinkingly throw out my arm and encounter his face, I will never feel his fingers in my hair again, we will never again be enclosed by these walls, for whose sake we came here today, not for my sake nor for his sake nor for the sake of our son but for their sake, to pay our last respects to this grave. We could have lived here to the end of our days and we did not, we could have had another child and we did not, we could have stayed together until we were old and gray and we did not, and now before we become refugees in other families we are here on the stained mattress in the depths of a pit into which we stumbled one after the other, not in lust or pity or rage or terror, but in the desperate haste of the fall, the urgent packing, as on the night of the exodus from Egypt, our loins girded, our feet shod, our staffs in our hands, for it seems that in our haste we left behind us here on the mattress the mute essence of our shared existence. So much of us is no longer here, looking with abhorrence at the empty bedroom, but this pale stain that no man will ever notice, and no woman will ever decipher, it alone will remain after us, and it is this stain that our only son will seek almost in spite of himself, trying against his will to reconstruct it in his adulthood, and out of it we now emerge to face each other, reaching out with arms like the dry twigs of the dead tree, we will never save each other, our bones break with the effort, but for an instant, like the crack of a tree trunk falling, lending it the illusion of life, we let our bodies add their voice to the deep sultry lament, the lament for the days of our family.

Let me be the first to leave, to turn my back on your sudden sleep, I came here alone and I shall leave alone, and nobody will ever know, heavy and quiet you'll lie and I'll get up silently and look at your familiar body sprawled with limbs outstretched on the mattress and steal outside as if I have murdered you in your sleep and robbed you of your most prized possession. Our separation is completed when I realize that it will never be complete, that to my dying day the sound of this lament will ring in my ears, in varying frequencies, stealing between the slats of the blinds and rising from the asphalt and falling like rain from the clouds, hidden under the wings of the birds and dropping from the trees and peeking between the blades of grass, stretching along the electricity wires and ticking between the hands of the clock and slipping from the pockets of the passersby, and it seems that your surrender today is reshaping the days to come, and those that have passed, completing mine as in an old habit, and these two capitulations immortalized in one contract are charting my course. Was it implanted in us from the beginning, this surrender, was it already there then, like a child waiting to be born, when you said to me, I know you from Thera, you're painted on the wall there in the Minoan site, could we already then have known that at the end of ten years we would shed one another, each in turn, disengage forever.

Slowly I drag my feet down the streets, like an object detached from its original context and immediately losing its full value, for only the context, the relation to the other data, are what give the finding its meaning. On the screen of my cell phone I see Oded's number and I don't reply, a mountain of disappointment that has grown as quickly as the mound of debris next to an excavation site stands between us, I don't like bears, or children who aren't mine either, it seems. The fresh rage climbs the stairs at my side, enters the apartment with me, will it ever be my home, the familiar objects offer slight comfort in their solid presence, the light canvas easy chairs, the carpet we brought from Sinai, the coffee cup from this morning, and I go into the bedroom, its blinds closed like a room left in haste, the blanket rumpled on the bed creating a human contour, as if a pair of lovers are hiding underneath it, and I push it aside and expose a soft, pale teddy bear, and sit down beside it as if it were my sick son. Unthinkingly I close my eyes, remembering the way he stood here with a tray in his hands, two cups of coffee and a cake, the way he said, I have a proposal for you, how warm and buoyant the happiness was, almost playful, like kittens in the bed, to this happiness I awoke one morning, and perhaps more surprises await me here, tucked between the sheets. When will the two of us be alone together again, to reconstruct the nights masquerading as nights of love, when movement gave birth to movement and word gave birth to word, when I believed in him. All I want is to believe in him again, it seems that if we were alone again it would come back, it's impossible that everything melted away as if it never existed, and I hug the teddy bear in my arms and rock it, it's too soon to give up, and for what, my happiness was complete one morning, and I think longingly of the coming weekend as if it were a precious memory, I'll ask Amnon to take Gili and we'll be alone again, we'll melt the icebergs of the new anger, it was preceded by love after all, there isn't a lot of love out there, someone said to me once, and here at home there is.

When I rouse myself to get to the school in time I hear a ruckus in the stairwell, Yotam's voice echoed by another childish voice, he must have brought a friend home from school, to make Gili feel rejected, but when they burst into the apartment and I look with a hostile eye at the threatening friend I recognize my own son, happy and excited, Oded picked me up too, he shouts gleefully, we live in the same house anyway, he says, and I kiss his flushed cheek, and even pass my hand over Yotam's hair, his status fluctuating rapidly, according to Gili's attitude toward him. Now that his presence is making my son happy I smile at them both, come and eat, we have schnitzel and pasta; but Gili shouts, later, Mommy, Yotam hasn't seen the new castle yet, we're going to play in my room first and then in his room, and already they take flight like mythical winged creatures, and I raise my eyes to the door as Oded walks in with the two schoolbags on his shoulders, the two coats, open pride on his face, eager to please, and when I see him like this, Gili's schoolbag on his right shoulder, and Gili's coat in his hands, it seems to me that the din of nervous drumming has subsided and made way for the hint of a blessed routine, even if it doesn't last for days or hours, the very knowledge that it is possible brings consolation.

I called you, he says, I wanted to tell you that I would pick them both up; and I say, I wasn't available, thanks for getting him; and he replies with exaggerated politeness, you're welcome, and he doesn't ask where I was, with Amnon a similar sentence would have given rise immediately to demonstrative unease, I wasn't available, but Oded calmly makes himself a cup of coffee, is it disinterest, or respect for the other's privacy, confidence and trust, what would I actually prefer, did Amnon's jealousy oppress me or reassure me, even if I shouldn't compare them I shall go on comparing them forever, and it seems that even if I were to say, I went to bed with my husband, I sold my house, he would go on calmly pouring the boiling water, adding milk and sugar, carefully washing the teaspoon. Do you want coffee? he asks, and I shake my head; I sold my house; and he takes his lips from the cup, really, why? And I say, because Amnon put pressure on me, he needs the money; and he asks, why didn't you tell me this was happening? And I shrug my shoulders, draping myself in a mantle of self-pity embroidered with heroic pride, the pride of a little girl hiding her distress in order not to burden her parents.

Ella, he says, please don't keep me at an arm's length, we moved in together in order to be closer, not further apart, and I sit down opposite him gratefully at the kitchen table, all my wishes flare up again, leaping wildly, you're with me, with me, you're still with me, and he asks, so is it final, did you sign a contract? Yes, I say, this morning, and he clucks his tongue, it's a pity you didn't consult me, you shouldn't behave rashly in these kinds of matters, and I look at him in surprise; what matters should you behave rashly in then, when you leave home, when you move in to live together? Already I can hear the rejection in his voice, you behaved rashly, and now you've been left empty handed, don't expect to build your home with me, you should have hung onto what you had because I have nothing to offer you in exchange, nothing between us is final yet; and my throat closes as I snap, don't worry, it doesn't bind you to anything.

What's the matter with you, he looks at me hurt, you're misunderstanding me; but I continue vehemently, misunderstanding? You want to shirk your responsibility, you know that if I hadn't moved in with you it would never have occurred to Amnon to throw me out of the apartment, it's all because you pressured me to come and live with you, and now you say to me, you shouldn't behave rashly? Sentences I didn't know existed march out of my mouth as aggressively as soldiers to battle, loaded guns in their hands; and he slams his coffee cup on the table, what on earth is wrong with you, you keep on misinterpreting everything I say, you imagine that every step I take is directed against you, I can't stand this hypersensitivity of yours; and I say, then maybe you should take a good look at yourself, what you do and mainly what you don't do.

I was only trying to help you, he says through clenched teeth, standing up abruptly and pushing back his chair; and I ask, where are you going? And he says, to get Maya from her afternoon class, and I remain frozen and fossilized at the table, drinking the dregs of his lukewarm coffee, I failed again, is it possible at all to interpret ancient data, reconstruct a reality that no longer exists, is it only from within ourselves that we interpret the nature and intentions of those who lived before us, and perhaps they were totally different from us. My head drops heavily onto the kitchen table, it seems that recently every day has been divided into dozens of very short days, each of which has a morning afternoon and evening, one full of anger and insult and the next full of hope and longing, with no lull of night between them. One after the other they assail me, wearing me out with their extreme reversals, did I read you wrong, now another day begins, and I will try to believe in you again because the children are playing so happily, because the old life is over, because I loved you up until two days ago, because my kitchenware is in your drawers, and my clothes are in your closet.

When he comes back after a while with Maya I welcome them warmly, hi, Maya, how are you, what a pretty sweater, and she says, thanks, Daddy bought it for me, everything looks different, she looks around her vigilantly, you brought a lot of furniture, she remarks sternly, as if I have upset the balance, and I say, yes, I brought everything we had, and she announces, it was nicer before, it's too full now. You'll get used to it, Mayush, Oded puts in quickly, giving me a tense sidelong look as she walks around the furniture examining it disapprovingly, touching it with a slender finger as if to make sure it's real, until she sits down with a loud sigh on their black leather sofa. Daddy, I'm hungry, she says, and he hurries to the kitchen at her command, opens the fridge and announces, there's schnitzel and pasta, as if he cooked them himself, and I watch resentfully as the pretty, slender girl who looks so much like her mother greedily devours the meal I prepared this morning for Gili, it looks like I'll have to get used to completely different quantities.

You're eating really nicely, Mayush, her father praises her, and she smiles at him with ingratiating innocence, although it is clear to me that there is nothing innocent about her appetite, it's all part of the conspiracy against me, for the moment she swallows the last bit of schnitzel Gili bursts into the kitchen; Mommy, I'm hungry, you said we had schnitzel; and I say, the schnitzels have just been eaten, I'll get you something else, it will take a while, next time come when I call you; and he's already screaming, I don't want something else, I want schnitzel; and I turn to Oded in an accusing voice, would you mind going and getting some schnitzels from the supermarket, all the food I prepared is finished; and he looks at his watch, I have to go back to the clinic, I'll bring them later, and leaves me alone in the apartment with the three children, like an inexperienced babysitter who arrived for a short visit and whose host took advantage of her presence to leave the house.

But when he's gone we're all more relaxed, even the girl tries to make friends, coming up to me as I unpack the last boxes in the kitchen and showing me the bead bracelet she made herself on her fair, tender wrist, and it seems that when he's not here creating miserable waves of longing in both of us I am able to like her, even if it's only out of pity, poor child, her world, too, has been turned upside down, and when she approaches me from time to time to ask how to spell a word, I help her gladly. Why don't you do your homework here next to me, I suggest, clearing a space on the table for her and sitting down beside her, praising her handwriting, her neat notebooks, and then Gili and Yotam come to join us, their hands full of toys that they scatter over the carpet, and I make them hot chocolate and fill a bowl with cookies, and every now and then I look expectantly at the door, come and see what a great babysitter I am, see what a happy, relaxed family is coming into being here without you, perhaps you'll double my salary, perhaps you'll forgive my rash accusations, perhaps you'll begin to take an interest in my child, but in a devilish turn of events, the moment he arrives and I go up to him and stroke his cheek, Maya opens her English notebook and discovers the crude crayon strokes.

Who scribbled in my notebook, she screams, and immediately levels an accusation, he scribbled in my notebook! Why me, Gili yells, it wasn't me, it was that stupid Yasmin, do I look like a baby to you? And I rush to his defense, it isn't his fault, Maya, his friend was here with his little sister, and the minute my back was turned she ran wild in your room, don't worry, tomorrow I'll buy you a new notebook; but Maya refuses to be mollified, if it was his friend's sister it's because of him, she says sullenly, if you hadn't come to live here it wouldn't have happened; and I try to quote Talia, it's like this in all families, children always scribble in their big brothers' and sisters' notebooks; and she stares at me disdainfully as if I've gone out of my mind, but we're not a family, she says, do we look like a family to you?

We all fall silent in the face of this verdict, forthright but surprising in its vehemence, how come it didn't occur to me to give Talia the update, to point out her mistake, we're not a family, what are we then, and he stands helplessly in front of his daughter, for the first time I notice the similarity between them, even though she is far fairer than he is, and her features are softer. There are all kinds of families, Mayush, he tries to appease her, or me, now that we're living together we're like a family; and she grumbles, what are we living together for in the first place, we were better off without them, and now her good-tempered brother interrupts her in a rare outburst; I want television in my room too, Yotam hangs onto his father's arm, it isn't fair that only Gili gets one; and Oded sighs, that's enough, calm down both of you, what's the matter with you today? I go out for a couple of hours and you fall to pieces, he gives me a rebuking look, as if I have messed up on the job, whereas it was actually his presence that disrupted the peace.

Mommy you promised, you promised me television in my room, Gili buries his face between my arms; and Maya yells, then I want one too, why should he be the only one to have one? And I want a knights' castle too, Yotam immediately joins in, why did he get a present for his new room and we didn't? Gili is already crying bitterly, I let him play with my castle and he won't let me play with his toys, and I look at the three gaping mouths, tongues and throats and lips, baby teeth and sharp incisors, the words pour from them dense and disappointing as a spoiled meal, each of them spits his bile into the common dish, around which we stand helplessly, and when I steal a glance at Oded in the expectation of a sympathetic look, an encouraging word, he avoids my eyes, purses his lips at me, and I hear myself saying, come on, Gili, let's get out of here.

Where will we go? he wails, apparently reluctant to part from the noisy chorus, and I drag him away almost by force, forgetting to take a coat, blind with disappointment and derision, and we rush out into the dark, Penitential Lane thin and fragile beneath our feet. What will I say to him now, where will I take him. I let him play with all my toys, he cries, and when I wanted to play with his he wouldn't let me, and I hold his hand, the smell of home cooked dinners floats from house to house, from window to window; and I say, let's go and have something to eat, you haven't had your lunch yet, do you want pizza? And he asks, to take home? And I say, no, we'll eat in the pizza parlor; and he says, it's more fun to eat at home, and I don't dare to ask him what he calls home, the place we just fled, rejected and unwanted?

Look how warm and cozy it is here, I say, sitting down with a sigh on the tall bar stool, helping him to climb up onto the one next to it, where he plops down, a little dwarf on tall stilts, and when I try to produce the simplest words, order a pizza with olives, the sentence turns out to be impossible to pronounce because suddenly the tears are gushing uncontrollably from my eyes, and I hide my disgrace with the paper napkins, pointing weakly to the desired portion, and he looks at me anxiously; don't cry, he begs, I don't need the TV, doesn't matter if you promised, I don't have to have a TV in my room, and I hug him with the frustration only growing in the face of his mature, considerate concession; honey, that's not why I'm crying.

Then why are you crying? he asks; and for the first time I admit, because it's hard for me, and he keeps quiet, examining the pizza placed before him; Mommy, I want to eat at home with everybody, he says gravely in the end, as if this is his considered response to my confession, let's get a big pizza and take it back for everyone, and I look at him in surprise at the feeling of belonging he has developed overnight, long before me. Are you sure? Maybe we should eat here, you must be hungry, I coax him, but he insists, happy to demonstrate his perfect memory, Maya likes with corn and Yotam likes with mushrooms and Oded regular and me with olives and you with tomatoes, and thus we once again compose the most diverse combination possible, a super-sized pie to satisfy everyone, and he insists on holding the huge cardboard box himself, marching in proud silence beside me, determined to succeed in the mission he has undertaken. His surprisingly mature behavior afflicts me, for in volunteering to sacrifice his wishes for my sake he has shown me how meager is his confidence in my strength, how small his faith in me, the determined delivery boy smelling of melted cheese, hardly able to see the road but hurrying as if bearing great tidings, rushing down the damp streets, teetering up the stairs, is it the fear of being alone with me that sends him hurrying toward them, is even this conflict-torn home a refuge from me.

Three pairs of eyes look at us in tense relief when we walk through the door, they are still standing in the middle of the living room, exactly where we left them. Pizza! Yotam swoops, did you bring me with mushrooms? And Gili sets the steaming package on the table, calmly hands everyone his slice, and only then is he ready to eat himself, and we sit down exhausted on the sofa, chewing tensely. It seems that the first to forgive are always Gili and Yotam, diving onto the carpet, racing toy cars with their free hands, laughing loudly, and after them Maya who offers everyone drinks, pouring coke into glasses just unpacked, and only the two of us, for whose sake these three children have convened here, sit frozen in our places, exchanging not a word or a glance, an estrangement that has sprung up overnight, separating us like a disgraceful stain, as if we have both been convicted of fraud, of deceiving a group of young children, and we stare at them perplexed and ashamed, who is to blame and in what way will we serve out our punishments.

Chapter twenty-two

But this week is a coiled serpent striking at my heel, and every passing day adds another vertebra to its cold repellent back, elongating it, empowering it, giving it purchase around my neck, the venomous tip close, and I wonder if I'll be able to erase this week from the ledger of time, for it seems that seven years have passed since the movers brought my things here, a sofa and two armchairs, a child's bed, carpets and desks, boxes of books and toys, clothes and dishes, more than half the contents of an apartment, all swallowed up in the new apartment without providing a feeling of home, rather an oppressive and humiliating exile shared by me and my possessions. The humiliation seems to swell from day to day, as if I have unconsciously absorbed a blow and the pain, rather than fading, it is increasing, renewing itself, like a body that eats of its own flesh, and I eagerly await the weekend, perhaps then everything will be different, in the children's absence we will try to heal our battered love, reestablish the intimacy that has hidden its face from us, for at night I sleep on the rug at the foot of Gili's bed, and during the short daytime hours when the children are at school, Oded is at the office, and when I try to talk to him upon return, it seems as if we are chopping the words with an axe from the block of ice standing between us. Jump into the water, he said, but it wasn't water that we rashly dove into but a frozen lake, our necks meeting the ice, our eyes dazzled by the glare, our lips trying to mumble through chattering teeth the banal words of love and hope that we have been practicing all our lives, but in their place all that our throats produce is a deep, angry growl, the sound of an animal whose cubs are imperiled.

And I wait impatiently for the weekend, for this accursed first week to end, to be alone with him, to wash the garish war paint from our faces and to return to the old intimacy, the memory of which lashes me with longing, did it exist, did I imagine it, and now on Friday afternoon I look out of the window, eager to see him hurrying home from work, a bouquet of flowers or a bottle wine in his hands, but instead I see him walking down the lane accompanied by his two children who don't seem to have a mother anymore, their schoolbags on his shoulders, his hands on their backs. I open the window all the way, a sharp, dry wind slaps me in the face, and I watch them, infuriated. They proceed as naturally as if this has always been their home, like all the other children coming home from school on Friday afternoon, Maya in front, brisk and energetic, her honey hair curling down her back, Yotam dreamily bringing up the rear, and between them their father, pressing a cell phone that has just begun to ring to his ear, and I, after anticipating a childless weekend, and accordingly sending Gili to his father, purse my lips in sour surprise.

I thought we would be alone, I whisper to him when they come inside, what is it that has molded my voice into a permanent scold; and he snaps, sorry, it wasn't up to me; and I probe his face, are you really sorry, because perhaps that would have been enough, to share a common disappointment at a missed opportunity with you, but why does it seem to me that you aren't sorry at all, that you're using your children to distance yourself from me, and I say, why is it never up to you? You could have told Michal that you had plans, that you were leaving town or something, but he lowers his eyes, it's clear that he can't say no to her, his guilt seizing his mouth like a muzzle on the jaws of a dog, again and again I hear him mollifying her over the phone, allowing her to set the child care arrangements and for her to change them according to her moods. I myself haven't seen her in weeks, ever since we had that picnic in the park together, and my perception of her has been distorted beyond recognition, turned her into a greedy and demanding figure competing with me for his attention, sending her children forth to spoil my plans, endlessly producing illnesses and pains, she and her children, an ancient snake goddess with an infinite number of limbs in need of perpetual bandaging, a relentlessly miserable creature, the more miserable she is the more relentless she becomes.

Actually we were thinking of taking a trip out of town, he says dryly, would you like to join us? As if they are the family and I am a casual guest, without any influence over the proceedings, and again I purse my lips in surprise, where are you going? To friends of mine in the Galilee, Orna and Danny, I told you about them; and I ask in an aggrieved tone, why didn't you tell me before? I would have kept Gili with me; and he says, Ora just called now to invite us, when I was downstairs, brandishing the cell phone as proof, if we were alone I wouldn't have bothered, he adds, but for the children it's a treat. So what are you telling me now, are you sorry, like me, that we aren't alone, do you miss our closeness like I do, a mask of pious fatherhood covers his face, and it seems that this demonstrative devotion to his children will always be interpreted as an affront, simply because they are not my children, because of course I would never condemn Amnon's devotion to Gili, especially if it were at the expense of another woman. My attitude changes with the circumstances, depending on whether I'm alone with Gili, I'm with all the children or only with his; one minute I'm a pedestrian crossing the road, and the next I'm a driver heading toward a crosswalk, in the blink of an eye the person is transformed, assuming a different role, her wishes changing with the circumstances, forever unsatisfied.

My bag's packed, Daddy, she announces, sitting down on their sofa, looking smug; and I hear his voice from the bedroom, great, Mayush, go and help Yotam get his things together; and she heaves a spoiled sigh, I don't feel like it, I'm tired, and stretches her slender body out on the sofa, her loosened hair curling charmingly like her mother's; and I go and stand in the bedroom door, you're leaving already? And he says, yes, you're not coming? Do you want me to come? I ask; and he replies cautiously, only if you feel like it, I can't force you. Oded, tell me the truth, I say, do you want me to come or not? And he straightens up over the sock drawer with a sigh, it depends which me you're talking about, if it's the tense, frustrated and insulted me then there's no point, but if you come willingly and try to enjoy the getaway, which isn't what you had in mind, but is what's on offer, then yes, happily.

Thank you so much for putting me on the spot, I hiss, now let me return the ball to your court, if you're hostile and ignore me and relate only to your children like some steroidal mother goose, then I'm staying here, and if you're prepared to pay me some attention and talk to me like you once did, then I'll be happy to come; and he looks me over with narrowed eyes, all week he hasn't given me one direct look, when the time is right we'll talk about all this, Ella, I see things differently, but now all I'm asking is for you to decide, I want to get going, before the traffic jams start. I'll be sorry to go without Gili, I say, maybe we can go next week when he's with us, and he cuts me short, we've been invited for today and we're going today, are you coming or not? I don't know, I mumble, my faltering voice betraying my distress, what's happening to me all of a sudden, over the past months I've made so many bold, extreme decisions, and, of all of them, this trifling decision suddenly seems almost impossible, terrifying and fateful.

I'm staying here, I say in the end, as he rummages in the fridge, collecting food for the journey, everything I bought so eagerly for our weekend, wine and cheeses, fresh rye bread, apples and bananas, a cinnamon cake, and he sets his jaw; as you wish, he says, his face expressionless, I've already learned my lesson with you, he adds, I'll never pressure you again with regard to anything, so you won't blame me. He quickly packs the groceries into the bags from which they were removed only a short while ago, emptying the fridge, preparing for a long journey to remote locales. Come on, he says, hurrying his children along as he puts his jacket on, make sure you don't forget anything, and they present themselves and stand next to him, waving to me in a ludicrous manner, as if they were already very far away, but when they leave, skipping lightly down the stairs, their packs on their backs, I am drawn to the alluring sight of a family in motion, landscapes flitting by, objectives shared, experiences amassed. What will you do here alone for two whole days, that's not why you moved here, why don't you try to fit in, to be more flexible, show him that you're with him in spite of the difficulties, get to know his friends, help him with his children, perhaps this is the ideal opportunity to draw closer to them, when Gili isn't around, and your oppressive sensitivity about him prevents you from seeing them as they are, after all they're not to blame, and maybe he isn't either, what could he do, he's as concerned about his children as you are about yours, and I shout after them, wait for me, I'm coming too.

A spasm of discontent crosses her face but she doesn't say anything, tightening her grip on her father's hand, and he says okay, hurry up, Ella, I don't want to get caught in traffic; and Yotam asks, is Gili coming too? He still hasn't taken in the fact of my individual existence in the life of the family, and I am grateful for his loyalty to my son; no, I'm sorry to say he isn't coming, he's with his father, I say reproachfully, as if to say, take note, children, weekends are supposed to be divided between the parents, and you two should be with your mother right now.

Lighthearted and relaxed, I say to myself as I throw my things together, that's what you need to be, otherwise you're going to lose him, his look couldn't have been more noncommittal, and be easygoing too, and patient with the children, and at the same time feminine, a hint of sensuality, charm, vivacity and *joie de vivre,* show him that he didn't make a mistake. I must have frightened him recently, over-reacting as usual, perhaps he's not guilty of all the sins I attributed to him, after all I used to be too quick to blame Amnon too, until we separated, and I am so eager to take all the blame on myself, to believe that it all depends on me, that if only I calm down and relax everything will go back to being the way it was before, quickly packing good resolutions in among the few clothes in my bag, for a moment everything seems simple, the main thing is that I'll be with him, the children will occupy themselves in the back seat, and I'll sit beside him, my hand on his thigh, I'll talk to him in a quiet, intimate voice, and anyone looking at us from the side, from the windows of the passing cars, will naturally assume that we're a family, this is what a family looks like, father mother and two children, and nobody will imagine that I have left my son behind, and that these two are not my children, and not wanted by me, as I am not wanted by them, and perhaps I, too, will be deceived by the seductive picture, I will believe in it myself and if I do, so will we all, and by the time we arrive at his friends' house we will be a real family, not one that is cast in doubt by each and every change in circumstance.

Daddy, you promised me I would sit in front, Maya announces in an aggrieved, demanding voice when I open the front door; and he answers weakly, because I didn't know Ella was coming with us, it's her spot; but I of course am already insulted by his feeble stance and I volunteer with affected lightness, no problem, I'll sit in the back, better to be the hurt party than the hurting one, better in this case than to sit beside him and feel her eyes drilling through the headrest, and he says wearily, are you sure? And I don't bother to reply and sit down in the back next to Yotam. Maybe you can switch places on the way, he suggests, and I keep grimly silent, leaving her to reject the suggestion; but you promised, Daddy, you promised all the way, she fakes tears, and I wrap myself in silence, in the robes of noble reproach, even though my face burns with rage. All my good intentions fly out of the window, beating their wings like birds on hearing the sound of an explosion, look, I'll say to him when I finally get the chance to talk to him alone, here's a perfect example of the anomaly you're creating here, a child of ten sits in the front and a woman of thirty-six sits in the back. Look at the distorted message you're sending the child, you're encouraging her to compete with me instead of setting limits for her, which would reassure her and prevent this kind of friction in the future.

Do you even know Danny and Ora? The little girl turns her porcelain face to me, aglow with the pride of victory; and I admit, not yet, I'll meet them soon; and she says, I've already been there lots of times, enjoyably demonstrating her superiority; and Yotam immediately chimes in, me too; and she is quick to assert, I've been there more than you, I went there with Mommy and Daddy before you were born, right Daddy? Right, Oded obediently confirms, but it's not important, it isn't a competition, Orna and Danny are crazy about both of you. And Mommy too, Maya adds; and he agrees, yes, Mommy too; and she protests in a spoiled voice, so why didn't she come with us? I'm used to Mommy coming with us to Orna and Danny; and he says, I'm sure that Mommy will still go there with you, but without me, parents who have separated don't go on weekend trips together; and I bite my lip, a foul wind is blowing through the car, why did I let myself be tempted to come with them, the children don't want me, and therefore I'll be a burden to him in spite of all my efforts, and now it turns out that our hosts won't want me either, especially if they're so attached to Michal, and I try to remember what he told me about them, once he complained that all their common friends had ostracized him since he left home, casually mentioning a few names, it seemed so insignificant then, a drop of sorrow in the sea of our love. Why did he invite me to come along in the first place, perhaps he was only being polite in the hope that I would refuse, and in my folly I agreed, to be a nuisance to everyone, only to Yotam am I of some use, his neck sways toward me, his eyes close, like a tired soldier on the bus whose head suddenly drops onto a strange, accidental shoulder, sleepy intimacy, does it mean anything, and for a moment I am ready to take comfort even in this modest function, but the childish head resting on my shoulder suddenly heightens the absence of my son, the treachery of going on this trip without him, I shouldn't give myself to other children, this shoulder is meant only for his beloved head. So many times we sat close together like this in the back with Amnon driving in the front, and I would hug his shoulder, gazing with infinite admiration at his delicate face, the narrow bridge of his nose, the almost imperceptible dusting of freckles sprinkled over his cheeks, the special radiance of his eyes, the sensitive molding of his lips, the waves of abundant brown hair, the comforting closeness of his body, and now I squint sullenly at the wide, gaping mouth dribbling onto my jacket, chapped fleshy lips with bits of peeling skin hanging from them, and suddenly it seems to me that my shoulder is starting to tingle, and I shift uncomfortably in my seat.

In the front seat the little girl babbles on, as if she is afraid that if she keeps quiet for a minute she will cease to exist, opening every sentence with Daddy and sometimes ending it that way too, Daddy, Orna and Danny like it when we come, right, Daddy, we can play with their rabbits like last time, right, Daddy, you remember how Danny once took us for a ride in his jeep and Mommy was afraid that it would turn over, how old was I then, Daddy? And he answers her calmly, careful to maintain a warm, patient tone without a hint of irritation. Does he really enjoy her babbling, why doesn't he shut her up for a second and say something to me, the itching in my shoulder is getting worse, as if I've been in contact with an animal I'm allergic to, my nostrils tickle and I begin to sneeze, I have to keep wiping my nose, and he looks at me in the mirror, are you okay? And as if he can read my thoughts he suggests, if you're uncomfortable like that why don't you move Yotam; and I answer heroically, no, it's fine, and these are the only words we exchange during the long drive, three hours on the road, with my regret intensifying throughout, sitting next to me like a concrete entity, laying its head on my other shoulder; why didn't you stay home; and I stare at the billboards with their crude advertisements, they're pursuing us, lying in wait to trap bored travelers, whose only hope of salvation apparently lies in a new flavor of fruity yogurt, or a new cell phone, a revolutionary laundry detergent.

The sun leans over the earth and sheds a melancholy, skeptical light on the loud, hollow promises of these times in this land, like feeble distractions for someone who has already gone out of his mind, the jerry-rigged housing projects huddled together like herds of frightened animals. From time to time the ancient cities of the land also arch up from the earth, steep hills, blunt-headed cones, settlements built again and again on the ruins of their predecessors, falling and rising, and it seems that the familiar mounds are waving to me with fingers warped by age, like a friend from the past who knows that his face is hardly recognizable, or perhaps it is my own face that has changed beyond recognition. A short while ago I saw the Gezer excavation site in the distance and soon I will see the blunt-headed cone of Megiddo, the mountain of debris next to the site like a double hump, and in the end we will pass Hatzor too, the biblical cities of Solomon, which set fire to the imaginations of scholars and offered them spectacular remains, palaces of hewn stones and stylish arches, sophisticated water systems, but in the end it was precisely these sites that proved that no united kingdom based in Jerusalem had ever existed, no mighty buildings and no magnificent capital, the legendary kingdoms of David and Solomon were nothing but a mini-state in the Judean hills, and it seems that my personal past is touching the past of these hills, excavated again and again, disclosing different faces, confusing findings with longings, truths with wishes, evidence with opinions, and I look longingly at the curving belly of the earth, pregnant with ancient fetuses that do not wish to be born. Here is Megiddo, growing palms and figs and carobs, we went down almost two hundred steps on the curving staircase, in the underground tunnel quarried to the bedrock, to the cave at the edge of the site, peeping a little fearfully into the chamber above the spring, where two skeletons were found, side by side. A single drop of water fell from the rock into the spring, again and again, with a muffled, rhythmic sound, like a heartbeat, no one was there but us, and Amnon said, if the earth trembles now and the entrance is closed our skeletons will be found here too, and people will think we were a father and his daughter.

Not far from here is Tel Jezreel, the damaged, eroded, disappointing site, which actually produced the evidence that resolved the controversy, the palaces of hewn stone could not be attributed to Solomon, but to the infamous house of Omri, they were the ones to realize the dream of the mountain rulers and establish a vast kingdom, and the memory awakens in me a profound, consoling feeling of home, a feeling I haven't felt for ages, giving rise to a forgotten possibility of life, how happy I was there, in that hallucinatory spot, ensconced in the depths of the excavation square, a shade net above my head, gray with dust, sieving the soil, sieving the soil again and again.

As the road approaches the fields, where the hazy hint of spring starts to flower, the light weakens and runs out, and I close my eyes, pretending to be asleep, and only then does Maya shuts up at last, as if her incessant babbling had been directed against me, and in the silence that falls in the overheated interior, the sound of a single cello is heard, alarmingly similar to a human voice, in a pattern that repeats itself like a persistent thought, gathering a suicidal force. How many faces there are to sadness, every note expresses a different shade of sorrow, and it seems that I am a solitary child in the back seat, my parents' only child, listening reluctantly to my father's explanations, accompanied by his vehement gestures, this is the mountain way, this is the king's way, this is the way of all flesh, did he really say that, the way of all flesh, the car was always blazing, the windows open, a hot wind hitting my face. Did we really only go on our trips in the summer, in pursuit of the prophets, the kings, the crusaders, the pilgrims, the wars in which bloodied words were spilled, unreal and hardly regrettable blood, the blood of anonymous multitudes, dead in any case, who, even if they hadn't fallen on their swords in those wars, would not have been among us today, and I would look at his well groomed hair that defied even the wind, would he ever stop talking? and tried to imagine his head without hair, his face without a mouth, would he shut up if I jumped out of the moving car, maybe he would go on talking without even noticing what had happened, maybe he would go on nagging my corpse. The Christians call this hill Armageddon, a corruption of Megiddo, he thunders, stopping at the side of the road with a screeching of brakes, in the New Testament it is mentioned as the place where the final battle will be waged between the sons of light and the sons of darkness, he turns his head to make sure I'm listening; you're sleeping, he scolds me, I'm speaking to you and you're sleeping; and my mother rushes to my defense, what do you want from her, she's tired, why shouldn't she take a little nap? And he complains as usual, she's tired because she came home late again, who knows what she did there, she's got enough vitality for parties but when I try to teach her about the history of this country it doesn't interest her; you had better listen, he warns me, it concerns you more than you know.

The darkness is already painting our faces a chilling purple when the car stops outside a low, rustic house at the end of the street, and Yotam's head detaches itself from my shoulder at last, I feel sick, he mumbles, licking his peeling lips, when are we going to be there? We're already here, you idiot, Maya says, can't you see? And he snuggles up to me, Mommy, tell her to stop, and only then he realizes that I am not his mother; and I whisper to him, don't listen to what she says, you're just a little confused because you were sleeping, perfectly ready to make an alliance with him against her, but the minute she relents he springs ungratefully over to her side, forgetting the shoulder that served as his pillow, and I follow them up the wooden steps leading to the house, Oded walking in front with the bags, Maya skipping behind him with Yotam on her heels, and me bringing up the rear, my status unclear, neither spouse nor mother nor *au pair* nor family friend, and it seems that their father, too, has forgotten all about me, not turning his head even once to make sure that I am there, not stopping for a moment to wait for me, until I feel like slipping silently away from the convoy, letting them disappear into the lit up house to the happy exclamations of their hosts, hoist my bag onto my shoulder and start walking, for any house whose door I chance to knock on will be more welcoming than this one. Perhaps I will sleep there tonight, in Tel Jezreel, in the ruins of the royal compound, covered with earth, and I stand and wait for the door to close behind them but it stays open, and a woman's graying head peeps out, Ella, she says as if we know each other, why are you standing outside? Come in, it's not as if we were expecting Michal, we're pretty up to date.

If you were really up to date you'd know I have no reason to be here, I say quietly, surprising even myself, mainly myself, for she smiles with ease and says, that bad? Don't worry about it, we'll get to the bottom of all that soon enough, and I examine her, her sharp face, heavy-framed glasses swaying like scales on her narrow nose, her faded lips, her tall body relaxed and comfortable in its frame, her short gray hair, her sloppy clothes, a bleach stain splattered down her pant leg, a spot the color of mustard on her assertive chin. Well, now that you're here you might as well come in, you're letting in the cold, she scolds me with sudden impatience, and I follow her into the warm house, heated by a hulking stove in the middle of the living room, pipes emerging from it in all directions, the children are already horsing around on a brightly colored rug in front of the lit TV, a tall, serious looking girl is sitting on the sofa holding a guitar, reluctantly answering the polite questions posed by Oded, who has already found himself a bottle of beer, set it opposite him, and is lifting it to his lips.

Are you hungry? she asks, Danny went to Nazareth to get hummus and pitas, we'll eat soon, she quickly clears the piles of newspapers from the enormous marble-topped table, I don't know why I read these horror stories, every newspaper should come with a pill against depression, how can anyone stand it? Tell me, do you have more patients now because of the situation? she asks, normal people can go crazy, too, from what's happening here; and Oded replies, on the contrary, the situation's actually convenient for sick people, suddenly everyone around them is depressed, everyone is afraid, they're not deviant anymore, they're almost happy to join in the collective anxiety.

Interesting, I never thought of that, she says, what about you, Oded, aren't you sick of looking after everyone already? Not at all, he says, smiling, I'm addicted to it, it's fantastic, you get to take a vacation from yourself for most of the hours of the day, without drugs, without medication, and sometimes you even manage to be useful, it's only when I leave the clinic that I suddenly remember myself, and when I see his slow, reserved smile I remember how long it has been absent from his face, and again that yearning for how he was before, for our brief period of bliss.

And what about you? he asks, are you painting a lot? And she lights a cigarette with stained fingertips, as much as I can, have you seen that one? She points to a big grayish painting hanging opposite us and he squints, empty shelves, she explains patiently, lately I've been trying to paint emptiness, empty cupboards, empty vessels, it's much harder than I thought, and Oded goes to stand in front of the painting; it's very impressive, Orna, he says sincerely, very disturbing, you know I read recently that according to the Kabbalah, it's precisely into the void that the divine can enter; and as I watch him talking animatedly my heart goes out to him and I promise his back in a whisper, you'll talk to me like that yet, you'll smile at me like that too.

Where is that bum, she interrupts their abstract conversation, how long does it take to get pitas, he's probably wandering around some church, forgot you're coming, I'm telling you, Oded, my married life is one long farce, you have no idea how fed up I am with him, what am I even doing with him still, and Oded chuckles; I've been hearing the same song for twenty years, you'll never leave each other, what makes you think you'd be better off without him? And it seems to me that he is speaking from his own experience, his short miserable experience with me, which has not yet left its mark.

Oded, don't play innocent, she waves a stained finger at him, that's exactly what you did, and you too, no? She turns to me, you've been through a separation too, haven't you? I nod glumly, trying to adjust to my new identity, I hardly ever meet people who didn't know me before, who didn't know Amnon, who are meeting me for the first time in my new situation and classify me accordingly, as a woman with a broken family behind her, a determined and decimated shadow, silently following her wherever she goes, even to this remote corner of the Galilee.

You have a daughter, don't you, the same age as Yotam, no? she asks, apparently trying to ransack her memory for everything she has heard about me; and I correct her, a son, not a daughter; and she asks, and how do the three of them get along together? So-so, I say, it isn't easy; and she immediately jumps in with an unpleasant crow, why should it be easy? I told Oded it was crazy to live together in such circumstances, why make things difficult for the children? But you know what men are like, they never think things through, even though he's relatively enlightened, he still has his moments, and the casual yet decisive ease with which she defines this move as a total mistake, as a step I should have prevented, chills me as I stand opposite her menacing painting. A mistake so obvious a child could have seen it, a simple human error, and now all that remains is for us to admit it and put it behind us, for each of us to go our own way, with our own children, and I turn slightly in his direction, waiting for him to say something in his defense, to justify the step he so strongly pushed for, but he sips his beer thoughtfully, his lips closing around the mouth of the bottle; I'm not sure that the problem is the children, he says in the end.

Of course not, she announces, the children are not the heart of the problem, they just reflect your own difficulties back to you, but they are more adaptable than you are, and they grow up quickly too, what can I say, who has the strength to deal with these upheavals in the middle of life, not me, that's for sure, my dream is to live alone, she declares, and immediately complains, where the hell is he; and Oded chuckles, you see, you can't even handle an hour without him; and she waves her hand dismissively, it's the pitas I need, not him, listen, just before you arrived I saw an amazing program about India on the Discovery Channel, about the untouchables, the way they live, it's terrible. You know what shocked me the most? she asks, turning to me, taking me by surprise like a teacher with a daydreaming pupil, that even in future incarnations they won't be freed from their predicament, even when they are born again they will be untouchable, isn't that awful? I nod, looking at her in embarrassment, is she trying to hint at something, the traces of her former beauty reveal themselves to me as I look at her face, traces that for some reason she enjoys concealing rather than magnifying as most women would do, her neglect is proud and challenging, as if to say, if I can't be as beautiful as I once was, I'd rather not humiliate myself trying.

Here he is, she announces as a tall balding man enters the room, his hands full of plastic bags, and I stare at him, astonished by his resemblance to Amnon, the same sloppy stance, the same loose, undisciplined limbs whose size gives them an immediate advantage, and it seems that this is the last thing I needed here under the prying eyes of our hostess, a face to face encounter with Amnon's twin, radiating an open, lanky relaxation as opposed to the tense, reserved Oded. So you're with Amnon and you're in no hurry to get rid of him, despite your rude complaints, I protest in silence, how pleasant it is to complain while he showers you with attention, hugs your daughter, fills your fridge, and now Maya and Yotam pounce on him; wow, he says, you guys are enormous, Mayush, you've turned into a bombshell, and Yotam you're turning into a little man, soon you'll be coming here on your own, without your mom and dad, you'll help me on the farm; and Orna makes a face, don't get carried away Danny, I'm not taking care of two small children, I'm not up to it anymore, you'll leave it all to me as usual, and when he comes toward us I notice that his upper lip juts out slightly, giving him a babyish expression, and he stares at me in frank curiosity, and offers me his hand. So you're the new girl, he says, shaking my hand, pumping it rhythmically up and down, nice work, Oded, and turning to his wife, you see Orna, everyone's taking young women and I'm still stuck with you; and she sniggers, you poor thing, my heart bleeds for you, nobody's forcing you to stay you know, and she rises quickly to her feet, wiping her hands on her shirt, why don't you set the table instead of standing there salivating, everything's ready, I just have to make a salad.

Can I give you a hand, I offer; and she says, why not, and once we're in the kitchen she places a chopping board and an enormous cabbage in front of me on the counter, do you know how to dice? she inquires before entrusting me with the task, and seems to be scrutinizing the clumsy movements of my fingers as she rapidly chops up parsley and throws it into a blue ceramic bowl. You two don't look like you're in love, she states calmly, her knife hacking a ripe tomato, it's not what I expected, I have to say, you look exhausted and depressed, I haven't seen Oded like this in a long time, even during the most difficult period with Michal he was more optimistic, and I bend over the white cabbage leaves; we're both a little stunned by the move, I mutter, and immediately add, I've been happier too, trying to hint that I also have a past, that I, too, have lost something, that once upon a time I too sat at home and entertained guests, just like her, teasing my husband and playing with my child, a situation that is definitely preferable to my present status as an unwanted guest, a questionable new woman who wore out her welcome in a week.

He described you completely differently, she complains, as if she has been cheated, he said you were strong and independent, and I'm afraid you seem no less fragile and needy than Michal, poor guy, I don't think he has the strength for another woman like her, and when she speaks these words, fragile, needy, she spits them out of her mouth with revulsion and condemnation, as if they were crimes, and I shudder before the mirror she holds up to me, let's see you in my place, I silently rebel, let's see you losing a home and family for a man who's grown alien and hostile overnight, as if I have already forgotten that it wasn't for him that I left Amnon, as if the separation only took place this week, with the selling of the apartment, with the move to Penitential Lane.

You're not angry at me for speaking like this, she says hurriedly, I know I sometimes go too far, I have a foolish compulsion to make people see things clearly, let me finish the cabbage, she pushes me aside and energetically attacks the frayed leaves, shredding them rapidly into tiny bits and throwing them into the bowl, you kids, scram, you'll get dessert after dinner, Danny, how long does it take you to set the table? And she whips an aromatic Pyrex dish out of the oven, chicken with rosemary, she announces, and for the kids I made meatballs, and a dish of potato gratin also immediately makes its way to the table, together with the salad to which I hardly contributed. There's too much food, what did you send me to Nazareth for, Danny complains, trying to find a place on the table for the dish of hummus, Ella why are you standing, he says, come and sit next to Oded; but Maya immediately shouts, I'm next to Daddy, and Yotam is already sitting on his other side and I go and sit at the end of the table next to their silent adolescent daughter, the more her mother talks the less she has to say, and I find myself facing Oded, who looks more relaxed after a few beers, and he participates in the conversation, which is occasionally interrupted by the children complaining, bickering, taunting, and mainly competing relentlessly for his attention.

Sorrowfully I look at him as if I have already lost him forever, would I choose him again, a man no longer young, who looks older than his years, his skin rough and his face marked with vertical lines, his soft deliberate voice drawing out the ends of the words, his language spoken in brushstrokes, his handsomeness slightly hidden, his eyes shadowed, avoiding me, and I hardly listen to their conversation, once I, too would make intelligent remarks about the situation and the chances for peace, the causes and the guilty parties, but in the past months I seem to have lost the capacity, like a sick person absorbed in her sickness, speaking of it endlessly and eagerly while every other subject prompts nothing but resentment and tedium. A deafening noise suddenly startles me, but our host hastily reassures us, don't worry, it's just planes taking off, we're right next to an air force base, something is happening in the North; those impotent idiots have finally remembered to react, he adds with satisfaction, and is immediately interrupted by his wife; what exactly do you expect to gain from their retaliations, more violence? she scolds him, the cycle of violence has to be broken; and he defends himself, but when we don't retaliate it sends a signal of weakness, and our weakness only makes them more aggressive, isn't that clear to you?

We should be magnanimous, Oded says, we should say to them, we've all made mistakes, let's start again, is he talking to me now, about us; and Danny pounces on him, how can you call yourself a psychiatrist if you don't understand the most basic things about human nature, it's all power struggles, the strong one wins, not the magnanimous one; and Orna points to him mockingly, look at him, as soon as his son's in the army he becomes even more militaristic, Oded, write me a prescription for some sleeping pills, ever since Amit was drafted I have a hard time sleeping five straight minutes; and Danny sighs, when will you understand that it doesn't depend on us, you think I don't want peace as much as you do? The problem is that I don't have anyone to make it with. A loud telephone ring prevents her from answering him, maybe it's Amit, she rushes to pick up the receiver, hello Amitush, she cries, and immediately her voice falls, Michali, how are you dear, of course, we miss you, next time you should come with the children, are you feeling better? Yes, I'll call you at the beginning of the week, do you want Oded or the children? And a long line forms next to the telephone, all of them eager to hold the receiver with greasy fingers and talk to her, and Maya, who naturally got there before her brother, gushes into the mouthpiece, Mommy, how are you feeling? Yes, we're having a great time but it's a little sad without you; and Yotam goes even further, why don't you come, Mommy, so what if it's far? I'm not used to being here without you; but their mother doesn't show too much interest in their feelings, and her conversations with them are surprisingly short in light of the excitement they aroused. It's with their father that she yearns to talk at length, it seems that she has a lot to say to him, that much has come up in the few short hours since their last conversation, and he walks around the marble-topped table and goes out to the garden, his voice trailing behind him, weak and worried, and even though I bury my face in my plate, shifting pieces of chicken around, drawing my own empty pictures with the trail of brown sauce they leave behind them, I know that in the face of his desertion they are all looking at me, even the children, some gloating, some in discomfort.

Can I pour you some more wine? Danny asks, and when I hold out my empty glass he says emphatically, poor Oded, I feel sorry for him, she doesn't give him any room to breathe, and I am surprised, is that the way things look from the other side of the table, and I thought they were secretly nodding, mocking my humiliation, and Orna quickly silences him, that's enough, not in front of the children, and I look at the sliding glass doors, through which Oded can be seen in his dark clothes, pacing nervously back and forth on the lawn illuminated in a yellow light, bending over the cordless telephone as if its weight is too heavy to bear and in a minute it will slip from his hand, coaxing the receiver with emphatic gestures, perhaps they are right, perhaps he is to be pitied, how can he cope with my difficulties when he is sunk in his own, and how can I, like two sick people who have wound up lying in a single bed, with no doctor to be found, which of us can afford to help the other?

Are you all right? Orna asks me when I rub my forehead, would you like a glass of water? I thank her and gulp it down while her husband pats her shoulder with a clumsy hand, if this is what a new couple looks like I'd rather stay with you, Ornaleh, and she shrugs his hand off; go away, you pest, but I smile at him in gloomy agreement as the glass door opens and Oded joins us, bringing with him a gust of cold from outside, and he puts the receiver down on its base with a sigh, like a defeated weightlifter.

Is it like this all the time, the phone calls? Orna asks in a whisper, while the children, who have already left the table, lick lollypops in front of the television; and he says, it's getting worse from day to day, she isn't getting back on her feet; and Orna twists her mouth angrily, obviously, why should she get back on her feet when you take care of her so devotedly, when you're at her beck and call all the time, she whispers, look at you, your face radiates guilt, you're begging to be punished, how thick-headed are psychiatrists, they can't see what's under their noses, and I surreptitiously cheer, ready to forgive her for all the charges she hurled at me earlier, especially when she goes on, look at what you're doing, you're hurting Ella, you're hurting yourself, but most of all you're harming Michal, she'll never get better like this, you know I love Michal, she adds quickly, but if you've decided to separate, then separate, make a clean break.

I'm just trying to be humane, he says quietly, looking, to my surprise, at me, I can't ignore her distress; but she rushes back on the attack, that sounds good, but it's too simplistic, you have to look further, it isn't going to work like this, Oded, maybe you don't really want it to work, she adds, maybe you want her condition to worsen to such an extent that you'll have to go back to her; and he smiles bitterly, you too, Orna? I'm always being suspected of ulterior motives; and she says, with you radiating guilt and doubt that's not so far off the mark, come on, let's put the kids to bed so we can have a real talk. That's what she likes best, Danny sniggers, putting everyone's life in order, except for hers, if anyone dared to say one word to her about what she radiates, God help him, and she shuts him up at once, Danny, did you bring cigarettes? No, he says, you said hummus and pitas, and she grumbles, go and get some at the gas station, and he gets up reluctantly, you didn't say anything about cigarettes, and she says, you're getting senile, I told you three times.

Did you really tell him to bring cigarettes? I ask her with an unforeseen urgency when he leaves, and she laughs, of course not, but why not torment him a little bit, it makes him more manageable; and Oded protests, take it easy, Orna, you don't have to teach her all your tricks in one sitting, it'll just come right back at me, and she gives us both a thoughtful look; relax, nothing's coming right back at you because it looks to me like you're not going to make it, she says quietly, and immediately covers her mouth with her hand, sorry, sometimes my mouth has a mind of its own, I really didn't mean it, but her words hover in the air like six black ravens, you're not going to make it, you're not going to make it, they caw, while I silently observe the commotion of the end of the evening, not taking part in washing the dishes or watching the children, in a house that I have never been to before and will never be in again, a guest for a single night, a guest for a few months in his life. From a distance I watch the commotion receding from my life, a man no longer young trying to put his children to bed, a woman no longer beautiful trying to restore order to her kitchen, and I am a stranger to them both, looking around me in shock, like an object preserved for thousands of years in the depths of the earth, in a stable environment of moisture and acidity, suddenly exposed to the open air, which inflicts physical and chemical shock, setting irreversible processes in motion, and I remember the wooden amulet, buried at the bottom of the sea in a capsized fishing boat, and the way it was pulverized by exposure to the light of day.

Why should you run your hands from one end of my body to the other, and I am like an old railway track, impassive, the voice of their adolescent daughter rises with surprising power from her bedroom, accompanied by thin guitar chords, just as everyone sits down around the packet of cigarettes thrown resentfully onto the table, and another bottle of wine is opened, even Oded has escaped his children, his pants wet from their stormy baths, and I look at him, rocking the wine in my glass like a baby in its cradle, now that the children are asleep we can play the role of lovers again, and when we go slightly tipsy to bed we will fumble in the dark for something to hold onto, a yearning deeper than desire will reconcile us tonight, from one end of my body to the other I will love you, but light rapid steps come pattering toward us and Maya emerges from the hall in a long nightgown, her hair curling wildly and her mouth pouting, and she seats herself nimbly on her father's lap, fitting her body to his, slipping into it like he is a coat, laying her head on his shoulder and murmuring, Daddy, I can't fall asleep, I'm not used to sleeping here without Mommy.

Mayush, come on, that's not like you, a big girl like you, Orna says, repulsing the invasion, go and try again, let your father sit here with everybody else; but she bursts into angry tears, Daddy, I can't fall asleep, come and lie next to me until I go to sleep, Daddy, and he buries his lips in her hair; I'm right here, as close as can be to you, sweetheart, go and try to sleep, I'm sure you'll fall asleep; and she kicks her feet, but you promised you would sleep next to me; and he says, I'll join you later; and she carries on, but you promised, Daddy, and he rises heavily to his feet with her hanging from his neck like a little monkey, her legs clamped around his waist, and he ignores the vehement signals Orna sends him with her mouth and finger, disappearing again into the green-carpeted hallway, leaving damp footprints behind him.

I ate too much, Orna complains, putting her hand on her stomach, and she immediately adds in a whisper, she's become difficult, Maya, she wasn't like this before, poor kids, how did I know not to get divorced, she marvels, however young and stupid I was I somehow understood that much at least, is your daughter having a hard time with it too? Son, I correct her, not daughter, the strong singing from the closed room accompanying the sadness welling up anew, why should you run your hands from one end of my body to the other, when I am like an old railway track, impassive, accustomed to the terrible weight, the sudden darkness, the abandonment.

Our daughter writes poems and puts them to music, Orna says, indicating the closed door with a movement of her chin, did she really stress the word 'our', or is it just my ears that seize on it, you have an our and I no longer do, the children of divorced parents are sometimes their father's and sometimes their mother's, they will never again be ours, and once more I am tortured by Gili's absence, how he would have enjoyed jumping up and down on that rug, licking a lollypop in front of the television, playing ball with Yotam tomorrow morning on the manicured lawn, Yotam will surely tell him what a great time he had and Gili will look at me in astonishment, why did you go without me, why didn't you wait for me?

I seem to see him through the vapors covering the glass door, prancing on the lawn between the three oak trees, his arms hugging his chest, his bare feet not touching the ground, and I get up quickly and go to the door and immediately return embarrassed to my seat, wiping my eyes, and she looks at me curiously, what did I say, is it something I said? And I sigh, it doesn't matter, everything you say aloud I've been saying to myself, only for me it's too late, and then I find myself telling her everything in detail, how we met by chance, and how wonderful it was in the beginning, and how he pressed me to move in to live with him, how he promised that his relations with Gili would improve when we were all together, and in the end it only got worse, the way he told him that he didn't like bears, my voice chokes as if I'm speaking of some cruel abuse, just imagine, the child shows him his teddy bear and he tells him he doesn't like bears, and I go on, presenting the new and at the same time age-old indictment, he doesn't even get up, and this may seem trivial to you, but I'm used to Amnon jumping up to greet us and hugging Gili, I'm so disappointed in him, Orna, I confess to this stranger, who is listening to me with a furrowed brow, I believed in him so much, I've never felt so cheated in my life.

So why don't you leave him? she asks coldly, puffing pale cigarette smoke in my direction, what do you need him for, his children get on your nerves, his wife is a millstone around your necks, he isn't capable of interacting with your child, why are you hanging on to him, this isn't what you left your husband for; and I sigh, but it's because of him that I'm left without a home, my husband pressured me into selling our apartment. So what, she says, buy a smaller apartment for you and your son. Finished, she claps her hands decisively, to signal the end of our relationship, and I say, but it's not so simple, it was good for us together, I loved him, we planned a future together, I can't give it up so easily, he promised me that when we were together everything would work out.

So he promised, so what. What will you do, sue him? For not liking bears? When he made the promise he believed it, and in the meantime he realized that he can't keep his promise, so what do you want to do, drag him to court? Can't you see how ridiculous you're being? I shake my head, why ridiculous? He should be responsible for his actions; and she says, but you should be responsible for yours too, he didn't force you, he didn't march you out of your house, you decided to go and live with him, you can't behave like a little girl and blame him for not being what you thought, he didn't deceive you on purpose, he believed it would work out and he was wrong, and you're paying for it, and again she feels her stomach, as if we are both guilty of overeating.

So what are you saying? I mutter; and she sighs, that you have to take responsibility for your decisions, you can't keep telling someone from morning to night what a disappointment he is, nobody would put up with it; and I say but what if it's true, what if he really is a disappointment?

Then leave him, she says, you can't change him. Or else change yourself, either adapt your expectations to reality or get out, those are your options, you have to understand, she leans toward me, her face close to mine, even if all your complaints are entirely justified, your attitude is fundamentally wrong, you think that he owes you something, that it's a game played according to the rules when actually it's a jungle. I look at her with hostility, it all seems so easy to her, as if we're talking about separating the yolk from the white of an egg, let's see her coping with a disappointment like this, and she goes on, listen, I've known Oded for years, I love him with all my heart, but I'm not blind to his faults. He really is misleading, he's one of those men who make you believe they'll fulfill all your yearnings, but he's far from that. He's suspicious, withdrawn, he doesn't really give of himself, in my opinion he's largely responsible for Michal's decline, the only way she could manage to keep his attention was by falling apart, but in the end that was how she lost him, too, it's a real shame, she's a brilliant girl, and I shake my head, as shocked as if she's told me that I've gotten myself involved with a dangerous criminal.

But that's impossible, I protest indignantly, he was so sweet and supportive at the beginning, I couldn't believe my luck, I couldn't believe it was for real; and she claps her hands in astonishment, tell me, were you born yesterday? It wasn't for real, don't you know that when a man is trying to woo a woman he does things that he'll never do again, didn't you take that into account? And I shake my head in shame, I thought those laws didn't apply to us.

Tell me something, do you have any girlfriends? she carries on, don't you have anyone to give you advice? I can't believe you're so naive, I'm not saying that he was deliberately putting on an act, or that he's a monster, he's a profound, interesting man, his intentions are good, but he has a dark side, he's very damaged inside, and around this inner wound he has built a superstructure of control, he has to control, interpret, mold, otherwise he feels threatened and he disengages. He was desperately in love with you, and maybe he still is in love with you, but you've reached a more realistic stage, it's impossible to escape from reality, either accept him as he is, and then you'll be able to enjoy him a bit, or leave him, your love story is just beginning, if at all, forget everything that was, it isn't coming back.

But there are some things I can't possibly accept, I say, I can't accept his attitude toward my son, and she lights another cigarette; perhaps you should examine your expectations, Ella; your son has a father, he surely doesn't need another one, and, by the way, I didn't get the impression that you were particularly warm to his kids, she says snidely; and I confess, believe me, I try, but whenever I get close to them something goes wrong, I'm sure that if he treated Gili differently it would be easier for me with them as well. I'm not sure, she says, and there doesn't have to be a linkage either, it seems to me as if you've gotten yourselves into a big mess, instead of being lovers you've turned into your children's lawyers, you identify with yours, he with his, and there's nothing left in common for you two to hold onto. You're also projecting your own needs onto them, but I don't think your child needs a warm relationship with Oded, you're the one who thinks that's necessary, either way you have to chill out about the children, let me tell you, they grow up, maybe you haven't heard about that either yet, they grow up in the blink of an eye, it's only yesterday that Amit was born and he's already in the army, the children aren't the problem and they aren't the solution either.

Loud snores rise intermittently from the rug in front of the TV, where her husband retired at the beginning of our conversation, replacing the strains of the guitar that have died down, her daughter has apparently gone to sleep too, and I glance from time to time at the hall, how long does it take him to put Maya to bed and come back here, instead of talking to him I'm talking to his friend, a strange woman, shrewd and cruel, as if we are the ones trying to weld the fragments of our lives together, weaving a shared future, and she sees me looking, are you still waiting for him? I'm sure he fell asleep long ago, let's go and check, and I follow her to the room set aside for us, where we find him sleeping on his back, his lips pursed, even in his sleep he looks troubled, his arms spread out as if he has been crucified, and on each of them the head of a child, and I survey the mattresses laid out for us gloomily, all that is left for me is to choose next to which of the children, neither of whom are mine, I prefer to spend the night.

After thrusting a big towel into my arms, like a rude chambermaid, she says, listen, it looks to me as if you still have no idea who you've chosen to live with, I chose to live with a rock, it has its drawbacks, but at least he'll never break, Oded is a lot less solid than he seems, he won't survive in a hostile environment, he has his own ways of detaching, I'm warning you, don't drag this out too long, give it a few more weeks and if things don't improve make a clean break, you'll only suffer, she sighs, it's a pity I didn't meet you before, tell me, can you still go back to your husband? I have the feeling that he was actually right for you, judging by the volume of your expectations you seem to have had it good, why did you leave him in the first place?

Believe me, I don't know any more, I sigh, it was uncontrollable, like a natural disaster, and she looks at me doubtfully through her glasses; I don't believe in that sort of thing, she says firmly, maybe you simply don't understand your own motives yet, can you still go back to him? No, I say, it's too late, and I didn't love him anymore anyway, I add hastily, trying to defend myself from her agonizing conclusion; and she snickers, love isn't something you feel, it's like health, it's only when you're sick that you notice its absence. Maybe it was too easy for you, she says, maybe you're looking for difficulty, for a challenge, who knows, if that's what you're looking for you've come to the right place, she points theatrically at the sleeping man surrounded by his children, good night.

I feel as if I have landed up in a youth hostel full of strange backpackers, disturbing body movements, a medley of mouth odors, panting breaths, the cry of a confused rooster at midnight, what am I doing here, if only I could detach one of the children, roll them onto the edge of the mattress and take a place next to Oded, at least to be close to him at night, maybe even wake him up and tell him in a whisper that I've understood something, that the letters are growing clearer, or just to show him by the way I touch him, the way I kiss him, but like vigilant bodyguards they cling to him, and I toss and turn on the edge of the mattress, I have no chance of falling asleep here, Maya doesn't shut up even in her sleep, muttering loudly, and even now her words seem bracketed by the word Daddy, and Yotam, while silent, kicks in all directions, I don't belong to them, I don't belong here, I want to go home, even if this home no longer has walls and a ceiling, for when I was a child I had no home, and yet I always needed to go back to it, not because it was warm and protected, but because it was unsteady, and it was up to me to keep it safe, to press its foundations together. Don't you have any girlfriends, she asked, and I have difficulty in answering, I always made friends easily and let them go with the same ease, only Dina has accompanied me through the years, and recently I have been avoiding her too, is this what she was trying to tell me then, that he isn't right for me, that I need a rock, to smash against again and again without breaking it, and I stand up, holding my blanket and pillow, and look for a place to sleep, in a house I do not know, hugging the walls and groping my way to the rug in front of the TV where a number of blankets are piled up next to the wall, and I lie down next to them, getting away from that tightly linked family is a relief, as if I have shirked a burden, and when sleep is already covering me like a vaporous cloud I see that the blanket next to me is moving, the man of the house's big limbs stiffen for a moment and immediately relax again, and my sleep fills with a dreamy, delirious merriment, look, Amnon, I've come back to you, the rug has turned into a magic carpet and miraculously taken me back to my former life, but if this is you, Amnon, then where is Gili, where is the child of our love, and his voice seems to answer me, he hasn't been born yet, he'll come in nine months time.

Chapter twenty-three

Children carry time on their narrow shoulders, between their eyes, along their calves, they hide it under their clothes, like a pocketknife, a blade, a pistol, who will dare to check and see if it's really loaded. Like miniature porters, midget slaves, they take up the load and advance in last year's sneakers, in dark rubber boots, in scuffed sandals, riding on bicycles, on scooters, on skates, their hair bristling in the wind, their clear features softening the blow, the enemy is not so threatening when it is etched on their faces, buried in their bodies, they are dependent not on us but on time, reared not by us but by time, faithful not to us but to it, obeying its commandments, leaving us behind, for they can exist only if they betray us.

The history of our lives is written on their skin, drawn with their crayons on crumpled pieces of paper, swallowed up by their changing voices. They mature more quickly than we do, we part for just a few hours in the morning but when we return at midday you're different, we'll hardly recognize you, your evasive looks, your shame at the displays of our love, and while you will always identify us from afar, the smell of our bodies, the sound of our voices, the map of our facial expressions, the gleam in your watching eyes grows dull. When will the day come when

I am a nuisance to him, when will the moment arrive when I make my vows of love to him and he does not reply, but remains politely silent, his body stiff, his muscles unresponsive, how brief this love story is, with its end inherent in its beginning, and then the tiresome memories he has no interest in hearing, the embarrassing longings, and we mothers, loved for the first time in our lives with a perfect love, without reservation, how will we resign ourselves to its end and how will we fill the void it leaves behind. How imaginary is our happiness, how doubtful, how pitiable, on whom do we pin our hopes, on whom did we choose to depend, on these enchanting creatures, compelled by a command as old as human history to wrench themselves from our grasp, and the harder we try to hold onto them the more violent the separation, will they cast us off like someone peeling a parasite from his skin, with our anxieties and frustrations, our hunger and thirst, never to be satisfied.

Is this the stick they fought over like a pair of puppies, holding it by both ends, shouting and crying, refusing to let go, still here, lying among the bushes like a dead snake, unwanted, damp from the rain, cracked by the sun, since nobody wants it I will take it, and I climb onto one of the rocks and stand up, the long stick in my hand, looking down at the commotion raging near the school gates, like a prophet before a city about to be destroyed, how doth the strong staff break, the beautiful rod, how great the uproar, lips smacking, car horns blaring, schoolbags lurching, juvenile crying and feet stamping, urgent running, proud of its independence, to get there before the bell rings, and nobody stops to part from the moment, to mourn this morning, swept away like a frail leaf in the mighty torrent of time.

Will I even recognize his face among the dozens of children still playing in the yard, his voice among the dozens of voices flying from strained throats, we have been through so many upheavals in these past months and yet from the heights of this rock the road ahead of us seems clearer than ever, it seems that this and only this is certain, in another few years or hours, in the blink of an eye, he will be like the youths striding before me now, their steps broad, their laughter grating, secretive, and I hold the stick close to me, will almond blossoms shoot from its cracks, to show the intentions of God amidst these vicissitudes, will it turn into a snake if I cast it to the ground.

The bell rings and I must leave now and make my way to one of the apartments on offer in one of the nearby streets, to walk through the empty rooms, to count floor tiles and paces, to peer through windows, and still I remain rooted to the spot, reluctant to abandon the familiar and at the same time terrifically impenetrable sight, the vantage point that distances my life from me, and yet accurately reflects its essence. A black dog runs through the park, ravens of the same color cluster around it as if they are its offspring; how many years does a raven live, how many years does a dog live, how many years does a tree live, how many years does love live; this is what the world looks like without love, a world ruled by time, that heartless tyrant, only total surrender allows the semblance we require for survival, reverence for what cannot be changed, and I, more than love, sought proof. I pounced on Oded like a rushed researcher seizing on the first bit of evidence that comes his way, the proof that I had not made a mistake, that all those upheavals were for the good, that life after the separation would justify its trials, but perhaps the time has come, at eight o'clock this morning, to call off the search, to accept the absence, for with my staff I will cross this park, with my staff I will leave your house, and even that provides no proof.

As has been my way in recent months, I marvel at the pairs of parents parting from the children at the school gates as at an inexplicable natural phenomenon, what do they know that I don't know, are they more patient than I am, better at adapting their expectations to reality, or are they simply lucky, what kind of morning did they have, what kind of night, and I think of our mornings, the children opening their tired eyes to a home of strife and conflict, can it be called a home at all, a place where you live next to people who are almost strangers, a building without forgiveness, without ease, with contradictory needs and opposing relations relentlessly tearing it to pieces, until it seems that we have already given up, as hastily and casually as we chose each other. The anger has given way to a despairing wonder at how incapable I am, how incapable he is, how irksome are the most ordinary, ostensibly most natural moments, sitting in the living room in the evening watching TV, while a small child in his pajamas plays with his toys on the carpet, his body warm and his hair damp from his bath, but this child is not mine, and his presence magnifies the absence of my son, and even the knowledge that he is not far away, that I will see him tomorrow or the next day, does not console me, and how oppressive it is to sit here in the living room with my own son, playing with his toys on the carpet, his tiny toys that are becoming more and more abstract, it seems that he is holding nothing in his fingers, knowing that Oded feels exactly the same as I felt only yesterday, that he is waiting for the little boy to go to bed and subtract his presence, and, to my horror, I find myself momentarily identifying with his wish, hurrying to put the child to bed in the hope that it will bring us some relief, but in vain, and how troublesome is the constant tension between the children when they are all at home together, the arguments, the unrelenting competition in which we join despite ourselves, fanning its flames against our will, and it climaxes in the kitchen, which has turned into a battleground. Like a gang of hungry juvenile delinquents we stalk around that room, stealing from each other's mouths, and when I discover that, again, there is nothing left of the food I prepared for Gili I fall furiously on the fridge, and the minute before they come home I drink Maya's favorite sweet yogurt, and the chocolate milk meant for Yotam, swallow the remains of the rice, and the nausea stirring in my stomach is the taste of the days in this house, their disrepute and their disgrace.

If only it were possible to shed the anger for a single evening, but it seems that every movement fans it anew, even if we're sitting in a restaurant with appetizing dishes before us, at the movies, in the homes of friends, the slightest gesture, the most casual word arouses it, and immediately the hoarse whispers, the accusations, the threats, the clumsy attempts at reconciliation igniting a new quarrel, and it seems that precisely the times without the children have become the most dangerous of all, because then there is no more need to maintain the facade and a bitter alienation reigns, because we have recently stopped trying. On the nights when his children are with their mother he sleeps in the clinic and we, Gili and I, find ourselves alone in the big apartment that heats up slowly and with difficulty, to whose smell and sounds we have not yet grown accustomed, how miserable is our victory, even the mirrors reflect our faces to me differently, with bitter accusations, yes, the occupants returned to the site again and again and built a new settlement on the ruins of the old, again and again people produced the same artifacts, a pot for cooking, a lamp for light, a coin, and thus we produce the same unease again and again, exhausted by comparisons, suffocated by disappointment, naked of all fraternity. Don't drag it on too long, she said then, and now the week has turned into weeks and we have not extricated ourselves, wallowing in the swamp of our lives that has been drained of expectations, facing each other hollowly, missing each other in the closed circle of stimulation and response, the words explode in the body long after they are uttered, shrapnel flying, and when we look at each other our faces arouse blood-boiling memories of empty promises, of failure repeating itself over and over, an ever deteriorating mistake.

A fancy jeep stops at the school gates and a boyish man climbs out, wearily despite the young hour, taking a pretty toddler into his arms, and after them a familiar child jumps out, their mother's beautiful eyes set in both their faces, and I approach them with a sudden urgency, how is Keren, I ask her husband, I haven't seen her in a while? Is it him at all, I am suddenly overcome by doubt, how haggard his face has grown since that Shabbat party at the beginning of the year.

Not so good, he says somberly, she's sick; and I ask in alarm, is it something serious? And he walks his eyes across my face as if wondering how much to confide in me, and blurts out, yes, I'm afraid it is, and disappears into the gate, holding onto his children who look at me with four worried blue eyes, yes, I'm afraid it is, and I try to remember the last time I saw her, was it then, when she dropped onto the lawn next to us, when she said, I can't eat a thing, her fingers playing with her hair, a sallow tinge to her skin, about our children's safety she spoke then, how concerned she was about the number of security guards at the school, and who was keeping her safe all this time, and immediately I take up my staff and hurry off, seized by an embarrassing sensation of health. Orna was wrong, actually we do feel health, and I still have mine, as far as I know, and perhaps one day I'll succeed in feeling love too, not only its loss, and I turn my back to the raven park and walk rapidly toward the address written in my notebook, the morning chill peeled from the streets, which are happy to welcome the mild spring sun, but will soon regret their welcome when the orb bears down on the stones still shivering with the memory of winter, and sucks them dry of every drop of moisture.

This must be the building, a stout, dark woman is standing in the entrance and dialing a number on her cell phone, the phone in my bag rings but I do not answer, walking past her as if it is not I she is waiting for, in order to show me in one morning all the apartments available in the area whose size is suitable to my needs and price to my means, apartments for two people, and only when I am far away I call her, something's come up, I have to cancel; if I avoid her will I avoid the sentence, was that how it was issued, and what will I say to Gili, how will I explain another move to him, but it seems that the time for questions has not yet arrived, just as someone fleeing a fire cannot stop or ponder, and I arrive at the junction, traffic surrounding the square, red tulips, densely planted, beginning to sprout, gleaming like a strip of velvet cloth in the golden light, will it really soon be too hot, too late.

For the first time I notice that the floor of the stairwell is tiled in black and white like my father's room, and I climb the stairs slowly, sending my stick before me like a blind person, and it taps rhythmically. Happily the secretary isn't there, the waiting room is as empty and silent as an abandoned army outpost, only the shrill buzz of the drill rises from the nearby dental clinic, and I approach his door, putting my ear to the absolute silence, apparently there's nobody there, I won't find him sitting and nodding, his mouth slightly open, as if he's listening with his mouth not his ears, and I knock discreetly and when there is no reply I slowly open the door and peep inside, my heart pounding. I was only here once, for a brief, vivid moment, so weak that my lids drooped over my eyes and yet I saw him, how quick and mysterious was my recovery, was it really all a brazen lie, a deliberate deception intended to pull the wool over my eyes, for even the well-appointed, reassuring room has changed beyond recognition, and it is dark and stuffy as a storeroom.

Does anyone still take the trouble to come here, does anyone still have faith in this room and the person manning it, and I sit down on the comfortable leather chair into which I once dropped, utterly exhausted, bewildered by the air of neglect, my eyes gradually adjusting to the darkness that is stained purple by the curtains, noticing a number of boxes stacked against the wall, and to my astonishment I see my own handwriting on them, short words written in hope and fear, bedroom, living room, kitchen, can he be removing his belongings clandestinely, leaving at his leisure, where is he anyway, I look around uneasily, as if peeking for the first time into his inner world, and finding there a threatening chaos.

Only then do I notice the figure lying motionless on the couch, is it one of his patients, forgotten here while he negotiates over his life, and I rise to my feet in alarm, examining in confusion the fragile profile, his face is steeped in the curious calm that I remember from our moments of love; Ella, he says suddenly without opening his eyes, you've come at last, I've been waiting a long time for you, his voice is rhythmic and monotonous, like a recording coming from the walls rather than from his lips, which remain closed; and I murmur, Oded, are you all right? Why are you lying there like that, why aren't you working? And again that strange voice when he replies, I'm on leave, didn't I tell you I was on leave?

There are a lot of things you didn't tell me, I say, why are you on leave? Because I'm waiting for you, he says, how can I work when I'm waiting for you, I have to talk to you, and I exclaim, talk to me? I don't understand, you've had countless opportunities to talk to me and you didn't take advantage of them, and suddenly it turns out that you've been waiting for me.

I didn't have any opportunities, he says, turning his face to me, you didn't give me any opportunities, I talk to you all the time and you don't hear, I ask you all the time not to suspect me, not to judge me so harshly, not to demand of me what I'm incapable of providing; and already his words are giving rise in me to the familiar anger and I snap, what did I demand of you, to say goodnight to my son? Is that such a farfetched demand? Spare me the sanctimonious speech, you're good at words but your words aren't worth anything, what does that mean, not to demand of you what you're incapable of providing? It seems that you're not capable of anything.

I'm sorry, Ella, he sighs, I was a fool, I thought that I could meet your expectations, maybe that's a good thing in a therapist, to believe in his powers, but outside the clinic it apparently doesn't work, I'm really sorry; and I yell, sorry? Is that all you have to say? As if you bumped into me by mistake and spilled my coffee, as if you made a date with me and forgot to come, are you out of your mind? And he sits up with a sharp movement and looks at me, his eyes brimming with black hostility, it's time you directed some of your criticism at yourself, you think it's such a pleasure to live with you? You came just to receive, you decided you deserved compensation for everything you'd been through, without paying a price, you saw every difficulty as a conspiracy against you, all you can do is blame others, go away, Ella, you don't want to see me like this, you have no patience for other people's problems, apparently you get along well with stones, but human beings are too much for you.

Spare me your diagnoses, I hiss, tightening my hands around the stick and groping my way to the door, you dragged me and Gili into an impossible situation, you made me extravagant promises, but then you turned away from me when I needed you most, it's no wonder I reacted badly, but don't worry, I won't burden you any longer, as soon as I find an apartment I'm leaving, and I open the door and in the neon light coming in from the hall I see his face twisting as he flips onto his chest, his shoulder blades sticking out through his thin shirt; you're right, he suddenly croaks, his voice as dull and destroyed as if it were coming from his stomach, I misled you, I have nothing to give you, I'm emptied out, I'm finished, I have nothing to give anyone, that's why I'm on leave. For a moment I believe that this is his way of continuing the battle, bashing the words back into my teeth, but his voice surges up to an alarming pitch, I ruined Michal's life and now I'm ruining yours, I'm not fit to live with a woman, I'm not fit to bring up children, I'm not fit to treat patients, his back heaves with wild sobs, and when I close the door and stand helplessly before him, leaning on my stick, I remember a distant rosy morning at the end of summer, standing at the door to my father's room, the palm fronds in his window glittering like silver blades, and I say to the back bent over the desk, Daddy, I'm leaving home, I'm moving into the student dorms, sure that he will wish me well in an official voice and hardly raise his eyes from his books, but to my surprise he suddenly rose from his chair and threw himself onto the bed, burying his face in the pillow, his back shaking, and I stood open mouthed before the sight that I had never seen before, and I never believed to have existed among the myriad sights of the universe, and I wanted to lie down next to him and burst into tears, to lament the strongest of loves, the bitterest of missed chances, why did my soul miss your soul, Daddy, why did yours miss mine, why did we alarm each other, in vain, in vain.

For long moments I stood there, rooted to the spot, leaning on the door frame, until I closed the door behind me and went on my way, in vain, and now, before the man heaving in a great primeval lament, I mumble, calm down, Oded, don't be so hard on yourself, you didn't do anything on purpose, but my words only increase his lamentation; I destroy everything I touch, I'm not so different from my father, my mother always said I was a fraud, that I was really like him, I was never good enough for her, I was never enough of a compensation for the suffering he caused her, and you wanted compensation for your suffering too, apparently I don't know how to compensate; and I sit down fearfully next to him on the couch, trying to stroke his shoulders that flutter like broken wings, my fingers straying timidly over his back, we don't really know each other, am I really ready to know you.

Calm down, I whisper, you're a wonderful father to your children, I'm sure you're an excellent therapist, don't be so hard on yourself, your intentions were good, we both came to this with heavy baggage, we both sought a refuge, it's no wonder we clashed the way we did, but all is not lost, not yet, there's still room for something between absolute failure and absolute bliss, calm down, I'll help you, I whisper as if my voice is afraid of being heard by my ears, I'm sorry, Oded, I don't even know what for, come on, get up, let's go home, but he won't stop the weeping that sounds more like soft, dry coughing; I want to stay here, he mumbles, I don't feel comfortable at home without the children; and I say quickly, then we'll bring the children, I'll go and pick them up from school this afternoon; and he sighs, but I don't want them to see me like this, it will frighten them; and I say, don't worry, I'll tell them you're not feeling well, let's go home, home, I say it again, and for the first time in a very long time the word sounds convincing.

I switch off the light in the clinic and shut the door, as if it's a bankrupt factory at the mercy of its creditors, carefully take his arm and lead him over the black and white tiles like an old man who has lost his way and requires the help of strangers. His eyes are lowered under his heavy brows, his lips are clenched, his back is as stiff as usual but his head is bowed, and he recoils slightly as we emerge into the busy street, shading his eyes against the sunlight, and I link my arm in his and thus we advance in the late morning, in the shadow of the bent, slanting pine, how slender its trunk is, no more than a human waist, and how tall it is, topped by its meager foliage, a solitary bird drops from the sky as if shot down, finding shelter among its needles, surrounded by the fists of brown cones.

Lean on me if it's hard for you to walk, I encourage him, but he remains stiffly erect, even if his feet can barely lift themselves off the black asphalt, his arm is as rigid as if bound to a wooden splint and tied to his neck, his breath is hot, a sour smell comes from his skin. Our figures are reflected on the glass wall of the cafe, dark, narrow, slow, like the hands of a particularly skeptical clock, at our corner table, under the plastic awning that will soon be removed with the coming of summer, another couple sits now, swooning with blissful happiness, this is the way of the world, I say to myself without resentment, we are walking now in the way of the world.

When we get home I lead him gently to bed, take off his shoes and put my hand on his forehead, you have a fever, I inform him, and I quickly make a glass of lemon tea, watch him sip it, do you want more tea, do you want something to eat? I ask, trying to coax an answer from his clenched lips. It's all right Ella, I just want to rest, he mutters at last, and his eyes close, his cheeks, dotted with prickly bristles like the skin of a fruit, slacken slightly, I'm cold, he whispers, and I cover him with the blanket, watching him with concern, stay away from him, he's sick, they told me once, is this what Dina meant, has the time come to talk to her at last, to find out what she was warning me against, but my hand hesitates over the telephone, recoiling from the tediously familiar routine, once more approaching her in my distress and avoiding her in my happiness, being dear to her in my misery and threatening in my joy, just as I always was to my mother, and instead of calling her I hunt around for the number of the telephone that is ringing now in the cottage at the edge of the country village, with the flat roof and the wooden steps leading to the door. It's Ella, I say when Orna's voice answers me impatiently, I came to visit you with Oded a few weeks ago, I have to ask your advice, I simply don't know him well enough to know if it's serious, and as soon as I begin to describe his condition she cuts me short; it was predictable, Ella, I warned you, he has his own ways of detaching himself, he's had a few brief breakdowns in the past and he recovered from them, no, he was never hospitalized, don't worry, he'll pull himself together and begin functioning normally again, it's not a reason to stay with him or to leave him either, but if you decide to stay with him you have to change your attitude, you have to behave as if everything depends on you.

When I return to the bedroom and sit on the edge of the bed, I remember how I used to cradle Gili in my arms for hours at a time when he was sick, not daring to put him down for a moment in case he woke up, denying all my needs as if I had become an inanimate object, and how much freedom there was in this absolute subjugation, how much strength, how it banished every other worry and demand with an outstretched arm, and when I look at the man lying under the blankets, a tranquil lull descends on the room as if I am watching over the sleep of my own child. Now my own child is growing up and needing me less, and in his place a strange, deceptive substitute has suddenly come into in my life, I expected him to protect me, I tried to crowd in under his wings and there was no room for me there, and now precisely his helplessness fills me with a rare serenity, a kind of happiness, a feeling more complete than love, which I never felt for Amnon. His Adam's apple rises and falls, his expressions change rapidly, his lips move as if he were begging for his life, and I seem to see photos of his childhood appearing on his face, and next to them photos of his old age not yet taken, an entire life hovering in the space between absolute happiness and absolute failure, and I cover him with the fallen blanket, sit down in front of the computer in the corner of the bedroom, and type quietly, as if whispering words into its receptive blue ear.

Who ultimately destroyed the most spectacular of palaces, the hall of the double axes, the vast labyrinth, what was the mysterious force that wiped out the first perfect European civilization, Plato's Atlantis, who annihilated the ancient people whose art was so marvelously stylish and subtle, the society that worshiped the bull that roared in the belly of the earth. Was it the mighty forces of nature, a chain of earthquakes and tidal waves, or did humanity rain destruction on itself in the form of invaders from land or sea, the Dorians with their iron daggers, the Myceneans setting sail from the mainland, for more and more evidence indicates that the Minoan civilization continued to thrive, in Crete, even after Thera was buried in volcanic pumice stone. True, the patterns painted on the urns changed, and the people grew less interested in art than in fortifications, in defending their water sources, but even as they made human sacrifices to appease the forces of nature, men came with fire and wreaked havoc on their prosperous society, on its magnificent palace, on its living people and on its painted figures, among them the Parisian, woe unto the inhabitants of the sea coast, the nation of Crete! Why did he tell me then, ten years ago, I know you from Thera, he must have known then that she hadn't been painted there, that her arrogant eyes had never gazed at the volcanic island.

When I enter the schoolyard in the afternoon Gili comes running toward me in surprise, a mischievous smile on his face, Mommy, did you come to get me? But I'm with Daddy today, did you forget? You're so mixed up, it seems that my mistake amuses him to no end; and I have to confess, no, I didn't forget, I came to get Yotam because his father is sick. To my relief he accepts the news naturally, offers to help me find Yotam, pulling me behind him through the yard, my mother's here to get you, he tells him in a calm, relaxed voice, obviously enjoying the upsetting of the natural order, and he does not seem to be at all envious of his friend for borrowing his mother, and I hoist Yotam's schoolbag onto my shoulder, your father's waiting for you at home, I explain to him, he isn't feeling too well, and his expression, a little frightened, but at the same time grateful, wrings my heart, and I stroke his hair that has grown wildly, covering the traces of that miserable haircut.

Holding hands we go up to Maya's class and find her standing alone at the back of the classroom, putting her books into her schoolbag with a pensive expression, none of the children talk to her, why doesn't she have any friends, I wonder, remembering that she has never brought a friend home. When she sees us her face tightens, what happened, she asks, where's Daddy? He's waiting for you at home, I say, he isn't feeling too well, don't worry, and when we leave the building I glance at the yard, to make sure that Amnon has arrived, and I see him standing next to the swings, talking animatedly to one of the mothers, gesturing energetically, since when has he become so friendly, but I can't go into it at the moment, two children have been entrusted to my care today, two human creatures that I have to take care of and bring home safely.

Wait a minute, Mommy, Gili comes running up, waving a white

page like a flag, I drew a picture for Oded, he shouts, and I turn to meet him, what a lovely picture, I declare even before I can make out what it is, a plump, smiling teddy bear, sketched in hasty crayon strokes. I know that Oded doesn't like bears, he says gravely, but he'll like my picture, and I say goodbye to him and leave the yard, without stopping to talk to Amnon, even though there was something I wanted to ask him, why he mentioned Thera then, on our first meeting, but what difference does it make now, there's no way back, there never was.

When we pass through the green gate upon which I found myself suspended one morning at the beginning of the year, trapped between heaven and earth, looking down on the lawns and the piles of garbage, I hold out my hands to the two children walking silently next to me, and they take them, and together we cross the road in the direction of the raven park, and although Gili is not with us I feel a surprising completeness, a vaguely remembered, innocent fullness, and it seems that as I gather these two silent pieces of a shattered family to me I am mending my own shards, even in the absence of my son, the absence of Oded, precisely when I am alone with the two unfamiliar children, who sense the weakness of their parents and cling to me.

Are you hungry? I ask, inviting them to sit down on the warm plastic chairs outside the falafel stand, buying them pitas stuffed with falafel and watching in enjoyment as they chew, how like his father Yotam is and how like her mother Maya is, as if they are intended to perpetuate the union that failed, and at the same time he looks like Gili too, and the little girl reminds me more and more of myself, the same supercilious look, veiling an unbearable vulnerability. So how was your day? I ask, and Yotam lets a half eaten ball of falafel fall from his mouth and says, oh, today Ronen told the class in the morning meeting that his mother is very sick, but she promised him that she would get better; and I ask fearfully, really, what's wrong with her? A disease, Yotam says, his mouth full, biting into his pita again, I don't know which, but she's in the hospital.

But Daddy's all right, right? Maya makes sure again, her spectacular curls close to my face, so that I can see the knots tangling them, creating dense lumps of hair, perhaps I'll comb them out for her, if she lets me. Of course he's all right, I say quickly, he has a little fever, that's all; and she says, maybe we should go home now, I want to see Daddy, and we continue on our way, walking down the steep lane untouched by the light of the sun, as dark and cool as the depths of the orange grove, and when we reach our home, and stand in the bedroom door, he opens his eyes at once, holds his arms out to his children as if he hasn't seen them for weeks, and they jump onto the bed with their shoes on, cuddling up to him in relief.

Leaning on the door frame I look at them, no, I won't join them for now, and perhaps never, perhaps we will never be like those families that climb naturally into bed together, and yet our achievement will be more thrilling, for every ordinary moment will be a victory for us. You'll see, I promise them silently, in a strange way life will become precious, and even though I don't go and lie down beside them the bed seems to be growing wider, indirectly including me, for beyond the contradictory needs and opposing attachments there is one hidden longing, and it seems that it depends on me, it is in my hands, I can work miracles if I want to, like a goddess who cured humanity with her wound, and I go up to Oded and hand him the slightly crumpled white page, Gili sent you this, I say casually, and he somberly examines the drawing, fantastic, he says, I'll hang it up here, right opposite the bed.

Touched, I leave the room and stand at the window overlooking the lane, a pregnant woman is climbing the steep slope, her face red with effort and her breathing heavy, almost audible, no, a family is born not out of doubt but of necessity, only perfect faith will be able to replace the ties of blood, overlooking our own needs and fulfilling each others', is this the union my father wished me all those months ago, the one that bestows peace and happiness, and why couldn't I achieve it with Amnon, how much better it would have been for us, all three of us, but it didn't happen, and perhaps I will never know why, for no absolute proof will ever be found, much as there is never an inscription testifying to the reality of a life that has vanished from the world, only the bare, daily effort, done for its own sake, like the priests of On shedding their shoes on the cliffs every morning, only it will provide the shards of meaning for us, step by step, line by line.

When I return to the room with another cup of tea for him I hear Yotam say, Daddy, did you know that it will be Passover soon, we learned about it today in school, the exodus from Egypt, do you think it really happened? And Oded replies, as far as I'm concerned it doesn't make any difference, but ask Ella, she knows about these things, and with the three of them looking at me I feel the pressure of a full lecture hall, and it seems that if only I can convince this small immature audience I will be convinced myself. Apparently we will never know if it really happened, I say to them, up to now no proof has been found to support this story, but I still believe that it was written in the wake of a real event, because the miraculous phenomena it describes of darkness and blood and all the plagues visited on Egypt are connected to a natural disaster that really happened thousands of years ago, and just as we tend to fear something that has already frightened us in the past, the ancient writers described this event in the form of something that once happened and frightened them terribly.

But the exodus from Egypt is a happy story, isn't it? Maya asks, the Children of Israel were freed from their bondage; and I say, yes, you're right, the ancient writers remembered a cruel, frightening story passed from generation to generation about a world that was destroyed, and turned it into a happy story about redemption and salvation, and she asks, and did the people who wrote it believe that it was true? And I say, I think they wanted to believe it very much.

Chapter twenty-four

How her eyes shone when she invited us all to a party, a clearly impersonal invitation, since she hardly knew any of us, as if she were standing on a street corner and persuading the passersby to come to her home, to see her happiness. What's the occasion, someone asked, and she said, nothing in particular, we just feel like celebrating, exchanging glances with her husband, as if sharing a secret with him, a faint blush on her cheeks, and I in my folly recoiled as if her happiness were stolen from me, as if she had dipped her hands in the general reservoir of happiness and grabbed bucketfuls for herself, not leaving a single drop for me. So how did that party go, how many bottles of wine were opened, what music was played, what refreshments were served, who showed up, how many of those gathered here to accompany her on her last journey attended her party, the stunned people getting out of their cars and starting to trudge, with a desert wind harassing their hair, blowing through their skirts and sleeves, tingeing their skins, just as her skin yellowed in recent months, suddenly we are all like her, we are all closer to death.

It was a Friday, like now, the day I first saw him at the Shabbat party, pale and reserved, and when I glance at him walking next to me I notice for the first time how much he has aged since then, the lines running down his cheeks have deepened, his neck has grown flabby, his hair has faded, and it seems that this new vulnerability is what brought us together, for it was by *my* side that he grew older, every change that takes place in his appearance from now on belongs to me, to us, for better or worse, like property accumulated during a life together, and I examine him with my newfound tenderness would I choose him again, did I in fact ever choose him, a powerful blast threw me at his feet and him at mine, together we crawled through the ruins, stunned, dragging three children behind us.

We advance on paths as yet unpaved, blazing a trail in the city of the dead, familiar faces merge with strange ones, sobs with coughs, slowly we walk behind her, behind her body wrapped in white cloth, prostrate on the stretcher, as if she has been urgently evacuated from a disaster zone and is being taken to a better place, where she will be healed. Grief darkens our faces as we gather around her plot, a storm of weeping passes from eye to eye, akin to the sand storm raging around us, trying to ruin the ceremony, in a moment the storm will return the piles of dirt to the waiting pit, and lift her light body into the air, into the sky pressing down upon us, how close the sky is today, heavy with dust, like a lampshade hung too low.

From our place on the fringes of the crowd we can't see what's happening, only the sound of the spades hitting the rocky earth reaches our ears, and in the stillness between strikes our senses sharpen, until we can hear the whispering of the tissues wiping away the tears, the sound of the tears being absorbed, the swallowing of dusty saliva, the rippling of hair, the dank scent of the depths of the earth. This is how she would work in her garden, and I remember how I came once to pick Gili up at their house and I found her leaning thoughtfully on her spade, just like the ones being used now by the people digging her grave, in her red shorts and flimsy tank top she looked like a girl, her calves streaked with dirt, look what I planted, she said, wiping the sweat from her forehead, a cherry tree. Her little son romped around her, tottering like a drunk, and she snatched him up and kissed him on the mouth and said, when Jonathan grows up there will be cherries on the tree, he'll be able to pick them and eat them, and when we drank lemonade in the garden, the gate opened and her husband came in, and she raised her face to him, you're home early, what a wonderful surprise, and he lifted the toddler up in his arms and kissed him, his lips seared by the taste of her lips forever, and now he looks down at us, her little son, swaying on his father's shoulders, interrupting the recitation of the *Kaddish* with shrill cries of joy, and suddenly I hear the voice of his big brother, Gili's friend, trying to pronounce the words of the mysterious text correctly alongside his father, as if he is reading for a strict teacher in the classroom, and for a moment his piping voice reminds me of Gili's voice, of Yotam's voice, one day they, too, will stand like this opposite a pile of earth and say the *Kaddish* for their mothers.

From our place at the edges of the crowd it is hard to see what's happening, I can only see Jonathan clearly, is he really sitting on his father's shoulders, it seems that the whole congregation is raising him up on hundreds of shoulders like a bridegroom on his wedding day, his eyes, blue as hers, beam with pleasure as he surveys the crowd surrounding him, the smile spreads over his face as if he is sure that they have all assembled here for the sole purpose of entertaining him, and the sight of the jubilant child who only yesterday lost his mother produces ripples of crying, and he looks around him in surprise and asks his father slowly and hesitantly, as if pronouncing his first words, Daddy, why is everybody crying? His father's reply is no longer audible, heavy sighs muffle his voice, the howling of the wind muffles his voice, and I wipe my eyes and look around me, from minute to minute we grow more alike, our eyes reddening like the eyes of a hamster, our hair turning yellow, our tongues cleaving to our palates, our mouths filling with dust, as if we were all taking part in a mass excavation, frantically digging tunnels beneath the built up city, yellow milk rains down on the world from the sky, the wind grows hotter, heavy with sand and spores, a charged, electric wind, like the volcanic dust that floats in the air, for days and days.

In the distance I see a tall man removing his sunglasses, revealing pale eyes and greeting me with a nod, the first time I saw him, too, he was covered with dust, in how many funeral processions have we marched, Amnon, how many dead have we accompanied to their final resting places, and it seems that his presence among the mourners makes me feel obscurely safe, like then, when he patrolled the excavation squares; look, we are together again, even if hundreds of people separate us, accompanying each other from a distance in the cycles of life. Next Sunday we are to meet at the Rabbinate to conclude our marriage, to stand before three stern-faced rabbis, exactly like the ones now busy burying her, asking forgiveness of her soul, and I will take the marriage contract from your hands, walk with my head bowed between the walls of the hall, accompanied by hostile stares, white beards pouring down black robes, cast off, cast off they will shout, no longer consecrated.

Keren loved Fridays, I hear her husband's voice rise with difficulty above the loud sobbing, she loved the *Kabbalat Shabbat,* with all the family together, we want to sing the song we always sang, I know you can hear us, Keren, I know you're singing with us now, I promise you that we'll sing this song to you every Friday night and hear you singing with us, and he clears his throat with an effort and gathers his voice, *Peace be unto you, ye ministering angels, messengers of the Most High, the supreme King of Kings, holy and blessed is He, may your coming be in peace, messengers of peace, messengers of the Most High, the supreme King of Kings, holy and blessed is He,* his voice is cracking, dragging behind it with difficulty the faltering voices of his sons, while the congregation hesitates over whether to join in, or whether the song is meant only for those closest to her, this song that conjures up images of a carefully laid table, children washed and combed, a cake in the oven, a woman in a dress, the Sabbath Queen, let's go and look for the Sabbath Queen, the beautiful bride who marries her husband each week anew, the teacher suggested then, and the children jumped up and disappeared into the rolling lawns, was it then that she said, we're having a party tonight, everyone's invited, there'll be lots of wine, great music, it'll be fun, and her husband stood next to her, his arm around her shoulders, and explained how to get there, and soon a merry group gathered around their happiness, yes, sure, we'll come, why not, what turn did you say to take, the first one after the traffic circle.

His strength seems to falter after the second verse, from the distance I see him collapsing into the arms of an elderly woman, apparently his mother, and precisely then the congregation rallies as one to his aid, *Bless me with peace,* we shout hoarsely, *bless me with peace, ye messengers of peace, messengers of the Most High,* and the toddler who has moved to other shoulders in the meantime waves a golden sunflower that has been plucked for him from one of the floral tributes, Daddy, won't I ever see Mommy again? he suddenly asks, more astonishment in his voice than grief, as if wondering at the way of the world, giving rise with his question to a new wave of weeping, and among all the sobs and moans I seem to recognize a familiar sound, which has been accompanying me now for many months, like the continuous wail of a memorial siren, and when I look tensely around me I see pale mango colored curls blowing in the wind, framing a contorted face that is covered by a hand. For months I haven't come across her, I avoided her in every possible way, and now she is here, sobbing uncontrollably, as if she has lost what is most precious to her, and it seems that the stifled weeping that rose then from the secret recesses of the bedroom has now been liberated from its prison, burst into the open air, and I find myself answering her with a weeping of my own, like a chorus of two voices telling a story that has no proof and no conclusion.

Twenty years have passed since I stood like this over the grave of Gilad, my mother tried to hold my hand, but I slipped away from her, hiding behind the headstones, seeing before my eyes the smooth body that shone in the dark like a phosphorescent candle, in vain you warned me, Mother, how could you have imagined that I didn't know about his sickness, and I wanted him so much, perhaps that was why I wanted him, drawn to the loss lurking within him rather than the youth, to the past rather than the future, was it fear that made it impossible for me to choose, which made me give up in advance? Behind the headstones I hid while his boyish ribs were covered with dirt, and when everyone left I took a little stick and turned the earth over, if I dug deep enough perhaps I would find a house there and it would be my home, I would find the bones of a boy there and he would be my love.

When the mourners begin slowly dispersing, their faces distorted with sorrow, their eyes red, with firm steps that reveal a sudden lust for life in spite of everything, a violent impatience, as if they had all suddenly had their fill of grief, I tug at Oded's arm, eager to fade into the crowd, but he stays rooted to the spot as if waiting, and as I stand by his side it seems that the fear of the encounter is gradually disappearing and an embarrassed need is even emerging, to mourn together, to lament everything we have lost together, and when the crowd dwindles, like a heavy wave ebbing from the shore, baring the flotsam left by the receding tide, it seems that we four have been left exposed, and I see Michal turning her back to us and walking slowly away, wearing a blue shirt that had once reflected the color of the sky, her skirt flapping in the wind, and I watch her with my heart full of pity, wait, I want to shout, don't go yet, I have something important to tell you.

As if she heard my words she suddenly stops and turns hesitantly toward us, and I lower my eyes to the ground and watch the approach of her high heeled black sandals, her wobbling ankles, now she shakes hands formally with her ex-husband, as if she is being introduced to him, her face has grown a little thinner and a mature beauty shows through her curls, and I stand next to him as if turned to stone, holding my breath, but she approaches me and gives me her hand, and I shyly stroke the soft white hand with the veins that twine like the branches of a river, I'm so sorry, I find myself whispering, as if she is the mourner here and it is her I must console, and she whispers, so am I, may we know no more sorrow, and when heavy, careful steps advance toward me I know that Amnon is standing next to me, and I lean against him for a moment, supported by his body, for the wind is whirling around us, assailing us as if to test how firmly we are planted on this earth, and we stand close together, will an outside observer be able to say who belongs to whom, will we?

The sandstorm chases the last of the mourners away, sends them to their cars as though a tempest is spilling from the sky and they retreat in haste, leaving behind them gusts of polluted air, even the bereaved family members detach themselves from the fresh, flower-covered grave, the toddler on his father's shoulders again, proudly holding his sunflower, which has sprained its neck, its magnificent head drooping, swaying with each step, and only we remain behind, reluctant to take our leave, standing at a short distance from the grave, around a plot of earth into which the spades have not yet dug, where no pit has been opened up, no body buried, and it seems that a transparent ring of children are dancing around us, children with smooth empty faces, seven times they circle us, like a bride around her groom, they are our children, those who have already been born and those who have not yet been born and those who will never be born at all.

Furiously the wind churns up the footprints of the hundreds of mourners who have just departed, effacing evidence and proof, until it seems that no one has ever set foot here, furiously it tugs at our clothes, and we start walking one behind the other between the gravestones, under the nearby sky, accidentally trampling the remains of memorial candles, the flowerbeds tenaciously clinging to the stone, Michal's heels dig holes in the earth, and now Amnon's footprints cover them, and they are joined in turn by ours, on the narrow paths between the tombstones, step after step, row after row, like an engraved inscription, one that only the earth will be able to read.

About the Author

Leading author Zeruya Shalev was born at Kibbutz Kinneret. She has an MA in biblical studies and works as a literary editor at Keter Publishing House. Shalev has published four novels, a book of poetry and a children's book. Her novels *Love Life, Husband and Wife* and *Thera* have received critical acclaim both in Israel and abroad and have been bestsellers in several countries. *Love Life* is included in *Der Spiegel's* prestigious list of "20 Best Novels in World Literature" over the last 40 years, together with Saul Bellow, J.M. Coetzee and Philip Roth. *Husband and Wife* is included in the French Fnac list of the "200 Best Books of the Decade."

Shalev has been awarded the Book Publishers Association's Gold and Platinum Prizes, the Corine Prize (Germany, 2001), the Amphi Award (France, 2003), the ACUM Prize three times (1997, 2003, 2005), and the French Wizo Prize (2007). *Husband and Wife* was also nominated for the Femina Prize (France, 2002). A feature film of *Love Life*, produced in Germany, was recently released.

The fonts used in this book are from the Arno family

The Toby Press publishes fine writing,
available at leading bookstores everywhere. For more
information, please visit www.tobypress.com